This book is dedicated to my favorite failures.

FIFTY

PATRICK

ONE

LOVELAND

FIFTY

prologue

Broken crayons rolled against each other and mashed together in Felix Brewer's wringing, trembling left fist, and his face was hot and clammy from crying. He had to will himself to stop squeezing and relax his hand. Crayon chunks and waxy smashed shards tumbled out, some still connected by torn paper sheathes.

Felix had been lying on his stomach and drawing, his knees and arms itchy from sweat and the blue and gray shag carpet in the living room of his dad's house.

The crayon pieces and paper wrappers had dropped onto his drawings, some less deformed ones rolling around. One rolled off the stack of papers and tried to hide itself in among the carpet's tiny jungle of distressed yarn tendrils and fronds.

Felix looked over the loose overlapping images and realized he didn't really remember drawing any of them— or the crying he must have done while making them. They were more roughly thrown around than he liked, too. He gathered them together in what seemed like an order that made some kind of sense.

Okay, so…. Car driving, woman inside. A big monster tank or something appears. Tank-monster drives toward little car.

Opens its mouth and bites the little car, chews it. A tooth comes out and stays in the woman.

There's red crayon all over the next page.

Looks like a fireman or something but it's messed up now. Next, the woman is coming out of the ground all white and blue next to a cross in the ground.

Then, a man and boy are standing at the cross. Oh, this probably went before the other.

The second to last is of a house. The boy is outside. Inside, the man sits. The woman is floating next to the man.

They look sad.

The last looks like there was a person drawn on it but now it's covered in swooping spirals of different colors. The spirals are densely layered, and he pressed hard enough that the paper is indented all over by the repeated strokes.

That explains the broken crayons?

It had been almost two years since his mom died. Felix knew that because he was almost ten now and he'd been almost eight when it had happened.

She would have been okay if they hadn't….

Felix heard his dad's door open down the hall, then the shuffling of his slippers.

It's been even slower lately…and he's got that one radio station on with all the great old songs but a weird name…. *"Soul," I think he said.*

His dad came into the living room smoking a cigarette. He took a drag and flicked ash into the tray on top of the TV. He exhaled slowly.

Felix coughed.

"I thought you were gonna stop that, Dad. You tol' Mom you would."

Dad looks so tired.

"Yeah…. Last one, little man. Promise."

He used to be so cool.

Felix knew his dad still loved him, but he was different now. His dad still tried for a while after his mom went away. Felix didn't think it was just because he missed Mom so much too. Something else had changed, and Felix didn't understand what that could have been.

His dad looked down at the TV.

"Why do you like this *Robot Tech* shit, Felix? It's unrealistic. Those eyes are huge…. Physically impossible. And they don't even fuckin' talk right," he said and took another drag.

It's Robotech. Robo-tech. *You always say it wrong.*

Felix would usually defend *Robotech* with all he had but today nothing felt important like it should.

"I don't know why. It's just cool."

His dad exhaled and scoffed gently.

"You should ask yourself why you like it…or anything else. Know why, little man. Be honest to yourself and others."

Dad never talks like this.

"You should always—"

Felix looked up and saw his dad staring above and past him. Felix looked at the corner behind himself.

There's nothing there.

He looked back at his dad. "You feel okay?"

Hand shaking, his dad raised the cigarette and took a long drag. He closed his eyes and exhaled. His eyes fluttered open before he was done, and he looked back at the TV. He took another long drag and let the smoke billow from his mouth, then inhaled some of it through his nose and blew the rest out as smoke rings at Rick Hunter on the tube.

"Hey, you should get some outside time today. Why don't you go play with Stacy down the street."

Felix frowned and said, "You mean Tracy?"

"Yeah. And tell her mom I want to talk to her for a minute if she wouldn't mind walking down here."

"I thought you didn't like her mom."

His dad let out a soft chuckle.

"I never said that exactly."

He started back down the hallway to his bedroom, then stopped and turned back.

"Hey. Come here."

Felix got up and walked to his dad, wiping his waxy hand on his shorts.

"I just want you to know that everything is alright. I need you to believe that, no matter what. Do you?"

Felix nodded.

"Say it then, Felix."

"Everything is alright."

His dad cupped the back and side of Felix's head in his big hand and mussed his blond hair.

"Don't forget to leave the door unlocked for Stacy's mom."

Something in his dad's expression stopped Felix from correcting him again. His dad patted the side of his head, then turned and walked down the hall to his room. Over his shoulder he said, "And turn off that stupid fuckin' cartoon, will you? TV is bullshit."

Felix watched his dad close his bedroom door, then crossed to the TV and shut it off. He stepped over his weird drawings on the way to the front door, put on his shoes and pulled the Velcro over just tight enough, then went out onto the porch. Before he closed the door, he heard something like sliding furniture from his dad's room.

Must be vacuuming or something.

San Jose sucks, thought Felix. He missed Santa Cruz.

Santa Cruz is nicer. San Jose is also flatter or something? Sucks is all I know.

Felix looked up the street and saw Tracy kicking a soccer

ball against her garage door. She'd kick it, run to catch it on the rebound, and kick it again.

She's kind of a tomboy. Pretty enough but it's annoying that she acts all dumb around me 'cause she thinks I'm cute or something. Whatever…. It's better than hanging out with Dad when he's like this.

He stepped off the porch and walked up the sidewalk toward Tracy's house. Looked over at the windows to his dad's room and saw him inside. Felix waved but his dad didn't seem to see him and closed the curtains tight. Felix lowered his hand, a little embarrassed. He looked around.

Hope no one saw, he thought, then moved on.

He was almost to Tracy's front yard when it started sprinkling. She squealed and kicked the ball into some hedges for storage, then ran inside. Felix chuckled.

That was cute.

Now Felix was kind of bummed that he couldn't play with her.

She'd kicked the ball a little too hard and it had kept going through the bushes. It picked up speed as it rolled down the driveway closer to Felix. He tried to grab it but it was going too fast and made it out onto the street, then down the gradual slope. It got shiny and threw off a little spray as it rolled through the fresh precipitation.

Felix walked up his porch steps and went back inside through the front door, closing it behind him.

Why did Dad want the door left unlocked anyway? Tracy's mom could just knock—shit!

Forgot to ask her to come down.

He looked down the hall at the closed door to his dad's room.

I'll tell him about the rain and hopefully he won't get all mad.

He took off his shoes with a ripping of Velcro and walked to the TV to turn it back on. As it warmed back up,

Voltron appeared.

Voltron *is all right. It's not rad like* Robotech, *but*—

There was a thump and crash from his dad's room.

"Dad?"

Felix crept down the hall, concerned but wary of angering his father.

"You okay?"

He knocked on the door, paused so he wouldn't get yelled at, then tried the doorknob. It turned but the door wouldn't budge.

The radio was still on and playing the soul-music station, muffled by the door.

Over the song, Felix heard a gurgle from inside—

"Dad?!" He turned the handle and pushed on the door, then slammed himself against it. He slammed again and the lock disengaged but he still couldn't open it. Felix pushed hard against it but his socks slipped on the carpet. He dug them in and pushed with everything his little body had. The door slowly slid open, pushing aside the desk that was blocking it.

"O-o-h Child" by the Five Stairsteps was playing on the radio, Felix's favorite song from that station.

"DAD!"

Felix's dad was hanging by his neck from a belt around one of the exposed rafters in his room, his body bucking and twitching.

Felix ran to his dad's legs, grabbed them, and tried to pull him down, not thinking. He wrapped himself around his dad's legs and pulled down hard again.

As he pulled, he saw the full-length broken mirror his father must have knocked over and started crying.

"P-please, Dad!"

He sobbed. The easier, brighter day the song on the radio promised couldn't come soon enough.

The knot of the belt on the rafter started to loosen—

It gave way and his dad's body fell like a big sack of

rocks, knocking down the radio and breaking it, then trapping Felix underneath. There was a sickening crunch as the head slammed down into his face, parts of his dad's teeth chipping off into Felix's jawbone.

Felix screamed. Blood from his jaw ran down his cheek and started to fill his eye as he struggled but couldn't escape the weight of his dad's huge, lifeless body. He tried to push him off, but he just couldn't. He tried and tried until his muscles hurt and he stopped fighting.

All Felix could see in this position was the broken-mirror image of his dad's empty eyes. With the radio busted and silent, he could hear *Voltron* playing out in the living room and started sobbing. He couldn't tell why that made it worse, but it did.

So much worse.

Then Felix got mad. The little boy started to fight again, pushing and pulling himself along the floor this time. He started to slide out just a bit. As he struggled, he stared into the spiderweb cracks in the reflection of his bloody face and blood-filled eye. He started yelling, angrier than he'd ever been. Felix Brewer yelled and cried and fought.

The spiderweb cracks got closer.

And brighter?

Then deep, inky black.

When Felix opened his eyes again, he felt older, larger. He was naked and the floor was cold.

The room is spinning? No, something is spinning around it. Around the outside?

Everything was blurry. Warping and twisting unnaturally.

It was like powerful wind whipping all around him—but a wind that warped and tore at the physical matter itself.

The floor was rubber, or the wind made it feel like it.

He felt like his insides were shaking in rhythm with

the sound of whatever was going around the outside of the room. Shuddering. Twisting. Pulsing.

Felix looked up and saw that he was inside a brushed metal dome. It was large enough that, near the inner apex, it was so dark he couldn't see.

A black, viscous fluid began oozing and sliding down the curved inner walls of the dome from the impossible darkness near the apex.

Felix started screaming but he could barely hear himself over the growing roar outside the room.

part one

> *"What we do here today...is for the good of our ancestors and, in the course of time, our children."*

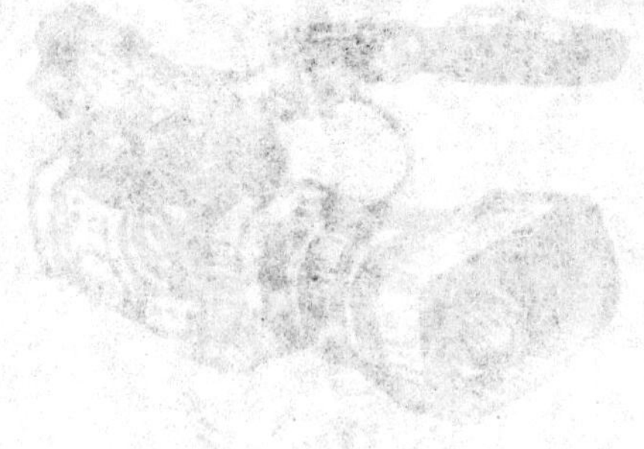

I jolt awake in a large futon in San Francisco, covered in sweat, breathing hard, and fighting off a thick comforter. As soon as I can steal back some amount of control from my subconscious, I slow and deepen my breathing. Then flex my calf muscles by pointing my toes up toward my knees like I've learned to do to not get charley horses.

I should drink more water. Maybe bananas too?

Audrey squirms next to me. She wriggles a bit more and makes a cute sound. I roll onto my side and smooth her glossy raven hair down. Lovely Audrey.

Even asleep and with messy hair, she's Louise Brooks–level stunning. Similar looks too, her mesmerizing dark eyes the only thing I can't see right now.

Don't want to wake her up, so I roll onto my other side and try to get comfortable. Before I can try to shut my eyes to get some more rest, they go straight to a tiny dimly silhouetted zebra toy on top of my dresser across the room.

I found the plastic figurine with its head down, half

buried in sand on a secluded stretch of beach up the coast. Had a Day-Glo green price tag on it marked "$ .10."

Random. Kind of amusing. Absurd, maybe? Kept it. Price tag still hasn't come off.

Then I remember my nightmare and shudder.

Why am I dreaming about Dad again? I'll get used to the nightmares someday, right? Yeah, probably not.

Audrey squirms again so I try to be still.

What was that other part of the dream about? A big, freaky metal dome?—

The alarm clock goes off.

I shut my eyes and act asleep. The digital bleating wakes Audrey and she groans. She gently slaps my chest as she tries to reach the alarm. I act like I'm just waking up. She grunts and reaches over me to slap the snooze button, collapses back on her side of the futon, then moans and grabs her head.

"You and your damned Olde English. 'Forty-licious,' my ass."

I chuckle. "The *forty water* is the *life!*"

"That's very *Yay Area* of you."

"I didn't put a gun to your head, girl."

"But you know I'm fragile."

"Fragile? You're too flexible to be fragile."

"Oh, what-ever, perv." She laughs, then breathes in sharply and rubs her eyes with her palms. "Ow."

"Don't act like it bothers you. You like it," I say as I roll over and tickle Audrey's underarm.

She locks up and giggles. "Don't!"

Audrey flings herself onto me and rolls her body back and forth. "Steamroller!"

I lock my arms around her and tighten until I've restricted her rolling, then smack her bottom. She mock-cringes like it hurts and I do it again. I'm getting a bit hard and she feels it.

"Oh, hell no, Felix. I'd love to, but my students gave me

dirty looks the last time I was late because of your little buddy there. It was like…."

She makes a face like she's aghast.

"It was like they *knew*!"

I laugh and let go. "Fine. I wouldn't want to get you in more trouble with the Brakhage and Deren wannabes."

Audrey scoffs, "And what's wrong with Brakhage and Deren?"

"Nothing. They're great. And it's great to have heroes. Just don't copy them almost one-to-one and say you're original."

"That's not all of them. Some are really talented this semester. Now, none will compare with your insects fucking, cars crashing, girls dropping ice-cream cones in slow motion 'stutter-cut' epic, of course."

"You joke. It will be powerful. It could change the world. It could make people cry."

We make our best pretentious snob faces and hold them up in the air looking down our noses at each other, until she snickers and we both laugh.

I say, "Hey, parody is a sincere form of flattery. Plus, I'd personally like to carry the torch for the Kuchars, Arnold, and Baldwin myself."

We kiss. I nibble on Audrey's neck and run a hand down to the small of her back, linger there, then keep going. She moans, then pulls away.

"Oh, uh-uh. What did I just say?" Audrey says before pressing the back of her open hand against my face, then wagging it back and forth like she's going to slap me.

"Not my fault! It's nature!"

"Control thyself, young man. Hey, speaking of talent— maybe you should get back to putting *yours* to good use again at some point."

I look at the ceiling and sigh.

Audrey puts her hand on my shoulder.

"You used to be so passionate about filmmaking. Your

illustration and painting too. Where'd your passion go, Felix?"

"I don't know. I'll let you know when I find it."

Audrey squeezes my shoulder and nods. "You do that. I think you were happier. Plus, it was sexy."

She makes a big, silly open-mouthed smile like she's drooling. Then a little gurgling moan.

I look at her and chuckle.

Audrey sits up and swings her legs off the futon, then gets up and walks to the bathroom in the hall that runs the length of her flat. Runs the water, washes her face. Takes an Ibuprofen gel tab. Combs her hair until it's smoothed out.

She has to look tasteful to critique her experimental-film students, now a teacher in the same program we met in several years before.

Audrey doesn't even have to work. Some sort of inheritance from a late relative in Europe. She makes her own money, though, and I admire that too. She only uses the inheritance when she really has to. She also really enjoys teaching others who are into what she is, which is cool.

The thing about Audrey is she's smart. Real smart, but chill about it. Some people know a little about a lot of things, a lot about a few things, everything about just one thing, not much about anything, or somewhere in between.

Audrey Eloise Myron knows a lot about a lot of things and everything about several things. Science, history, math, and, of course, art. She uses that knowledge to make incredible art pieces and short films. Her shadow boxes can make people weep.

But she'll also just smoke a few bowls and hand the controller back and forth on *Shadow of the Colossus* with me for hours on end. She still kicks my ass at the hard time attacks. She's especially wicked on the huge bird; the fifth one. She pulls the vertical wingtip transfer drop perfect every time.

I don't say it much, but I love Audrey. She seems to feel

the same. Even says so sometimes. Enough to let me move into her Victorian flat, at least. We live together well.

Audrey slips on a tank top and a sweater, then some old, well-worn jeans. She grabs her Pumas and sits on the edge of the futon. Audrey pulls over the left set of Velcro straps.

"You still down for H and K's party?"

I nod. "Yeah, wouldn't miss the big unveiling for anything. Took long enough."

"Right? Okay, I'm gonna take off. Wannabes' dreams to crush and all that."

She leans in and we kiss again.

Audrey gets up and walks toward the hall and I watch her butt as she goes. She stops and looks back, catching me.

She shakes her head. "Pig. Hey, have fun with your new toy, by the by. Maybe it can lead you to back to Passion-ville."

I smile. "Maybe so…. Yeah, might get it going and take it out for a spin later."

"Good, you do that."

She nods, smiles, and walks down the hall. I hear the front door open, then close. My smile fades as I stare at the ceiling.

chapter 2

I'm in the shower on the edge of the bathtub. Water runs down my body as I stare through the tiled wall into my memories. I look down at a slightly darkened ring of birth-marked skin around the base of my left ring finger.

The mirrored medicine cabinet door is propped open so that I can't see it.

I hate mirrors.

Mostly because I have complete heterochromia iridum. My left eye is a deep, bright blue and my right a dark brown. Sometimes in that combo, the right would be more of a light brown or hazel or the blue would be darker, which would have looked less distinct.

That would have been a little more forgiving. Kids never miss an opportunity to call attention to something that makes someone appear different, to put it nicely.

When it first developed, doctors my grandparents took me to had trouble determining if it was congenital or acquired. Some gibberish about autosomal dominance as opposed to blunt trauma from my dad's head slamming into mine. Either way, it didn't come on until after that. Before, my eyes were both blue like my dad's. Within a year of my father's death, my right eye had turned a deep, almost black, brown.

My hair also went from baby blond to a dark, reddish brown but that's way more common.

So, between my dad's death happening how it did— trapping me staring at the reflection of a dead body's empty eyes and my own blood-filling, blinking pair as I screamed—and my discomfort with my eyes from a delayed result of it, I really dislike looking at my reflection. I haven't intentionally looked at it in about fifteen years.

Because of all that, I shave from touch and memory.

Currently, with an antique straight razor I found in an oddity shop years ago. As I run my fingers down my cream-slick jaw line, I feel the scars from Dad's yellow teeth chipping off into me. Most days, I just tune them out. After a nightmare, it's not that easy. I rub the scars and stare at the razor. It's sharp.

So sharp you could….

My hand trembles. I sigh and shake my head, then start shaving my neck.

Two Pop-Tarts shoot up, jump half out of the toaster, then drop back into place. I quickly snatch them and drop them on a small plate. I blow on one and start to nibble at it as I walk down the hall to the living room.

I stop and feed Ganges and Yamuna, Audrey's two butterfly tail goldfish. They're kind of ugly and pretty at the same time. One is black and white and one is orange and white with splotches of blue-black. I can never remember which is which.

I turn on Audrey's ancient twenty-seven-inch Trinitron TV and it takes a while to warm up. Slap in one of my similarly antiquated *Robotech* collection VHS tapes for about the hundredth time. The intro music alone is pure comfort.

I still love *Robotech*. I learned years ago about its hatchet-job origins from other unrelated series that were all by the same company in Japan and had the same mech designer. I watched those and dug them too.

Then *Cowboy Bebop* and *Neon Genesis Evangelion* usurped it as my favorite anime, along with their own fantastic intro tunes.

But something about *Robotech* always keeps me coming back. Not what the original creators intended, yet it exists as its own version. Something about that made it almost more special to me, but I'd have trouble explaining why if asked.

I see my "new toy" on the table: the Victor HDV-426 SSD camcorder I had shipped over from Japan.

Was not…cheap.

Audrey won't let me pay rent, so I had a little money in the bank from freelance illustration jobs, designing and making merch for local bands and such, and part-time retail jobs I get here and there—mostly for product discounts.

I don't know what I actually want to make with my new toy—maybe a documentary if a subject strikes me or short horror films or even a no-budget midnight/cult-leaning feature—but after trying the camera out at a tech convention I went to with Audrey, Hirofumi, and Kaori, I just needed one.

H and K's beta party should be interesting. They've been working on their damn game in one way or another since I met them on a travel-study semester at an art school in Japan years back.

I spend most of the day fiddling with my camera and watching *Robotech*. As late afternoon starts transitioning to early evening, I decide to take the camera out for a test run.

I unplug the camera and stow it, the attachments, and instructions into their special carrying bag, then grab my jacket on the way to the door.

chapter 3

I step out into a cool, mostly cloudy, somewhat foggy San Francisco approaching early evening. Lock the front door and look around.

Perfection. You can keep your "clear blue skies" bullshit. If it's not at least partly cloudy and comfortably cool, I'll be grumpy all day.

I hike up Greenwich a couple blocks and climb a set of old wooden stairs up to Pioneer Park and Coit Tower on top of Telegraph Hill.

Take my new camera out of its bag and get some shots all around from the panoramic views of the city and surrounding Bay Area.

Continue to the Greenwich Steps, one of two sets of steps that snake down the east side of Telegraph Hill. On the way down, I hear dozens of whistles and squawks and the flapping of wings in the trees all around.

The famous "Wild Parrots of Telegraph Hill," as they're most commonly known, but I've seen them all over in different parts of the bay, when I think about it.

I stop and get some shots of the colorful, talky birds, then keep going down the steps.

I reach the bottom and head to the waterfront, fiddling with my camera and getting more shots as I head north along a wide, pier-flanked sidewalk that runs along Embarcadero.

Pier 39 is good for some fun shots, with its mixture of arcades, novelties, and themed retail shops. The ferry to Sausalito arrives soon after I get to Pier 41, and I get some footage of it filling up with passengers and leaving as the sun is going down.

Fisherman's Wharf is becoming backlit and silhouetted by the last of the sun's setting in the west, as I arrive.

Shit, I should probably head back so Audrey doesn't have to wait for me—

"Hey, stinky!"

I look toward the voice. Audrey is leaning on a newspaper rack, grinning.

How does she do that?

She's dressed for a funeral with a Lindy Hop wake.

Damn she's fine.

I laugh and shake my head as I walk over to her. "I am not stinky."

"Eh, I think you are."

Audrey smiles, deep red lips stretching across her almost perfect teeth. Glimmer in her lightly glazed eyes.

Must have smoked a bowl or two before coming to find me. After getting all done up like she is. Guess I just missed her getting home.

"Whatever. I showered and everything."

She makes a show of thinking hard for a moment.

"I don't believe that…but I have decided that I shall keep you anyway. So, the Swede is thataway."

She points over her shoulder with her thumb. "Shall we?"

I narrow my eyes. "What about my stench?"

"I'll crack a window."

She takes my hand and leads me toward the parking area.

The "Swede" is Audrey's 1963 Volvo 122S. Cream paint with pale-blue interior.

She loves that car to death. Any maintenance that doesn't require a hydraulic lift, she does herself. The way she fawns over it, you'd think she was the original owner.

We get in and Audrey drives the Swede south through the city.

I take out my camera and focus my attention on it, so as not to have a panic attack.

I get the convenience and comforts of driving in concept, just not how people can stand it.

There are cars everywhere, sometimes just inches apart. Hurtling instruments of death, is what they are.

After what happened to my mom, I never could get used to driving being normal. I tried to get my license in high school and got so worked up I fainted during the road test. The DMV examiner had to grab the wheel to get us to the side of the road, then pulled the handbrake.

Needless to say, I failed that one. Never tried again. Living in the Bay Area, there's not much need for cars anyway. Have transit pass, will travel.

I have the camera bag open and I'm checking out a detachable remote viewfinder. Part of it fits in and around the ear and doubles as a recording monitor. Also has controls for zoom, focus, etc.

I sync the viewfinder with the camera and adjust the camera settings remotely, causing a big smile to stretch across my face.

Audrey glances over and notices my excitement.

"So, what's the verdict? You stoked on your toy?"

"Hella stoked. This thing is tight."

She smiles too.

"Good. Make something cool with it."

My smile fades.

"We'll see…."

The Swede pulls up to one of many old warehouses in the South of Market area. There are people outside the door smoking cigarettes—and various other things, probably—and I get that old urge.

Have to hurry by them or I might try to bum a smoke. Nah, Audrey would kill me. She quit so I would too.

I suspect she sneaks one here and there like I do, though.

We get out and walk toward the smoke-clouded entrance area, and I hear throbbing, bass-heavy music as we get closer to the door.

A few drunken skaters are busting tricks over a spot densely littered with shattered beer bottles.

One tries a three-sixty flip and almost snaps his ankle on the landing, then flops against a parked jeep, setting off its anti-theft alarm. I try not to laugh at the impaired trickster as we enter the warehouse.

Glowing images dance across large sections of the warehouse ceiling and upper walls. Digital projectors throw shots from movies, cartoons, bomb tests, and instructional-video compilations up all around, working as atmosphere and the main light source.

There must be three hundred people in the open shop-floor area. A DJ spins records on the north side of the warehouse near the stairs up to the old offices and observation deck. The music is a cross between trip-hop, goth-industrial, and chopped-and-screwed hip-hop. "Witch House," I think it's called.

People dance all around the DJ table and open area in dense throngs that only break up at the edges of the central area, which is lined and filled with rows of nice computers and monitors. The people on the dance floor are lit up by a glow from below, but I can't see how.

All of the computers are taken. I see a girl leave a computer, and a guy who's been waiting takes the seat. That must be H and K's game.

Past all that, there's a projection on the back wall that doesn't seem to be a part of the atmospheric video collage. More like an impromptu and unrelated film screening.

Audrey guides me through the dance floor. I look down as she pulls me by the hand and see that we're walking on glowing, pulsing LED panels interconnected on the floor.

Cool.

We emerge from the sea of people at the far side and find a long metal shop table covered with various bottles of hard liquor, liqueurs, and mixers. Several ice-filled coolers below filled with canned and bottled beer. Even some wine. White in the coolers, red up top.

The music dies down a bit as an outro crossfades into the next intro.

"I thought I saw him," Audrey says, twirling slowly.

She stops and smiles, looking past me.

I feel long, slender fingers gently clasp my shoulder muscles from behind and rub like a masseuse.

"You know…men have nipples too," a Japanese-accented voice says. The hands stop rubbing and start sliding down my chest. "Ever wonder why?"

"Nhnngggah!" I cry as I spin out of Hirofumi's grasp.

Hiro shambles zombie-like toward me and I push him back repeatedly.

He smells like a brewery.

"N–nipples!" Hirofumi bellows as he advances.

I make gun shapes with each hand and dual-wield, firing with mimed recoil at my friend's head.

Hiro makes a sound like a deflating balloon with his mouth and crumples to his knees, dropping his chin to his chest.

Audrey laughs and says, "And…*scene!*"

Without raising his head or moving anything else, Hiro's right arm raises toward me like it has a mind of its own. I take it and pull him to his feet.

Hiro's eyes open crossed, then he uncrosses them. "You have *freed* me!"

We all laugh and Hirofumi slaps me on the back and squeezes Audrey's shoulder. I go to return Hiro's back slap and hit a ratty old backpack.

"*Irrashaimase!* Thanks for coming!" Hiro says, casually nodding a little bow.

Having a second to breathe, I notice that Hirofumi is wearing a puffy hooded vest, thick sweater, scarf, bright orange camouflage BDU pants, and unpolished secondhand combat boots. His already punky hair is also messier than usual.

I turn Hirofumi by his shoulder and see that he has a bedroll strapped under a tattered backpack. A miniature metal shopping cart the size of a small shoebox dangles from the pack by a rusty carabiner.

I smile. "What is this getup?"

"It will make sense. Here, what should we drink?"

Hirofumi crosses to the table and picks up two bottles. He squints at them through his drunken haze. He makes a face and sets down one bottle. Audrey and I approach the table.

I chuckle. "Do your worst."

"Same," Audrey agrees.

"Famous last words," Hirofumi says while he studies the bottles.

Hirofumi grabs bottles of juice, liqueur, and rum from one of the coolers and three plastic cups, then proceeds to make a trio of stiff drinks with a big cocktail shaker. He hands me and Audrey ours and starts toward the computer area.

"Okay! Let me show you!"

We follow Hirofumi but don't make it ten steps before

Audrey peeps and stops abruptly. Hiro and I stop and look back. Two small, camouflage-sleeved arms are clamped around Audrey's waist from behind and her arms are raised, trying to steady her sloshing drink.

A very drunk Kaori pops her head around, looking up at Audrey from just above her waist. She's bent over and leaning into her.

Audrey shakes her head, smiling.

"You guys are faded!"

Kaori moans and scrunches her face up. Audrey puts her hand on Kaori's big knit cap. She has the same weird hobo look going on.

"Oh," Audrey coos while stroking Kaori's head. "You okay, cutie?"

"*Ijo nashi!*" Kaori says as she sticks the thumb on each little gloved hand up.

Hirofumi narrows his eyes at her and says, "You should vomit and be in bed," then follows with something long and fast in Japanese that I can't catch all of. Loving and concerned yet stern is all I can glean from it.

Audrey laughs.

Kaori makes a playfully indignant face.

The DJ transitions into another track. Kaori's face lights up and she stands, almost spills Audrey's drink again, and teeters for a moment but succeeds in regaining stability.

Kaori exclaims, grasping Audrey's dress.

"Ah! I love this! Can we dance?!"

"Do I have a choice?"

Kaori smiles big and shakes her head. She takes Audrey's free hand and pulls her back toward the heart of the dance floor. The captive Audrey waves with her drink as she is whisked away. I wave back and Hiro makes a sound of mild disgust, then shakes his head and chuckles.

"Come here," Hirofumi says and continues toward the computer area.

Hirofumi and I emerge from the crowds of dancers into

the rows of people and computers, then Hirofumi leads me down one aisle and stops. He takes a big sip of his drink and casually gestures around at the glowing widescreen monitors.

Looking over several shoulders in quick succession, I gather a few things immediately.

Third-person view behind the character. Highly stylized, and gorgeously so. All of these people are playing together but the style seems different from one screen to the next. Sometimes subtly, sometimes more pronounced.

"We call it *Home Free*. For now, at least. With slash in between. *Home, slash, Free*."

Hiro takes another sip and I can feel him watching me for reactions.

I lean closer and focus on one screen at a time.

Cityscape. Skyscrapers, moving cars, and large areas of the streets and neighborhoods are stark and minimally detailed white, black, and gray like a high-contrast photocopy. Many of the skyscrapers are tall enough that they disappear into the fluffy, swirling clouds high above. In contrast, the player characters are vibrantly colorful. Exaggerated human forms. Ridiculously short or tall, round and squat or gaunt and slender. Huge or tiny eyes, noses, mouths. Everything in between. They all share one thing, though. They're caricatures of homeless people. Scarves, hoods, parkas, camo, backpacks, shopping carts, books, sleeping bags.

The atmospheric non-player characters share the photocopy look of the buildings and lack the exaggeration of the players. They are unisex and uniform, very tall, and walk too fast. They don't react in any way to the players. Players get knocked over if they don't move out of the NPC paths.

I watch the screen of a girl who's controlling a tall, thin character with huge eyes and a tiny mouth. A bright blue bird balances atop the character's head, and it sings as he digs through a large wire trash receptacle on the corner of an intersection. The trash in the can is photocopy stark, but recyclable bottles and cans and edible, practically untouched food all glow colorfully. The character collects them, placing the recyclables and food in separate bags with quick keystrokes of *R* and *F*.

On another screen, a cartoonishly obese hobo sits and drinks a huge beer in an alley. In reality, it would be over a hundred ounces, but he holds it one-handed. After every chug he takes, digital urine soaks his pants. So much so that he's sitting in a puddle of it that grows a little every time. His tongue hangs out over his huge, gap-toothed grin. Clouds of stink form from each breath, and his little eyes are red and glassy.

I laugh and shake my head.

"What the fuck have you done, Hiro?"

"You don't like it?"

"I love it! You guys made a damn massively multiplayer homeless role-playing game! How could I not like it? It's funny. Strangely cute too. Great graphics. If it's fun to play and has something to say, you're set."

"I hope it is fun. I think it is. Other thoughts?"

"I'm not sure if you'd be worried about it, but some people might be a little offended by it."

"What I say to that is, play it. It's more than just… supposed to be funny. Like how you just put it—it says something. The style and silly things bring you in, then over time you see more meaning."

"Let's play it then, motherfucker!"

Hirofumi laughs and nods, then gestures for me to follow him, so I do. We come around to the next row of computers.

I sip on my drink and wait for a seat. Before too long, a guy logs off and gets up. He heads toward the film projection as I sit in the seat.

Hirofumi slaps my shoulders.

"Now, you play!"

The login is set to default entries. I click through and see a character customization screen. Seeing how many slider bars and options there are, I just click a button for RANDOM, and after a moment, a tall, thick character appears. Regular-size eyes, huge nose and mouth. I take a swig from my drink and click again. I get a medium-size woman with huge eyes, tiny pupils, and a big mouth that hangs open.

I laugh. "Tell 'em Large Marge sent ya."

Hirofumi chortles behind me.

I notice the young woman's screen next to me is different. Glowing faeries flutter around, and her view has a subtly rolling distortion and pulse to it.

"Why does her world look different? With like the faeries and stuff?"

"When you roll a new character, randomizer attaches a mental illness or condition to it. Almost always. Her character got something like…delusional. Kaori programmed all that. Crazy complicated."

I click the RANDOM button again and get a medium-size man with intense eyes. He's wearing a camouflage tarp like a cloak with a large hood and combat boots with spats. The eyes reflect light as they dart around cautiously in the shadow of the hood. His pack and bedroll hang low under the back of the tarp and there's another pack slung low around the front like a forties parachute pack.

I type UNCLE SALTY in the name box, then press READY.

Hirofumi laughs behind me and slaps my back.

"Perfect!"

Uncle Salty is sleeping on the bedroll in the corner of a fenced-off, abandoned lot. I move the cursor and see that it changes when hovering over him. I click and Uncle Salty wakes up. He stretches and hauls himself up. The bedroll rolls itself up and glides into place as the packs zip up and do the same.

Using standard WASD and mouse controls, I guide Uncle Salty through and out of the lot, the character grumbling the whole way.

Uncle Salty gets to the sidewalk, and I guide him through the city as he admires the beauty of the impossibly tall, stark skyscrapers.

I nod. "It really does look great."

"You have only seen the beginning. As you play, it becomes more and more—"

"Hiro!"

I see Oscar approaching, another school friend of ours who works on H and K's game now.

"What, man?" Hirofumi asks, "I'm showing Felix," then takes another sip of his drink.

"Sorry. Hey, Felix. You makin' me hella nervous, as always."

I blush a bit and nod a greeting.

Hirofumi raises his eyebrows in a "Well?" expression.

Oscar catches the look.

"Alright, shit. Zhenya's having trouble with the gravity apparatus upstairs. I've never smoked that way either, so I'm no help."

"You just have to sink it, light it, pull it up, and…." Hirofumi curses in Japanese and shakes his head. "Okay, I'll come up. Hey, you should play more, Felix."

"Totally."

Hirofumi wades back through the dancers and is quickly out of sight. Oscar extends his open hand and I lightly slap it, then we bump fists.

"Watching Hiro go off on Yev is epic hilarity. I'll see you later."

"Later, man."

Oscar takes off after Hirofumi. I steer Uncle Salty around the stark city and sip on my drink—until I notice it's almost empty.

I get up and make my way back through the dancers to

the bar table.

chapter 4

I make a stiff gin and juice, then head back to the computers.

Through the smoothly writhing limbs and bodies, I see Audrey and Kaori dancing in the glow of the LED floor panels. Audrey does love dancing. All kinds. I'm not big on it but she doesn't seem to mind.

There are guys dancing behind her, probably enjoying the view…but she always seems to dance for herself and no one else.

I continue my journey back to the computers but find my seat is taken. A bookish but tatted hipster girl wearing 1950s cat-eye-style glasses has usurped me and is now guiding Uncle Salty around.

How dare you, Salty. I thought we were tight….

I look around and one of the projections on the ceiling grabs my attention.

Eye surgery.

I wince and look at another. Time-lapse of flowers blooming.

My eyes go from one to the next.

Little Richard performing. A bald politician having a bullet for breakfast in front of a lectern. A 1980s commercial for M.U.S.C.L.E. wrestling action figures.

Another property with a *Robotech*-like history.

Home video through a living room window of a trash truck collecting an alley dumpster. A foreign reporter having his head sawed off by an extremist. The *Gummi Bears* cartoon intro. The very last shot of Tarkovsky's film *Stalker*.

My favorite part. I enjoy and respect his film but prefer the Strugatskys' *Roadside Picnic* novel.

A plane dropping water on a forest fire. That commercial where an old lady "returns" a tire through the shop window. Anthony Bourdain smoking and laughing after a meal in the late-night glow of a food stall in what looks like Southeast Asia. A space-shuttle launch that ends in a fireball.

Cheery.

My eye movement combined with the randomness of the video clips creates its own narrative. It strikes me that it would be all but impossible to ever experience it the same way twice.

Each shot would inform my interpretation of the next, recontextualizing differently with every change in order. Shot *A* plus shot *B* affects how I feel about shot *C*, and so on.

Then eventually—

I cringe and shake my head.

Nah, forget that film-school overthinking shit. Too much of that pretty much ruined it for me.

My eyes come to rest on what I can see of the film projection on the far wall. Curiosity kicks in and I start heading that way.

There are several large couches of varying designs and states of repair and a few big recliner-style chairs. They are arranged in a series of rough concentric half circles around a big sheet tacked to the wall with its bottom edge a few feet off the ground. On a rolling cart near the rear of this area is a sixteen-millimeter projector clacking and ticking away. A large speaker on the ground near the cart is connected by a quarter-inch cable and pumps out the mono soundtrack.

I find a spot on a big, puffy couch next to a guy who is passed out. The guy squirms a bit when I sit, then settles.

The current film is a faux documentary. Animated diagrams and charts, a disheveled, wired person looking into the camera earnestly in some kind of bunker set, and grainy footage of extreme violence.

Soon after sitting down, I'm laughing to the point of tears.

The part that pushes me over the edge is an animated sequence of humans walking through a jungle. They come across a slow-moving sloth. Take pictures. Laugh. The sloth becomes almost invisible, running and jumping back and forth from one side of the couple to the other, and ends up hanging from a draped vine above them. After a pause, the people unravel into chunks and ribbons of organs, flesh, and blood, *Fist of the North Star* style. The sloth empties its bowels down onto the pile of viscera, drops to the jungle floor, and crawls off.

Huge, wavy red block letters fill the screen:

THIS COULD BE YOU

My laughing wakes up the guy next to me. He looks around and glares at me, then gets up and leaves.

Hey, it's not my fault that shit is hilarious.

A girl who was standing and watching the film from the periphery beelines toward the open seat—

But someone else beats her to it.

An odd-looking young woman wearing big, mirrored aviator sunglasses hops over the back of the couch from behind me and flops down into the vacated seat.

The approaching girl starts to protest but the odd girl

casually flicks her hand at her a few times in a "shoo" gesture.

"Hey, I was—"

"Bzzzzzzzz!" the odd girl says and shoos the girl away again, so she storms off.

"Oh, don't cry, Nancy!"

I'm unsure how to peg this odd woman's style down other than maybe under the general umbrella of dark and weird—

Like…if Macy's had a Thrift Store Homeless Crusty Goth Pirate Tribal Warrior section, she'd be the poster girl.

Two thin chains run from one of her many earrings to a nose ring, the lower one running through a string of beads that look like full-size translucent human teeth. The hair on the front half of her head looks to have grown back a bit from being buzzed short and what is there is dyed all different colors and patterns. The rest is a black and blue tangle that drapes down between her shoulder blades and rests on the hood of a threadbare jacket. She also wears old-style loose, puffy-around-the-thigh jodhpurs tucked into knee-high combat boots. I notice the material the pants are made of catches the light—dark, shiny, smooth.

She rummages through something like a messenger bag and pulls out a Zippo lighter, then pulls a half-finished smoke from behind an ear. It reminds me of a beedi, only thicker and crimson.

The young woman lights her smoke, then slowly and deliberately closes the Zippo as she takes a deep pull and holds it for a moment. She moans in an almost obscene manner as she exhales out through her nose and mouth.

Watching her enjoy her weird beedi so much is like torture to me.

I need to get an electronic cigarette or whatever you call them. I've been curious about those but Audrey's big on cold turkey.

The odd young woman looks over at me, and after a

quick glimpse of myself in the two big mirrors on her face, I wince and look away. I pretend to be interested in the screen while she rummages through her bag some more.

She says, "Some people are just rude, you know?"

"Huh?"

"I mean, you tell a person to fuck off and they just look at you like, 'Uh….' I think I'm pretty good at it but shit…. They don't get it."

She glances at me.

"You're cool. A bit of a staring problem but I can live with that."

She takes another drag and exhales the thick smoke as she stubs the beedi or whatever it is out again on her boot heel. She tucks it back where it came from, then digs back into her bag.

I chuckle. "Sorry. Your style is a bit…unique."

"Maybe I'm just ahead of my time."

She takes off her sunglasses.

Damn. She is stunning.

I'm struck by her large, lovely eyes—and of course there is something odd about them too. I can't tell what color they are because she's wearing some sort of specialty contact lenses. Reflective but also translucent.

Not like the B movie–monster-style contacts some goths and rivetheads wear. These look like expensive, custom kit.

I also have trouble guessing at her background.

Maybe Anglo and East Asian? Arab?

"Oh wow, I love your eyes," she says.

I blink a few times. "Gee, thanks."

"Ooh! You know what would be great right now?"

She looks at me expectantly, her eager familiarity disarming.

I also notice just a touch of an accent I can't place, almost like she's consciously masking it with an "American" accent like a British crossover actor.

"What?"

"One of those cheeseburgers where the buns are donuts! Maybe a breakfast one with eggs and bacon on it too. Holy *shit* that sounds so good!"

A few people at different couches and chairs look back at us, then go back to watching the screen.

"Seriously?"

She frowns at me. "What, are you a vegetarian or something?"

"No, but—"

"Never mind. You killed it."

She rummages in her bag some more.

I shake my head. "Do they miss you in the magic forest?"

The young woman narrows her eyes at me and looks around like I just blew her cover, but I can't tell if she's joking. Satisfied, she turns back.

"Siobhán," says the odd young woman.

It sounds something like Shiv-awn, but I remember seeing that name spelled once and it didn't look like it would.

I make eye contact again, reluctantly.

Her eyes are a little hypnotic.

"That's me…," she says, then lowers her chin and raises her eyebrows. "And you?"

"Uh…Felix."

She laughs. "Adorable. You hot?"

Siobhán opens up her jacket and pulls it apart some, revealing a worn black t-shirt with the sleeves cut off. I catch glimpses of what look like old-school Yakuza-style shoulder tattoos that disappear into her upper jacket sleeves, and parts of others peeking out from the ragged arm openings in her shirt. I wonder how much of her body is tattooed.

Then I feel a sharp pang of guilt when I realize I would very much like to see all her tattoos. I look back at the screen, now determined to let the conversation end.

"Hmm…so." Siobhán shifts her butt, spins, and kicks

her booted legs up onto my lap and leans back against the puffy couch arm. She nestles in, rubbing the boots against my thighs, then interlacing her fingers on her chest and crossing her legs. The boots have intricate, colorful designs worked and layered into the leather—various atom bombs and nuclear missiles, from what I can make out in the flickering light of the film.

I'm stunned by her presumptuous intimacy. I've never met anyone like this before and feel almost helpless.

"What kind of undies do you like a girl to wear?"

"*Excuse* me?"

"When you're walking behind a girl and checking out her ass, which style do you hope-slash-imagine she's wearing?"

"Are you all right?"

"I'm fantastic. Are *you* all right?"

I try to lift Siobhán's boots off my lap but she presses them back down. I stare at the screen and try to ignore a slight stirring in my pants.

She narrows her eyes a bit.

"Hey, if I'm making you uncomfortable, I can stop. Honestly, say the word. I have no interest in an unwilling naughty-time participant. You don't want me to stop, though, do you?"

If I'm being honest with myself…no, I don't.

I shake my head. "You don't make any sense. And I think maybe you enjoy making people uncomfortable."

"Only if there's a damn good reason, prickly pear…. So, I think I have you pegged but I've been wrong before. Honest question."

"Why do you care?" I ask.

"You can tell a lot about a person by what gets them all hot and bothered."

I frown. "Can you now?"

"Certainly. Those naughty, possibly embarrassing little preferences and fetishes that really get you going say a lot.

Different for each person, though, other than resulting from imprints of sight, smell, strong emotion and such. There's an enormous but finite mesh of possible triggers. Biological imperatives guided or confused by details of a formative moment."

I chuckle and raise my eyebrows. "What, you're a shrink or something all of a sudden?"

She pauses and appears to be watching something moving behind me. I turn and look back at the area she is staring toward. In the glow from the ceiling and sloth-movie projections, I see some stacked plastic chairs, a sealed box of paper-towel rolls, and Zhenya's folded up Ping-Pong table against the wall.

Nothing there....

"Then there's partialism. For instance, you're obviously a butt man 'cause you barely glanced at my chest when I opened my coat, and you can keep eye contact almost effortlessly. You gauged general size and maybe shape and moved on. You took a lot more time trying to figure out what material my silky trousers are made of like you were, I don't know, trying to imagine what it would feel like to palm and squeeze the aforementioned butt in it maybe? Your focus on the material leads me to believe you might not mind seeing a woman wearing sexy little undies. I can't fault you for that, if that's the case, as I share that fondness. For your information, my trousers are made of a material you are not familiar with, and it feels *phenomenal*."

She lifts her hands and makes an exaggerated squeezing gesture and opens her eyes real wide for a moment, then relaxes them.

"So, you gonna ask me what kind of unmentionables I have on or you just want to get lost with me so I can show you?"

She winks and smiles seductively, then licks her left upper canine tooth gently. Her boots slowly, rhythmically rub against my thighs.

I'm really turned on and hating myself right now. It's like no matter what I say or how I say it, she knows she's getting to me and I actually really don't want her to stop. Ok, Hail Mary—

"My girlfriend might not—"

"Wait, girlfriend?"

She drops her hands to her chest. The mischievous gleam leaves her eyes for the first time and is replaced by a hollow stare.

Like she's looking through me. It's almost eerie.

Siobhán says, "My, my, aren't you just a cruel joke."

"What?"

"I guess after long enough things do start to come back around…or maybe I finally burnt my brain with all those lovely drugs."

Siobhán closes her eyes and sighs deeply, then opens them and the gleam mostly returns. She smiles again but seems different. She looks exhausted now.

"If you have to, think of it as a survey question. I'm just doing a 'cute guy on the street' survey on how you like your presents wrapped—"

"He likes his presents wrapped and given by *me*, you fucking slag…," Audrey says from behind the couch.

I all but jump in my seat.

Siobhán looks unfazed.

"Hey, it's the lucky lady! You know, your boyfriend's a cutie patootie. You should keep a closer eye on him."

Oh shit!

I push Siobhán's legs off my lap and stand, careful not to straighten all the way too fast.

Siobhán uses the momentum from the movement to spin back up to her original sitting position and crosses her arms and legs with a flourish.

Audrey steps around the couch and leans over, getting right in Siobhán's face from the side.

Siobhán ignores Audrey's intense glare and watches

sloths fight over a gnawed-on severed head on the screen.

Audrey gets even closer.

"Find someone else, or I'll jam my thumbs into your eyes, crack open your skull, and piss on your brain."

Siobhán raises her thin eyebrows and gives a sarcastic frown, then puts her big sunglasses back on and jabs them gently with her thumbs as if to test their effectiveness as armor.

She uncrosses her legs, pulls two shiny, straight objects out of her boot tops, and stands, forcing Audrey to straighten up. Siobhán has almost a head on her, but Audrey doesn't seem concerned.

Siobhán raises her hands, moving quick and smooth and the objects in them come apart, flipping on pivot hinges and glinting in the reflected light.

They must be balisongs, AKA butterfly knives, but their dark, double-edged blades look strange to me.

Kind of see through and…opalescent, I think the word is.

The handles and pivots also look intricately detailed and almost ornate, and I can tell she didn't buy these cheap in some shop in Chinatown or on Pier 39.

They look almost like weird, dangerous pieces of art or artifacts from a museum.

She fans them expertly, flipping them between and around fingers, over her hands, then transfers them from one hand to the other with an aerial, slaps them into her palms, fans them around the backs of her thumbs and closes both with a final flip-lock, then slides them into her jacket pockets.

"Blow me, 'fugee," Siobhán says, then cocks her head and makes a smooch sound.

Audrey doesn't look scared at all. Not even a slight flinch. She just stares at where Siobhán's eyes must be behind her mirrored glasses.

Siobhán picks up her bag and looks at me, then points

at Audrey.

"Now, this girl knows how to tell someone to fuck off. She's a keeper."

She steps around Audrey and walks through small groups of gawking partygoers toward an exit door to the street.

Over her shoulder with a hint of an accent, Siobhán says, "Later, boyo."

The "boyo" hits me like a slap and I flinch. I'm confused for a moment and struck in a deep, ineffable place.

"There won't be a later, wanderer cunt," Audrey says.

Siobhán reaches the door and raises her middle finger toward us without looking back as she uses her other hand to open it and leave.

chapter 5

"What the fuck was that?" Audrey stares at the road ahead as she drives us home in the Swede, speeding the whole way.

That's the first thing she's said directly to me since the thing with Siobhán at the party. Audrey stormed smoothly through the *Home/Free* and dance area, then went upstairs and I followed. She said goodbye to our friends. They protested her early egress. I also said goodbye and left with her.

"What?" I ask, knowing exactly what.

I'm back to fiddling with my camera and have the eye-patch viewfinder attachment on as I mess with more settings.

"That weirdo whore back there! Do you know that fucking wanderer slut?!"

"'Wanderer'? What does that even mean, Audrey?"

This is the other side of Audrey. When she feels wronged, she loses it. The insults come out. Almost like a mean old woman. Audrey unhinged. But this one, she's never said before.

"Doesn't matter what it means—"

"I've never seen her before. She just sat down and started talking nonsense."

"It made perfect sense, Felix. She wanted to get some, and you know it! Why were you even talking to her?!"

"She was coked out or something. I didn't say a word to her. She sat down and started babbling."

"Why didn't you tell her to go away?!"

"I was watching the fucking sloth movie, okay?!"

I couldn't think of anything better to say. Nothing true.

Audrey gets real quiet. It's like she just expects me to take it and take it until she runs out of steam. When I start to stand up for myself, she sulks.

I see a small circular button on the lens without a marking. It's almost flush with the surface and recessed just a bit.

"Hey, am I the one who was dancing with other guys?"

"Not fair at all. We both know half of those guys would be more dangerous if they were dancing with you, and besides, not one of them gets to touch. If you didn't hate dancing, I would do it with you. I would rather dance with you, actually."

I finally realize she might just act like she isn't bothered by something because she cares about me.

Okay, maybe I should try dance lessons to surprise her on McValentine's Day™ or her next birthday. Or the one after that, with my lack of talent.

When is her birthday again? She never brings it up herself and I could swear it was different one year. Audrey doesn't talk about her childhood at all.

Maybe she was an orphan and doesn't really know what her birthday was.

I press the recessed button on my new camera.

There is a tiny jolt like haptic feedback or static electricity.

I pan the camera out the window view speeding by. There is no obvious change in the eye-patch view.

What does that button do?

I set the camera down and take the manual out of the bag. In the viewfinder over my eye, I see an angled shot of Audrey fuming from my lap level. I try to read the table of contents in the light from passing cars and streetlights. The different input from both eyes at once is disorienting, so I close my left eye and focus on reading the manual.

Can't find that button described in the contents or in the diagram of the camera. As I flip through to find a more lens-specific diagram, I relax my left eyelid and let it open some. I find a diagram of the lens.

Okay, this diagram would have to—

Wait…. What is that about?

Audrey's eyes look different.

Her eyes are naturally a dark brown, but right now they look jet black. And they're…pulsing.

With each pulse, the black spreads. The whites of her eyes are almost completely black already.

I shake my head and blink a couple times.

No change. Black and pulsing.

Still holding the manual up, I close my right eye this time for a better look at this special-effect filter.

Or whatever it is. It looks so real. Match moving and rendering based on facial recognition or something?

I raise my left hand and search for the focus dial. Find and adjust it. The black pulsing gets blurry, then sharp again.

Fumble for the zoom lever and nudge wide by accident, then telephoto a few times. It zooms in a bit each time and I see that the black is not just black. It's subtly shimmering and iridescent.

The whites are covered now and it's still growing.

What look like curved seams and holes appear all over her face and head in rhythm with the pulsing black in her eyes. A dark mist wafts from her nostrils illuminated by a glow from up inside them.

Audrey notices me holding the camera manual and whips her head toward me—

"HEY, FUCKHEAD! YOU AREN'T EVEN LISTENING!"

Her voice is shrill and abrasive but has roar-like added depth. It echoes and reverberates until being absorbed by the metal frame of the car, which hums in time with it.

As this bellows from her mouth, her face and head warp and distort, breaking apart while burning and melting into organic chaos. Parts implode. Others burst. Some just float in place where they should be while this happens around them—or go translucent making some of this more visible.

A cross-section of Audrey's cheekbone and muscle are melted away by an avalanche of bubbling liquid flesh. A triangular prism of ocular cavity dripping down to her teeth. A sliver of nasal cavity widens and stretches open exposing brain matter before rolling like mercury down into her throat and showing a cutout of glowing, sizzling esophagus, larynx, and neck muscles.

The glow and lambent smoke now coming from her mouth, nose, ears, and behind her inky, blue-black eyes is almost blinding.

This all vibrates and glitches in rhythm with the persistent throbbing I realize must be Audrey's arterial pulse.

What kind of sensor picks that up?

It takes less than two seconds for this intense, blazing maelstrom to occur.

This camera was worth every penny. The real-time audio effects are incredible too.

After it "speaks," the distorted mess of light, smoke, and flesh calms a bit and looks back at the road.

How much did it cost to slip this much effects tech into the camera itself…not to mention why would they with so many programs for "pro-sumer" postproduction?

I zoom back out.

"QUIT PLAYING WITH THAT FUCKING THING AND TALK TO ME!"

The voice is louder this time and the distortions even more intense.

I take off the viewfinder, detach it, and throw it into the bag on the car floor, then exhale sharply and turn my head to complain—

It's all still there—blurry, but there.

A deep chill washes through my whole body and I shudder. I can't look away.

The blurriness of the bright—yet somehow also dark—pulsing mess makes it even more horrifying.

"THANKS FOR COMING BACK TO THE REAL WORLD, FELIX!"

She notices my stare.

"WHAT? DON'T LOOK AT ME LIKE THAT! IT'S NOT FUNNY—STOP!"

I tear my eyes away and lock them on the street ahead. For the first time since childhood, the view of cars rushing through the night all around me is almost soothing.

Careful not to see myself, I look sideways at the reflection in the windshield of the swirling thing that was so recently my lovely girlfriend. The glowing and burning make it easy to see, even though the car is dark inside.

I watch the whole thing undulate rhythmically. Feel nauseated. Head hurts. The organic glitches and cutout views swell and shrink. Every pulse of the thing makes my nausea worse and my head hurt more.

"WHAT THE HELL IS WRONG WITH YOU?!"

When it scream-talks at me, both feelings multiply. My mouth fills with pre-vomit saliva—close my eyes and try to breathe it away.

"HOW MUCH DID YOU DRINK?!"

The voice is too much. It vibrates through my skull and the pain is awful—turns my stomach the rest of the way. I roll down the window as fast as I can and lean out.

"YOU BETTER NOT—"

I do my best to project my stomach contents away from the car and I'm…mostly successful. A car behind us in the other lane honks.

"DAMMIT, FELIX!"

Somehow its voice is worse every time.

I heave again. Someone in the car that honked laughs loudly and yells, "Lightweight bitch!" out their window.

Fuck you!

"FELIX—"

It starts to speak but I raise my hand in a cautious pleading gesture. I hang out the door and spit a few times.

I see the asphalt rushing by below.

How fast could we be going? We're on a regular street. Couldn't be that fast, right?

"ARE YOU OKAY, BABY?"

The intonation tells me the thing is trying to sound concerned, but the voice is more shrill and booming than ever and the vibration of the car frame is almost deafening as it absorbs it. My insides convulse a bit but there isn't anything left to purge.

It's almost unbearable….

It's so loud….

Why can't I feel it vibrating? I ask myself in a distant part of my mind that isn't overwhelmed by pain, sickness, and horror.

"TALK TO ME!"

I moan against the door, then lean out and try to heave again.

The door is unlocked, I remember that much.

I'll have to be quick. Who knows what it can do. Why hasn't it attacked me yet?

I close my eyes and take a deep breath, then let it out slowly.

I look over at it again to be sure. It gets brighter, darker, and weirder by the moment. Wipe my mouth on my sleeve. Steel myself.

"What's there to t-talk about?"

As quickly as I can, I unbuckle my lap belt and try to open the passenger door—but it sticks with a creak.

I steal a panicked glance at the pulsing inferno behind the wheel.

The thing looks over and its twisted, melting face forms into the closest thing it can muster to an astonished expression.

Lost my chance—I'm so dead!

No—try again!

I slam my shoulder against the door and it swings free, then grab the top of the frame and pull myself up and out of the seat and flop my left arm up onto the roof.

The HDV-426 falls out of the car and breaks apart into several snapping, whirring pieces of varying size and complexity.

We're going faster than I thought!

"FELIX!"

That last scream makes my insides contract and my head hurt so bad I can barely see....

I jump.

I try to get footing and run to slow myself down like jumping off a runaway skateboard as a kid—

Instead, my feet tangle immediately and I slam into the asphalt fast and hard, which forces my body into a rough roll. Feel and hear a *pop* in my left shoulder and the distant part of my mind calmly decides it's probably dislocated. My limbs flail and the pavement bruises and tears my flesh. Cars honk and swerve to avoid me as I roll to a stop.

I lift my head off the asphalt and feel pieces of it detach from my face and shower down, glistening with blood.

I look down the street—the creature with Audrey's body is running from the stopped Swede and screaming my name.

The sickness and pain in my head keep coming when I hear the thing wailing.

Fresh injuries and all, I use my good arm to haul myself off the street and try to back away from the approaching abomination—

A sharp pain in one of my ankles collapses me back to the ground—

I try to stop my descent with the wrong arm and it crumples, useless.

I slam temple first into the pavement—

I shake uncontrollably as I stand on the cold rubber floor of the dome chamber with the dark ceiling. The sound of the thing going around the outside of the huge chamber's base is a roar that vibrates and penetrates my bones.

I look up. The apex is still too dark and fills me with dread. The liquid is gone and the apex now gapes like an abysmal maw.

The whole chamber shudders and the hum of the unseen revolving thing gets louder again and the vibrations stronger. The chamber grows darker in time with this and everything blurs again.

Somehow as it gets darker, I can see the inner surface of the dome more clearly.

Machinery installed at irregular spots across it connected by cables and pipes and conduits. Some mechanical and antique while others could be electronic—and some a fusion of machine and organic material.

In that fleeting glimpse of clarity, these disparate technologies appear to connect and function seamlessly.

I feel a presence to my left and realize there is something warm in my hand. I look down—

I come to on a gurney in the back of an ambulance, my head still pounding but nausea mostly gone.

Paramedics check my vitals and gingerly examine my

injuries.

Audrey sits to my side explaining what happened but I can't make out the words. She looks at me and gets emotional.

The distortions start again, her face burning and collapsing inward and apart, and just the sound of the shrill, pounding voice turns my stomach again. I dry heave hard. The paramedic gently presses me back down onto the gurney and I lose consciousness again—

There's another hand in mine. I look up to see whose it is but the chamber is too dark and blurry.

A woman's form but the face has no clear definition through the gloom. All I can make out is that her mouth is moving like she is speaking but I can't hear what she's saying over the deafening howl of the dome chamber—

I regain consciousness again with a cute nurse pressing me down and a pretty doctor on top of me. *Kinky*, quips the distant part in my mind.

The doctor has her foot wedged in my armpit. She aligns my arm and pulls up hard and then down, wrenching it back into place with an audible, sickening pop.

Ouch....

I let out a guttural moan and slip away again—

The silhouetted woman won't stop speaking but I still can't hear her.

Something on the cold, dark rubber floor catches my eye. Sitting at our feet is what has to be a cat—almost totally dark in the chamber now but I can make out the shape. It must be bright white.

As my eyes adjust, I see the cat's eyes more clearly. They are entirely black and reflective, like obsidian. With no light left in the room, I can't help wondering what they are reflecting off of.

The cat cocks its head and examines me.
Everything goes black.

chapter 6

I wake up. Recovery room bed. Left arm in padded, secured sling. Face and left eye ache. Ankle wrapped but doesn't hurt.

Must have given me the good shit.

I look around.

A young woman in scrubs sits in a chair across from the foot of my bed reading a tabloid.

TOM CRUISE HAS TWO PENISES AND A MIND CONTROL BEAM! THERE'S A UNICORN BOY TRAPPED IN A WELL! THE EARTH IS ACTUALLY HOLLOW AND SPACE ALIEN EXILES LIVE ON THE INSIDE SURFACE!

Fun bullshit. Hope she doesn't believe any of it….

Audrey sits in a chair next to the bed reading a book.

She notices I'm awake and sets the book down on an end table.

"Hey," Audrey says, then smiles, happy but cautious.

"H-hey."

My voice is hoarse. Throat is dry. I rub it with my free

hand.

Audrey pours some water from a pitcher and hands me the cup. I drink it all, so she takes it back and refills it. I shake my head and she sets it down.

"They say you'll be fine. Just need to relax and heal. How did you sleep?"

"All right. Had the worst dream. Well, weird at least. About like a big metal dome room."

Audrey blinks and furrows her brow, her eyes taking on a hollow look like she's thinking about something. But she recomposes herself and just says, "Weird."

"My shoulder hurts...."

"Yeah, that's to be expected, y'know? They said you shouldn't wear that sling too long. Don't want your tendons to atrophy or whatever."

I nod toward the attendant reading her tabloid.

In a hushed tone I say, "Who's that?"

"She's here to watch you."

"Watch me what?"

Audrey scrunches her face a bit, then seems to catch herself and actively relax it.

"They've had someone watch you since they brought you to this room."

"Why?"

"Why...?"

The shimmering black starts as pinpoints in her pupils and pulses outward, overtaking her eyes.

"SO YOU DON'T TRY TO FUCKING OFF YOURSELF AGAIN, FELIX!"

Warping, glitching, translucent cutout mess pours out of her eyes until it twists and burns—like striking a huge road flare of impossible blue-black flame and light.

I draw back in the bed, a twinge of sharp pain in my head causing me to cringe—and nausea comes with it.

The young woman looks up from her tabloid.

I expect her to shriek and run out of the room—but she

doesn't seem to notice Audrey's weird inferno of a head at all and shoots me a look like *I* make her uncomfortable. Then she looks at Audrey with sympathy or pity in her eyes.

Oh yeah, she's the one stuck with me! I can't believe this....

I look back at Audrey and she's crying quietly into her hands.

The effects of the distortions are lessened with her eyes covered but it's still cutting through her head and hands, and the glow pours out from between her fingers like she's covering a big flashlight with them. Through a prism cutout, I can see one of her black eyes through her translucent finger bones and eyelid.

Audrey lifts her head and locks eyes with me. The iridescent black of those eyes piercing into my own sends that deep chill through me again.

They're like shark eyes. Empty. Cold. You wouldn't think they could see anything but they see just fine.

I can't look away, even though I'm desperate to.

"WHAT DID I DO? WHY WOULD.... HOW COULD YOU DO THAT? THAT'S ALL I NEED."

The windows and long light bulbs in the ceiling panel vibrate hard with each syllable.

Why can't that stupid girl see or hear this? Wait....

Maybe I'm going crazy like my dad did. Is this in my head? It seems so real.

"Audrey, I didn't—"

There is a knocking on the frame of the open doorway.

An attractive middle-aged man enters wearing an expensive, tailored suit and carrying a medical chart.

I honestly can't peg down his age. He has a shock of gray hair and some wrinkles around his pale blue eyes that make him look distinguished more than anything else.

Somewhere between forty something and a very fit seventy?

When Audrey sees this man, the distortions change from one indescribable color to another and retreat back into her eyes.

The man pauses upon seeing her. He nods at her and she returns it.

Is that recognition or familiarity? They must have met for a consult while I was under. Audrey likes mature, charismatic types. I'm not really much of either. Another thing she seemed to be okay with.

Dance and etiquette lessons it is then.

"Hello, Felix. I am Doctor Fleischmann. I am a psychiatrist and psychotherapist."

The man has a Central European accent—also a plus for Audrey, as we've joked about while watching movies....

I say nothing, so as not to embarrass myself with my barely there SF / Bay Area accent I picked up from being raised by my grandparents in the Richmond (after my parents...no longer could). A lot of people don't think there's a local accent, 'cause it's almost extinct, but you know it when you hear it if you're from around here.

Audrey stands and extends her hand and Fleischmann gently shakes it. A little too gently for my liking and I think I see the doctor subtly caress her hand as she takes it out of his.

I'm right here! What a slimy prick....

Or am I just being sensitive?

Audrey sits back down, and I'm just here hoping she doesn't slide off the chair and hit her head or something.

Doctor Fleischmann extends his hand to me and smiles ever so pleasantly. I weakly raise my hand and the doctor shakes it firmly. A little too firmly and I feel my metacarpals grind together just a bit before the doctor releases my hand.

"Do you mind if I sit, Felix?"

I shake my head.

Doctor Fleischmann pulls up a chair and flips the thin metal cover of the chart he is holding over to the back.

"Actually first, just as a matter of personal curiosity…."

This better not be about my fucking eyes.

I say, "Sure."

"I have always wondered—with mismatched eyes like those, does one seem to function at all differently than the other…or both the same?"

I can tell that he could have said that more politely… but chose not to.

"Pretty much the same, doctor."

"Hm…. I might have to research that further at some point."

Dr. Fleischmann glances at Audrey and I notice her narrowing her eyes at the psychiatrist. Subtle, but I caught it.

What am I missing?

"Now, just to check a few things. Your full name?"

"Felix Andreas Brewer."

"Your address?"

"Six forty-two Greenwich Street."

"Mmhmm. Your date of birth?"

"December seventeenth, nineteen eighty-five."

"And what year is it currently?"

I study the doctor's face. "Two thousand eleven."

"Great. Thank you. Now, do you understand why I'm here, Felix?"

Quit saying my name.

"I guess because I…jumped out of Audrey's car."

I look at Audrey. The pinpoints are back and pulsing in her pupils but she's trying to stay calm.

"Audrey's quickly moving car?"

"Yeah."

"And why did you do that?" Doctor Fleischmann asks, still pleasant and with that incredible calmness that screams, "I am so objective right now."

The shimmering black grows in Audrey's eyes but still only pulses gently.

61

Doctor Fleischmann studies my face.

"Audrey? It was Audrey, correct? Could you please step out for a bit?"

"If you think that would help."

"Yes, I believe so. Thank you so much."

Audrey gently squeezes my left hand, careful not to move my slung arm. Still holding it, she turns and gives the doctor a look I can't really decipher.

Cautious? Protective?

The doctor nods and closes his eyes slowly and deliberately, seeming to respond to the nonverbal question or statement with reassurance.

Satisfied, she stands, takes her book, and leaves the room.

Doctor Fleischmann turns toward the young woman reading her tabloid.

"You may leave as well."

She keeps reading.

He loses his air of soothing tranquility for a moment when he notices she isn't paying attention to him.

"Excuse me!" the doctor exclaims with the disdain of a king scolding a commoner.

The young woman looks up, visibly startled.

"Yes. Please *leave*."

She looks too confused and embarrassed to be angry as she gets up and hurries out into the hallway.

Doctor Fleischmann turns back to me, cool and calm once again.

"Better? Now, why did you jump out of Audrey's car? She seems to be quite pleasant."

I do my best to ignore his "quite pleasant" comment and lean over to look and make sure Audrey isn't near the door.

"You didn't see that? Her face?"

"Her face? Was there something wrong with it?"

I notice the doctor observing my reactions now.

"You would have noticed."

"Something strange?"

"You could say that."

"So, you jumped out of Audrey's car because something about her face troubled you that much?"

I know where this is going but I figure it was settled before the doctor walked in anyway.

My asphalt bodysurfing experiment was pretty out there. Might as well be honest.

"Yes—but I didn't try to kill myself, if that makes any difference. I was just confused and…scared."

"Scared. Of Audrey? Her face frightened you enough to cause you to throw yourself out of her car?"

How many ways is he going to rephrase the same basic question?

Must be a trick of the trade.

"Yes."

Doctor Fleischmann studies my eyes to be sure, then writes a few things on the medical chart and flips it closed.

"Alright, Felix. I feel that we have a great deal more talking to do on this subject. I will have you transferred to my facility for a few days so that we may do that and so that you can get some more rest. How does that sound?"

"Is it up to me?"

"Is your health and well-being important to you?" the doctor asks pleasantly and smiles at me.

"I guess that sounds great then."

"Wonderful. I'll have your transfer arranged."

I watch the view out through tinted rear windows of an ambulance. Tree tops. Power lines. Cloudy sky.

A dirty Jack in the Box antenna ball on a car behind us sometimes gets close enough to smile at me. Mostly at stop signs and lights. Then we start going and it tries to keep up and catch us again.

My shoulder aches.

Hopefully they'll give me some more painkillers at the facility.

I look over at an EMT who's in back with me, then back out the rear windows.

The doctor explained that I have to be transferred in an ambulance for legal reasons but it seems like overkill to me—especially now that I'm strapped securely on a gurney.

I'm the only one who knows I'm not a danger to myself or others or whatever they have to say to make me go there. Although, I guess that's how a crazy person would feel. Shit. Maybe that is what I am….

I imagine Fleischmann's facility as a scary, dilapidated horror palace filled with dungeons and deranged, drooling psychopaths.

I just hope the huge, no-neck orderlies and evil nurses don't torture the patients at night.

How far away is this place, anyway?

"Excuse me."

The EMT looks up from a chart.

"What's up, Felix?"

"Is this a decent facility?"

"We had to look that up ourselves, actually. Pretty specialized, I guess. You a depressed superhero or spy or something?"

I chuckle and say, "Nope."

The EMTs roll the gurney out of the ambulance and the legs slide down and lock in place. The driver closes the rear doors and the other hooks a metal crutch on the side of the gurney and steers me toward the main facility. The driver checks some charts as he follows.

The facility is two levels high, and half a city-block wide at this end. The outer surface is seamless mirrored paneling.

Simple. Stylish. Elegant, even.

The EMTs wheel me onto the sidewalk and toward a set of automatic mirrored doors. Backlit white letters installed flush in the mirrored wall near the doors read FLEISCHMANN MEDICAL CENTER.

After reading it, I have to close my eyes, seeing my reflection being inescapable this close to the reflective building.

They roll my chariot into the facility lobby and ease to a stop near a large, tasteful reception desk. The whole lobby is minimal, modern, and clean. Nice leather chairs line dark coffee tables in waiting areas that flank both sides of the entry walkway.

The driver approaches the desk and speaks with a

young redhead who gives him directions. We follow the receptionist's directions down a few stretches of corridor and arrive at two large, mirrored panels the width and height of the hallway that must serve as doors.

Backlit letters above the doors read LOCKED WARD.

I wonder how well I have to behave to get upgraded to the *un*-locked ward. Or is that just everything out here that's not locked in there? I picture a worldwide Matrix Cave Rave of dancing lunatics, all us weirdos the Locked Ward hasn't taken…yet.

The driver looks for a way to call in but there is no obvious panel.

–Felix Brewer?– asks a female voice from near the glowing letters above the doors.

Concealed speakers? Must be priceless when the really paranoid patients arrive.

"That's him," the driver says, obviously ready to leave.

I look down from the letters and flinch—

There is someone standing on the other side now, looking out through one of the mirror doors.

I realize then that the mirrors aren't opaque. The translucent tinting of the mirrors makes the person's face a vague oval and I can't see any detail. Just the rough silhouetted impressions of a head, face, and body.

The person steps back away from the doors and they hum and click, then open inward smoothly and quietly.

The person in the ward hallway is a young woman with light pink thick-rimmed glasses, crystal-blue eyes, a nice tan, and baby-blond hair pulled back into a tight bun. White skirt suit, flesh-colored stockings, white heels.

She is attractive and seems pleasant but there is something about her that really bothers me. It takes me a moment to place it—then it hits me.

She looks a lot like Audrey. Like a blond, blue-eyed snow-bunny version of her.

Audrey is shorter and built a little differently but if this woman had brown eyes and black hair, they could be sisters. The facial structure is that similar.

"Welcome, Felix. I am Sasha Menlo."

I'm just relieved she doesn't sound exactly like Audrey. That would cross over from kind of weird to genuinely creepy.

"Bring him in."

She gestures to the EMTs to enter, then turns around and walks toward the main desk.

Three of the four rooms lining both sides of the entry hall are dark. The lights are on in the second on the right. There is a curtain around the padded table in the room but it's partly open and I can make out what must be restraint cuffs installed in it.

Do they leave that open to nudge you toward good behavior?

We make it to the desk, and the driver has a short, all-business exchange with the head nurse. Name badge reads PEGGY. Paperwork signed as Sasha observes.

The EMTs unbuckle the gurney straps and adjust its angle, then help me up and off it and hand me the crutch.

I shift around on my left foot until I get the crutch under my right arm and stable.

"Thanks."

A large orderly approaches from the hall to the right of the desk. Taller than me and twice as wide. Not fat, just big. He wears his hair in cornrows and looks tough, but has large, friendly eyes.

The man's name badge reads RAY.

"Thank you, gentleman. Have a nice day."

The driver is already halfway to the door as the other EMT rolls the gurney after him to the doors. Peggy presses something at the desk, which opens them. They leave and the doors close again.

Ray scans the chart the driver left at the desk.

"How's it going, Felix? I'm Ray. Uh, I'm looking here

and I don't see…. Who's your doctor?"

"Hi, Ray. Doctor Fleischmann, I think."

Sasha Menlo nods. "That's correct."

"No shit? The man himself?"

Sasha frowns. "Raymond. That is hardly appropriate language to use in this facility."

"I apologize, Doctor Menlo. I meant to say, *gosh whillikers, really?*"

He said that last part all nasally like Steve Urkel.

I almost laugh but hold it in. Sasha Menlo seems a little humorless.

"Raymond will see to it that you are situated and inform you of our policies and schedule, Felix. Please don't hesitate to report any inappropriate language or behavior on his part to Doctor Fleischmann or myself."

She looks at Ray.

"He is quite good, but he has the potential to offend patients and we cannot have that."

Ray meets her glare for a moment, then relents and looks down to the side.

She nods, then turns and walks down the hall to the left of the desk. She enters a doorway down on the left and closes it behind her.

Ray mumbles something under his breath.

Peggy chuckles and shakes her head. "What was that, Ray?"

"*Nothing, Peggy.*"

I chuckle.

"There you go! Keep your sense of humor and you'll be fine. Oh, hold up. Lemme get your shoes, man."

"My shoes?"

"Policy. You'll get 'em back."

"Uh…okay."

I slip one of my sneakers off easily, then gingerly nudge the other off from around my taped foot and ankle.

Ray picks up my shoes and hands them to Peggy over the

desk counter. She puts them in a large bag, which already has my last name and first initial on it. Ray reaches behind the counter and produces a pair of disposable slippers in a plastic bag, then takes them out and places them by my feet so I can step into them.

"Alright, let's give you a tour. It's kinda lean right now, population-wise, which is probably a good thing, I guess. Come on, I'll try not to lose you."

Ray walks down the hallway to the right of the desk. I limp after him on my crutch, taking in his descriptions and guidelines.

North hall, males. South hall, females. No fraternization. Group therapy room. Dining room, breakfast at seven fifteen—they'll wake the patients. Common room with a big TV and a dozen comfy chairs. Tables near there for visits, big boxes of board games near those. Ping-Pong table—nice.

As we're finishing up, I see a woman through a partially open door. She's sitting on her bed watching something on her wall.

It's like there's a spider and her eyes are following it but there's nothing there other than striped wallpaper and a generic painting of some flowers.

Ray says, "That's Gina. She's getting out later today. Probably should stay a little longer…. Should be fine, though."

She's not spooky. Not drooling or cackling. More sad than anything else.

Then it hits me that the strangest thing about this creepy mental hospital is that it isn't creepy at all.

More boring and generic than anything.

Instead of concrete walls smeared with blood and/or feces or disintegrating water-stained wallpaper, the only bad thing about the décor is that it's a cross between bland office building and sweet old grandma's house. No long, open rooms lined with rusty, wrought iron beds with dingy, scratchy sheets.

Scariest thing about the rooms is their disturbing ability to emulate a pleasantly inoffensive guest room.

As I follow Ray around to the male rooms on the north side, I sees someone on the far side of the visitor tables common area I hadn't noticed initially.

There is a man standing stock still, staring out through two large, tinted doors, which take up the center third of the east wall past the common area. Looks like an outdoor area from the vague shadows.

"What's past those doors?"

"That's the patio. Practically a small park. Usually used for smoke breaks and lunch on good weather days. A lot of times people take visitors out there. Mostly smoke breaks, though. Facilities in this area usually don't let you smoke but Doctor Fleischmann doesn't see a need to add any stress on top of whatever a patient is going through. You smoke?"

"Used to."

"Good for you. Don't do it or at least keep it moderate. You don't want to end up like Mitch over there. Barely eats. Never does anything but smoke and wait to smoke. Like it's his job. Then, when he's finally smoking...."

Ray lowers his voice a bit.

"He doesn't think I notice, but he wastes half the time he's smoking going through the ashtrays for butts he can smoke. Problem is, I distribute and light all the cigarettes so after he gets back in here, he's got a pocket full of nasty butts he can't use."

Ray chuckles and shakes his head.

"Let me show you your room."

"Sure."

Ray leads me to an open door with a backlit "7" set flush in the floor at the base of the threshold. The carpet is cut perfectly around the number. To the left and right of the door are slick electronic readouts. Black background, pale blue letters. The left one reads J. OLDHAM and the right already reads F. BREWER.

I can't vouch for their behavioral-science skills yet but I'm pretty sure they would sweep the Mental Hospital Style Awards.

"Alright, you're in room seven with Jesse. He's cool. Runs up the water bills a bit."

"Huh?"

I hear a toilet flushing from the bathroom in the room.

"Dammit. Jesse, come out here!" Ray yells, loud but not threatening.

A muffled curse and one more flush are heard, then Jesse comes out of the bathroom. He's probably in his late fifties but he could be younger. He has thin gray hair, and his unshaven face has deep crags in it and the dark skin is leathery.

"Wh-what's up, Ray?" Jesse says, guilt written on his face.

"I know it's hard, but please stop flushing the toilet, Jesse. It's a huge waste of water."

Jesse's eyes dart sideways and he watches the bathroom through the open door.

"But—"

"I know what you think is happening. This all got worked out last time, remember? Once the meds have time to get back in your system, you won't see it anymore. And this time, keep taking them. I know it's comfortable here but you should try to find a shelter or something, man. Anyway, this is Felix. He'll be rooming with you for a while."

"Hi," Jesse says before looking sideways at the bathroom again.

"Jesse," Ray says.

Jesse looks at him again. "Yeah, what's up, Ray?"

"Just try for me."

"Yeah, definitely. For sure, man," Jesse says, practically vibrating due to the intense effort it must be taking not to look back at the bathroom.

Ray gives me a nod, then walks off shaking his head.

Jesse peaks into the hallway, waits for Ray to get a certain distance away, then rushes back into the bathroom and starts to close its door.

Just before it closes, I think I see something blurry whip around from where the toilet must be. More a disturbance of the air than an actual thing. The lockless door closes with a click.

The toilet flushes.

I sigh, then set my crutch against the wall and sit down on the bed that isn't messed up.

The toilet flushes again.

When placed in proximity, can crazy sync up and multiply?

chapter 8

I look around the dining area as I eat salmon and rice pilaf from a tray. I learned some names when Peggy handed out the meals.

Delores looks half asleep. Picks at her spaghetti and meatballs like she is revolted by them but knows she is expected to consume some sustenance.

Mitch is forcing down some food because Peggy is watching him. I figure there's an agreement that he can't go on smoke breaks if he doesn't eat at least a little something.

Mitch bothers me but I can't place why.

I glance over my shoulder at Shasta and Candy.

Shasta looks like a runaway or gutter-punk girl. So far, it seems like Candy has a motherly thing going with her. Maybe had a similar "misspent" youth and went down her own longer stretches of rough road. I wonder if Shasta's sisters Tab and Rite will be coming to visiting hours.

A slight young man enters the dining room and makes his way to the meal cart. He has thin ungroomed facial hair.

Probably been in here a for a while.

Peggy looks at the stylish clock with the glowing blue numbers on the wall.

"Rudy, you just made it. Try to make it in for lunch earlier tomorrow okay, hon?"

Rudy just looks at her.

"Salmon, spaghetti with meatballs, or portobello—"

"Spaghetti."

Peggy hands him the sealed package. I watch Rudy walk around the tables and sit in the back corner. As he's sitting down, Rudy notices me watching him. He gives me the finger and holds it in the air until I look away.

I lean on my crutch as I wait behind Delores in a line for medicine. Peggy stands by a cart with a clipboard handing out duos of little paper cups of pills and water.

Delores takes her pills with the water and starts toward the TV area.

"Delores," Peggy says.

Delores looks back at her. Peggy gestures her back with a finger. Delores returns, opens her mouth, and Peggy scans the inside of her mouth with a small LED flashlight. Delores lifts her tongue and moves it around.

"Thanks, dear."

Delores heads for the TV area.

I hop up to Peggy and lean on my crutch again.

"How are your shoulder and ankle?" Peggy asks.

"Painkillers from earlier are wearing off a bit but I'll be fine until tomorrow."

"If you're sure."

I nod.

"Okay. Just these then."

She hands me a little pill cup and holds the water cup up in front of me. I take the pill cup but don't try to hide my confusion.

"I just got here today."

"Uh huh," Peggy says, still pleasant.

"I haven't even seen the doctor yet. How could I have a prescription?"

"If Doctor Fleischmann had you transferred here, this *is* your prescription. He's very good at what he does. Y'all are in the best possible hands."

I look down into the little cup.

There is a circular pill and a long blue pill. The circular pill is black with a small white dot in the center. I tilt the cup and shift the pills. The circular pill flips over the blue one. On the rounded outer ring of the circular pill, it becomes white and the other side has a black dot in the center.

"What are they?"

"The half-and-half ying-yang-lookin' pill is called Harmonia. The other one just helps you sleep."

It's *yin*-yang, but okay.

Then it hits me that I hadn't even considered taking medicine. It makes sense, just didn't occur to me.

Not thrilled about the idea—then I remember the whole glitching, bubbling distortion inferno face with Audrey's body thing.

I tip the pills into my mouth and take the water cup from Peggy.

I roll the pills around in my mouth, still a little hesitant.

Swallow them with the water and let Peggy look in my mouth with her little flashlight.

I limp to the TV area on my crutch and sit one row in front of Delores and a few seats over. We watch a documentary about cotton-candy production.

Riveting.

Ray's loud knocking wakes me up.

"Breakfast in fifteen, squares!" Ray bellows.

Man, that sleeping pill worked wonders. I feel completely

rested.

Jesse looks like he's been up all night and just jumped in bed.

Ray moves on and I hear him repeating his wake-up process down the hall.

Jesse gets up and creeps into the bathroom, then shuts the door. I hear the toilet flush and shake my head.

It should be a felony to waste that much water in California. Anywhere, really, but California is a delicate setup.

Careful not to hurt my shoulder, I sit up and slide my legs out of the bed and rest my feet on the floor—but I feel something by my foot and look down. My shoes are next to the bed.

The laces have been removed.

For the first time since the restraint setup in the entry area, I'm reminded of where I am and how serious it can get.

It's not a bed-and-breakfast or a hotel.

Sasha Menlo wears a lime-green suit today and seems distracted as she leads the patients in group therapy.

Preoccupied with something?

Group therapy consists of Shasta and Candy trying to out-cry each other while describing how their lives have been damaged by delusions and hallucinations. Shasta's floating bugs and dark shapes in the sky. Candy's monsters on flying cars and black vents that spit out mind-control gas.

I listen and daydream, my mental images informed by what I think of as The Madness of the Hotties.

Rudy is silent. Mitch's eyes dart around, probably desperate for a smoke. If Delores is awake I would be surprised. Jesse is almost as distracted as Mitch for different reasons.

Oh, here we go.

Shasta is on to her cutting problem now. You see, the bugs can go *through* things. She had to know if they could be inside her.

Ray gently knocks on the therapy-room doorframe.

"Excuse me, Doctor Menlo. Doctor Fleischmann is here and he would like to speak with Felix."

Sasha Menlo brightens visibly at the mention of the doctor.

"Of course," she says.

Doctor Fleischmann clears his throat and scans over his notes. He sets the notepad aside, uncrosses his legs, and leans forward, resting his elbows on his knees and interlacing his fingers.

"Everything you have told me today has reinforced my initial impressions and helped me form a more accurate diagnosis."

I blink and nod. "Okay."

"You have just experienced the effects of an acute schizophrenic episode. A kind of *break*, as some call it. This can manifest in the teens and into the twenties while your brain chemistry is still developing and changing consistently. Even later, in some cases. Your father's issues and regrettable suicide show family history. This is not something you should be ashamed of or blame yourself for. And with the right medicine you shouldn't ever have another episode like this one."

"I understand. I'm confused, though...."

"Yes?"

"Why do I feel normal? I feel the same and it's just Audrey that's been...strange to me."

Doctor Fleischmann leans back and crosses his legs again.

"That is a good question, actually. That is the reason you were brought to this particular facility. What you have is a very specific form of schizophrenia. I have been working on it almost exclusively for many years now. I generally refer to it as *situational schizo-dissocia*."

"What does that mean? Like, it's not all the time?"

The doctor steeples his fingers.

"It begins with a focus. Usually, based on some form of trauma. Your focus is Audrey."

"Why?"

"The source will take more study and therapy to deduce. Right now, treatment is paramount. Untreated, it would eventually spread, perverting and warping the whole of your perception. Hallucinations. Paranoia. That is why I spearheaded the development of Harmonia. It's a revolutionary new combination of specialized antipsychotic and antianxiety medicines with a twist of—"

"Will I have to take it for the rest of my life?"

The doctor blinks and flexes his jaw a bit.

He doesn't like being interrupted. Most people don't, but there's a flash of actual emotion in his eyes for just the slightest instant, then it's gone.

Fleischmann takes a breath and lets it out.

"Honestly, it is quite possible that you will have to, yes. Although, I believe it is preferable to the alternative. Wouldn't you say that is so, Felix?"

"How long am I going to be here, doctor?"

"Currently, you are here for a seventy-two-hour evaluation hold. However, I would recommend—"

"Can I stay longer?"

Doctor Fleischmann's jaw twinges but his expression is more curious than angry.

"Longer? That is a new one. Other than Mr. Oldham, but his motives are obviously not about treatment."

I say, "How long does it take for the medicine to kick in?"

"It varies. About three to four weeks for the full benefit."

"Can I stay that long?"

"Why so eager to stay, Felix?"

"I…. I don't want to see Audrey until the medicine is working. Or talk to her."

Doctor Fleischmann considers this.

"I see. Yes. I will explain the situation to Audrey discreetly. I will take responsibility for the idea so as to avoid any animosity toward you. For now, just relax and keep taking the medicine."

"Thanks, doctor. I appreciate it."

"Not at all. I usually have to fight patients to stay here as long as is needed."

That evening, I wait my turn in the pill line, then hop up to Peggy. I take the pills without hesitation and down them with the cup of water.

I feel better than I have since this all started.

I just want things to go back to normal.

The medicine is my ticket.

chapter 9

The next day, Ray leads the group in a game I've decided to think of as "beanbag therapy."

We throw square-cut beanbags through holes on a large, colorfully painted wooden board on a stand. With different-sized holes.

The top is probably five inches in diameter. Below that, seven. Bottom hole, nine or ten.

Delores is up and she's terrible at this.

I'm next and do better than Delores but not by as much as I thought I would.

Out of my five shots, the first three litter the base of the board on my side. Then I get one into the big bottom hole. The last one gets stuck in the middle hole, straddling it.

It's just taunting me.

Some beans inside it shift and the beanbag drops out of the hole on my side, flopping onto the other failures below.

After lunch, I lie on the bed in my room reading a book

of haikus I found in the nightstand drawer under a white Gideons Bible and another Gideons with a blue digital-camouflage cover some navy guy must have left here.

So far, my favorite is about resting beneath cherry blossoms during a journey. I'm not quite sure why I like it so much but I do. It's pleasant and tranquil and all that but there's something else. My mind wanders to cherry blossoms. A falling storm of light petals swirling down around a long, lovely female form topped with a wild half mane of black and blue—

The toilet flushes in the closed bathroom. I hear a muffled "ha!" through the door.

Jesse opens the door and comes out. He's more relaxed than I've seen him.

Jesse flops on the bed, exhausted, and I rest the book on my chest.

"You finished just in time for visiting hours."

"Kid, I get visitors all day, hours or not," Jesse says, his voice muffled by the comforter his face is half buried in.

There's a knock outside the door. Peggy pokes her head in. "Felix, uh…*Hero* and *Kerry* are here to see you?"

"Really? Okay, I'll be out in a minute."

I set the haiku book down on the nightstand and get up carefully, then limp down the hall on my crutch.

Hirofumi and Kaori are sitting in chairs near the main doors speaking quietly to each other in Japanese. I look at the restraint rooms. The doors are closed and lights off. Good.

Wouldn't want to worry them…more.

Kaori notices me first and squeezes Hirofumi's thigh and nods toward me. Hiro turns and looks over and his face lights up. Both stand and hurry over to me. They each give me a hug, careful not to squeeze my shoulder too hard.

Hirofumi laughs and says, "You look like shit, man! You are all busted! Does your arm still work?"

"It's getting better."

"Where are your shoestrings?" Kaori asks, looking down at my shoes.

"I guess they take 'em so you can't hang yourself with them?" I say, not realizing how bad it sounds until I've finished. I let out a nervous chuckle.

Hirofumi nudges Kaori with his elbow and makes a sound of disapproval.

She shrugs and grunts softly as if to say, "I didn't know."

"Enough of that. We came to cheer you up!" Hirofumi says.

"Sorry. Thanks for coming, guys. Hey, let's go out in the park thing. I haven't been out there at all."

"Park?" Hirofumi asks.

"It's like a big patio…. You can smoke."

They both nod in approval.

"Sorry about your shoes," Kaori says, still a bit embarrassed.

"Doesn't bother me. I'm no danger," I say.

She smiles, cautious but hopeful.

Hirofumi and Kaori follow me around the central area, through the common room, and out through the propped-open patio doors.

Once again, Ray was not kidding.

The patio is like a small park. It's only as wide as the ward interior, but it's longer.

The "park" is actually several small artificial islands in a large pond connected by ancient-looking step-stone bridges. The islands are covered in landscaped grass and have abstract rock sculptures here and there. There are nice benches and tasteful ashtrays on each island as well. Beautiful, colorful koi fish swim lazily through the pond all around. A shallow bamboo forest lines artificial banks, which border the entire rectangular area, the trees placed meticulously to look naturally arranged. The facility walls just past the trees are mirrored, giving the illusory effect of almost endless depth containing millions of ponds. The trees and mirrors stretch up to the edge of the roof. The trees peak a bit up over it and they sway a bit in the breeze.

Hirofumi mutters something in Japanese about his grandfather's house.

"Yeah, this whole place is pretty slick. Makes sense they'd go all out on a glorified smoking patio. It's like they're trying to win an award," I say, still fond of my little award joke but happy now to be able to vocalize it.

I chuckle and start down a path of subtly connected stepping stones to an island on the left.

We reach the smooth wooden bench and Kaori and I sit. Hirofumi watches koi swim past the shore of the island as he takes out a pack of those Double Happiness cigarettes he gets in Chinatown. He takes two out and lights them together with his worn blue Zippo. When he offers one to Kaori, she shakes her head. Hirofumi shrugs.

"Why did you let me light the two then?"

"I'll take it," I say.

"You didn't quit?" Hirofumi asks.

"Still have one once in a while. Don't tell Audrey."

"She would beat me for giving you one, so don't worry."

Hirofumi hands me the lit smoke and I take a long drag and cough a little in my throat. Getting rusty at smoking? I guess that's a good thing, strange as it is to me.

"Audrey has one sometimes too," Kaori says with a playfully guilty expression.

I chuckle. "I figured."

I shake my head and look around. Mitch is walking from island to island searching the ashtrays for smokable butts. Delores is sitting at a bench on the far side with a young woman who's probably her daughter. The rest must be inside.

I take another drag and sober a bit.

"How is Audrey?"

Hirofumi straightens up. "She's okay. It's hard for her to understand, but—"

"She just wants you to get better," Kaori finishes.

Hirofumi grunts at Kaori's interruption and continues, "She loves you, Felix. I don't know why, but she does. Anyway, she was upset when your doctor called but he must have convinced her it was needed. Why is it needed, though?"

"It's a part of my condition."

"What is your condition? What happened?" Kaori asks.

I take a drag and hold it. Maybe if I hold it long enough, I won't have to let it out?

Defeated, I exhale, smoke rushing out of my mouth and nostrils as I speak.

"I guess I have something like what my dad had. Saw some crazy shit. Audrey's…. Actually, I don't really want to say much more right now if that's okay. Maybe not at all. It's just in my head. The medicine will control it."

"That's okay," Kaori says. "Yeah, we understand."

I notice Mitch approaching, staring at Hirofumi's mostly finished cigarette. Hirofumi notices Mitch too.

"Are you finished with that?" Mitch asks. His own cigarette is down to the butt but still burning.

Hirofumi looks at his own smoke. He takes his pack back out and gives Mitch a fresh cigarette. Mitch's eyes get big.

"Really? Thanks, bro!" He lights it with his almost dead smoke and sucks on the fresh one hard as he takes a few steps away. Mitch stops and turns around. He says, "Hey, could you go get me a real big coffee and bring it back in like it's yours and give it to me? I need a coffee, man."

"Is that okay with them?" Hirofumi asks.

"People do it for me all the time."

"Then get someone *else* to do it, Mitch," I say. It comes out harsher than I meant it, but something about Mitch really bothers me, so I'm not too broken up about it.

Mitch looks crestfallen and goes off toward Delores and her visitor. Hirofumi shakes his head and lowers his voice a bit.

"Just don't stay too long or you will be like that guy."

"Yeah, I'd hate to see him when he actually drinks some coffee," I say and we all chuckle softly.

We hug by the doors, both at once this time. It hurts my shoulder a little but the friendly intimacy makes it worth the pain. They release and Hirofumi pats my good shoulder.

"Watch your ass, *aniki*. You are a precious little flower," Hirofumi says.

I laugh and Kaori shakes her head and squints at Hiro.

"So, we are going traveling to different countries to oversee server setups for *Home/Free*. People really do like it," Hirofumi says, with an air of modest pride.

"That's rad. Have a great trip."

"Yeah, we will be back in a while. Just let them help you and come home to Audrey soon," Kaori says.

I nod and smile.

They walk to the doors and Peggy opens them.

I look down toward the common room. Rudy is sitting with a pretty girl who has her hands around his neck and shoulder and her face against his chest. He holds her tenderly.

Hirofumi and Kaori step through the doors and turn back toward me and wave. The mirrored doors close and I watch my friends turn and walk away in stark outlines through them.

Because of the shallow translucence of the doors, it looks like Hirofumi and Kaori are gone almost instantly.

chapter 10

I sit at a long table with the other patients, all of us drawing and painting. I had heard the term "art therapy" before but figured that's kind of what I do when I'm sketching anyway, so I never really thought about it much.

This is a little different. Most of the others have almost no artistic talent. Not in graphic art at least. They "got no hand skills," as one friend used to put it.

The purpose seems to be to relax the patients and allow a different way of expressing…well, something.

Most of the other patient's images are simple.

Candy draws a big, silly puppy with oil pastel sticks. Mitch, swirls of red and black, also in pastels. Delores makes abstract blobs of color with tempera paint.

Shasta has managed to draw a skyline and abstract, almost cubist San Francisco with brown and blue crayons. Above the city are black blobs of varying shape rendered in black crayon.

Kinda cool, actually.

From what I can see over Jesse's arms, he's drawing something mildly lewd.

Peggy told us to draw whatever we felt like.

I've had a bad association with crayons since I was about ten, but decided to mess around with them because I despise tempera paint, and the oil pastels Candy and Mitch aren't hoarding are broken and smudged with other colors. Plus, Rudy grabbed the only colored pencils.

Having had so long to learn other graphic mediums, I quickly figure out tricks I can use to bring out the potential of these cheap, drugstore crayons. I actually really enjoy the strangeness of the resistance and waxy sliding they do between intended strokes.

My drawings depict some of the different states the distortions Audrey's head and face went through during my "episode." The quick portraits of melting prismatic cutouts and light distortions are vivid and almost impressionistic. I'm channeling some of my favorite Francis Bacon paintings, I realize, but that's just fine—and disturbingly appropriate.

Something moving in my peripheral vision catches my attention and pulls me out of my focused artistic state.

Rudy's right hand is shaking and the red-colored pencil in it is wavering back and forth. I look at his face.

Rudy is staring at my drawings, visibly disturbed.

Our eyes meet. Rudy looks confused and upset. He looks over at Peggy. Texting someone on her phone. He subtly spins his drawings around so I can see them.

Rudy seems untrained but isn't without talent. His images are a little crude and they have a distinct flatness but—

I feel a chilly tingle through my body, and furrow my brow.

It's unmistakable….

Our styles and skill levels are different, but we are drawing the same basic thing. The same distortions. The transparent cutouts and the bubbling and melting. Lifeless black shark eyes. Rudy even tried to pull off the paradoxical effect of the bright darkness with dark-blue, black, pink, and white pencils.

We make eye contact again, then Rudy thinks for a moment. He writes something on his drawing and spins the drawing more so I can see what he's written.

GUESS WE SHOULD TALK

CHESS LATER

I consider a moment, then decide I have to know what this means. I nod subtly to Rudy, who returns it and quickly draws over his note before looking at Peggy again. She didn't notice.

Dean Martin slides down a fireman's pole and lands on a stage on the common-room television. Delores lets out something approaching the enthusiasm of a light chuckle.

She also formed a whole sentence in group therapy after lunch. They must be stepping her dosage down or something.

She is transfixed by Mr. Martin as he sings and jokes with his Rat Pack friends and popular guests of the day on *The Dean Martin Show*.

I usually hate these long ads for video collections of ancient comedy and prank shows but it's taking my mind off my meeting with Rudy.

Dean stands with Dom DeLuise who's dressed up like a magician with a cape and big turban hat. Dean tries not to laugh, fails horribly. Then Dean stands in front of a board with a vague human shape painted on it and Dom throws knives at the board around him. Delores is enthralled.

Rudy enters the common area from the male-section hallway and I watch him make his way to a board-game box near some padded tables and chairs past the Ping-Pong table. He sorts through the box, looks around, meets my gaze. Nods.

Fuck. Don't talk to him, Felix. It won't do you any good to talk to him.

I look back at the screen. Dean busts swinging saloon doors down on a western set and struts in with a cigarette in his mouth.

I want a cigarette.

Dean smashes a candy bottle on a cowboy extra's head.

I always want a cigarette when I'm nervous.

Dean saunters to the bar, smashing more glasses on the way, and fires a blank from his cowboy gun, and Don Rickles as the bartender cracks wise, but what he says is hard to make out.

My stomach twists into itself from an aching dread I can't shake.

Don Rickles breaks the fourth wall, joking about them both flubbing their lines.

Delores chuckles.

Roy Rogers shows up and Don Rickles goes round in a circle behind the bar joking about having Roy Rogers pictures up since childhood, then proceeds to mock Roy about his bad acting in the sketch.

Delores sniffles. I see that she's crying silently.

I think about *Robotech* and *Voltron*.

Fuck it.

I get up and walk with a slight limp toward the padded table where Rudy is setting up the chessboard, my ankle having improved with the amount of rest I've been getting in the ward.

Rudy gestures for me to sit, then takes the black and white king pieces, does something with his hands behind his back, and holds his clenched fists toward me. I tap his right hand and Rudy gives me the black king piece.

As we set up the rest of the pieces, Rudy notices that I'm slower because of my slung arm. He helps me finish my side, then sits.

"Cheap plastic set. You play?"

I nod. "Badly, but I know the basics."

"Then we won't bet on it."

Rudy moves a pawn near the center two spaces forward.

I move my corresponding piece two forward to block.

Rudy moves a bishop to the same row as the pawn, one over. I can tell just from Rudy's quiet confidence that I'm going to lose—and badly.

Only a few total moves later, I have.

"Checkmate."

Even expecting it, I'm still confused. I must look it too because Rudy gestures around the board to show me how I lost so quickly.

Rudy chuckles and says, "You weren't kidding. I haven't gotten anybody with a School's Mate in years, man. Alright, I'll just mess around from here on out."

We reset our pieces and Rudy starts again.

Knowing I have no chance, I tune out on the game and just move reactively.

"They really had me going, man. Felix, right?"

"Yeah, Felix. And you're Rudy. What do you mean?"

"What do you do, Felix?"

"I went to art school. Studied art and film. Work freelance and shit jobs. Why?"

"Just trying to break the proverbial ice."

Rudy toys with me on the board but I don't really care.

"Fine. What do you do?"

"Going for my masters in journalism at State. Almost there…. Bad timing." Rudy shakes his head. He looks at my sling and arm. "How'd you get so busted up, anyway?"

"I jumped out of a speeding car."

Rudy studies my face, probably not sure if I'm serious. I move my only remaining pawn.

"What did you mean when you said they had you going?"

"I mean I was almost convinced. I was starting to believe I was a nutjob. Schizo-discombobulated or whatever she called it."

"She?"

"Doctor Menlo."

Why am I the only one here that I know of who has Fleischmann as a doctor?

"So…you think our drawings mean we *aren't* crazy?"

"Hell yeah. I'm not the Dave McKean you are but we were drawing the same thing. If I could draw like that, they would have been almost exact."

I try to come up with another, more rational solution.

I'll settle for anything remotely rational.

"I don't know, man."

Rudy thinks. "Okay, look. Where did you see yours? Who was it?"

"My girlfriend."

"Day-um. Sorry. Anyway, it started when she got emotional, right? Like when she got pissed off?"

I become uncomfortable.

"Yeah."

"And it started in the eyes?"

"Yeah…it did."

I pick up a piece to move.

"And I'll go out on what's lookin' like a sturdy limb that it all started after you pressed that little button on the lens of the HDV-426."

I knock a few of the other pieces over. Rudy looks around. No one seemed to notice.

Rudy sighs. "Yeah, I just got that camera. I was doing an interview on the street for an assignment. The sun was going down and I hit that button to see if it did any good with low light or something."

I stare at the board, but I'm seeing Audrey's freaky face and head in the car.

"The guy seemed homeless. Had a dead eye and a big face scar. A little vacant but coherent enough. The questions were about world politics. Oil and water as finite resources.

I thought it would be funny to get a bum's opinion on world affairs. The guy got hella heated when I brought up.... I think I asked him about nuclear proliferation. The fool went ape shit. That's how it started. First from the eyes—then it fucked his whole face up."

"What did you do?"

"I flipped, man. Thought I got dosed at the coffee shop or something. But listen, I saw some even weirder shit after that and made the mistake of asking random people if they saw it too. Somebody called the po-po I guess. I was in SF General, then got transferred here. This place gags on it but General was a nightmare by comparison. Been here a couple weeks."

I lock my eyes on Rudy's.

"So, if we *aren't* crazy, what's going on?"

Rudy shakes his head slowly. "I do not know. All I do know is that I was ready to take those pills forever just so I would never see that shit again."

"Yeah, I know what you mean."

I look around the common room. "It has to be some sort of defect or something. Some glitch or surge in part of the camera that causes, like...temporary hallucinations? That shit can't be real."

Rudy stares at me. "What if it is?"

"Do you still have your camera?"

"Nah. I think the cops broke it when they cuffed me and I don't remember seeing them pick it up. Now I'm not sure it was an accident. How 'bout you?"

"Mine broke when I.... Mine broke too."

My mind races. I look around the common area again to escape Rudy's intense gaze, then toward the patio doors, and I see Mitch leaning against the wall to the right of the doors, just staring out.

He must be pining for his beloved, sweet cigarette. I wish I had one....

It finally hits me. Something about this angle and his

partial profile.

Mitch kind of looks like my dad.

Not that much but enough to bother me. Watching Mitch lust after another smoke and the similarity to my dad makes me angry. I don't want to end up like either man.

"If that stuff is real—"

"It's not," I say, never more sure about anything.

"Woah. We saw the same damn thing, Felix. We need to—"

"They're just drawings. You probably just copied my drawings as best you could and you're fucking with me."

I lock eyes with Rudy. "I have an illness and I just need to…. I want my life back."

"That's bullshit. Where is this coming from? A minute ago—"

"Shut up!"

I swipe my good arm across the table, throwing the chess board and pieces onto the floor, then stand up from my seat.

Mitch is staring at us now and even Delores looks back. I see Shasta peek out through the door of the room she shares with Candy over in the female section.

"Don't talk to me anymore," I say and start limping away.

"Not just a river in Egypt, huh?" Rudy asks behind me.

I stop and look back. "What?"

"Denial," Rudy says.

"Fuck off."

I turn and limp toward my room.

chapter 11

Two days later, early afternoon. Jesse sleeps on his bed, covers flung around but not on him, snoring.

I read a haiku book on my bed, wearing big hi-fi–style headphones attached to an MP3 player they had at the desk. They had enough players for a full ward population, all loaded with soothing nature sounds and the like.

I listen to the sounds of a thunderstorm. Rain. Wind. Thunder rolls sporadically.

Something catches my attention. Rudy is waving at me from the doorway, so I set the book down and take the headphones off.

Rudy holds a big department store bag.

"Hey, I'm getting out today."

"Great. Have fun," I respond.

"Yeah, fuck you too."

Rudy steps into the room and hands me a slip of paper.

"What's this?"

"My deets and mail. In case you need it."

"I won't."

"Better to have it and not need it."

I scrunch my face and shake my head. "Whatever. Take your medicine and have a nice life."

"Don't worry about me, bitch."

"Oh, I won't," I say with a smile.

Rudy shakes his head and walks back to the doorway. "No wonder your girlfriend kicked your punk ass out of her car. Yeah, I figured that one out. You're an asshole, man. Have fun dying alone and unloved."

In a singsong way like a mother reminding a child to brush their teeth, I say, "Take your med-ih-ciiiiiine."

Rudy walks out of the room still shaking his head. As he walks down the hall, I hear him grumble something like, "Fuckin' bitch."

The slip of paper has an email and phone number like he said but there's also a note on it that reads, "Keep an open mind."

I crumple it up and throw it in the metal wastebasket by my bed, then put the headphones back on.

I shall now let the forgetting of Rudy the fellow mental patient begin....

After Rudy leaves the FMC, I feel better. Take my medicine, read, watch television, draw pretty pictures of Audrey and other innocuous things, and play Ping-Pong with Ray. I'm a lot better at Ping-Pong than beanbag therapy.

I even have a couple productive sessions with Dr. Fleischmann and open up at group therapy about my mother's death and father's illness and suicide. Have a few good cries a long time in the making.

Maybe this is just what I needed.

Two weeks after Rudy left, I sit in a chair across from Doctor Fleischmann's desk watching him jot down notes on a pad. The doctor finishes his notes, then looks up at me and studies my face.

"So, you have not seen or heard any more of the distortions or warping you had spoken of?"

"No, not at all."

"And no voices or strange ideas? Paranoia?"

"None."

The doctor jots one more note, then flips his notepad closed.

"Excellent. Now, today will be different, Felix. You have been here nearly the amount of time for the medicine to take full effect. You seem to be doing quite well. Would you agree?"

I nod. "Yes. Just fine."

"Splendid. I will cease tiptoeing around it—Audrey is in a room down the hall."

My stomach tightens and that dread comes back.

Doctor Fleischmann watches me closely as he says, "If you feel up to it, I would like for you to see her. We have already spoken and she understands that if, after this meeting, you don't feel like returning home yet, you can stay with no ill will on her part. If you do feel ready, you may be discharged immediately. Moving forward, we can schedule outpatient appointments as needed but you should be fine as long as you take the Harmonia on schedule."

I shift in the chair.

"If you don't want to see her yet, I will have her return on another day."

I rub my hands together in my lap and my eyes dart around while I try to get used to the idea.

"You seem quite anxious. I'll have her come back another—"

"No. I'd like to—I want to see her."

Doctor Fleischmann smiles.

The doctor opens the door to a small interview room and lets me step in past him. Audrey sits in a chair at a small rectangular table.

She looks great. Nervous, but great. At least the anxiety's not one-sided.

We smile sheepishly at each other.

"You two play nicely now. He is mostly healed."

Audrey and I let out polite laughter. Doctor Fleischmann winks at us.

Or was it just for her? I wish I could shake the weird feeling I get when Fleischmann is near Audrey.

The doctor closes the door behind him as he leaves.

I sit down across from Audrey.

Awkward silence.

"How have you been?" I ask.

Audrey studies my eyes, then forces a little smile.

"Okay. Good."

"You have a new boyfriend yet?"

Audrey glares at me in disbelief.

"That's not funny. How could you say that?"

She starts tearing up a bit.

This must have been hard on her. So far, so good?

"I'm sorry, Audrey. I didn't mean to...."

I sigh.

"Okay, that's a lie. This is gonna sound really weird but...I need you to get mad at me."

"What the hell, Felix? Why? I'm trying really hard to keep it together here."

"I just need to know something. Please."

Audrey shakes her head and looks around the room, thinking. I watch her closely. Tears form as she begins and roll down her face.

"Mad, huh? That's not so hard, I guess. First, you jump out of my car and bust yourself all up. Then in the hospital, you look at me like *I'm* the crazy one. They put you in here and your doctor calls me up and says you don't want to see me for like a month! I get to sit at home like a fucking military wife or something! Then—" Audrey chokes up, then laughs through it sarcastically and continues, "Then I see you for the first time in forever and you want me to get *mad*!"

She looks up at the ceiling, then locks eyes with me.

"I love you, Felix Brewer, but there's only so much bullshit I can take!"

Nothing. No distortions or shark eyes or cutouts or glowing darkness.

Not even a little.

I take one of Audrey's hands and kiss it.

"Thank you. I love you too, Audrey. So much. I'm sorry."

Audrey squeezes my hands with hers, then gets another tissue. She dabs at mascara tears with the fresh tissues.

"You're welcome, twitchy. So…now what?"

"If you'll have me, I want to come home. I'll take the medicine for the rest of my life if I can spend it with you."

She chuckles softly.

"Aw, mushy poetics will get you everywhere. But you bet your ass you will. I don't think I could go through this again."

"You won't have to."

We lean over the table and kiss.

Audrey stands at the main desk with me while I sign discharge papers.

Peggy did a double take when she saw Audrey and she keeps looking back at her in between changing papers out for me.

I have my sling and some underwear in a Macy's bag on the floor at my feet. Sign for personal effects and Peggy hands me a small bag containing my shoelaces.

I chuckle and look down the hall toward the interview rooms and offices. Sasha Menlo is standing in the doorway of an office speaking with Doctor Fleischmann who has his back to us.

Audrey says, "I guess we'll have to get those laced back

up quick. Wouldn't want you to trip and…."

She trailed off, so I look back at her.

Audrey is staring down the hall at Sasha. She cocks her head and takes a few slow steps past me and the desk to examine closer. Sasha looks at her and Audrey stops. Sasha stops talking and Doctor Fleischmann notices. He looks back and sees Audrey, then blushes and his expression changes to one of something like boyish guilt.

"Felix, can we go? I'd like to go."

"Yeah, just have to go to the pharmacy."

She just says, "Let's," then turns and walks past the desk and down the entry hall, only stopping when she gets to the big mirror doors.

Who knows how that would feel? Seeing someone that similar? Weird for sure.

Ray approaches the desk area. "Hey, man. Getting out, huh?"

"Yeah."

"Take care of yourself. And no more street diving, right?"

"Right. Hey, work on your backhand smash. Way too easy to defend."

"Yeah, whatever. I was rusty. Hadn't played Ping-Pong in years before you got here. At least I didn't hit Delores with a crazy ricochet."

"It was off your paddle, though, so you sorta did. Anyway, I doubt she noticed."

We laugh.

Ray grabs and squeezes my good shoulder.

"You just take care."

I nod. "Bye, guys."

Peggy waves.

I pick up my bag and walk toward Audrey at the mirror doors.

Or as I like to think of them—the entrance to the Unlocked Ward.

As we walk through the parking lot to the Swede, Audrey seems relieved to be out of the facility.

I look back as we walk and notice the dense woods behind it again. Think about the patio pond with the islands, bamboo, and mirrors in the facility.

I never want to come back, but part of me will miss that trippy setup.

Audrey reaches the Swede first and opens the door for me. I get in and set my bag down at my feet.

It is a little odd to be back in this seat.

She walks around to the driver's side and gets in. After she is situated, she presses a new button installed under the dash left of the steering wheel.

I hear a little clicking sound in his door. "What was that?"

"Open it."

I try to but can't. I look at Audrey.

"Aftermarket child-safety locks. Cuts down on unwanted injuries, deaths, or sleepless nights caused by lying in a cold, empty bed."

She forces a smile to lessen the blow of her mean but deserved joke.

I hope it's a joke anyway. Return the forced smile and we both look forward.

Audrey starts the car and drives out of the parking lot.

She turns the key in the lock and swings our front door open, jumps in a bit, and makes a sweeping gesture with her arm like a showman.

"Surprise!"

I don't see anyone in the hallway, and give her a confused look.

"Just kidding. I was going to have some sort of surprise party but I didn't know if you would actually be coming home today."

"That's cool. Not sure I'd be up for it."

"Yeah…well, there is one thing. Stay here."

Audrey prances down the hall and whips around at the kitchen opening about halfway down, an excited gleam in her eyes. Her left hand disappears into the kitchen and something lights up in the ceiling hallway above her that I hadn't noticed. It has a towel covering it, which Audrey pulls down like a dramatic magician.

A Nixie tube sign glows:

I LOVE YOU FELIX

Bright orange I LOVE YOU, blue-tinged orange FELIX.

"So you don't forget," she says, a little misty eyed.

I step inside and close the door, then walk down the hallway, smiling.

"I love it."

"You better. I paid Crescent in the sculpture department to make it for me. Had to flirt a little even. Show some leg."

I chuckle.

"What are the different colors for?"

"Oh! I forgot. So, on the occasion that you beat me home or something…."

Audrey fiddles with something in the kitchen.

The FELIX tubes progress through a quick sequence and form into a glowing AUDREY—the EY at the end one tube to make up for the letter count difference.

I laugh. "Perfect."

Audrey beckons me closer with her finger. I lean in and we kiss. I slide my arm around her and start for her bottom. She pulls gently away.

"Nope!" Audrey yells.

"Aw, what?"

"You get comfy in the living room. I'll put your stuff away."

"Okay."

I walk down to the living room and sit on a couch.

Across from me in place of the old Trinitron standard television and funky entertainment center is a huge HDTV that must be over fifty inches installed on the wall. The newest game systems from three major console companies are installed below it and hooked up, each with several sealed brand-new games neatly organized in a holder.

"Surprise," she says.

I look over and see Audrey holding a decent-sized box covered in wrapping paper. She walks over and sits next to me on the couch.

She hands me the box and I unwrap it.

It's a new HD camcorder. Not an HDV-426, but basically the Panasonic equivalent.

"Oh wow! You didn't have to do that. Really."

"You busted your ass to get that camera. Okay, listen now. These things are not to be seen as rewards for…strange behavior. I just wanted to make you more comfortable in my evil web. Plus, that TV was pretty much done."

Audrey is adorable. Worse, though—she's gorgeous.

She sees the look in my eyes and winks at me.

I set the camera box down on the coffee table and let the wrapping fall to the floor.

I grin. "I think you're gonna get it."

"Really? Are you sure it'll still function with all that medicine in you?"

"Oh, it'll work."

"It better."

We make out a bit before she stands and pulls me off the couch, then after her down the hall toward the bedroom.

I look up as she leads me and catch the glowing Nixie tube I LOVE YOU AUDREY.

Yes, I really do.

part two

*"Even if we, and they, are fortunate...and we defy all manner of
laws and idols to accomplish our Herculean task,
they will not remember us."*

chapter 12

"Did you take your medicine, baby?" Audrey asks from the bed.

I stop brushing my teeth and lean on the sink, brush still in my mouth. The mirrored medicine-cabinet door is propped open, so I stare at pill bottles, Audrey's razors, cotton balls, and nail clippers while I shake my head. I'm happy she can't see all of me at this angle across the hallway in the toilet room.

It's been almost three months since I got out and she asks me every night.

Everything else has been great. Better than before even. We've been doing more fun stuff out of the house like we used to, like going to see friends' bands and art shows, the movies, zoo, Marine World, hiking, swimming, bowling, going on long drives in the Swede, etc., plus watching a lot of movies and playing board and video games.

Not to mention our other "indoor sports," which are better than ever.

I've even been sneaking to dance lessons here and there. Lindy Hop, swing, foxtrot.

I hate it and suck really bad but I'm trying. Just once I want to impress Audrey instead of the other way around. Sweep her off her feet, let's say.

I understand that what happened was serious and I need to take the medicine—I just hate being harped on.

I'm an adult.

Well, an adult that jumped out of a moving car because I thought my girlfriend was a psychedelic space demon out to get me…but still.

Yeah, she has the right, I decide grudgingly.

I take the toothbrush out of my mouth, lean back so she can see me from the bed, and say, "Yep."

The next evening around six, I set down my game controller and tear Audrey away from a 16mm optical printer in her workroom and we start making dinner.

I finely slice cabbage for fish tacos—one of the few nonvegetarian meals Audrey still enjoys.

She's basically a pescatarian at this point. Mostly vegetarian but eats eggs, dairy, seafood. If I sneak a burger she says she can smell it on me and it might even be a couch night.

Audrey fries battered fresh fish and watches me slicing. I'm trying to do the tucked finger thing she showed me and almost pulling it off. I notice that she's watching, and I make a funny face. She makes one back and we focus on what we were doing again. The doorbell makes a sound like a string of wind chimes.

I look at Audrey. She acts like she didn't hear it.

"Expecting someone?" I ask.

She makes an exaggerated "not me" face and shakes her head slowly.

"You're full of it."

I shake my head and set the knife down, wipe my hands

on a towel, and walk toward the hallway.

In a cutesy, mocking voice, Audrey says, "Let me just… finish these…so there's no…blood in them…when we… eat," each pause stepping a tiny bit closer to the cabbage on the cutting board.

I chuckle. "Whatever."

I walk down the hallway to the front door and reach for the handle—

Something slams into the small glass windows set high in the door.

I flinch and look up.

It's an adorable stuffed plush octopus.

Through the door I hear,

"Let me in! I want to touch your niiiipples!"

I laugh and open the door to see Hirofumi and Kaori crouched down on the doorstep holding stuffed shopping bags and smiling, and Oscar and Yevgeny crouched behind them.

Hirofumi pushes the octopus doll into my chest and rubs it around.

"Ooooh! Tasty nipple meat!"

I can't help but laugh. "You're gonna get me all worked up and then what'll you do?"

Hirofumi moans. "Whatever I want!"

Yevgeny shakes his head and laughs. "I am already disgusted."

Audrey pops her head out of the kitchen and laughs.

Kaori holds up a pink plush octopus and smiles big. "And you get one too!"

"Thanks, Sweet Tea!"

I push Hiro's blue doll away from my chest and we all laugh. Hiro and Kaori both give me a big hug and I let them step in past me, then slap and pound Yevgeny's and Oscar's hands as they step in.

Hirofumi sees the I LOVE YOU sign in the hallway ceiling and hurries down to it. Audrey turns it on and Hirofumi and Kaori both let out sounds of amazement and approval.

He rubs the octopus against the glowing sign.

"I love you too, Felix-kun!"

Kaori shakes her head. "Sometimes I think Hiro only stays with me because Felix likes girls."

Audrey laughs. "No doubt in my mind."

"So, how's the game going?" I ask.

Hiro says, "Fucking awesome!"

Oscar nods. "Yeah, they got us going as a free-to-play where you buy full skins, parts, accessories like different backpacks, and tricked out shopping carts with different ornaments and stuff. Customizable stuff too. Fuckin' funny shit, man."

"I made one with Weyland-Yutani–symbol wheels and motion tracker installed on the handlebar even," Yevgeny says, smiling big.

Oscar chuckles. "This fool even made a Colonial Marines helmet for his hobo. Ob-sessed, homie."

"It's true. We are doing well with Home/Free so far. Our server setup trip was worth it," Hirofumi says.

Kaori scoffs. "Hiro just likes drinking too much in different countries."

"Speaking of which...." Hiro stuffs the octopus in his bag and pulls out a sealed bottle of aged single malt whisky.

Kaori does the same, pulling out a big pint bottle of expensive craft beer. She rubs it up and down on the side of her face, eyes big and shaking her head slowly.

"Why did we get so many beeeeeers?"

Food consumed. Whisky sipped and shot. Bowls sparked. Beer imbibed. Terrible straight-to-streaming horror movie *Vacuum Cleaner Killer* thoroughly mocked and enjoyed. More of every consumable consumed.

"That's why *Aliens* is best movie ever. *Alien* is a masterpiece for sure...but it's more like best *feelm* ever. Three was great potential, too much interference. *Alien* and *Aliens*, both masterpieces," Yevgeny concludes.

Yevgeny's favorite movies are the first three Alien films. He's like that super-obsessed Star Wars or Star Trek person a lot of people know…just with Alien. Also the Dark Horse comics, alternate film scripts, original novels, etc. I know way more about those movies than I ever would on my own. They're great but…damn. He's pretty extra about it.

Hiro and I sit on big black beanbags near the TV. Kaori and Audrey are on the couch. Oscar sits cross-legged near Hirofumi, and Yevgeny is sitting on the floor with his back against the couch by Kaori's legs.

Audrey jokes, "I'm glad we got that settled."

We all chuckle.

Yevgeny frowns. "I'm just saying. Masterworks."

Oscar nods. "Yeah, Seamus really likes *Aliens* too. He was making Vasquez jokes about this butch girl at church one time—"

Yevgeny interrupts, "See…I still don't understand this. How you can be such a faithful, practicing Catholic and so gay?"

"I don't see the conflict. I believe in God as the Trinity of The Father, Son, and Holy Spirit. I just think They…or He, I guess, made me gay."

Yevgeny shakes his head. "So weird.…"

"It's kind of like how you're a Jewish atheist," I say.

Yevgeny scrunches up his face.

"What? No, it's not. For me, being Jewish—it's culture and family thing. Oscar lets himself believe that his vengeful, crazed God will be okay with him because he wants to think He-Three is nice and fluffy and won't mind that he likes boys."

Oscar scoffs. "That's not true. I like men."

Everyone laughs but Yevgeny, who just shakes his head.

Kaori hits a glass color-changing bong and passes it to Yevgeny like a peace pipe. He takes a hit and hands it to

Oscar. Oscar hits it, then stretches and gives it to Hiro.

Audrey and Hirofumi are playing *Nazi Zombies* on a map that looks like an old German movie palace or theater. Audrey has something like a space pistol from a fun box but gets swarmed on a long, curved staircase and goes down while reloading.

I say, "See, you have to stick together and cover each other."

"She's better than you are, bitch," Hirofumi says with a smile.

Audrey says, "Ha!"

"Maybe," I respond, smiling.

Now alone, Hirofumi runs for it, kiting the swarm in a long trail behind him and turning to fire on them at choke points before kiting away again. Audrey hands the controller to Kaori in exchange for the bong.

Hirofumi eventually whittles the zombie horde all the way down and the other character comes back to life at the start of a new round, now with Kaori in control.

Hirofumi says, "Hey, Felix."

"Yeah?"

"We were thinking maybe you could work with us on the game."

Audrey smiles. "Finally."

I frown, a little taken aback. "I thought you weren't into my style. Too dark or whatever."

"You could do more general work at first. Maybe not major designs, but we are planning to make it bigger. Expand. There are some new ideas we have that could be good for your style. Like the player characters start seeing spooky shit like you always draw. For like a big expansion update or DLC down the road."

I sip my beer and think. Balance my slight bitterness at their longtime stance on me working with them and the excitement of actually working on a creative new project with good friends.

Doesn't hurt that *Home/Free* is really cool, either, but….

"Can I think about it?"

Audrey cringes. "Do you even have to?"

Hiro looks annoyed like he didn't expect any hesitation.

Oscar looks at Yevgeny and raises his eyebrows. Yevgeny fishes in a pocket and shakes his head as he hands Oscar a crumpled five-dollar bill.

Kaori says, "Of course you can."

"Cool. I'll let you know."

Kaori isn't paying enough attention and she's brought down by the brain eaters.

I stretch for the controller. "Alright now. Next spawn let's see who's better at killin' zambeez."

The next day, I'm eating at Sushi Boat. I watch little wooden boat-plates drift steadily in their endless rounded rectangle of a river and can't help but hear "Ride of the Valkyries" in my head. Grab a couple more unagi roll pieces, salmon nigiri, and inari to finish it off.

My phone vibrates so I take it out of my pocket. Not a number I know, not a name from my contact list. Usually don't answer those.

I watch the little sushi boats float down their river.

I press ACCEPT.

"Hello?"

"Felix Andreas Brewer. You didn't drown yet?"

"Rudy? I didn't give you my number."

"You didn't tell me your middle name either, genius. I'm a journalist, remember?"

"Whatever. What the fuck do you want?"

"I got another four-two-six."

"And you pressed the little button and saw absolutely nothing because you were on meds, right?"

"You wish. Camera works, pills or not. Like it forces the eyes and brain to see and ears to hear. I think that's why it makes you sick at first. It doesn't even show you everything there is to see. It's limited, especially with the medicine. After that poison's out of you, I can show you some shit that'll—"

Before I can stop myself, I slap the counter next to my small plate-covered tray.

"I'm hanging up and changing this number. They shouldn't have let you leave. Start taking your meds again and leave me alone, you delusional shithead!"

There aren't many other people in the establishment, but those who are either glance over at me or listen without looking, acting like they're not.

I end the call and stare at my phone.

That night, I sit on the couch in the living room playing *Flower* through for what must be the sixth time. It usually relaxes me.

In it, I am the wind, blowing a stream of petals from different flowers through beautiful and majestic landscapes.

Normally I'd be soothed by all this lovely, painfully Zen shit. Can't stop thinking about Rudy's call.

Audrey walks down the hall and looks into the living room. "You, okay, lovey?"

"Yeah, what's up?"

"You just seem preoccupied."

"Just a little stomachache."

"I told you Sushi Boat is hit or miss."

"I'd lean toward it being the breakfast burrito from the liquor store."

"Eek. Gotcha. Hey, if you aren't too sick, I'll let you touch my heiny later."

"If I'm up for it."

Audrey looks concerned.

"I'm almost done with this part."

"Okay."

Audrey walks back down the hallway.

I brush my teeth with the medicine cabinet door propped open. Finish, rinse, spit.

I pick up my Harmonia bottle, open it, and shake a pill into my palm. Examine the black-and-white pill, then close my hand into a fist around it.

I breath in deep and sigh.

From the bedroom, Audrey asks, "Did you take your medicine, Mister 'If I'm up for it'?"

I fill a cup with water and take the pill.

"Yeah."

I close the medicine cabinet door without looking and turn off the light.

The next day, I stand in line at a Best Buy electronics store.

I've heard this one on Harrison will take back any piece of new, unopened equipment as long as they can figure out what it is.

I just so happen to have an untouched Panasonic HD camcorder under my arm as I wait at customer service.

Never opened it because, as cool as it is, it isn't nearly as badass as the 426. Didn't have the heart to tell Audrey.

The person in front of me finishes and walks off.

"How may I help you, sir?"

I step up and set the camera box down on the counter.

"Yeah, this was a gift, but I never opened it. I was hoping to exchange it for a JVC HDV four-two-six and pay the difference."

"Do you have a receipt?"

"No, but this is where she said she got it."

"That's okay. I don't think we have the one you mentioned, though."

"Your site says you have three," I say, still pleasant and patient.

The young woman taps and types at the terminal for a full thirty seconds.

What's the problem?

"Yeah, but I don't think….Hold on one moment please."

She approaches a guy wearing business casual and a tie. They both come back to where I'm standing.

"What's up, boss?" he says.

"I want to exchange this new camera for a JVC HDV four-two-six."

"Sorry, sir, no can do."

I gently tap the camera box.

"This camera's brand new and sealed."

"Oh yeah, that camera's no problem. Looks great."

"Okay?"

The supervisor leans toward me.

"The four twenty-six was recalled. The ones in the system just haven't been shipped yet. They're lagging I guess."

"Recalled? When?"

"About two months ago. There were some problems with it."

"What problems?" I ask.

"Fires or something. Battery problems. Hey, this one you have is nice, though. I can show you some other camcorders we have that totally rival the four twenty-six on all fronts. Not much more expensive than this Panasonic. What do you say, boss?"

I sit on a park bench reading about the 426 recall on my phone.

The official story seems to be a power-supply problem, so the Best Buy guy wasn't far off. There were fires and exploding batteries.

Enough to cause a full recall, though? That's like accidental terrorism.

I fight the thought forming in the back of my mind.

What if the camera made a lot of people flip out like Rudy and I did?

No way. That wouldn't just get a recall. There'd be like a federal investigation or something, right?

Unless it was like a large-scale behavioral experiment. Or maybe they know weird stuff is going on already and it was an accident? Like an industrial accident.

Shit, did I just label some unknown force "They"? Let's not get paranoid now, Felix.

But I can't shake the feeling that I have to know for sure.

I have to press that button and not see anything.

I have to.

I check eBay and Amazon. There is a vague message about the recall and suggestions for similar cameras.

Craigslist?

I navigate to the page and search for JVC HDV-426. Nothing found. HDV 426. Nothing.

Damn.

In frustration I scoff and look around. Reflected light glints off a passing car window and I blink. My eyes open and rest on some graffiti on a wall across the street.

One of the tags reads:

SHRMP

TIKLA

Those real tweaked, cryptic letters. Great style and colors.

I try to imagine tickling a shrimp and chuckle.

That name gives me an idea, though.

I search for HDV 462.

Nothing found but I keep going.

HDV 642
HDV 246
DVH 426
DVH 642
DVH 246
HVD 426
HVD 642
HVD 246—

That's got one. They're only asking three hundred dollars, though. It's either broken badly or they don't know what it is. Looks brand new in the pics.

I dial the number on the listing. The name for the seller is Sonja.

The dial tone purrs in my ear. Someone picks up.

–Hello?–

"Hi. I'm trying to reach Sonja."

–I'm Sonja. Is this about the video camera?–

"Yes, I'm very interested."

–You are the first person to call. I was beginning to think my price was too high.–

I say, "The listing has it as HVD two-four-six. It's actually H-Dee-Vee-four-two-six."

–Oh, heavens above. That was silly. I guess you are in luck.–

"Could I maybe come by to see it?"

–Of course. How is tomorrow afternoon?–

chapter 13

I'm half-heartedly editing video at home later, shaving a few frames off between a shallow depth-of-field macro close-up of strawberry and chocolate ice-cream scoops splatting down onto the hot sidewalk and two European cars crashing into each other and whipping apart in slow motion, glass spraying everywhere.

Audrey enters my workroom, which used to be her sewing room and still has cloth and sewing machines and scissors neatly stored about.

"Hey, we're pretty much out of fishy foodz. I'm hand-processing some sixteen in the tub."

I keep editing. "You want me to pick some up?"

"If that's cool. Fishies look hungry."

I make another trim.

Needs more insect murder fuck action.

"I mean, like, eat-your-face hungry."

"Sure, I'll get some."

"Whenever you aren't so busy."

I keep working.

She cocks her head. "Because you look *so* busy."

I finally stop and look back at Audrey.

"Fishies could starve…but I'm sure they would understand. *Daddy was too busy editing insects screwing and car crashes together to save our lives with delicious foodz.*"

Audrey cracks a smile. I smile and shake my head, then get up and walk to her. We kiss and I step past her into the hallway, grabbing a jacket on my way to the front door.

"Yay! You're their little fishy savior! Go save the fishy day!"

Audrey claps her hands a few times and does a little mock cheerleader jump.

I laugh and say, "You could just ask."

"This—much more fun."

I walk through North Beach and come to a pet store where we usually get our fish supplies, then try the door but it's locked. GOING OUT OF BUSINESS SALE sign in the window dated two weeks ago.

Weak. At least the evening is fixing to be a nice one. Might as well wander around and look for another store.

I head south on Grant and enjoy the crisp coolness in the air as I walk through Chinatown. It starts to rain lightly a little before I reach Grant and Sacramento.

A few built-up droplets sprinkle down onto my face from a row of lanterns hung above the street. I squint up at them and stick my tongue out while pulling my eyelid down with a middle finger.

When I look back down, I see a shop up the hill on Sacramento with the words FISH STORE in thick red block printing bordered by strips of Chinese characters.

I cross the wet street and climb the hill to the storefront. The windows are blacked out and there are big, silly caricatures of fish on butcher paper pasted up with deal signs in English and Chinese characters. I open the door and go inside.

Little bells on the door tinkle together as the door closes behind me. The store is lit almost exclusively by a few long rows of bright, colorful aquariums. They glow from beautiful fish, florescent artificial coral, real aquatic plants, fake mushrooms and anemones, and resin aquarium decorations. Sea caves and outcroppings, shipwrecks, deep-sea divers, etc.

The aquarium stands, floor, and walls are painted black, and the ceiling is dark blue with "schools" of bright, caricatured fish similar to the storefront deal displays painted on it. They are lit by black light and glow like the aquariums. They seem to be a work in progress.

Like eventually they'll meet and be a full mural the length of the ceiling.

A song is playing from what must be a record player.

"Yesterday Is Here."

It's from my favorite Tom Waits album, *Frank's Wild Years*. I'm a big fan but don't listen to him as much as I used to because Waits doesn't do much for Audrey. She thinks his style borders on shtick, while Waits's music is one of the few things that has ever given me hope for humanity.

The music and soft, colorful lighting combine, swirling and dreamlike as I walk down one aquarium-lined aisle looking at all the aquatic creatures as I go.

I emerge on the other end and find the fish-care products, on racks at the end of each row of aquariums and along the last stretches of wall before a dark back-counter area.

I go through the fish food and find a medium container of the type Audrey usually gets. Compare the prices by size and stick with the medium.

I haven't seen any employees in the store yet, so I look around, then lean over to look through the aquariums. I turn and glance at the dark counter area and do a double take—

There's a young woman sitting behind the counter in the dark staring at me.

No, wait....

Sleeping mask. Eyes printed on it.

I step closer.

There's a book in front of her on the counter and she's... rubbing it?

I say, "Uh, how do you read like that?"

"What?"

"The mask."

"Oh, it's—here, let me...."

She fumbles for a bare bulb above the counter and pulls the chain. Soft, low light.

The young woman pushes the sleeping mask up to her forehead revealing large, lovely eyes covered in translucent contact lenses with an odd reflective quality. She blinks a few times and squints up at the light bulb.

Oh shit. It's Siobhán.

She has a lot less makeup on. Black eye shadow and mascara and dark blue lipstick with a vertical strip of hot pink in the center.

I can see a smattering of light freckles around her eyes and across her face from cheek to cheek.

Oh damn—you are just a lovely creature, aren't you?

She wears a thin pink and gray plaid shirt with short sleeves over a black tank top and jeans. The top few buttons are open on the plaid shirt and the tattoos I saw suggested before are visible, as are her sleeve tattoos, which end about halfway down her forearms and smoothly transition into streams of blossom petals that dissipate along the backs and bottoms of her hands.

Thick, layered waves like old yakuza styles creep down out of her short sleeves. Where there would be mountain demons or dragons or something else from Japanese folklore over the wave strips there are what look like long, warped humanoid sea creatures with a mix of tendrils and limbs and too many eyes. The creatures are run through with spears, hacked partially open, have their weird heads smashed in, etc. Whatever they are, the artist must not have been fond of them.

Siobhán looks down from the bulb and flinches—seeming confused as she studies my face. Then she cocks her head.

"Wait—you're the guy from that party a while back. Oh shit…," she says, lowering her voice as she scans the aisles, "…is your girlfriend here?"

I chuckle. "No, you're safe."

"Oh, man. I was so spun that night! Sorry. I usually don't remember things so clearly on a big bender, but your girl was fuckin' pissed!"

"Can you blame her?"

"Yeah, I guess not. Sorry I harassed you. I'm not real super clear on the particulars, thankfully."

I make a show of thinking back and say, "There was the donut burger and…the panties thing and…oh, you decided I'm an ass man and then—"

Siobhán raises a hand to stop me and covers her face with the other, then lowers her hands back to the book.

"It's coming back now, yeah. Wow, I'm a charmer, right? My only defense is that I took a break from all that crap because of that night. Mostly. For dance parties I let myself have a little."

I smile. "Naturally."

"Also, I had just come back into town after a long time away."

"What brought you back here?"

"I left my heart, of course. Really, though, I had just gone through a rough breakup and this place has always been comfortable. Like an old sweater or some shit. I needed that, so I came back."

"Must have been a hard one."

"Yeah, she was something…." Siobhán drifts away for a

moment, then snaps back and says, "Anyway, hope I didn't get you into trouble with your lady."

"She was pretty intense that night…but I healed."

I look for a subject changer and notice the beads on her lower ear-to-nose chain. They were like translucent teeth the night we met, but now they're little pieces of cartoonish sushi with silly expressions.

"Hey, isn't it a conflict of interest to have sushi displayed so callously around all these fish?"

Siobhán frowns and thinks.

"Oh, these? They were *bad* fish. If the fish are nice, they need not fear the blade. If they're bad and mean, the use of blades is a promise."

She lowers her voice.

"And, secretly, the other side of this building is a sushi restaurant, so it's a brilliant setup."

"Blades like those crazy butterfly pigstickers you had?"

Siobhán cringes. "Forgot about that too. I should never have brought those out. They're mostly just for flash anyway. Distract somebody before you kick 'em or punch 'em and run off. Maybe just scare 'em, if that does it."

"I don't know, you looked pretty dangerous with them. You sure you've never stabbed anyone?"

Instead of laughing, Siobhán looks uncomfortable for a moment, then it's like I didn't say anything about the knives.

"So, how's your relationship with Lady Sourpuss going? You guys pretty serious? Seemed like it."

"Yeah, definitely."

"You love her?"

"I do."

Here I was having a laugh pretending I could still flirt with girls and not have my testicles removed without anesthesia by my one and only fair maiden Audrey.

I look down at Siobhán's book on the counter and see that the pages are blank. Look closer and see rows of tiny bumps.

"Braille?" I ask.

Siobhán studies my eyes with another confused look and then looks down.

"Oh, yeah. Besides my prowess as a simultaneous lover and sociopathic murderer of fish, I'm a substitute teacher at a school for the blind near Concord."

"That's cool. Any special reason?"

Siobhán thinks. "I've just always been amazed how people take what they see for granted."

That makes me think about meeting with Sonja to check out her camera tomorrow.

There's an awkward silence and Siobhán starts ringing up the fish food. I take out my billfold and hand her a twenty.

As she takes the bill, I see a small, shiny curved metal piece on the top of the ring finger of her left hand. She makes my change and counts it back. I notices that there's a similar piece on the underside of that finger to give the illusion it goes all the way through. I've never seen a body mod like that before.

"Thanks," I say while I tuck my change.

"I better send you packing before your woman comes looking for you and they have to call the coroner for little ol' me."

We laugh as she bags the fish food, puts the receipt and a coupon on colorful paper inside the bag, and hands it to me.

I nod. "Yeah…hey, have a good night."

"Come in any time. Now that I'm back in town, I'm not going anywhere for a while," Siobhán says and smiles.

I nod, then turn and walk down the center aisle between the bright aquariums toward the door. I hear the chain for the light bulb and look back over my shoulder.

Siobhán is in the dark again, already reading her Braille, and those fake eyes on the sleep mask seem to watch me leave.

That night, I stand in the bathroom studying the Harmonia pill in my hand. Then pour some water and take it.

I extend my hand to switch off the light but hesitate. I shut my eyes and slowly close the medicine cabinet door so that the mirrored surface faces me.

I just stand there with my eyes sealed, my hand trembling a bit. I let out a sharp sigh, then shut off the light and leave the room without looking toward the mirrored cabinet door.

I have to lean back a bit as I hike down the steepest stretch of Hyde.

You know, the Rice-A-Roni street. One of them anyway.

A cable car comes down the hill behind me and I ignore thrilled tourists calling and waving toward me as they pass.

I come to a gated doorway displaying the address Sonja gave me and press the call button.

While I wait, I look down at the empty JVC camera bag slung around my neck and right shoulder and resting on my left hip. Audrey had stuffed it in the back of a cupboard. Occurs to me now that I maybe should've kept the Panasonic camera's bag, at least.

My thumb is hooked in the strap where it meets the bag, and my arm is resting on it. Drum my fingers on the outer padding. It reminds me of the sling I had to use after my shoulder was dislocated and I think about how it went the last time I used one of these cameras with that special button pressed.

–Felix?– Sonja asks through the callbox.

"Yep."

–Just a moment.–

A buzzer sounds and I open the gate, then climb a short staircase. Sonja opens the door at the top. She is probably in her late fifties or early sixties.

Seems tired. Sad maybe?

"Please come in."

I nod. "Thanks."

I follow her into the large townhouse. We reach the living room and she gestures for me to sit on a large couch, so I do.

"I'll go get the camera. Would you like anything to drink?"

"No thanks."

She leaves down a hallway.

I casually scan the room. Cooking, style, and home magazines on the coffee table. Tasteful furniture and decoration.

There is a large chair across from where I sit. I can see steam rising out of a fresh cup of tea on a small table next to the chair.

On another table in one corner, there is a shrine with a teenage boy's photograph as its centerpiece.

Sonja returns with an HDV-426 box and hands it to me, then crosses to the large chair and sits.

"It's all there. Practically brand new," she says.

"Do you mind if I…?"

"Please do. I'm sorry, of course. Inspect as thoroughly as you need to. I charged it last night so that you could. I had to read the manual just to do that simple thing. I'm so bad with technology."

I open the box and take a quick look at all the accessories and the camera.

"I am techno illiterate. What do they call it? 'Technophobic'?"

I smile. "Nothing wrong with that if it's not what you're into. I'm more of a film person myself but video's cheaper and easier, so I do more stuff with it at this point."

I turn on the main power.

"Really? My expertise with film only went as far as popping in the cartridge."

"Super eight?" I ask, always curious about the home-movie period before video.

"Yes, I believe that was the name. I couldn't even make the projector work with it. My husband had to thread it. I guess I have always been a bit technophobic. Now, cooking I understand. I know that sounds mighty old fashioned but it just makes more sense. To me, that is."

I check all the wheels, then the buttons. All but that one on the lens. "That's at least as complex. I can boil water and chop stuff. My girlfriend doesn't even trust me to chop by myself, actually."

We chuckle. Sonja seems happy to have company, even just for this. Realizing this, I feel a little guilty as I pack the box back up and close it.

"Everything seems to be in perfect working order. I have to ask, though. Why so cheap?"

Sonja looks out the window and the sadness I noticed before blossoms into obvious heartache.

I continue, "It's just that…. I mean you could sell this for ten times what—"

"I know what it's worth. It isn't about money. I'm not worried about money."

She looks over at the shrine and her lower lip and chin quiver. She looks down at her tea.

"There is nothing wrong with the camera. I just don't want it here anymore. I was going to just throw it from a bridge…. But I decided that if it can be put to some good use, that would be better. You seem like you could put it to good use. That is more important to me."

Sonja tears up.

"I didn't mean to upset you."

"Just be careful."

"I'm very careful with cameras."

"I don't mean the camera," she says and looks out the window again.

"My grandson James saved for a long while to get a camera like that one. He mowed lawns, washed cars, and worked at a movie theater on Van Ness Avenue. The old historical landmark one that used to have a car dealership in it. He was almost finished with high school and planned to go to film school near Los Angeles. He had already been accepted and offered scholarships for his short video movies."

I look down at the box.

"He finally saved enough for the camera that was perfect for him…." She locks her hollow gaze on me and I meet it reluctantly.

"I am not generally a superstitious person…." She looks at the shrine again and I'm a bit relieved.

"Within a week of having that perfect camera, he became very strange. Antisocial. Agitated and paranoid. I thought it was some form of bad flu because he was having a lot of stomach sickness at first. He wouldn't let me take him to a doctor. Halfway through the second week, he took an entire bottle of my sleeping pills and went into a coma. If I hadn't found him…."

I fight the thoughts that are trying to fit what she is telling me in with my own fears. "I am so sorry."

She locks eyes with me again.

"Three hundred dollars is all I will take. Just do something good with that awful thing."

I walk down the stairwell and step out onto the street, closing the gate behind me. Then walk farther down the hill out of sight of Sonja's place, since I figure she should be left without any reminders of what she's been through.

I see a recycling can and hike down to it. Open the camera bag and take a small bottle of Pepto Bismol out of it and tuck it in my back pocket.

I figure there won't be any need for the packaging since I couldn't return it now if I wanted to, so I take the camera and all its attachments and such out and put them neatly into my camera bag in their respective spots. I open the recycling can and toss the empty box in. After opening and swigging half the Pepto bottle, I return it to my back pocket and start down the hill. I come to the Bay intersection and stop.

There's a lot of people around. This should be as good a place as any.

I take the camera out of the bag. Close my eyes and take a deep breath, then let it out slowly and open them. I press the recessed button on the lens and wince slightly at the weird feedback vibration or shock.

At least I expected it this time.

I raise the viewfinder to my eye.

People walking by with dogs, children, grocery bags, etc. Cars driving. People riding bikes.

All normal. So far, so good.

I continue down the hill. A cable car passes. Nothing strange about the driver or passengers. I pass a rental place for bike tours and little tourist GoCars with a decent amount of people in and around it but don't see anything odd.

Good stuff.

I continue down the hill and it starts to flatten out quickly as I approach Jefferson and the Fisherman's Wharf area.

Oh, that will totally settle this. There are tons of people around this area today, no doubt. If there was going to be weird stuff, which there's not, my chances of seeing it would be in dense groups probably. Right? Right.

I pass locked gates and fences, leading to the real docks

and piers, and themed seafood restaurants and tourist shops full of postcards, camera supplies, and "Pier 39" and "Fisherman's Wharf" imprinted clothing. There's even a wax museum if I remember right. I only come here to use the ferry at this point.

Touristy or not, it would probably seem weird for me to just be pointing my camera at random people, so I attach the wireless viewfinder earpiece. After I finish that, I move on down Jefferson, looking casual and shooting from the hip.

I pass the In-N-Out Burger and moan.

Smells so good.

Haven't seen a single weird thing yet and I've pointed my camera at a few hundred people already. I decide to grab a bite and start again before I give up and happily accept that I wasted my money.

Okay, so the burger wouldn't be worth the harassment if Audrey smelled it on my breath. What else would be good? Maybe a bread bowl or crab or something? Sounds good.

I keep the camera on and carry it by the top handle, just in case, as I cruise down the sidewalk. I cross the street and walk through the Tarantino's overhang to the smaller fish-vendor stalls. Get in line at my favorite and casually pan the camera around while I wait. There's an argument at the next vendor stall.

I listen in, which isn't hard because the vendor is getting louder, and pan the camera over from my hip.

The vendor says, "I told you, Bizmark! You ordered two chowda bread bowls and two drinks. You gave me a twenty. That's four bucks change!"

Oh no....

As the gaunt vendor gets more upset, his eyes pulse red and wisps of something like dark smoke come out of his mouth.

The German tourist responds, "I gave you a fifty-dollar bill."

"The hell you did!"

The vendor's eyes are all red now and, as his voice rises, jet-black smoke billows from his mouth. The voice is odd but nothing like Audrey's was. There is also a strange glowing thing pulsating behind his ear.

I raise the camera and zoom in. The vendor notices.

"Hey! You gonna order somethin' over here, cameraman?!"

The smoke pours toward me and what look like small translucent many-eyed serpents slither from his face and neck, then burrow into another part of them.

"N-no," I stammer.

"My sog card's all full so you gotta fuckin' pay to film me, awright?!"

The little serpents burst out of him this time, squirming and twitching obscenely before burrowing back in.

I step back and bump into someone in line behind me.

The vendor at the stall I was waiting at says, "It's SAG card, moron, and there's kids here, for Chrissake."

"You know what I meant, jagoff!"

I turn to the person I bumped into.

"Sorry."

The track-suited Midwesterner says, "That's alright, honey," but her look is more like, "Stupid shithead."

There are translucent, glowing sacks on her neck, which pulse like slugs or huge, nasty amoebas. Her eyes are oozing a greenish iridescent fluid.

Does she feel that? Doesn't seem to.

The German tourist starts back in, "I want thirty-four dollars now please!"

"You gave me *twen*-ty!"

I'm getting a bit queasy and my vision is blurring. I leave the line and rush through the rest of the vendor-stall area, not stopping until I'm across Taylor and halfway through the parking lot on the other side.

I take deep breaths and try to calm down.

I wasn't supposed to see anything! This is bad.

I'm sweating now and my head hurts a little.

The nausea and head pain are tame compared to the Audrey thing at least. The Pepto's probably helping too.

A one-man reggae-band busker watches me recover as he sets up his equipment for a show.

Back at the vendor stalls, there seems to be a new argument about the spider-serpent vendor costing the other one a customer. I raise the camera and zoom in all the way. The nasty little snake things are still wriggling and tunneling back into the thin, jerky vendor while he yells.

Something buzzes through my zoomed in shot. I zoom out and, after a struggle, get it in frame. It's blurry and hard to see clearly until I let my eye relax.

Its head resembles a spider's, but its eyes are less symmetrically placed. The wings flap fast enough to buzz but it's more sporadic than, say, a hummingbird. It makes the thing kind of bob around in the air, and thin, glowing tendrils below the start of its long tails flutter and seem to keep it up and steer it.

The outer body is similar to a dragonfly's but I can see tiny organs rhythmically pumping inside that I'm pretty sure dragonflies don't have.

I guess it's silly to apply normal insect biology to something that isn't even real....

But wait. If the camera is making me see these things even with my medicine fully functioning, are these things actually there?

The vendor and Midwesterner obviously don't notice them. Is it a question of reality...or perception?

Or are we back to insanity? Do I need a stronger prescription? I still feel completely normal.

The spiderfly, as I decide to think of it, moves closer to me, bobs up and down in front of the camera curiously, and then the one-man reggae band starts up with his one-two chords and the creature jolts and flies off south toward the buildings.

It becomes blurry as it gets farther away but it looks like it joins a small swarm of similar blurry creatures, and they all disappear up over the Shell Vacations Club building.

"Woah."

I rotate the viewfinder up on its swivel and it locks in place over part of my forehead. Lower the camera and move on through the parking lot. I don't know whether to laugh or cry or pull my hair out and scream. My hopeful bravado is completely gone and I'm missing it already. Confused and more than a little dazed, my gait is languid as I pass through a long strip of a parking lot.

As I reach the intersection of Jefferson and the Embarcadero at the acute angle tip, I notice a group of break-dancers doing their thing on a big rectangle of linoleum on the sidewalk.

I stop to watch.

I tried it when I was in high school but never got anywhere. Love to watch it, though. I have the same relationship with skateboarding. Much love, no talent.

The well-matched breakers battle, one-upping each other with their sets of moves escalating in difficulty and crowd-pleasing flair.

More applause from the tourists and locals, and I join in.

This is a nice distraction, but I'm here for a reason.

I swivel the viewfinder back down into place in front of my eye and pan the camera around.

Lots of tourists with shopping bags and cameras. Taxis and cars. There's nothing obviously strange in this immediate area so I frame the camera shot on the battling breakers and watch some more—then I notice something on the ground through one breaker's controlled windmill flailing.

It looks like a cat.

It's bright white and sitting on its haunches and has shiny, dark eyes and…it reminds me of the cat—

No. It *is* the cat from my dream.

The obsidian eyes reflect the movement of the dancer.

I'm transfixed. The cat isn't paying any attention to me and seems to be watching the B-boy spin around on his hands.

The B-boy blocks my view of the cat by executing a big suicide flip and landing on the ground.

The crowd applauds and cheers and whistles as the panting break battlers squash it, one helping the other up and hugging them.

Dammit!

I lean back and forth trying to find the cat but it's already gone, then step out of the spectator circle and walk around looking for it.

There it is! Pattering off toward Pier 39.

I follow from a distance. The cat cruises smoothly between the legs of the tourist throngs as it makes its way onto the pier.

Or is it going *through* their legs? Can't be sure.

The wind is picking up and big flags above the pier flap in it.

I keep my distance but pace the little cat.

Tourists and locals here and there shop in the stores and eat and walk around.

A fat man with huge, entirely blue eyes and a large glowing leech-bulb thing on the back of his neck and upper back passes me. I watch the man exhale blue mist in big huffing clouds.

As I watch the man lumber away, something else catches my attention. A woman is sitting on a bench consoling her little daughter who seems to be pouting.

Dark, translucent centipede-like creatures crawl into and out of the girl's mouth, nose, and ears. Some burrow into her skin and disappear, only to reappear from a different part of her face or neck.

I zoom in.

They glow like the spiderflies, and each has at least two dozen long, thin legs. And there are tiny eyes of different sizes all over what has to be the head area of their long, bulbous bodies—which are filled with pumping little organs like the spiderfly.

"Burrowpedes" seems to suit them. Might as well call the serpent ones "slints" short for "slither serpents" while I'm at it.

Dark, reddish fluid oozes from the little girl's eyes and mouth, which she obviously doesn't notice.

The little creatures seem to feed on the ooze?

A spiderfly buzzes into the shot and most of the burrowpedes dig into the girl's face and hide. The few that don't notice the spiderfly swoop-bobbing in are quickly preyed upon.

The spiderfly's mouth area breaks apart and a slimy stalk of tendrils whips out, snatching the smaller creatures up in quick succession as the spiderfly crawls across the girl's face. The spiderfly catches one last straggler as it's trying to burrow for freedom and pulls it out after a struggle and sucks it into the slimy tendril stalk.

The girl starts to whine and cry for unrelated reasons but the synchronicity of the events has me practically hypnotized. I'm just glad she can't feel that for real.

Shit—lost the cat again!

I look all over the first level of the pier but can't find it. I rush up the stairs, careful not to trip and break my only way of seeing these things I don't really want to see.

The cat is nowhere to be seen on the second floor. I look down at the first floor, hoping to catch it pattering through the crowd.

Nothing. It's gone. Shit.

I see a bench near the railing on the bay side. Might as well rest for a minute and think this through. I cross to it and sit.

Could it actually be a practical joke or something?

Maybe by a disgruntled or crazy designer or worker at the company or manufacturing plant?

It could be an incredibly elaborate augmented-reality experiment, like a guerilla art piece.

I shake my head and lean back against the bench and look up at the thick, dark clouds.

"Or are you really just too batshit crazy for the meds to work right?"

I hear the sounds of sea lions snortling and honking on the short floating docks in a little artificial harbor and look down at them.

Well, at least the sea lions haven't joined forces with the sloths yet.

On that day, humanity's reign is at an end, I think and chuckle.

I adjust the camera on my lap so that it's pointing down at the sea lions. It's still zoomed in from searching the first floor from the second and the shot is pretty tight on one of the floating docks.

The sea lions are just splayed out. One keeps arching its head up and harassing or just responding to one or all of the others. I'm not real familiar with sea lion behavior but that's what it seems like. There's a weird distortion on the edge of the frame, so I zoom out some—

Crouched on a dock near one group of sea lions is an impossibly dark figure.

Any playfulness I felt is instantly gone and that now familiar tingly cold wave flows through me. Like a cocktail of disbelief and profound terror downed on an empty stomach.

It isn't just dark but even seems to suck light in and distort it at the edges of its vague, humanoid form. A warped, living silhouette defined by its gaping maw of absence.

The figure stands. As it does, it takes on the form of every shape it creates in space as it moves at once, becoming a tall, amorphous blob of impossible negative space before the movement catches up and absorbs the multiple shapes and reforms into its humanoid silhouette.

I zoom in on what would be its head area.

It seems to notice somehow, and it "looks" directly at me. The view goes black. I look at the camera. I was almost okay until I couldn't see the thing. Like a nasty-looking spider crawling behind something out of sight you just know is going to get you later.

What the hell is wrong with this thing?

I check dials and settings.

Everything's the same. It's still on. The battery life and other info are still displayed in the remote viewfinder attachment. It's just totally black past that.

I tilt the camera up to look at the lens with my uncovered eye but what I see in the remote viewfinder is what helps me understand.

The camera is fine—

The dark figure is standing directly in front of me.

Even this close, there is no definition or discernable features but from its outline it seems to be looking down at me.

I jolt and almost drop the camera. It wobbles in my hands and I steady it, then shut it off and practically rip the viewfinder piece from my eye and ear.

Slow and cautious with a shaking hand, I swipe the air in front of me.

A little boy passes with his hand in his father's.

"Dad, a mime! Can we watch?"

I force a smile, then get up and rush away.

chapter 15

I was off Pier 39, down the Embarcadero, and almost to Pier 27 before I even considered slowing down. As I did slow, though, my hunger came back.

I guess if that spooky fuckin' thing wanted to hurt me, it would have. Shit, I need some comfort food....

So, I ended up at the Fog City Diner eating a big burger with a fried egg and bacon on it and downing a six-dollar chocolate malt.

'Cause fuck it, right? You probably only live once and who knows when a tall, dark "Nothing Man" is gonna sweep you off your feet—and decide to eat you, or whatever?

Anyway...sorry, Moz. That was too much for me and I need some selfish, evil comfort at the moment.

My hands are still shaking but I'm making do. This isn't the best burger I've ever had but after what I just saw you'd be hard pressed to convince me of that. Tastes like unicorn meat on an ambrosia bun to me.

I finish the burger and eagerly suck down the malt refill

in the metal mixing cup.

I step out of the diner and walk down the sidewalk. I see Coit Tower up on Telegraph Hill and stop. The hill is like a protective barrier between me and home right on the other side. Protective because I don't want to think too hard about the implications of any of this being real.

If it is real…what the fuck is Audrey? Some kind of monster?

I walk a little farther down the sidewalk and think. Try to. Now that I've attached this silly function to Telegraph Hill, I can't help daydreaming about the "World Famous" Parrots of Telegraph Hill up there in the trees. Picture the feral, squawking birds flying up out of the trees en masse to combat a Godzilla-big Crazyface Audrey looking over the hill from the west side or at least confuse her by pecking at her backyard-satellite-dish-sized shark eyes.

I cross the street and pace in front of Pier 23, fighting myself to stay on task and come to terms with what I've just seen.

Even though the pier is closed right now, I realize I must look pretty crazy just pacing and thinking hard, so I stop and lean against the big pier roll-up door.

I take out my phone and navigate through the contact list. Find the personal contact number Doctor Fleischmann emailed me for use in case of issues.

My thumb hovers over the touchscreen. I close my eyes and sigh. Then back out of the contact list and shake my head when I realize what I'm going to do.

Call history it is then.

I find the number that came up when Rudy called me in the Sushi Boat and steel myself. I press that number and put the phone to my ear.

Dial tone….

You're going to regret this.

Dial tone….

This is a bad idea.

Dial tone....

You should hang up and call the doctor.

Dial ton—

The line opens and a young woman says, –Speak.–

"Hi. I'm…uh…. I'm trying to reach Rudy?"

–How do you know him?–

"Uh…from school."

–Are you sure about that?–

"Yeah. Why? Who are you?"

She pulls the phone away some.

–Hey, Rude Boy! It's your lover! Tell him to clean up after himself next time. That's nasty when it's like dried on.–

Farther from the phone Rudy says, –Lacy, what the fuck are you talkin' about?–

Lacy says, –I am so fuckin' baked,– laughs, and then, –Just take it. Here.–

There's muffled shuffling.

–Why do you always answer my phone, girl? Fuckin' paranoid, man.–

Now she's farther from the phone.

–Because you're so sexy. Whatever, I was just playing with you.–

–Whatever yourself,– Rudy says to Lacy, then, –Who is this?– into the phone.

"Rudy?"

–No, that's me. Once again, who is this?–

"Felix. It's Felix."

–Felix? I don't know a Felix. Who are you?–

"We met at—"

–I'm just fuckin' with you. So, what's up? You gonna talk some more sense into me?–

"No. Actually, I…saw some more stuff. I got a new camera and—"

–Hold up. Baby, could you get me some Oreos? And

milk.–

I hear shuffling sounds as Lacy gets up.

Her voice gets farther away as she says, –Lazy ass. Does sound good, though.– She laughs.

–You know Union Square?– Rudy asks.

"Yeah."

–What time can you make it there?–

"Anytime."

–Then leave now. Later.–

Rudy hangs up.

I end the call and put my phone away. Then bang my head back against the roll-up door one more time and keep it there while I look up at Coit Tower.

I hop off the F Market at Kearny and cruise down Geary to Union Square. As I climb some steps up to the square proper, I study the statue of the goddess Victoria atop the high column in the center.

There's an open bench so I cross to it and sit, setting the camera bag down. I look around for Rudy but don't see him.

I take out my phone.

It was on vibrate so it's possible I could have missed a call or text with the streetcar shuddering like it was.

No messages or missed calls.

Might as well kill some time and take my mind off this all for a minute. Load up a game on my phone. I've beat it twice already now but it's really addicting once you get used to the touch controls. I combine pieces of cartoon sushi into groups of three or more to clear a circular area. I get a good run going and I'm on my way to a new high score—

"Boo!"

I jump in my seat and exclaim, "Shit!" before whipping around to see Rudy grinning down over my shoulder.

Rudy laughs. "Damn, fool. Relax."

"It's not my fault you're like a fuckin' ninja!"

"Just wanted to feel out your nerves. Guess I did."

"Whatever. Don't do that shit again."

"Yeah, yeah," Rudy says and sits next to me, leaning forward and resting his elbows on his knees before looking around.

"Alright, so…what did you see?"

"A bunch. This guy bitches me out and black smoke comes out of his mouth and little like see-through snakes pop out of his face."

"Uh-huh."

"Flying spider-head things that glowed and ate centipede things out of a little girl's face. A bright white cat with obsidian eyes that can walk through things."

"Anything else?"

"Uh…more glowing see-through growth things on people. Guy with big, all-blue eyes. The worst was this really, really dark thing. Freaky."

Rudy turns his head and looks me in the eyes. He looks nervous.

That's got you all ears.

I continue, "Human shaped pretty much. Dark doesn't do it justice, though. Seemed like it absorbed light. And when it moved, it like—"

"Were you recording?"

"No."

"Damn. Why not?"

"I wasn't out there to make home movies. Didn't seem important. Hell, I didn't want to see anything at all."

"Too bad. Shit…. He won't even tell me about those. Come on."

Rudy stands up.

I hesitate.

"Wait. Who's 'he'? What are you saying?"

"I met you here to make sure you were cool. You are, so what we're really doing is going to see a man about some upgrades."

The BART car shudders a bit as it cruises quickly through an underground stretch of tunnel heading south.

Rudy looks around at the other passengers.

Apparently satisfied, he opens his backpack and produces his own HDV-426. I immediately notice some differences.

It's subtle enough but there is a slightly glossy pattern or intricate symbol over the solid-state drive housing. There's a different pattern on the lens. You probably wouldn't see them at all if not for the lights right above our padded bench seats.

There are also some foam and plastic parts glued on that make it look different. They look cosmetic.

Rudy extends the camera and remote viewfinder to me.

"I've got a four-two-six," I say.

"Not for playback. Yours needs some…accessorizing."

I take the viewfinder and put it on.

"Ready?" Rudy asks.

"Sure, why not?"

Rudy reaches over and presses the play button.

Raw shots. Some just quick glimpses out a car or bus window. Others are longer like Rudy was able to really study the subject.

Most of the shots are of things I've seen or similar. Spiderflies, slints, burrowpedes, amoeba growths, etc. There are growths I haven't seen, like slithery translucent suckerless tentacles and bulbous sacks that glow and pulse and pump with those strange little internal organs on people's faces, necks, and backs.

One bulbous sack wriggles and pulls itself loose from a person's neck and pumps away through the air like a flying jellyfish before attaching to another person's face down the sidewalk and nestling in.

Larger flying creatures fly over the streets and in the sky, similar in makeup to what I've seen, but more like many-eyed translucent porpoises with pumping visible organs under their glowing skin and thin, tentacular appendages streaming behind them in long bunches where fins would be.

Another shot starts with a large bulb over a man's eye that's so full of little pumping organs and fluid that his eye is barely visible. When the man turns more toward the camera, I can see a group of thick tentacles sprout from behind his ear and disappear into his cheek on that side and come out his mouth when he speaks. After his mouth closes, the tentacles stay there, writhing on his chin. A woman enters the frame and leans into him, and they kiss. I can see the tentacles squirming around and through her mouth and cheeks.

A homeless man downtown near the bus station gesticulates. He jabs his finger toward the growths on one woman walking down the sidewalk and tries to get others to look.

The wall of a building near him shimmers subtly and shudders, then breaks open like horizontal window slats, only darkness past the openings. I feel my ear tingling and realize I can just hear a mechanical creak from inside the dark openings.

A faintly glowing, sickly green gas or mist belches out of the wall, enveloping the man in its murky clouds. He tries to swat the gas away from his face, but his breathing is heavy due to his excited state and after only a few breaths, he relaxes so much that he slouches against the wall next to the openings. When he exhales what's left of the gas, it comes out thinner and dark blue.

He looks drunk or high as he stumbles away down the sidewalk, seemingly oblivious to whatever was bothering him before. The slats close and the wall looks normal again.

Okaaaaay....

The sky on a partly cloudy, sunny day. There are dark

discolorations passing through the fluffy clouds and open sky. Some float slow enough that they stay in roughly the same area while others cruise smoothly through the air like asteroids in a belt. Different shapes and sizes and hardly visible.

An intersection in the Mission District. The camera tilts up, framing a low-angle shot of the space above the traffic lights and bus wires, then pans left as if to follow something moving through the shot in the air but there's nothing in sight. Something about that bothers me more than anything else I've just watched.

I hit stop on the camera during a shot in a BART station of a bald, trench-coat-wearing man in the distance walking through station support pillars like they're not there.

I remove the viewfinder and hand the camera back to Rudy, eyebrows raised.

"Wow."

"That's just a few shots since I wiped it," Rudy says.

"Wiped it?"

"I take it to the man and he loads it into this big master drive and cloud system; then I wipe it and fill it up again."

"Who is this guy?"

"He goes by the name *Var-height*. He's like a zoologist for this shit."

"How did you get hooked up with him?"

"There was a guy in the FMC ward before you got there. They stuck us together. Like a 'gutter punk' or whatever? Smelled like it. Anyway, he told me that he heard there was some guy who knows what's really going on. Said it was impossible to find him without help. I'm good, but he was right. After I got out and tried the camera thing again, I eventually found him or.... Probably vice versa, actually."

"You sure he's for real?"

"As real as any of this."

The BART train slows. Signs that read COLMA flash by outside the train windows.

Rudy stands, finishes securing his HDV-426 back in his bag, and says, "This is us."

"Colma? Does he live in a cemetery?"

Rudy chuckles. "Not quite. Close enough, though."

chapter 16

Colma is a small city south of San Francisco composed largely of cemeteries segregated by ethnicity and/or religion, a necropolis set aside for that purpose sometime in the 1920s. I looked it up one time and was tripped out to learn that there are more dead people there than living. "City of the Silent" is what some call it, which makes sense if you are there in certain parts for more than twenty minutes.

Most of my experience with Colma was from hanging out there with different goth and death-punky girls in high school.

Now I only come down here once in a while to bowl with Audrey and our friends.

Cheap pitchers of nasty beer make bowling three to five times better, no question.

I follow Rudy out of the BART car and through Colma Station.

"So, what was up with that shot of an intersection?

There wasn't anything in it."

Rudy cringes. "There was when I took it. Well, sort of...."

"I don't get it."

"Me neither. I could see it...but the camera couldn't pick it up. Spooky shit, even by these new standards I've been forced to develop."

"I heard that. Why don't you just ask this Var-height, though?"

Rudy shrugs. "There are still some things he won't tell me. Not yet, anyway."

We cruise through the odd, sleepy town and end up on Hoffman Street, which borders one of the largest cemetery areas.

I notice that Rudy is visibly nervous. He keeps glancing sideways into the large cemetery to our right, then closes his eyes, opens them again, and locks his eyes on the street ahead until he can't help looking again.

I look out into the cemetery and see nothing but grass, grave markers, trees. "What's up? You cool?"

"Just keep walking."

I look into the still of the cemetery again.

"What's wrong?"

"I should just cut through on Chester, one over. Totally forgot. Yeah, I'll do that next time. I hate this walk now."

"Now?"

"Now that I can see."

I start to open my camera bag.

"No. Not here. Just walk."

We pass a condo complex built into and bordering the northeast corner of the cemetery. On the other side of that is a gatehouse and stop sign at the entrance of what must be a gated community.

Rudy rounds the corner and passes the gatehouse, waving to the guy in it.

The guard looks at Rudy like he is confused but doesn't

say anything to them as they enter the community.

It's gated, but instead of mansions or nice houses, it's a large, protected community of double-wide mobile homes.

Basically, a nice trailer park.

We walk down the street we came in on, passing several possible left turns and probably twenty-five or thirty homes on the right.

As I walk behind Rudy, I wonder what it would feel like to have a cemetery for a backyard.

Cooler than a golf course.

Stranger than a golf course, though, too. Probably pretty eerie at night.

I bet full moons are creepy as hell.

I'd keep my south-facing windows totally covered for sure. I would…uh…..I….

I realize I don't see Rudy anymore and stop. Head feels foggy. As if heard from the bottom of a deep pool someone yells, "Hey, Felix!"

I turn around and see that Rudy is standing several house widths back down the sidewalk.

He's in front of a…kind of vague…um….

I look up at the mostly cloudy sky.

Nice, crisp day.

I look across the street at the row of houses.

I wonder….

Has there ever been a two-story mobile home? That would be weird. How would you build it—?

"Felix, come back here!"

Someone's calling me? Oh, it's Rudy. He's standing down the sidewalk in front of a…uh.…

"Felix, just walk back to me! Don't look at anything else!"

Okay, sure.

I start down the sidewalk, resisting the urge to look at anything but Rudy. I make it to him but feel dizzy.

Rudy puts a hand on my shoulder.

"I know this is weird, but…look to your left."

I try to look left but it makes me really tired and dizzy. There's nothing there anyway, so I look back at Rudy.

"There are two mobile homes to your left. I know it's hard to look at them. Keep trying. Knowing they're there should help."

What? He must be messing with me. He probably won't quit unless I do what he asks, though.

I try to look again.

Rudy points to his right and says, "There's the porch and front door. And windows there and there." I focus on Rudy's finger because everything else that direction is blurry.

It's like pointing a finger at the moon. Focus on the finger and miss all that heavenly glory.

I chuckle.

I should watch *Enter the Dragon* again. It's funny how the end part with the mirrors and the evil claw guy is so much like the end part in *Lady from Shanghai*—

"Felix!"

"What?"

"Keep looking. There are two double-wide trailers to your left. I promise you. Look."

I sigh and look at where Rudy is pointing again. Rudy starts gesturing and making angled rectangular shapes with his hand motions. He describes as he gestures, "There's the lawn…kitchen windows…fence between the two…. Lawn, windows, fence, the roof on the house…."

There are two mobile homes to my left?

"They're there, Felix."

There are two mobile homes to my left.

I see vague boxy shapes through the dense murk of confusion. They become clearer in the wake of the hand gestures Rudy is making. I shake my head to clear it and decide I'm seeing what's actually there.

Rudy's right. What the fuck?

There are two vague and blurry mobile homes to our left. A seven-foot-tall wood slat fence between them gives the impression they are one large combined unit, but it looks like a rough do-it-yourself job. I can also see a patchwork of tarps between the houses' roofs over the yard, which creates a layered shady canopy covering.

"I see them now. What's going on?"

"He keeps this suggestion field amped up so they can't find him. He said it's like what they use to failsafe outbreaks of perceptive clarity, only cranked to eleven."

"What…?"

"Just follow me."

Rudy takes a step forward, so I do the same.

For a moment it feels like walking toward the fan in a wind tunnel. The blurry fog puts up some kind of resistance and I want to look away. There is a flash and now I desperately want to turn around and forget what's in front of me—

Then my foot touches down on the turf of a little front "lawn" and the resistance is gone.

I look around, seeing the connected mobile homes clearly for the first time. The one we're closer to is a pale yellow and the connected one a pale green. The fence is painted pastel blue. I look through picture windows closest to us and see a living room with teacups on an old oak table. Floral print chairs.

I take a few steps into the short turf yard and look into the smaller kitchen windows. One is up halfway, and I can hear humming through the screen. There's an old white woman in a grandma muumuu wearing thick bifocals with a neck chain washing dishes.

The murk is totally gone. I look around for any signs of it but there are none.

It was so overpowering.

I notice several black devices installed along the roofs of the two mobile homes that resemble rotating pinwheels on casual inspection—but I see layers of wire mesh and thin electronics cables snaking down to their boxy bases.

Rudy says, "This way."

I follow him back around the closer house to a low wooden porch under an overhang that stretches almost the full length of the house.

Rudy presses a doorbell in the frame.

I notice a small camera mounted above the door. Then look around and see that there are more mounted in two corners of the overhang.

The door buzzes and clicks. Rudy opens it and steps into what looks like a short hallway with shiny walls. He turns back and gestures for me to follow.

I step in and close the door behind us. I hear the door click again.

The small hallway is lit by a dangling bare bulb emitting soft white light. There's another bulb that's not on and it looks like it's covered in dark blue paint with parts scratched out almost like scrimshaw.

The walls are stainless steel from the looks of it and there's a thicker metal door at the end of the short hall. It doesn't have a knob or handle. Above it there's an array of cameras and less recognizable equipment.

Some raw electronic patchwork mods and some sort of wire-pulley and mechanical-movement rig?

I also notice that the walls and ceiling have rows of small holes cut out of them. Even, symmetrical, ten rows each top to bottom.

There is a ticking and whirring sound and I look back up at the camera array. The cameras are zooming in and out and moving on their gears and pulleys.

In almost perfect sync the holes all around make mechanical clicking sounds.

The white light goes out.

"Rudy, what the fuck?"

"Chill. It's cool."

Small lights in the camera array strobe through a set of different colors and at three different speeds simultaneously, and then it's dark again. Mostly. I notice a faint orange glow coming from an intricate circular pattern on the metal floor.

The blue-painted scrimshaw bulb blinks on and—other than bathing us in eerie blue light—it laces the walls, floor, and ceiling in bright symbols and patterns projected out through the etchings.

The pattern on the floor glows bright orange now.

A small speaker in the camera array crackles and a choppy, distorted voice asks, –Who's the pink, Rudy?–

"Felix. I met him in the FMC. He saw some things."

–And?–

"I thought you could drop some logic on him and maybe give him some camera upgrades."

There's a few full seconds of silence.

–Felix.–

"Yes?"

Rudy looks at me.

The largest camera zooms in more.

–If a tree falls in the forest, does it make a sound?–

I furrow my brow. "What?"

–If a tree——

"I heard you."

I shake my head and think.

"Uh...."

–Uh...?–

Talk about being put on the orange glowing spot.

"Does the tree make a sound? Well...I guess scientists would say 'of course,' philosophers would say 'how could you know?' and nihilists would say 'who gives a fuck?'"

The distorted voice laughs over the speaker. It's not a pleasant sound but the holes in the walls and ceiling make a different clicking sound from before, which I assume is a good thing. The laugh cuts out abruptly.

The blue light and symbols cut off and the bare white bulb flicks back on. I can't see the symbol on the floor anymore at all.

More mechanical sounds are heard, and the door opens, revealing a smiling black man with dreadlocks.

Looks middle-aged but could be older. Salt-and-pepper chop sideburns that connect in a mustache and there's stubble growing in that threatens to complete the beard. The salt and pepper continues into thick old-school dreadlocks, some of which are wrapped and resting on his head, the rest reaching down his back.

He wears a silk kimono bathrobe over a tank top, sweat shorts, and fuzzy frog slippers.

As the man leans into the little hall holding the door, I glimpse a large revolver in a shoulder holster under the robe.

Wahrheit says, "Enter freely and of your own will, bitches."

chapter 17

Rudy and I step past Wahrheit into his long, large living room. It smells strongly of patchouli oil or incense and the lighting is low. *Abbey Road* is playing on a turntable that crowns a large, old component stereo system with waist-high floor speakers.

Other than the stereo and some chairs and couches on the far end of the room, there isn't much normal about this room.

Live monitors and electronic equipment glow and beep all over and some of it looks like it would be right at home on a submarine or space shuttle.

Something like radar? Something else like a seismograph?

A set of several translucent spheres rotate into each other. Peas in a plum in an orange in a cantaloupe surfacing past an internal tangent and creating a large bump on the outer surface of a basketball. All of this hovers over a baseplate like a hologram but I don't see any small projectors or lasers in it.

Then I see all the guns and I'm not worried about the glowing spheres anymore.

The first set I see is on the long window lining a strip of the porch we were on. All the windows are barred on the inside and gun rigs are installed between the bars. The gun rigs are simple and boxy and have wire-pulley systems like the camera array and seem able to be remotely manipulated and aimed. They don't have handles or grips. Just small barrel-sprouting metal boxes.

Some of them have other add-ons that look like ampules of bright blue and green fluid and small, clear piping for distributing it into the gun. The blue globs float in the green fluid like oil in water.

What the hell is that and what could it possibly be for?

The guns must have been custom made to work in the rigs. I can see more of them on the windows in the kitchen, which is visible through the openings in a hallway that must bisect the mobile home parallel to the length of the living room.

Then I realize a few strange things at once—there is no old lady in the kitchen and it doesn't look at all like it did through the windows. It's dim and, other than a fridge, stovetop oven, and a small table, it's more like the living room in that it's lined with more strange equipment. There's even a shortwave radio setup on the small kitchen table that takes up most of its surface.

The small section of table surface remaining is taken up by an ornate chessboard that looks to have a long-term game in progress.

Must eat a lot of ramen and TV dinners.

The other strange thing is that the mobile home looks larger inside than it did outside. Subtle, but enough to be unsettling.

I look sideways at Rudy.

He notices and returns with his "it's cool" face.

Wahrheit closes the metal door and re-engages the lock, then chuckles.

"You know, I just asked that to see how your mind works, but that might be the best answer I've heard to that one."

I turn toward Wahrheit but something else catches my attention.

The short hallway we were in is constructed from a metal frame and layered bulletproof vests under a few layers of brazed-together chain-link fence, all brought together with rows of smaller gun rigs lined up with the holes I saw in the metal sheeting.

My jaw drops open.

Wahrheit smiles. "This ain't for you, man. You're a guest."

My hands shake and I feel a flush of adrenaline from realizing I was one decision by someone else away from a horrible death. "I heard you c-cock them."

Rudy puts his hand on my shoulder. "It's c—"

I push Rudy's hand away. "Cool? You think that's al-*right*? I came here for answers, not to get mulched in Scary McFuckjob's Entryway of Death!"

"Oh, you came for answers?" Rudy gestures toward Wahrheit without looking at him. "This is the man with the *answers*, so chill the fuck out!"

Wahrheit steps away and hums to the song on the stereo as he walks away from the entryway toward the living room proper. He arrives at a large purple couch on the left side of the long room and sits.

"Damn, Rudy-Rude. This kid is spooked. Doesn't seem like the fightin' type, but this has got him all worked up. Back off, will ya?"

I look away from Rudy's glare and see Wahrheit produce an ancient-looking bottle of scotch from below the long coffee table. He pours a few fingers of the whisky into a lowball glass.

Curving around from the end of the coffee table to the left of Wahrheit on the couch is a stack of monitors.

There must be fifty of them. Different sizes but the largest is probably only twelve inches diagonal. Most are about five to eight inches. Black and white, color, and some just shades of green and black.

The stack starts on the floor to the left of the couch and the lowest ones are angled up for viewing and must be in some sort of custom rack. The stacks reach up to one layer above Wahrheit's seated head level and spill over onto his coffee table, five or six in a neat, angled pile on one corner of it.

There is also a joystick on the table by this pile that reminds me of one I had to play flight simulators when I was younger, but I imagine this one is for controlling Wahrheit's little death machines.

On the far wall of the living room past Wahrheit and all his electric eyes is what amounts to a small armory of strangely modified firearms mounted on gunracks and hangers.

Pistols, rifles, submachine guns, assault rifles—all with strange aftermarket fittings and tubing for ampules filled with odd-colored fluids.

Wahrheit takes a big sip of his scotch and lets out some breath. "Ah, much better. Hey, why don't you toughies take a damn seat?"

Wahrheit takes another sip, then pours some of the whisky from the bottle into another glass. He extends it toward me, still standing by the entryway.

"Here, sip off this. It's good for your heart."

I just look at him while Rudy crosses the room and sits in a large chair placed kitty-corner to another big couch that's across from the one Wahrheit's on.

Rudy shakes his head. "You should turn down that ninja-field shit out there, man. He got a few houses past yours before I was able to get his attention. Even then, it was hard to get him to come back to it and even harder to get him to see it."

Wahrheit chuckles. "That's the idea."

I titter and scoff, amazed at how nonchalant they are about all this hardware and weirdness.

After taking one more look at the entryway deathtrap, I relent and make my way to the sitting area, taking the glass and sitting on the couch across from Wahrheit with Rudy to his right.

Hand trembles as I take a big sip. It burns but it's still smooth and clean. I welcome the warmth and the coming soothing effects. Clear my throat and breathe out like it's hot. Haven't had this scotch before.

Very, very nice. Feeling better already, actually.

I lean back into the comfortable couch and nestle in. Gloomy daylight streams into the bisecting hallway from what has to be a window at its end. The shadows of droplets falling steadily from the edge of the roof are visible and I can hear the thrumming sound of them hitting something solid in the yard.

Must be raining now.

Wahrheit nods toward me.

"Better? Thought you would be. Alright, so, I am truly sorry to shake you up but if you're here I assume you've figured out that not everything looks like what it is."

"I understand. Sort of. Anyway, sorry I freaked out."

Wahrheit nods, takes another sip, and taps something into a nice laptop on the coffee table as he frequently glances at his stack of monitors.

He picks up a two-foot glass bong from near his feet.

"You smoke?" he asks as he packs a big bowl from a silver dish of prepared marijuana on an end table to his left.

"Sometimes."

"Right answer. It's good for your soul. It's like soul medicine."

He lifts his scotch.

"This stuff is lovely, but you have too much of it...." He makes a whistling bomb dropping sound with his mouth and lowers the glass like it's falling.

He sets the glass down on a coaster and picks up a lighter. Takes a large hit and rises, extending the bong to Rudy. Exhales as he sits back down.

Rudy takes a hit with his own lighter and hands it and the bong to me.

"Soul medicine? I thought it just fucked you up."

Wahrheit smiles and raises his eyebrows. "That too."

The coffee table is also covered in what look like tools and materials needed for making homemade bullets.

I gesture around. "So, what is all this for? These guns and equipment and shit?"

Rudy stretches a hand toward him. "Hey, Mr. Microphone. Puff-puff, give."

I remember the bong in my hands. Take a small hit. Stretch to pass the bong back to Wahrheit over the table.

As I hand the bong over, I glance at a few of the monitors and notice two people in their underwear who seem to be working in an indoor garden, a different view from a camera that bobs up and down as it makes its way through the air high above the city streets approaching the Transamerica Pyramid building, and a view from one of the night vision cameras showing dark canyons or something? Then a little white crab skitters by the view and I realize it must be underwater.

I really want to examine the views closer but notice Wahrheit staring at me with a serious expression that seems to say, "Can I help you with something?" It reminds me of Hirofumi tapping his foot but this man seems far more capable of causing someone bodily harm.

"Sorry," I say and sit back down.

Wahrheit sets the bong down by his feet without smoking again. "So, now that we're a little more relaxed…I assume you acquired a special camera recently and that ultimately led you here."

I take another sip of scotch. "Yeah, the HDV four-two-six."

Wahrheit turns his attention to making bullets while we speak. The process involves making organized groupings of symbols on thin, old paper, shaping them into rough cone shapes, and soaking them in a bluish solution. The finished symbols look like equations in a foreign form of math.

Like an artist's abstract interpretation of math formulas written by aliens. Mindfuck math calligraphy.

The wet, conical pieces are then placed into empty prepared shells. He puts those into a special forming press, depresses the handle until a little beep is heard, then opens it, releasing a puff of steam or smoke and places the finished rounds into a bullet tray.

Like a lot of Wahrheit's contraptions that I have recently seen, there are elements of antiquated and ornate etched metal, plastic model kitbash, scrimshawed molded resin or ceramics, and RadioShack-level electronics.

I notice a smell kind of like surf wax mixed with something between a smoking soldering iron and that musty, metallic smell just before or after rain comes. Petrichor, I think it's called.

Who knew Colma had such interesting living denizens?

Wahrheit says, "We'll definitely have to upgrade that before you go."

"Upgrade?"

"You must have noticed that the odd things you've been seeing quickly fade from the shots they're in upon playback."

I look at Rudy, then back at Wahrheit.

"I...haven't recorded anything yet."

Wahrheit glares at Rudy.

Rudy shrugs. "I know, right?"

Wahrheit shakes his head and says, "At least tell 'em something, man."

"Sorry. He wasn't ready until today."

"Whatever. Hey, you know where I keep the upgrades,

right? You wanna try it?"

"Hell yeah."

Rudy stands and crosses to the door kitty-corner to the gun-rack wall and he's out of sight down the hallway.

Wahrheit says, "Okay, let's start again. What's that expression? 'Do over'? So, what brings you here, Felix?"

"A few months ago, I got that camera. The first one I had, I mean. My girlfriend was driving us home from a party. I pressed that one button on the lens, and her face and voice started to like distort and…and…."

"Break apart and warp and such? Twist and pull? Glowing and weird dark…brightness? Started in the eyes and got stronger when she got more upset?"

"Yeah. Exactly."

Wahrheit seems sad and lost in thought for a moment. It's the most serious he's been since he opened the door by far. Then he shrugs it off, grabs his lowball, and drains what's left in it.

He sets the glass down and asks, "What else have you seen?"

"Glowing, see-through bugs and animals. People with smoke coming out of their mouths and they have like growths on them and sometimes glowing creatures…in them. I mean…what the fuck are all those things?"

"Where to start? Your entire life and well before it, those things and many more have been around. You just couldn't see them until you pressed 'that one' button. Well, see is just part of it. Without chemicals, an intense maybe life-threatening experience, or whatever that camera does, you can't see, hear, smell, feel, or taste any of this stuff that you would think of as out of the ordinary. I still don't know what that damn camera triggers exactly…."

"Okay. Why couldn't I?"

Wahrheit takes the bottle of scotch and pours another couple of fingers into his lowball. He sets the bottle back down, then takes a sip and I do the same.

"Think of it like this. At any given moment, you are sharing space with other realms as complex, diverse, and, well…fucked up as the one you know. There's a symbiosis between some things but our side doesn't know about them because they're generally benign. Now, whoever made those cameras…. It forces you to see and hear these neighbors and stuff but, believe you me, they are always there. We don't see them due to the power of suggestion. Or, more accurately, a lack of any suggestion or reason to think they are there. Why would we, right? So, the camera kicks in and forces you to see just enough to put the suggestion needed in place. Then the fun starts and the wild weirdness opens itself to you."

Trying to keep up, I say, "Like ghosts or lost souls or something?"

"That would be oversimplifying one small element, but it is part of the bigger picture. The things you are describing are nothing like ghosts. More like interdimensional flora and fauna."

Wahrheit takes another small sip. "From what I've observed, there is no supernatural. It's all part of the same complex thing. *Natural* natural."

He grabs the whisky bottle and stretches to refill my tumbler without asking, then sits back down. He goes back to making his bullets. Rudy returns and extends his hand expectantly toward me. After a long stoner moment, I catch on and open up my camera bag. I tear the Velcro securing straps off of the HDV-426 and hand it to Rudy who then sits down and starts upgrading it.

He gingerly applies decals and stickers to the solid-state housing, lens, and viewfinder. Then he starts applying the foam and plastic cosmetic pieces, and it occurs to me that those must be to disguise it more than anything else. One of the pieces goes over the tiny red light that comes on when filming, obviously for stealthy shooting.

I sip and think. "What about a figure that sucks in light?

It was a creepy, human-shaped black hole that moved like liquid. Completely silent too."

Rudy stops upgrading and looks at Wahrheit. Wahrheit stops writing a weird symbol equation and looks at me.

Rudy asks, "Yeah, what about that?"

"What you saw was different, Rudy. Felix, where did you see this 'figure'?"

"Pier thirty-nine. It was on one of those docks by the sea lions. I watched it checking one of them out and then it noticed me. Then it was just right in front of me."

"The fact that it knew you could see it and you are sitting here says a lot. About what, I'm not sure."

"Why?"

"That's one of the old guard, you might say. Hey, finish that up, Rude."

Rudy shakes his head and goes back to placing mostly clear decals in certain spots on the camera.

"Old guard? What, like angels?" I ask.

Wahrheit grimaces. "Why do you keep trying to jam the huge circular-peg shit I'm giving you into a tiny cross-shaped slot, man? I know religion is a kind of forced assumption for most people from their upbringing and shit…but none of that is true. None of the religions you know of are true. None of them.

"In my experience, the closest it gets to religions being accurate are small outbreaks of people getting the sight or people misinterpreting things and coming up with their own stories about them. Religions are bullshit. Nothing wrong with that—until the knives, guns, and bombs come out."

Wahrheit makes a gun of his hand, his thumb coming down as its hammer a couple times.

"What's funny is that even a tiny amount of the reality of things as I see them is far stranger and more frightening than the wacky shit religions come up with to scare people into giving them money or being good for selfish reasons to get into some fluffy afterlife Disney-verse. If you believe any of those lovely religions out there, feel free to hate me. All I ask is that you hate me for the right reasons."

I shake my head. "Not my thing, no. I mean, I don't know what I believe exactly but I know it's not what other people try to tell me. I've read at least a little about every religion I've heard of and none have seemed like much more than cool stories and instruction manuals for behavior, like you said. If I'm going to read stories, I prefer the horror and sci-fi section. At least they don't try to convince you what's in them is real, past suspension of disbelief, I guess."

Wahrheit nods. "That's a good start, actually. You ever read any of those pulp magazines from back in the day?"

"I had a collection of shorts from like *Weird* and *Amazing*, yeah. It was my dad's copy, and it was real old. From the seventies I think."

Wahrheit laughs.

"'Old, from the seventies.' You're too funny. I read those magazines as a boy and they scared the living shit out of me. Toothy, gooey creatures and cosmic boogeymen and shit. My point is, people would be better off reading those old, spooky pulps than scripture but that would still only leave them slightly better prepared for the true horrors under the existential bed and in the pitch-dark closet of the great beyond. The big things with real power are not something to be worshipped. Although, that doesn't stop some from doing just that.

"Anyway, all that said—no, Felix. These old guard I mentioned are nothing like angels. Referees in an endless cosmic soccer match, more like. Or maybe secret police… space…ninja…demigods."

Your basic SPSNDs. Spaznoids? Spaznoids, definitely.

Wahrheit finishes a bullet and stores it. "Alright, so who was your head-fucker in the FMC ward?"

"Uh, sometimes Doctor Menlo."

Wahrheit chuckles softly.

"Sasha Menlo ain't no doctor. Anybody else?"

"Mostly Doctor Fleischmann."

Wahrheit winces a bit and gently rubs his robed forearm. He's lost in thought again but instead of sadness, now he looks angry. "The man himself."

I chuckle.

Wahrheit flashes on me and his eyes seem to glint with the reflection of an unseen light and I could swear the table and monitors vibrate as he says, "Somethin' funny?!"

"N-no, no. Sorry. That's just what one of the orderlies said too."

Wahrheit takes a deep breath and lets it out. Everything goes back to normal as he relaxes. "Sorry. Took it the wrong way. Well, it makes sense someone else would say it too because he almost never deals with patients anymore."

"Why did you call him a 'head-fucker'?" I ask.

Rudy chuckles. Wahrheit rolls his eyes toward him with an annoyed expression, then looks back down at his bullet work.

"In a nutshell, unbeknownst to almost all of its members, one the main jobs of the mental health industry is to keep pinks who start seeing what surrounds and interacts with us drugged and believing it wasn't real. Now, don't get me wrong—there are genuinely mentally unwell, delusional people. People who need real empathy, compassion, and help.

"It's just that what they see or hear *isn't* real. Well, in a nitty-gritty way at least. Gets even weirder when one of the genuinely quote-unquote crazy can see too, I'll tell ya. Although, crazy and sane are relative as well."

I frown. "How so?"

Wahrheit thinks.

"Hmmm…how to explain? So, let's say you got a normal mental ward. Not concentrated with people who definitely see like in FMC. Regular, real crazies mixed in. You got Shlomo Jenkins in a padded cell 'cause he gets real worked up about TV sets watchin' him in reverse and sending the sound-and-image feeds back to a giant ice-cream cone floating at the center of the hollow Earth. This ice-cream cone judges us and sends big maraschino-cherry people after the ones it doesn't like—they got cherry-stem arms and legs and shit. Follow so far?"

I nod slowly. "Sounds pretty crazy."

"Hear me out. So, you got Shlomo and then you got Rosetta Lim, a nurse working in that ward. She pities Shlomo because he's *so* crazy. She prays for him. She prays to a man who died two thousand years ago. There are stories about this man collected in a book that many people like herself have believed for a long time.

"They believe this man is the creator of everything or the maybe the son of that creator and somehow a ghost too and that he listens to every little prayer they make and really cares about their decisions and guides them every day.

"He created everything—the whole universe…and he did it only a few thousand years ago for the sole purpose of giving these little people-things—which bear a striking resemblance to a few other types of creatures he created at the same time—a place to make decisions and be judged and work off a debt he created for them to damn themselves with."

I nod some more, following.

Wahrheit sets a tool down and spins his finger in a wide circle in front of himself.

"For some reason, he also made an unfathomably huge, vast empty space filled with planets and other stars like and unlike ours and apparently that's all just scenery or a mistake or waste products—maybe trial runs in the first couple days of the *week* it took to do this?

"Now, she also believes that anyone who doesn't believe that this magical man is the one true badass of the universe should go to a bad place and be tortured forever. Those who do believe in it but don't make the right choices go to the same bad place, so these believers are real careful to do good things because they don't want to be tortured forever. She believes this because she has been told to from a very young age and it's been reinforced every few days for her since then in church.

"Oh, and there also happen to be millions of other people who believe the same thing so it couldn't possibly be untrue. It's like a big club. And I'm picking on this group, but there are also many other groups of millions of other people who believe variations on this same setup or totally different, no-less-ridiculous ones—rival clubs with their own agendas.

"They argue, yell, and fight based on differences in opinion on whose version of this dead dude or other ones is most correct. Some really zealot-level, fanatical fuckers are willing to *kill* each other based on differences in these beliefs. Saw the head off a living human being and shit.

"You have any idea how filled with the magic of faith you have to be take a knife or machete…and saw a person's head off? Noises coming out of him like a terrified animal while his hot blood pumps out and his body is jerking. Tendons. Arteries. Spinal cord. That's a fuckin' human being, man. His eyes are wild and he's pissing and shitting and…and I know you don't want to know what that whole situation feels like. But put yourself in his place. Just for an instant.

"You can't see the knife that's working through your neck…but you sure as shit can feel it. All you can see are masked men and a camera and your blood pouring and spraying out onto the floor and pooling like a bright red rain puddle. All you can think about is a perfect summer cookout you had with your family when you were seven or skiing or a girl or boy you never got to kiss again. Think about that horror and pure, real evil that's being enacted upon you based on differences in belief in one form or another. Faith—faith is where you find that special brew of accepted, encouraged delusion and blind, furious self-righteousness.

"Then, when questioned for proof of there being anything to these magical guys they believe in so much, they get real angry and defensive and try to turn it around by saying, 'Prove they don't!' Some people say, 'You can't prove a negative!' That gets into messy things like inductive arguments and blah, blah, blah—doesn't matter. What they fail to see is that the burden of proof is on those who believe the un-logically-believable, you feel me?

"Not to mention that people should and very well can be moral and good for the sake of it. What's more selfish—being good because you're afraid of punishment from on high, or being good because it's the right thing to do? The human thing to do. If you're only good because you believe you are being watched and someone's keeping score, then fuck…you. You're not good. You're a hypocritical, self-serving parasite.

"That's not to say there aren't genuinely good religious people. I'm cool with those. If they respect others' beliefs or lack thereof and can bring themselves to be rational or at least not bring it up, sure we're cool. Like Rudy here. He's still convinced there's a Bearded Hippie God hiding in the sky but he's open minded about the rest. We've had some fun talks…."

Rudy smiles sarcastically while he struggles with an attachment. Wahrheit continues, "Now back to Shlomo and Rosetta. Millions of people believe in their heart of hearts that the crazy-sounding stuff Rosetta believes is completely, literally true or close enough and they should make decisions in daily life based on those beliefs.

"Only one person believes the nonsensical stuff Shlomo believes, which also makes him act strangely, so Shlomo is insane. Maybe he should start preaching about it. Convince a few others to do the same. Start franchising to even it out over another few thousand years.

"All the while, both of them are susceptible to the brutal effects of, say, falling off a high building. The concrete at the bottom believes in you whether you believe in it or not. Try praying it's not there on the way down. Good luck with that. It rests, just waiting to kiss your skull and you *will* lose that fight. But Shlomo and Rosetta let their imaginations and fears rule them in this world where concrete being hard is a constant."

I furrow my brow a bit as I think about all this.

Wahrheit studies my face and eyes.

"That's a gross oversimplification for rhetorical purposes, but I stick by the core logic of it. Obviously Shlomo is playing with a light deck, but how far is he really from people walking down the street believing it's genuinely important what celebrities wear or think or what work they've had done—or believing that the Holocaust never happened or we never went to the moon. Or that the shadowy powers-that-be secretly employ rappers and R&B singers as a part of some unknown part of their global domination schemes…and then let them fill their videos and tracks with multiple references to said shadowy organization? Might as well call them reptoids and jump off that cliff the whole way.

"Just keep the thought in your mind and listen to things people say. Make a little archive of the nonsense people say or think or believe because they can't be troubled to do any real research or…they don't *want* to. With animals as complex as we are, sanity is relative."

"Sanity is relative. I like that. It's just…."

"'Just'?"

"Well, my girlfriend is like a casual Buddhist or Daoist—"

"As is the case with Abrahamic groups, there's a lot of positive philosophy in those but as far as the religions go, same bullshit, different details."

"I get you. But what I'd say is, I try to be logical and rational as much as I can. On my own, I lean toward what you're saying, minus the shit that's new to me since it's new. And I'm also pretty skeptical, especially when others tell me what to think. I'd say, if there is a God or gods, I just figure they're something we wouldn't be able to understand or maybe just like a force flowing through everything that isn't conscious, y'know?"

Rudy snickers and says, "This shit ain't Star Wars, man."

"Don't act like you know so much, Rudy. Sounds kind of like animism, which is a fun way to see things, and many do. Kind of like a more spiritual sidestep or inversion of my leaning toward what I guess you could call cosmic materialism."

Wahrheit chuckles at himself, seeming to feel his liquor and smoke now.

"Anyway, Felix, please continue."

"I just…. I guess what I'd have to say is that I'm curious enough about everything that the nature of everything should interest me more probably. But past a certain point, I'd have to say I enjoy leaving a lot of mysteries as just that."

Wahrheit chuckles again.

"You need to re-evaluate where that line is drawn. Believe me, knowing more about the reality of our existence only opens up more mysteries and questions. Questions that most people have already decided they have the answers to. I think you might also be assuming a few things. What might surprise you is I'm not an atheist in the strictest sense. In the basic area of 'is there a supernatural, white-bearded capital-*G* God' or anything similar, I am very much a doomed, heathen atheist.

"But even if there is a God like that, with no evidence of any kind that that being actually does have any effect on our lives, I'd have to say—what good is it? It could have made absolutely everything, then fallen asleep or fucked off to somewhere else it made or maybe it really did create us with the sole intent of testing us for no good reason to get a ticket to a better part of this whole multiverse thing. But what does it matter if fear and disease and pain and chaos are the constants it leaves for us without explanation.

"As far as what is going on outside of all the crazy shit that, as I see it, falls under the realm of the natural, pencil me in as a skeptical, yet fearful, agnostic."

Wahrheit's eyes go hollow and distant.

"I know there must be scientific explanations for the strangest, wildest shit I've seen. I just don't think I'll live long enough for human scientists to explain it. Not even the ones in the greater know, as it were. Like those things in the cemetery. So much we still don't know...."

He shakes his head.

"But whatever is really going on at higher levels, what most religious types truly believe in is just an elaborate crutch to help them sleep at night. To get through the day without wanting to eat a bullet or kiss that concrete back on purpose, really. I envy them sometimes. Seeing things the way I do is a little depressing to others, I've found. Angers still others. Can't see why myself. The beauty I see in things as I see them is far more lovely and comforting than anything I ever came across in church."

I can't picture this man sitting in a church. Then I remember that I just met him, which also seems strange. There's a welcoming, honest charisma about him.

"I have this theory, actually. Sorry, this hypothesis. I have this hypothesis that we evolved in such a way that the magical feeling some people get in their heads that makes them so sure there's a God is actually a survival instinct deep in the old meat. As in the more hardwired parts. Maybe as we got smarter these fantasies made some of us more resilient and stronger when nothing else could. Because of their comforting abilities. Get too smart and you become harder and harder to comfort. Gave them a sense of control and order.

"Existential apophenia, let's say. 'That glowing circle in the sky sure is bright—must be the reason for all this' and shit like that. No need to think past that point when growing those crops that the sun god gives you is the concrete thing you need. But now that we know what the sun is and why it makes them grow, why can't we move on and keep learning?

"The sun won't be offended if we move on. It doesn't give a shit about us. It just happens to be helpful to us in this sequence of its lifespan as a side effect of its natural, physical processes. Anyway, just an idea of mine. Never looked into the science of it. My specialty is everything other than humans and the pink world.

"Now, the religious types that *are* in the know worship things I don't think count as deities. They are nothing like us and have nothing to do with us. They're just big, old, and scary as shit. Any interaction they've had with us is, I imagine on their end, like one of us meeting a particularly intelligent dust mite."

Wahrheit seems to notice he's piquing interest in me about things he must not want to elaborate on.

"Then again, I am just one man—one stoned, liquored-up man and billions of people believe in those things I truly don't. I just happen to have a few added layers of perception. Enough to ignore such meticulously cultivated, deep-seated ignorance and focus on the bigger picture."

"I think I get you." I sip more of the lovely, warm scotch and think as it burns pleasantly. "So, if you know all this stuff, why don't you do something? Like tell all us 'pinks' or put it on the internet or something?"

Wahrheit scoffs and shakes his head. "And what good would that do? I mean, first off, the internet is a huge cesspool of misinformation and idiocy as it is. These truths would have to compete with complete fabrications, and they'd probably lose.

"Even then, the average person doesn't even want to

know how fucked up this world, as they believe it to be, really is. Now, you take that person and tell them, 'Hey, bro, you're infested with a colony of psychic parasites, there are dozens of planets laterally sharing the same general area in this phased layer of this 'verse while they weave all around, and things are really run by very, very old forces there aren't any books about, which also happen to be nothing like what you would think—but at the same time, nothing is really *run* at all….'" He shakes his head and chuckles. "Probably get you back in the happy house faster than if you just copped a squat and took a shit in the middle of a busy intersection."

Rudy laughs.

I ignore my mild embarrassment and say, "Then why do you have all these guns and shit? Hobby? Sport?"

Wahrheit narrows his eyes. "Felix, I like you so far, but don't get too cute. You're gonna have to keep in mind that even with all this *new*, *exciting* stuff being thrown at you, you can still feel safe in the knowledge that you know almost nothing about what's 'really going on,' as they say.

"It didn't just start when you pressed the button. You could fill a whole bookcase or ten with the history books of what's really been going on and still call it the Cliff's Notes version. Reverse or maybe inverse lateral thinking is the key, you could say."

Riiiight….

"As far as what my weapons and equipment are for, without going into details that are really none of your business or concern, it's sufficient to say that I'm not exactly popular. There are those who know that I know about them. Best to leave it at that."

I finish my drink and set my glass on the table. "*Wa-ka-ta*. So, with these upgrades, I'll see more stuff and it won't fade away from the drive?"

"If that's all you want, sure. The camera will work much better. All I ask is that you come back once in a while and unload the footage. I promise no 'entryway of death' next time."

I chuckle. "What do you use the footage for?"

"Patterns and trending research," Wahrheit says with a look that adds a bit of "like I said, best to leave it at that" to it.

"You said 'if that's all you want'?"

"The other thing I can offer is a way to see all the time. That's a bigger…commitment. You have to decide how much you really want to know. How important is it to you to see what's really out there…and *why* is it important to you?"

"I don't have a choice now."

"Yes, you do, Felix, believe me. You can leave right now and convince yourself *we're* the crazy ones. You'd probably be happier. You could live the rest of your life without advancing your understanding further than this point. Hell, I could set that fog shit outside to blank this whole time you've been here. Rudy can act like it didn't happen. You'd leave the camera here. It would be confusing, sort of like when you drink too much and you don't realize that you don't remember the night before until someone mentions something. Only, Rudy ain't gonna mention it and you'd never find this place again even if you wanted to. Then it'll just be gone completely, and you can live free, oblivious to any of it."

Wahrheit calmly looks at me. No humor or malice or sarcasm. He means it. Rudy has finished the upgrades and looks at me too.

I think about my lovely Audrey. The temptation to only think of her as *just* Audrey is strong. But the scary glitch face keeps popping into my mind.

Then I think about my shithead father twitching at the end of a belt, then falling on me, scarring me for life in more ways than one.

What could lead a loving father to that? Was he crazy

or could he 'see' or both?

It's settled.

"I have to know. I'm sure."

I follow Wahrheit and Rudy down the bisecting hallway, through a small laundry room with a warm, humming dryer, and out through a door into the connecting yard created by the wood fences between the mobile homes. The yard smells like dryer sheets due to the exhaust port in the outer wall.

The yard is entirely covered in gray-green gravel and there are concentric rings or grooves in it that give the yard a Zen-rock-garden feel. The rings start around a large blue-black sphere near the north fence that's peppered with bright green specks. It must be three feet in diameter and it rests in a wide conical pile of the gravel that reaches about half a foot up its lower surface and would resemble a crater if the sphere weren't there.

We trudge through the rings of gravel and scatter them in our path but Wahrheit doesn't seem concerned.

A wind chime tinkles together, the sound hollow but soothing.

Broken streams of rain droplets fall from the edges of the thin ceiling created by the stitched-together tarps and the dull gray light comes through them with muted hues of their different colors. Blue, green, purple, yellow.

Near the south wall are several large machine parts covered by ratty blue tarps and a rolling metal cart covered in tools and smaller components. Most of the larger parts are covered enough that I have no idea what they are but I could swear one of them is a jet turbine.

I see a big tortoise or turtle crawling slowly through the gravel near the machine parts. There are several smaller ones milling about by it, all with colorful patterns on their shells. A small one with red irises near the center of the yard notices the three men crossing through and sucks its legs and head into its shell and watches us.

The patchouli smell hits me again as we reach the porch of the other mobile home. Without thinking, I make a sound of mild disgust.

Wahrheit looks back at me and says, "What, the patchouli? I hate the stuff myself, but it's like a pesticide for the glow bugs. You can't see on your own yet, but you wouldn't spot them around here either way."

We step onto the porch and Wahrheit presses a button on an intercom box above the doorbell and says, "Coming in with Rudy and an FNG."

I look over at the sphere near the fence again.

Is it…rotating?

I look back toward the other mobile home and notice that the footstep impressions and the mess we made of the gravel in our path are gone. The grooves are there again as if we never walked across them.

Upon looking at the dark sphere again, I notice that the tarp ceiling doesn't shield the whole thing. Water dropping intermittently onto the small section of exposed surface near the fence bursts into steam and wafts around it before quickly dissipating.

A voice over the intercom says, "–Roger-roger.–"

Wahrheit opens the door, and we enter a lush indoor farm. I'm engulfed by a wall of warm, humid air and have to take a deep breath.

Basically, the same layout as the first house but, instead of furniture, monitors, weapons, etc., this long former living room is filled with perpendicular rows of raised platforms topped with pots filled with growing cannabis plants. The walls are lined with floor-to-ceiling racks of growing wheat grass and herbs. The rows between the walls, though, are all weed.

Special lights with metal shrouds are installed in the ceiling over the rows of plants. There are tubs of nutrients under all the raised platforms and I see about two-dozen ports in the ceiling, which must be part of an elaborate ventilation system.

A young, dark-skinned Asian man with large eyes and severe features and a tall, tanned woman with dirty blond hair tend to the plants wearing only underwear and holstered pistols. I have to tear my eyes away from the blond's lean, fit body just before she looks back over her shoulder at us.

"Kveta, Sujit. This is Felix," Wahrheit says and makes a little vice-versa gesture.

Sujit bows his head slightly at me and Kveta says, "Hallo, Fe-licks," in what sounds like a Slavic accent.

I nod. "Hi."

Wahrheit continues into this mobile home structure's bisecting hallway and Rudy and I follow him. I notice a long stack of sealed, brand new HDV-426s five high stretching down the hallway against the wall.

We enter what would have been the laundry room in this mobile. Instead, it's a dense, intricate chemical lab. Beakers, tubes, burners—even a circular pill-pressing machine.

Wahrheit opens a glass case above a machine that is spinning long vials that radiate diagonally down from its head, like one of those rickety rides at a county fair, and takes out a clear bottle full of pills. He opens it and shows me the contents. The pills are half-black, half-white rounded discs with dots of the other side's color on the center of each half.

"Those look just like my pills. How did you—"

"Relax. Harmonia is for *special* cases. It's the only thing they would have given you. It's perfectly mixed to keep you from seeing.

"Now, these here do the opposite, and damn well too. You only need them to balance out, then overtake, the Harmonia, but they can be taken indefinitely if necessary. After they start working, you'll see at least some stuff until you die or take more Harmonia, basically. I made them to look just like Harmonia upon casual inspection so you won't have to worry about any meds questions. One difference, though," Wahrheit says, then shakes a pill out into his palm. He shows each side to me by flipping it over with his thumb.

Upon closer scrutiny, Wahrheit's pills have an extra pinprick inside the white and black dot on either side. The white dot on the black side has a tiny circular spot of black at its center and the other side has the opposite.

Wahrheit drops the pill back into the bottle.

"Replace yours with these and you won't have to worry about people getting suspicious. Make sure you keep picking up prescriptions, though, so as not to alarm the good doctor or anyone else."

He puts the cap back on the bottle and shakes it like a rattle.

"Last chance to say no. Once these kick in, you'll see more than you might like."

I extend my hand, palm up. Wahrheit gently slaps the bottle down into it and I pocket it.

Wahrheit says, "Okay, a couple things. It can take time for these to build up in your system and the Harmonia to leave it, but when the sight kicks in it can be…overwhelming. Just ride it out and you'll be fine."

I nod affirmative.

"And in the future, don't ever let these things know you can see them. Just think of it all as educational, not something to freak out about, alright? You've been just fine until now with all these things swimming and crawling around and on you. Just go about your business and absorb and study. Do not interact. And…."

He walks out into the hallway and disappears for a minute. I look at Rudy and say, "Sorry I flipped like that when we came in."

"Nah, I should have said something. I just didn't know if you'd come in if I did."

Wahrheit walks back in holding a filled canvas satchel that looks like an old WWII medic bag.

"And this is for if anything hinky does come up. It's like a survival kit. If you're smart and go easy, you shouldn't ever need it."

I take the satchel and strap it around my neck and shoulder.

Wahrheit hands me a small key and I add it to the ring on the karabiner I usually keep hooked to one of my rear belt loops, then tuck all the keys back into my back pocket.

"Don't open it until you would hypothetically need it. It's complicated, but the contents won't be there the next time you open it if you do."

What the hell?

"Just please...*please* read the instructions before using anything in here. And if you're smooth, this should just gather dust."

"Understood."

Wahrheit opens the metal door at the end of the special entryway and Rudy steps in past him. I hesitate.

Wahrheit chuckles. "Don't worry, man. They can't go off unless I want them to."

I step in.

"Oh, another thing. Don't spend too much time together, if at all. I don't need anyone getting suspicious that I'm in this area now. Two of you walking around together with those cameras after being in the FMC is a dead giveaway for anyone paying attention. And don't come around here just any old time. I'll let you know when you can come by at my discretion."

Still feeling a little buzzed, I say, "Hey, rhetoric aside— is there anything like a 'capital-*G* God' out there?"

Wahrheit scratches his left salt-and-pepper mutton chop and thinks for a moment like he's trying to find a simple way to explain once again.

"Like one OG motherfucker more like us? Maybe. It's not in charge of anything or judging anybody, and I really doubt it created anything other than empty bottles, but the closest thing I've come across to a 'God' was surfing off the island of Antigua, last I heard."

I just blink a few times, trying to process a serious answer I didn't expect. My confusion isn't lost on Wahrheit, who chuckles and closes the metal door, sealing us into the entryway. I look at the holes in the walls and ceiling. I imagine what it would feel like to be caught in Wahrheit's deathtrap when it goes off and shudder.

Wahrheit comes over the speaker in the camera and equipment array with a crackle and in that distorted, choppy voice.

–Now you boys stay out of trouble and remember: Minds are like parachutes.–

He buzzes us out.

Rudy and I are silent for several minutes as we sit in a shuddering, rocking, empty northbound BART train car. My mind races and I'm grateful that I still have a bit of the drink and smoke in my system or I might cross over into real anxiety. I'm already on the edge as I try to get a handle on having to see and think of things in a completely new way.

You made your decision. You have to know.

Rudy sighs. "I know it's a lot to swallow."

"Yeah," I say and chuckle.

"He tells me a little bit more every time. Doesn't want to overload me, I guess. The more he tells me, though, the less I feel like I understand, y'know?"

"Man, I feel like I don't understand anything now. I've spent most of my life just trying to get a decent grasp on the world the way it was. Now…."

"It helps to think of it, like, everything you do know is true. The stuff in front of us is real, true sight or not. You just have to add layers to your understanding. Like learning another language or being a child again." He laughs. "Listen to me…those are totally *Var-height*-isms."

"Makes sense, though." I catch myself gently rubbing the base of my left ring finger.

24 STREET MISSION signs flash by in the windows. Rudy secures his camera bag and stands up.

"The Mission, huh?"

Rudy nods. "Yeah. Hey, lemme know if you're gonna be around here with a four-two-six so I can lay off it for the day and it won't look suspicious."

"No problem."

Rudy extends his open hand at an angle. I slap it and we close fists and bump them together. Rudy crosses to the doors and holds the support bar.

I say, "Hey."

"What's up?"

"Sorry. And thanks."

Rudy chuckles. "We'll see."

"What do you mean?"

"I know why I want to see. Because it's the truth. It's what's real. I just hope your reasons are enough for you. Hey, if you still want to thank me and apologize in six months, I'll take it."

"That's a little ominous."

"I don't mean it to be. It's just, there are some things I wasn't prepared for. If it gets to be too much, I'll just ask Var-height to flash me back to a pink." He chuckles but it lacks mirth.

"Right." I feel a little less sure now.

The BART train eases to a stop and the doors open.

Rudy says, "Hey, don't listen to me right now. Just a little shook up from something the other day. There's a lot of beautiful, awesome stuff to see. Take it easy and enjoy, man."

"Take care of yourself."

"You too."

"Hey, one thing."

The doors start to close and Rudy grabs one and it slides open again. "What's up?"

"What did Wahrheit mean, 'minds are like parachutes'?"

Rudy chuckles again. "He means that both those things 'only work when open.' Old quote by a noble scotch brewer if I remember rightly."

"I guess that makes sense from him."

"Exactly," Rudy says, then shoots me a peace sign as he exits the train car.

The doors close and the train starts on its way again. I watch Rudy climb the escalator out of sight.

I open the front door of the flat and see that the I LOVE YOU FELIX sign is on. Since I've been back, it's always made me feel good to see it when I come in. This time, I just feel confused.

I gently close the door and lock it, then make my way down the hallway past the living room. I stop by my workroom, take off the camera bag and Wahrheit's survival kit, and tuck them by the chair next to my drawing table near the hall door before continuing down the hall toward the sound of a creaking wheel.

I wonder what's in that kit Wahrheit gave me. Probably like interdimensional goggles, a travel guide, and a towel.

I chuckle to myself, then poke my head into Audrey's editing room. She's working with 16mm film on a large flatbed editor.

"Hey, lady."

Without looking back at me Audrey says, "Where you been all my life, loverman?"

"Just went to a movie with a friend."

"'Friend'?" Audrey asks.

Mostly playful, but there's a tiny barb on the back end.

"My friend Rudy. He goes to State. Haven't seen him in

a while. Used to work with me at Game Crazy, years back."

"Cool. What did you guys watch?"

Shit.

"It was a chop-socky flick at the Kabuki Eight in J-Town. Thirteen fists of some shit. Special engagement. He heard about it through his school. I don't think it was even publicized."

There's a pause like she's trying to decide if she believes me, then she says, "I got you a six-pack of a new Imperial Stout I saw at the Whole Foods. It's like ten-something percent so I thought you'd be down. Also, some coffee ice cream and—oh, some great-looking shramps we can whip up with baked potatoes and maybe a salad with the last of the romaine?"

"Sounds great, thanks."

I walk down the last stretch of hallway and duck into the dark bathroom. Open the medicine cabinet door before turning on the light. I grab my legit Harmonia prescription bottle, open it, and empty its contents into the small wastebasket. Then I replace them with Wahrheit's alternatives, close the bottle, and put it back in the cabinet.

I pull the drawstring on the mesh-can liner, turn off the light, close the medicine cabinet, then walk to the backdoor.

The sound of the flatbed creaking and the lower sound of sprocket holes fluttering is still audible intermittently from Audrey's editing room, so I go out through the door.

I walk through the grassy fence-separated common backyard area to a staircase down to a long, narrow stretch of concrete that cuts back under the east side of the building back to the street.

I walk down a line of trashcans, passing the two or three I've seen Audrey use most frequently, and open one.

The creaking sound is just barely audible through the window above me as I lift up a small pizza box, empty the mesh liner into the can, cover the contents with the box, then walk back down the concrete strip toward the backyard.

chapter 18

I store the HDV-426 in the closet in my editing room so Audrey doesn't get suspicious about why I'd buy another camera when she got me a new one. I decide to just see how I feel about 'seeing' through my own eyes before I start traipsing around as a camera operator for Weird Shit Weekly.

Things are normal for almost two weeks. Too normal. I keep waiting for something to show up. Even just a spiderfly or something would stop me from becoming more and more suspicious that Wahrheit and his pills are some big joke or prank.

When I do start to suspect this, I just have to recall the big, spooky ball in Wahrheit's yard and the fog surrounding his houses that keeps you from knowing all of it's there. And the solid bubble machine and the see-through bullets with the formulas inside like insects....

Yeah, Wahrheit's for real. What he's all about is another matter.

I hang out with Audrey and our friends. Still have fun with her but know that soon I'll probably have to deal with seeing Crazy Face Audrey or whatever that is. That's the only part I really dread.

During this time, I watch Audrey real close during sad movies or when I "accidentally" leave the TV on a really political channel to get a rise out of her. Nothing yet.

I take long walks around the city looking for just a hint of strangeness through my own eyes.

Walk through the forested areas in the Presidio in the evening because it's the creepiest normal place I can think of, so I figure I'd be more likely to see something there. Nothing.

Hang out by one of the old, decaying windmills in Golden Gate Park hoping for the same but only get propositioned by guys wanting to get nasty in the bushes. My mistake, so whatever.

Take a tour of Alcatraz figuring there could be ghosts or something. Not that I can see yet.

It occurs to me that there's no sound logic to my tactics and it's more a question of chemical buildup, but I'm impatient.

I walk north up 3rd, returning from one of these spooky recon trips down by the waterfront. Had intended to visit one of my old favorite abandoned spots in the city. It was a lot down by the waterfront where old MUNI streetcars had been rusting and decaying for decades across an inlet from a little park that always seemed out of place in the industrial nightmare that is the Central Waterfront on the southeast end of San Francisco proper.

Friends and I would sneak through a cut in the fence over the inlet and crawl through some brush to another cutout that led to a ledge to the streetcar graveyard. We'd get fucked up and hang out in the old, creaky husks. It was nice because some of the streetcars had only metal skeletons where the ceiling used to be and you could see some stars from inside on the rare clear night.

It must have been longer ago than I thought since I had been there last, because the streetcars were all gone. It was repaved and converted into another parking lot for whatever the factory is there.

I just sat at a concrete table in the park across the water cursing the bastards who took away one of my favorite old spots in the city. I'd noticed a paperback copy of *Dune* sitting at the far end of the table, its cover half ripped off from the binding edge and flopping in the wind.

I left my book in San Francisco? I thought and chuckled to myself.

So, I'm heading back up 3rd and all I'd got for my trouble was disappointment, nostalgia, and a steadily worsening headache.

My phone rings, playing the original zither version of "The Third Man Theme" until I take it out of my pocket and pick it up.

"Hello?"

–Hey, studly!– Audrey says.

"Hey, sweetabix. What's up?"

–Fishy filter needs new cartridges. Can you get some?–

I cringe, not looking forward to having to do something that will keep me from taking some pills for my head.

"I have a headache, baby."

–Aw, I'm in a time crunch and it would help a lot. And I didn't ask you to bed me, Felix. Get your excuses straight.–

I chuckle through the pain and say, "Fine. No problem."

I make my way up 3rd, stopping at a newsstand shop near the Moscone Center to buy a little packet of ibuprofen gel tabs and a bottle of chocolate milk. As I continue on, I drink half the bottle, swallow both pills with a mouthful of the milk, and finish the bottle off.

3rd becomes Kearny up past Market, so I cut one over to Grant and make my way into Chinatown.

Gel tabs usually work fast for me but my head actually feels worse as they kick in and they're beginning to make my stomach feel off. I start sweating badly and my vision blurs. Slow my pace and it hits me that all the sounds around me seem distant and quiet even though most of the sources are right in front of me. Blurry Chinese locals and tourists shuffle softly by and cars gently putter up and down the street. One honks at another that apparently isn't turning fast enough in front of it and the horn seems polite and almost pleasant.

It's not just that everything is quiet. The sounds are being forced out by a low pulsing that vibrates through the base of my skull up through my brain's reptile parts and lobes, searing everything behind my eyes and what must be the inner workings of my ears in past the drums.

As this pulsing becomes more intense, my stomach goes from a little off to queasy and ready to revolt. I just want to find a spot to catch my breath and let the medicine do what it's supposed to.

Going through the intersection across Pine, I get a face full of all-day-cookin' dumpster juice fragrance from a nearby alley and it's over. Battle lost.

I moan and speed up, looking around for a place to hurl.

Through my blurred vision and tears forming in my eyes, I see a short street and concrete stairs that cut up the hill at a slope between a camera shop and a Chinese bargain bodega.

I duck up the alley, trying to get as far from the view of passersby as I can but my legs get twitchy and wobbly and I lose almost all of my strength. I collapse, catching the stairs' metal rail wide with both hands at the last second and accidentally slamming my abdomen down against it.

I vomit chocolate milk, half-dissolved pills, and stomach

acid down onto the stairs and base of the bargain store's outer wall. Heave hard repeatedly until almost nothing is coming out and my chest and throat hurt.

The need to expel finally subsides and I hang against the bar, breathing heavily but feeling a sense of release that seems to come from more than just throwing up. A light breeze hits me and my eyelids flutter closed.

All the tension that's been building up in me has washed away and I realize for the first time since a day or two after I started taking Wahrheit's pills that a feeling was building up along with the stress of anticipating an effect.

Like existential constipation, finally passed.

I open my eyes and chuckle, then press down against the bar, lifting myself up. Feel strong again and my legs are stable. Head and stomach feel fine. I feel great, actually—other than my mouth and nose being a little gross but I can fix that.

A spiderfly flutters down into the alley and comes to rest on the upper edge of a vague, dark rectangular shape on the wall behind me.

Finally!

I turn toward it and get closer. Hear a vague hum coming from the blurry, wall-poster-sized rectangle. My approach spooks the spiderfly and it pumps and flutters off into the street, quickly out of sight.

I extend a hand toward the rectangle but stop when I notice its horizontal shutters fluttering a bit and hear odd mechanical sounds coming from inside. I step back.

A low, deep sound rises above the bustle of people and cars back on the street. Like a long moan that frequently changes almost like humming or maybe di-tonal singing. As it gets louder, I realize it's getting closer.

I look up in time to see a huge, translucent creature gliding through the air above the buildings—

It's long and bulbous like a glowing, deformed whale. I can make out most of its big pumping internal organs and what must be its digestive tract. The head is covered with several big eyes, which seem to have multiple spherical layers of flesh moving around inside. Suckerless tentacles and misshapen finlike appendages sprout from its dorsal and ventral side, and an asymmetrical cluster of both make up its rear end, some trailing far behind as it glides away above Chinatown. The undulating tentacles and fins give it the appearance of swimming through the air. At a quick glance, it's like a submarine-sized paramecium flying gracefully through the air.

I shake my head and blink deliberately, then open my eyes and see the last bit of tentacles disappear over the rooftops only to be followed by smaller, similar creatures. The smaller ones seem to be trying to keep up with the really large…uh…"blimpwhale"? Blimpwhale it is.

The small blimpwhales try to keep up with the largest one, singing in a higher pitch as they go. They also seem to be trying to harmonize with the larger blimpwhale but aren't succeeding.

I can't help but laugh as I shuffle back down to the sidewalk. Wahrheit didn't tell me about the euphoria. I'm not sure if it's more a side effect of feeling so much better after throwing up or the pills themselves or both, but I feel fantastic.

Colors even seem brighter and lusher. I look up at the sky and the tiny patch of blue I can see peeking through clouds is vivid and lovely. I notice the vague impression of the strange, dark shapes in the sky but they are even harder to see and make out than they were in Rudy's footage. The beauty is I'm too blissed to care what the ominous, unsettling shapes might actually be.

As I reach the sidewalk, I notice several people with translucent, pulsing bulb growths and one with burrowpedes cautiously pecking around on his face.

I remember my mission for Audrey and continue on toward the fish store, stopping once for a soda and a pack of tissues at a store filled with Chinese kitsch. I stand by a trashcan with a pyramid top for recycling and blow my nose and then rinse my mouth with Future Cola.

I bend over and spit the cola into the trashcan, then straighten back up and look at the soda can.

Parallel to the "Future Cola" written perpendicular top to bottom, it has the motto "Future Will Be Better" printed smaller. I chuckle again while taking another sip.

Which camera we on—I'll hold it up and smile.

I make my way through the intersection across California and cruise down the sidewalk to Sacramento, noticing more growths on other people. One of the bulb growths detaches from a person's back and pumps through the air after a cat that seems to see it and run away down the sidewalk and then into a touristy store. The bulb undulates and thrusts through the air after it like a creepy flying jellyfish.

Is that why cats are always tripping out on what seems like nothing?

I reach Sacramento and hike the short stretch up the hill to the fish store. Hear strange squeaking sounds and look up. One of the seal-sized air swimmers with the whalelike mouth that I saw on Rudy's video footage is chasing a swarm of spiderflies through the sky above the Chinatown rooftops.

I open the door and enter the fish store smiling. Walk down the center aisle and marvel at how beautiful the bright, colorful aquariums are. There are more glowing, fluorescent fish on the ceiling, frozen in a tableau as if they're swimming through the dark blue light. All of these things are even more vibrant and vivid now, which also makes them dreamier. A Cocteau Twins song is playing loud on the record player, which makes the fog of dreaminess even worse. Can't remember the name but I've heard it. Something about tragediennes and meridians or something? Their stuff is pretty but I've always had trouble figuring out what it means. Great song anyway.

I'm halfway down the aisle when I spot something out of place in one of the aquariums and stop. There's a tiny, glowing creature swimming with the fish in the tank like it's maybe trying to socialize but doesn't get that they can't see it.

Or can they? That cat thing was weird.

I smile even bigger and titter to myself as I lean forward to get a better look. It's like a baby crawdad with so many miniscule organs pumping in it that it's only vaguely translucent. There are lots of thin antennae stalks and several eyes on its head and it swims backwards with the help of a curved stalk of many fine tentacles. In place of claw arms it has more tentacles with asymmetrical groupings of nodules all over them. The weird, almost cute thing notices me watching it and swims out of the aquarium through the glass and into the air between the aquariums in the aisle. I watch it swim through the air down the aisle away from me, into another tank on the right, then out of that one into the parallel aisle and out of sight.

I continue down the aisle. As I emerge from the aisles into the back counter area, I look around and see Siobhán with her back to me on a ladder near the wall of aquariums on the left. She's painting a fish on the ceiling with bright fluorescent paint. There's a strong black light on a tripod near the ladder that is aimed up at her work area on the ceiling. It's stronger than the installed ones that are always on to light the fish paintings. She bobs her head to the music, practically entranced.

That's just unfair. She looks fucking great.

She's wearing tight and shiny dayglow lime pants, a thin pale blue sweater that's stretched and loose, and hot-pink zebra print creepers. Her black and blue half mane is pulled into the tightest bun I suppose you could pull wild hair and thin dreads into, and it's secured with crimson chopsticks.

I notice that in the sections of skin exposed on her

shoulder, neck, and arms I can see intricate patterns glow in her tattoos. Like another layer of intricate design only visible under the black light. It's beautiful and makes the whole effect even more entrancing than just the flowing petals and Yakuza-style sea-monster designs I've already seen.

The song goes into a breakdown, and it's just drums and backing.

Siobhán stops painting and drifts off for a moment.

Antici…pation?

The guitar arpeggio line comes back in hard and Siobhán swoons, swaying back and forth on the ladder and closing her eyes. With the brush still in her hand, she starts dancing on the ladder, rhythmically undulating and curling her arms near her sides, then raising them to "sweep the cobwebs" as they used to call it at the goth clubs I frequented when I was younger. Her arms end up bent and together behind her head like she's stretching, and the paintbrush leaves little fluorescent orange strokes between her shoulder blades and on the back of her sweater as she sways. As into it as she is, I assume she wouldn't care even if she knew.

I clear my throat as gently as I can and still expect her to hear me.

Siobhán jolts and spins partway back toward me and almost loses balance.

"Fuck!" she yelps.

The ladder sways from her startled motion and I step toward her with hands outstretched to help.

The ladder lifts off the ground on one side and the can of fluorescent paint almost tips from its foldout platform—

But she grabs the ladder top and can and recovers expertly with the balance and muscle control of a highly trained gymnast. I stop advancing and marvel at her agility.

Siobhán sets the brush down on the tray next to the can and steps down off the ladder. She points back at the ladder and narrows her eyes like she's scolding a child or telling a dog to stay, then makes an exaggerated hand-dusting motion and turns toward me.

Over the bright fluorescent work light, Siobhán's face is aglow with the beautiful patterns that radiate out and around her from a point above and between her eyes on her forehead. The pattern starts as a fine circular design of entrancing complexity and whips out from it like layers of a fractal mandala.

Siobhán walks toward me and away from the work light and the glowing tattoo fades from view as she smiles big.

"Hey, Mister Spoken For. How goes the war?"

The beads on her lower nose chain today are tiny plastic eyeballs of varied size and iris color.

Those unsettling contacts of hers seem glassier than usual and she looks really happy to see me.

Must be a little "enhanced" at the moment.

I say, "Uh…I'm cool. How are you?"

She smiles, sizes me up.

"Better now…wowie-wow. Be even better when I get off, though."

I raise my eyebrows. "Get off?"

The song comes to an end, and I can hear the sound of the tone arm automatically raising and clicking back into place on its holder.

"Off *work*. I'm going to a party later. I know about your pervery, Felix. Don't you dare tease me unless you mean it. I'm delicate."

Yeah, right.

"Anyway, what can I do for you? Fish product-wise."

"I just need some refill cartridges for my filter."

In an "oh so professional" voice, Siobhán says, "Right this way, good sir."

She leads me over to the rack of filters and refills. She looks back and catches me watching her walk in her shiny pants. She narrows her eyes.

"Just as I suh-*spected*. You vile fiend. If it's not in a tank or on the racks, keep your eyes off. I ain't down with O.P.P. To you, I am the fish-store girl, glamorous mistress of all things aquatic. Well, at least those we have here."

I chuckle and say, "Sorry. Guess I was hypnotized by your ridiculous pants."

"Oh, come on. You and I both know they're draining your brain of blood as we speak. I'm watching your grubby hands for attacks of entirely unsolicited freshness."

She points at her eyes with her left index and middle finger, then gestures toward my hands.

I laugh. "Speaking of draining blood, can you even feel your legs at all? Those look pretty damn tight."

"I'd say they're just tight enough. A perfect fit."

Siobhán cocks her head and looks at me, playful and expectant.

Instead of following her further down this dangerous road, I swallow and scold myself for letting it get this far. She picks up on my new shyness and moves on.

"So, what type of filter do you have?"

The door to the store opens with a tinny jingle and I hear feet shuffling down the center aisle.

"HELLO?!" a raspy, distorted voice calls out.

I wince, then look toward the mouth of the center aisle. The woman waddles into the counter area and I stifle a gasp—

Her face is barely visible through what look to be deformed, glowing smooth tentacles. They're layered enough that almost no facial features can be seen.

The wriggling tendrils twitch and wrap around each other, slithering together as they fill her mouth, obscure her nose, and pulse in her unseen eye sockets.

Darker versions of the burrowpedes I've seen crawl around in the mess of tentacles, careful not to be crushed by the constant swelling and pumping of the tentacles and the odd organs inside them.

I do my best to act casual but know I must be visibly nervous. Siobhán notices and looks over at the woman. Her playful, flirty demeanor drains instantly and she seems to swallow a yelp but recovers just as fast and puts on a stoic face.

Siobhán forces a smile and says, "How may I help you?"

"I NEED SOME FOOD FOR MY TURTLES!"

Siobhán winces slightly as the woman speaks. I notice the aquarium glass all around vibrating with a weird, low hum as the woman speaks—reminding me of the Swede's frame the night I jumped out of it.

"You can help her first," I say, watching Siobhán's reactions closely. She looks at me and I nod.

"O-okay," Siobhán says, then crosses to a different rack closer to the counter. The woman walks over to stand next to her.

I try to act interested in the filters.

"Do you know which type you need?"

"THEY'RE AQUATIC!"

Siobhán fingers through the shelf and finds a sealed plastic cylinder to her liking.

"This one then."

I can't help wincing at her gravelly, unnatural voice.

It's like metal grinding on metal in her throat.

I look at the counter and see Siobhán ringing her up. Siobhán is staring at me in an unsettling way. I look back at the filters and grab the first box of cartridges that looks even close to what I need. Then I walk closer to the counter and stand behind the woman.

"Do you need a receipt?"

"YES, THANK YOU!" The words are pleasantly intoned but the sound of them is so grating.

I notice Siobhán's eyelids flutter a bit as the woman speaks.

So…she can see and hear this shit too?

Siobhán places the receipt in a bag with the turtle food

and hands it to the woman with a smile. The woman turns to leave and seems to give me a rude look, but it's hard to tell through that squirming mess and burrowpedes playing wacky wall crawlers in it.

Siobhán and I watch the woman leave. I set my filter cartridges down and act like nothing happened but I'm relieved the woman is gone.

Siobhán focuses her gaze on me now and looks like she's fighting herself internally.

She starts, "Did y—"

"*Tshee-fohn?*" A female voice says in a thick Chinese accent from the dimly lit stairwell behind the counter to the left. A middle-aged Chinese woman comes down the stairs.

"What's up, Mrs. Long?" Siobhán asks.

"Hello, sir," Mrs. Long says to me.

"Hi."

Mrs. Long smiles at me, then looks back at Siobhán and releases a stream of Chinese at her. I think it's Cantonese but can't be sure.

To my surprise, Siobhán responds with what sounds like perfect fluency. If I had closed my eyes and heard it, I would've thought she'd been switched with a Chinese woman who was raised speaking it. It's undeniably her voice, but the mastery she has makes me think she must have lived in China or somewhere in Asia for years.

Their body language leads me to think they're talking about me at first, then it's on to something about the aquariums. Siobhán gestures toward me again and Mrs. Long says something agreeable and starts inspecting the aquariums closest to her.

Siobhán starts to ring up my cartridges. I give her a twenty. She makes change and hands it to me. As she places the cartridges and receipt in a small paper bag, something seems to occur to her and she grabs another square of paper from behind and under the counter. Looks like a coupon.

She hesitates for just a moment, looks at me, then puts the coupon in the bag and hands it to me.

I say, "Have a good time at the party."

"Always do," Siobhán says, studying me with a look of suspicion and confusion that has a defensive quality about it. This is not the playful flirt I'm used to. I feel like I'm under the keen eye of a beautiful but dangerous predatory creature.

I really have to be more subtle about noticing the weird stuff…and fast.

I turn and walk down the aisles closest to the register. When I open the door to leave, I look back and see Siobhán leaning on the back counter on her crossed forearms, watching me down the length of the center aisle.

The little cute thing from before pumps out of the row of aquariums on my right and back through the air between the aisles about halfway between me and Siobhán. I try not to look at it while Siobhán stares me down, not looking either.

Staring contest? No problem. I can go all—shit.

I can't help myself and my eyes follow the fascinating little thing for just a sliver of a moment. Then I look back at Siobhán and she narrows her eyes at me, sure now.

Fuck! You suck at this! Just go!

I turn, step out onto the street, and let the door close behind me.

I enter the flat and lock the door behind me. My trip home was filled with more beautiful and fascinating spiderflies, growths on people, blimpwhales, etc., but all I could think about was flubbing the whole subtlety thing with Siobhán.

Oh well…. Why should I care what she thinks she saw anyway?

I LOVE YOU FELIX glows in the hallway ceiling and I hear Sigourney Weaver's soothing voice coming from the living room. She's talking about frogs? I round the corner and peek in.

Audrey sits cross-legged on the couch with a bong between her legs, wearing only a sweater, knee-high striped socks, and panties. The other half of a big hit of smoke licks at the top of the bong, waiting to be inhaled. Audrey slowly leans down, lifts the stem a bit to release it, and sucks the smoke out.

She looks really high. I'm in for it now.

She notices me watching her and smiles. She exhales, letting the smoke billow up past her face and says, "Heeeey, cutey." Audrey pats the couch next to her. "Sit down."

I cross to the couch and sit. She rubs my thigh.

"Thanks for getting the cartridges. Fishies will be thrilled."

"No problem."

"How's your head?" Audrey asks.

I watch frogs climb around in a jungle on the screen. "Oh, I got some meds at a store. Much better now."

"Good. I missed you today." Audrey sets the bong down, uncrosses her legs, and leans against my shoulder. She rubs my chest gently and kisses my neck. "I'd hate to pressure you into anything with your head throbbing. I mean, headaches are the worst, am I right?"

"Uh, yeah," I say, then move my hand up under her sweater and start gently rubbing her side up and down, hip to ribcage. She moans in appreciation.

"I was watching this Planet Earth about jungles and there's this part about frogs mating and it got me really horny." She chuckles softly near my ear, then nibbles the lobe. "Is that weird?"

"Maybe...but not bad." I chuckle.

I lean into Audrey and kiss her neck and jawline. Then guide her onto my lap, and we grind into each other while we kiss and touch. She moans into my neck, then says, "Futon."

I pick her up and carry her out of the living room and

down the hall with her legs wrapped around my waist, kissing her as we go.

About halfway down, I lower her and duck a bit just in time to avoid smacking the back of her head into the neon and Nixie tube sign and we laugh.

She wraps herself around me and nestles her chin over my shoulder and for a moment I feel like a firefighter saving an anonymous young woman. She sighs, sounding content.

We make it to the bedroom and I ease her down onto the futon. I kiss down her neck, then slide my face down the length of her sweater to her hips and kiss them down to her thighs. I kiss the inner parts of them as she looks down at me through half-open eyes. Normally I'd linger there longer, but she doesn't seem to need any more encouragement.

I hook my fingers through the panty straps and guide them off her hips, then, with a little help from Audrey, up her legs and off over her toes. Quickly undo my silly stormtrooper-helmet belt buckle, unzip my pants, and push my pants and boxers down.

I enter her and we move together like this for a long time, then I roll onto my back and she straddles me. She rides me, eventually going into something like a trance and closing her eyes. I close my eyes too.

Audrey's moans get louder and more frequent and I know she must be close. I grip her thighs tenderly, guiding her hips and helping her along.

Closer…closer…clo— No. Not now!

Audrey's moans have changed. Low, powerful hum and I hear the window vibrating.

I open my eyes just before she does. Hers slide open like windows into a psychedelic dream world. The distortions pouring out of her eyes this time are more awe-inspiring than disturbing.

Parts of her head and face do break apart or become see-through but the glow is gauzy and pastel. Her legs and hips and hands do the same and I can see parts of tendons, muscles, and bones as if through a fuzzy lens. I'm too far over the line to lose my arousal and, as I slide over the edge of the falls, that distant part of me decides this should prove to be the trippiest orgasm I ever have.

Audrey is already there and it shows.

The windows are vibrating stronger from some force I can't pretend to understand and I wonder how they don't shatter.

As she moans and arches her body back, she tightens up all over and I lose it with her, digging my fingers into her thighs. The pleasure and release are intense, paralleled by my anxiety and wonder. As it subsides, I realize my toes have curled and I deliberately relax them.

Audrey collapses onto my chest laughing and breathing hard. She nestles down into me and it occurs to me she wants to cuddle. I curl my arms around her and hold her but in my mind I'm still trying to process what just happened.

She kisses my chest and giggles, making her way up to my mouth. Still a little dazed, I forget to put my guard up again and I look down at her to see if she looks even near normal again.

"Felix, what's wrong?"

She raises herself up on her hands to look at me.

"N-nothing. I'm just tired."

The scary distortions must have felt upstaged because they pour out too fast, warping and melting everything into see-through cutouts and dripping, splashing gore. The burning dark glow is almost blinding in an instant and she locks those pulsing, dead shark eyes down on me. I shudder, unable to stop it.

"BULLSHIT! YOU LOOKED AT ME LIKE I HAD TWO HEADS JUST NOW!"

She studies my face.

"ARE YOU TAKING YOUR MEDICINE?!"

I try to stay as calm as possible even though her anger

pulses down onto my face and it feels like I stuck my head into an oven set to broil. It's more like radiation than heat, though. Plus, those eyes scare the shit out of me.

"Of course."

"FELIX, ARE YOU TAKING IT?!"

"You don't have to ask me twice! I'm not lying, dammit!"

The whole mess swirls, burning darker and brighter for a moment. Then she sighs hard, and it slowly starts to subside and she lowers herself back down to his chest.

She says, "I'm sorry, baby. It's just…. You have to take the medicine. I just need you to."

"Don't worry, Audrey. I'm taking it."

A little while later, I stand in the bathroom examining one of Wahrheit's pills. I look back into the dark bedroom. Audrey is snoring softly. I look back at the pill and think.

I look back into the bedroom again and it looks like Audrey is watching me through mostly closed eyes from the futon like I used to do when my grandparents checked in on me on Christmas Eve. It's not the same feeling at all, but I can't shake the memory.

I pour a glass of water and take the pill, then turn off the light and go to bed.

chapter 19

It's bright again and the thing is circling the dome room faster and faster and getting louder with every revolution. The vibration is so strong I can barely feel my limbs. I'm doubled over on my knees on the floor shaking violently and I can feel my teeth humming in my mouth in sync with that damn revolving thing.

I hear a new sound rising from the inner apex of the dome where it's too dark to see. A shrill, distorted hiss that harmonizes with the vibrations and hum of everything.

I force myself to look up.

Something in the darkness—or the darkness itself— slithers, and tendrils of pitch grow and swallow the light. The impossibly dark ceiling breaks apart and I can see what must be stars.

I wake up face down and alone in the futon. Look at the alarm clock. Almost 1 p.m. Roll onto my back and look around. Audrey is in the bathroom. She finishes brushing her teeth, rinses, and walks into the bedroom.

"Hey. Good morning."

"Morning," I respond cautiously.

"Gotta get a move on to my one-thirty class."

She crosses to the futon and sits. She tenderly places her hand over my heart.

"I'm sorry about last night. I ruined a really good thing."

"No, you—"

"I did and I'm sorry. I'm just paranoid because I love you so much, Felix. You just need to remember that the medicine is like a…necessary evil."

"I take it every night." Hey, it's sort of true.

"I know you do. I love you, Felix."

"I love you too."

Audrey leans in and we kiss. She gets up and walks to the bedroom door, then stops and looks back.

"Oh, you got the wrong cartridges. Too small. Could you go back and get the larger ones?"

"I have a pretty busy schedule today, but I might be able to pencil it in."

"Thanks."

"Ehn peeh."

"Geek."

Audrey leaves and I stare at the ceiling, thinking about my dream.

It's almost 3 before I get out of the house and into a foggy day in the city. Banks roll through the lower elevations and pour over the tops of the hills and cut the visibility like soft, seventy-foot dividers.

Usually, I love this kind of day, but I don't know what to feel today. The thick mist at street level as I walk down Stockton is cool on my face, so that's good at least.

Blimpwhales play and chase each other through the sky, disappearing into the fog banks and popping back out from a distant part a little later. There aren't as many spiderflies or those bigger swimmers out and about but there are glowing bulbs and tentacle growths on people all around.

I should probably start carrying my 426 again, I think as I enter the hustle and bustle of morning business in Chinatown's market area.

I reach Sacramento, cross the street and walk down the hill to the fish store. Enter and walk down the center aisle, half expecting to see the little crawdad thing but it's not around.

Siobhán is with a customer.

She notices me and her expression changes but she's still in control of it and she continues to help with the customer's problem.

I walk to the filter rack and find the right cartridges, then make my way to the counter.

Siobhán's customer seems satisfied and walks down an aisle and out of sight.

Siobhán walks behind the counter. The back of her shirt says "Killing Time" in thin white print that has faded from dozens of washings, and I realize the image on the front is the cover of an album by The Creatures. She turns back toward me and for once all she says is, "Hey."

"Hey. Yesterday, I got the wrong cartridges. Can I exchange them?"

Siobhán studies my face but this time it's more curious than nervous or defensive.

"Yeah, you seemed a little out of it yesterday."

"Must be getting a cold or something," I lie.

Siobhán watches the customer she was helping leave out the front door.

"Sure, I can exchange them, but it'll probably cost more."

"That's cool."

She takes the bag containing the filters from yesterday and the correct ones I found. She looks in the bag and winces a little.

What was that about?

She takes the box out of the bag and scans it, then the other. "It'll be three twenty-seven more."

I give her a five and she makes change. Siobhán places the new cartridges in the old bag, picks up something from under the counter and produces another of the colorful coupons.

"I think there's already one in the—"

"I'll honor both," Siobhán says and smiles. It's a strange little smile and I'm really confused now.

Hopeful with a touch of sad desperation? What happened to the long, tall vixen from Toughbutsexyville?

"Great savings, those. Make sure to check them out." There's even a slight wavering of the "American" accent she always uses, and I can almost pick out what her natural accent is.

I take the bag and say, "Thanks," then walk down the center aisle and leave without looking back so I won't have to return any more weird looks from Siobhán.

I enter the apartment, lock the door behind me, and walk into the living room. I take the cartridges out of the paper bag and set them down on the aquarium filter.

Then walk down the hall to the kitchen and look at the dark I LOVE YOU FELIX/AUDREY sign. When it's turned off, the letters in the display wiring in the name Nixie tubes look meshed together. I LOVE YOU [FAUEDLRIEYX]?

I crumple the fish-store bag into the circular hole atop the silver-bullet trashcan in the kitchen and walk back to the hallway. Then make it to the living room and pick up a PS3 controller to play some *Flower* before remembering the coupons Siobhán seemed so intent upon me using. I cruise back to the kitchen with the blinking controller still in my hand. Set the controller on the refrigerator, then reach into the trashcan and pull out the bag. I take out the two dayglow blue coupons and laugh.

The coupons have silly, cute fish sitting at a table playing cards and smoking cigars printed on them from a drawing like that one dog painting. I can tell Siobhán drew the original because the fish share similarities to the ones on the fish-store ceiling and in the cases outside the door. GET $5 OFF YOUR NEXT PURCHASE OF $20 OR MORE is written in hand-drawn block letters at the bottom. I shake my head and tuck the bag back in the trashcan, then press the coupons against the refrigerator to place a magnet over them. I detach a circular magnet that looks like a Royal Air Force roundel and place it on the coupons.

As I'm taking my fingers off them, I feel something I didn't expect. Roughness?

I rub them between my fingers and feel little bumps on the paper. I feel a flash of nostalgia for some reason, especially strange because I don't even know what they are.

Upon closer inspection, I find a strip of organized rows of tiny bumps on each coupon.

Braille?

"What the fuck...?"

I pull the coupons off the fridge and the roundel magnet falls to the tiled kitchen floor and skitters into a wobbly spin. I'm in my editing room before it stops.

I move my computer's mouse and the desktop appears, the background a blown-up, color-inverted image from a Tank Girl comic of her kicking someone's head off. I minimize a windowed video clip of a car crashing into a crowd of people at a race in Europe and open a browser. After a quick search, I find a Braille alphabet key and explanation.

It's hard to make out the arrangements of the bumps, though.

I think for a moment, then roll the computer chair over the hardwood floor to my drawing table and grab a pencil and a utility knife I use for sharpening.

Then place the coupons side by side on the desk next to my monitor and use the knife to shave some graphite into little piles of powder on each. I rub it across the rows of bumps, giving them more definition.

After consulting the Braille explanation, I start deciphering the messages on the coupons and writing down the letters under them with my pencil. I work quickly, going back and forth between the information on the screen and the groupings of bumps out of a possible six, two vertical rows of three, which, when raised, make up each letter. I finish the strip on the first coupon and sit back in the chair. The first message reads,

I KNOW YOU SEE THEM TOO

I take a deep breath and let it out slowly, reading the words over repeatedly. Confusion. Formless dread. But still, nostalgia.

Why the secret messages? Why Braille?

I decipher the strip on the other coupon, quicker this time. It reads,

DO YOU REMEMBER

Remember? Remember what?

How can Siobhán even see all this spooky weirdo shit, anyway? Who is she really?—

My phone rings in my pocket and I jolt in my seat. I take it out and check the caller ID. 650 area code. The only person I know in that code anymore is in Colma.

What now?

I KNOW YOU SEE THEM TOO
DO YOU REMEMBER

"Hello—"

Wahrheit interrupts, –Felix. I need you down here.–

"Sure. What's—"

–I'll tell you what. Just not until I can see your face. Then there's some shit you need to explain to me.–

"Are you okay?"

–Come now.– As Wahrheit hangs up, I hear Sujit say something in the background in another language. Then responses from other voices I don't recognize.

I hang up and set my phone down. Then read the coupon messages again.

I KNOW YOU SEE THEM TOO

DO YOU REMEMBER

I KNOW YOU SEE THEM TOO

DO YOU REMEMBER

I KNOW YOU SEE THEM TOO

DO YOU REMEMBER

I sigh and rub my eyes before picking up the coupons, leaning in the chair, and roughly stuffing them in my back pocket. I'm up and almost to the hallway before it occurs to me to bring the HDV-426, then I retrieve it and head down the hallway, grabbing my jacket and heading out the door.

chapter 20

I watch late afternoon San Francisco rush by out through the BART car window.

Look around the car to take my mind off Siobhán's messages. There are a few people with growths I'm familiar with but one woman down a few benches on the right has a type I'm not.

They're like glowing, translucent flowers that cover half of her face and all of her mouth. They run down her neck and down into her blouse. Tiny, lambent creatures flutter through the air around and disappear into them like bees on regular flowers.

I try to act casual as I take the HDV-426 out of its bag, set it on the bench seat next to my thigh, and aim it at her. Open the flip-out screen to adjust the zoom and framing, then rest my hand on the camera loosely and look out the window to complete the illusion that I'm not filming her. I'm thankful for the little cover piece Rudy put on the shooting indicator light.

The dark discolorations in the sky are clearer but only slightly. I watch them drift through sky, the different shapes and sizes rotating as they seem to revolve around multiple unknown central points, rarely interrupting each other's paths. Some even seem to pass through each other, and some disappear into the city and land all around, while others appear out of the bay water and East Bay, farther down what has to be a semicircular path of revolution with a central point somehow deep under the surface. Some paths are much larger and the groupings of discolored shapes stretch high into the sky and toward the horizon.

Do I even want to know what those are?

The BART train enters the mouth of a tunnel and I repeatedly study the route map and safety posters so I can continue to act casual while filming the flower lady.

I step out of the BART car onto the platform and make my way to the escalator and up to street level. As I send my transit card through the turnstile and the thick pizza-slice barriers open, I look at the BART attendant in her booth. She seems familiar but with just a quick glance, I'm unsure why.

A small blue hatchback picks up the flower-face lady at the station curb. The sun is almost down as I exit the station and follow the route I took with Rudy. I do my best to ignore the vague, dark things gliding through the sky all around above because they give me an uneasy feeling. As I cruise down A, I think about Siobhán and her secret messages. She went from flirty guilty pleasure to a source of real anxiety and confusion in the blink of an eye.

Maybe I should just avoid her. There are other fish stores around.

I can't help being super curious what her damage is, though....

I cross at a four-way stop and cut down another street. The streetlights are coming on and the mercury-vapor glow is picking up the mist in the crisp air.

As I walk on the long strip of dirt and dying grass between the cars and cemetery fence, I look over into the cemetery to my right, curious what Rudy was so bothered by.

Wait…what was tha—

Oh shit!

Keep walking—maybe they didn't see you. Shit-shit-shit.

I lock my gaze forward, stealing quick glances over without turning my head.

The cemetery is inhabited by dozens of faintly glowing, eerie figures.

They are translucent and hard to see until they move because they distort the air around them and become clearer in sporadic glimpses. Their actual shape is vaguely humanoid, but some are tall and gaunt while others are more hunched and all of them have some amount of physical abnormality. One crawls, pulling itself along with one long arm and hobbling with the elbow of its other crooked, warped arm and its mangled, useless legs. One is trying to drink from a puddle of rainwater from earlier in the day but doesn't seem to be succeeding. It lets out a long, tortured moan. When I can see them more clearly, I notice that their orifices ooze a thick, dark liquid and their black eyes glint, reflecting the streetlights. The ooze glistens in the light too, seeping from their mouths, noses, ears, and half-filled eyes.

One pulls itself up out of the ground near a grave marker. Most of them just roam aimlessly around the graves. There's one up in a palm tree between two rows of graves. It's among the fronds and appears to be watching over the cemetery eastward toward Wahrheit's trailer estate.

A few seem to have noticed me and they move silently, keeping pace with my advance along the fence line. They move like they're walking but the ones that aren't as warped and twisted sort of glide along the ground as they make the motion. Their eyes never leave me and rarely blink.

I can't take the proximity anymore and cross the street, then continue up the sidewalk.

When I look over again, I lock eyes with one of the wandering spirit ghoul things that's crouched by the fence and hanging its long arms over it. My blood goes all ice water. The shiny black eyes aren't actually opaque and there's a crimson hue in their depths. I can only just see them because the only movements it makes are its head moving to follow me. The look in those deep, crimson-black eyes is one of deep, haunted longing and I can't stand it, so I look away.

I'm relieved to reach the condos at the northern edge of the cemetery. A quick glance confirms that the ghoul things have stopped at the fenced boundary and are just watching me leave.

The guard on duty watches me enter the trailer estate through tinted aviator stunners but doesn't say anything, so I start down the main street toward Wahrheit's house.

I cruise down the long sidewalk for about twenty-five or thirty mobile homes, telling myself to remember the memory fogger thing.

There's a large white van with no side windows parked on the other side of the street that sticks out because the roof is covered with equipment, long antennae, and a little satellite dish, all blue-black with lines of stark orange symbols printed on them. Tiny blue and green lights blink on and off at the base of each rig.

Would I see that without Wahrheit's pills? Seems like crazy government or military equipment or something.

I get closer to the blank area my mind and eyes don't want to acknowledge, and my mind starts to drift and I just keep walking.

Why is that guard back there still wearing his dark sunglasses? Can he see? Not well, at least.

Seems like it might rain. That would be nice.

A glowing spiderfly flutters down toward the gaping maw of vagueness on my right, then bobs up and down for a bit before flitting away.

It must have smelled the patchouli—stop.

Wahrheit's houses are right there.

I stop and repeat that to myself until the two fence-connected mobiles are vaguely visible in front of me. I step toward the house and push through the suggestion that I should turn around and forget, successfully touching down on the artificial lawn.

I can see the nonexistent old lady through the kitchen window, drinking a cup of tea and reading a tabloid in the dim light of an also nonexistent low-wattage lamp in the ceiling.

As I make my way around to the porch, I notice that one of the surveillance cameras on the corner of the house looks busted somehow.

Weird.

I step onto the dark porch and reach for the doorbell in the entryway doorframe but stop when I notice the cameras on the interior of the overhang and the one above the door are busted too. The lens on the camera above the door is shattered and electronic guts are hanging out through the hole like it exploded from the inside and there's a smell like melted circuits. The smell is strong enough that whatever happened to the cameras must have been recent.

Oh, I do not like that.

I take out my phone and check the call history. Wahrheit's number didn't register, probably due to some secret device he has, and I'm not getting any signal this close to the house anyway.

Perfect. Shit.

I put my phone back in my pocket and look around the neighborhood, then push gently on the door, which swings inward a bit.

Under my breath, I say, "Oh, come on."

As I take a step down the porch to look in the dark living room windows, my feet crunch down onto broken glass. I crouch and examine the porch and yard. There's shattered glass everywhere and there are a few spots that look like scorched wood and grass that glisten and have bits of fleshy pulp in them. That smell mixes with the burnt-out electronics aroma and I cringe as I stand and back toward the entryway door.

I accidentally back against the door and it opens further, revealing a fresh kill zone. The metal walls of the entryway are riddled with thousands of small dents, blood spray, and more of the fleshy scorch marks. The camera array above the far door is busted like the others and the metal door is dented and partially open. The floor of the entryway is completely covered with spent lead pellets and small, deformed bullets, most of them scorched and bloody. A repetitive, rhythmic sound can be heard through the partially open metal door but it's hard to make out.

Fuck *this*.

I'm off the porch and almost to the sidewalk when I see the gate guard cruising down the street toward me in a golf cart. I stop dead. The guard is shining a flashlight around and keeps trying to point it toward Wahrheit's houses but lets it drift away to linger on other houses. Each time he tries towards me, it flashes across my chest, face, or eyes. I just stay frozen in place, letting the fog barrier do its thing.

The guard stops the cart near Wahrheit's houses and looks around. Every time he looks toward the houses, he gets a dreamy look on his face and looks away.

Must have seen me come over here but can't get through the fog in his head.

Dammit. Just go away.

I look back at Wahrheit's porch, then down the street toward the entrance/exit.

That's the only way out from what I can see. This fucker's

not leaving. I do not want to try to explain what I'm doing here. I'm not the best liar, so he's gonna think I'm a burglar or something.

Plus, I don't want him somehow stumbling onto Wahrheit's place. Seems really persistent.

I look at the porch again, then study the rest of what I can see of the houses.

Maybe whatever happened is over. Wahrheit might be in there smoking a bowl in the garden part waiting for me. And if not, maybe I'm far enough down that I'm past the cemetery and I can just hop his back fence and head back to the BART station.

I watch the guard's face, hoping for a sign that he'll leave any time soon but I'm not seeing one. I take a deep breath, then exhale and turn back toward Wahrheit's porch.

I half creep as I cross to it, knowing full well that if the guard was going to see me he would have, but I can't help it. I hesitate and sigh and it catches in my chest.

I don't know if I can do this.

As I step up onto the porch, the light hits me again. I freeze and look over like a caught possum but the light is already drifting away as the guard unwillingly aims it back down the row of houses.

I push the entryway door open and tiptoe through into the long living room.

The record player is stuck in a locked groove and continues to play the same part from a psychedelic rock song I haven't heard before.

——oaring…in a bright paisley sky….—

The only light source inside is from the stacks of monitors near the far end of Wahrheit's couch and on the coffee table. Most of the monitor feeds display glitchy static that bathes the room in eerie, low gray that shifts and dances on the walls and furniture. A few still appear functional.

——oaring…in a bright paisley sky….—

As I creep in, I step on shattered glass and shell casings. Then take out my phone and bring up a flashlight app, leave it on low, and pan it around.

There are casings everywhere, and not just from the fixed gun rigs.

They must have fired all those bug-in-amber equation weirdo bullets.

Several of the modified weapons are missing from the mounts on the armory wall at the end of the living room.

——oaring…in a bright paisley sky….–

I crouch and feel some shell casings. Still warm.

Some of the strange equipment has been damaged or destroyed. There's a steady whir and hum from the equipment that is still on.

I advance toward the couch and coffee table, hoping to see at least Wahrheit on one of the video feeds. His big bong has tipped over and broken into a few large pieces at the foot of the coffee table.

There's a prescription bottle of Wahrheit pills on its side on the carpet. I pick it up and shake it gently. Full. I put it in my back pocket.

I see the tone arm on the record player reset in the groove as I pass the big component stereo against the near end of the couch.

Probably better leave that on to cover my steps on all this glass and stuff.

——oaring…in a bright paisley sky….–

The few video feeds still on display aren't much relief. One maybe five-inch color screen and two probably seven-inch black and whites. Another, a partially functioning monitor, isn't showing a visual feed but I can hear what must be the big turtles scuffling slowly through the gravel between the houses. The sound is loudest when the tone arm resets in its groove and the music stops momentarily.

The small color monitor and one of the black and whites display different angles of the interior of the "garden" in the other house across the yard. There must be a busted light in the garden because there's a really dark corner in the shots of it. The other black-and-white view is one of the POV shots from a spiderfly—or swimmer, more likely, from the side-to-side movement of the shot. It's swimming through Candlestick Park above a 49ers game.

No Wahrheit in sight; no one on the screens at all.

——oaring…in a bright paisley sky….–

I wince, regretting that I didn't turn off the turntable as I was creeping by it. I shift my weight to take a step back toward the stereo and step on something softer than the glass and casings all around. Crouch and pick up a packed manila envelope. Turn it over and frown when I see what's written on it in thick block letters in black permanent marker:

OBRIST'S HEXE

I flip it back over and untie the red thread, then slide out the contents. I set down the bundle of notepaper, drawings, prints of old paintings, photographs, and printouts of photographs on the coffee table and leaf through them.

——oaring…in a bright paisley sky….–

There are Post-it notes and older notes on the scanned photo printouts in different languages, like they've been annotated by several people over a long time period. Russian, Polish?, Japanese, Chinese, Arabic, and others I'm less sure of.

The photos are from different time periods and locations, and they seem to begin in the middle of the nineteenth century. There are even a couple ferrotypes and a slightly blurred daguerreotype. The drawings and paintings date back even further. Possibly hundreds of years.

In every image there is a lovely young woman. In some images she is the subject or one of a few. In others, it's like someone played Where's Waldo? and found her in crowd shots.

France, Italy, Germany, Switzerland, Russia, India, China, Morocco, Egypt, South Africa, Cuba, Peru....

That's just what I can recognize from landmarks. It's the same with the time periods.

Eighteen thirties up through seventies, eighties, nineties, and upwards into the twentieth century.

In every image, she looks the same. Other than the fashion of the time and hairstyles, she looks exactly the same. Roughly twenty-five to thirty years old, deep brown eyes, glossy raven hair.

On a couple of images marked "1914," this young woman speaks with a bald, mustachioed Serbian military officer in a palace. She turns and sticks her hand out to block her face from the camera's eye.

——oaring…in a bright paisley sky….–

After World War I, she is spotted in Prague several times. A few images of her in Palestine in the background of a family photo shoot. Then she's in Switzerland consistently for a while.

Then it's all out of order for some reason.

She's having a conversation with Nikola Tesla and Mark Twain in a parlor in the early 1900s. Both men seem quite fascinated by what she's saying. To go with that, there's an image of her in one of Tesla's big labs sitting in a chair. Fifteen-foot tendrils of electricity flash through the air around her like lightning and it looks like she's laughing as a little girl might if surrounded by adorable puppies.

——oaring…in a bright paisley sky….–

Out in front of a rundown hotel in Paris with a note of "1959," William Burroughs and Brion Gysin are stepping out of a '57 Peugeot 403. Gregory Corso is standing on the sidewalk waving to the person behind the wheel of the car, a sleek Euro-beatnik version of that same young woman. Then she's a colorful hippy in San Francisco and looks high off her ass on acid or mushrooms maybe. A little post-it on this one is marked "Duboce Park 1967." I swear the Swede is in the background, parked by the sidewalk.

She's back in Paris in the next few, amidst overturned cars and police barricades. She's on a bullhorn, then chucking a brick at riot police. "Mai 68."

Then she's wearing a big coat and circled in red in a crowd shot marked "Christmas Eve, Moscow 1979." She's speaking with someone who's partially obscured by a pillar. Another shot seems to go with this one. Its Post-it reads, "Moscow 1988."

——oaring…in a bright paisley sky….–

In another black and white, she's well dressed and wearing a small clamshell hat and veil as she disembarks from a German transport plane on a landing strip. "1937" is written in faded blue ballpoint pen in the corner. There's a full shot with the whole plane in view as she makes her way down the short stairs placed at the base of the door hatch. There's a swastika on the vertical stabilizer. The next shot is a zoomed in close-up.

"Audrey?"

I'm trying to grasp at what all these images mean. It seems obvious but I can't get my mind around it.

——oaring…in a bright paisley sky….–

I cringe again, remembering the stuck record I've been tuning out.

I take it back. That racket is not helping.

With a dark image of re-photographed Polaroids in my hand, I cross slowly to the turntable. The Polaroids look like they were laid out and re-snapped in a hurry.

The notes read "south shore - Cayo Largo del Sur, CUBA '73" and there's a part of a finger in the edge of a frame on one of them. There's a rough vertical ellipse of red permanent marker around the blurry sliver of finger and "OBRIST?" written in the same red on its edge.

——oaring…,–

I reach for the tone arm.

–…in a bright paisley sky——

Then lift it off the spinning record and set it on its holder.

;',.',.',,.',.——

I catch a slight movement in my peripheral vision and look over at the monitors. On the two garden views, something moves in the shadows I saw in the corner—

No….

What looked like a shadow is really a large, dark figure that has a warped humanoid shape—and it moves like it's made of thick liquid. It's deep black but lacks the light sucking quality of the thing on Pier 39—and it's much larger.

This big, inky-black figure has pulled away from the corner it was blocking, and I can see what looks like a person's dark-skinned hand on the floor near the base of what serves this horrible thing as a leg.

I lean closer to the monitors and take a step toward them. I kick a shell casing across the floor, and it tinkles against the base of one of the monitors. The monitors glitch and sputter and the faceless figure seems to lock its gaze on the black-and-white garden camera, effectively looking straight at me—at least that's how it feels.

The movement of it looking toward the camera reveals a kind of vague luminescence in its depths.

Like watching lightning flash over the deep ocean…on a moonless night…from a hundred feet below the surface.

Kind of beautiful, actually….

The black-and-white garden feed vibrates and shudders, then cuts out to static.

Shit.

I snap out of a trancelike state that must be caused by looking at the figure too long and shift my focus to the small color monitor.

The figure is moving toward the door to the central yard, its limbs flowing and jerking like it has a bad limp, and it's hobbling across the bottom of a deep pool.

As it lopes away from the corner it was blocking, a scene from an abattoir is revealed. I cover my mouth as my eyes take in a mound of severed flesh, intestines, blood, and other fluids that very recently must have made up a human being. The garden, floor, ceiling, and walls in that corner are covered in blood and severed bits like someone took a buzz saw or five to the victim, and bits of bloody bone and viscera were flung every which way. I didn't know what I was seeing before, because on the black-and-white view the blood was just another dark gray. The color makes it almost unbearable to look at.

I could swear I see a severed finger drip down from the ceiling and drop into the blood-slick intestines below.

As the warped figure lumbers out of the color-camera view, the image shakes hard, then cuts out to bright blue.

OH, FUCK ME!

I take a couple steps toward the entryway but stop myself.

No! It'll come through the laundry room—laundry room is closer to the entryway—fuck! Go for the window in the hallway!

I backpedal and turn, rushing around the coffee table and monitor stack and into the hallway.

I look over my shoulder and consider grabbing one of the guns that's left on the wall and using it but I've never fired one before, don't know if they're loaded, and don't know if they'd even work on this huge, nasty creature—

Then I slip and try to regain my footing but my feet slide out from under me at an angle. I slam into the hallway wall with my face and nose, then shoulder and flop down to one knee hard and my body slaps against the wall.

My upper lip feels warm and I realize my nose is bleeding.

Dazed enough to forget why I was running, I look down at what I slipped on.

This end of the dark hallway is a messy slaughterhouse like in the garden and I can smell the coppery stench of drying blood from the spray and gory slop all over the walls, ceiling, and the puddle of guts and snapped bones on the floor.

In this haze, I notice that I slipped on the puddle and a loop of burst intestine. I smell the contents and it mixes with the odor of blood, causing me to retch.

Then I smell something far worse than that and feel an odd vibration. It's low and reverberates through the wall I'm still partially pressed against. Feel it in my fingertips first, then up my arm. It quickly becomes strong enough that I can hear it too from the laundry room opening down the hallway and I remember why I was running.

The window at the end of the hall is barred on the inside. NO! NO! NO!

I look down the hallway, then back at the window. My eyes adjust just a bit more to the dim moonlight coming in and I see that the window is in the top part of a metal door. YES!

I'm quickly on my feet and cross to the door. I hear the hum behind me get much louder in one distinct step and the smell causes my eyes to tear up. I look back and take in a sharp breath.

The figure has come in through the laundry room and stopped, slightly hunched with its head region cocked and resting up against the ceiling at an angle. I can't tell if I'm looking at its back or front. It starts to turn, and I realize that was its back, but it doesn't matter....

The video image didn't do it justice. Probably just couldn't. Its form is a swirling mass of something between liquid and squirming matte-black flesh and it seems to shift between these states and combine them sporadically. The flashes I noticed before aren't as pretty when seen with the naked eye. More like lightning in a tornado of terrible energy.

The closest thing to a constant in its ever-changing form and the reason it doesn't matter which side was facing me are the creature's eyes. There are dozens of them, and they glow faintly all over the thing's warping body. Concentrated on the head and chest areas but peppered less densely all over it. Varying sizes, from marbles up to tangerines. Some are cloudy and dead gray. Some a sickly orange. A rough dozen red ones range from bright and candy-like to deep and dark. Some of the eyes stay in roughly the same place but shift around like they are bobbing in the waves of living muck. The others close only to reopen in a different spot a moment later.

As it turns around, the head region against the ceiling undulates and reshapes like animals in a sack, as if it's filled with multiple limbs and joints straining against the humanoid shape. An eye-covered belly pregnant with dozens of squirming, amorphous fetuses.

I shake my head to clear it. I don't know if I could look away from the figure at all if Rudy hadn't taught me to push through Wahrheit's memory fogger.

I fumble through the locks and chains on the metal door and try the handle—but it won't open.

The hum behind me is getting louder and closer and it's vibrating the door now, but I can't look back. I choke back another retch as the smell gets even nastier.

I close my eyes for a moment and whimper in complete terror, expecting a blow or slash any moment.

Just be quick, you big, weird bastard....

I shudder and feel like I might start urinating on myself. Then I realize I'm about to die for no good reason in a trailer park in Colma, joining the rest of this dead town's majority population.

You know what? You're gonna work for this gut sack, motherfucker!

My eyes snap open again, focused and desperate for a solution.

There aren't any more locks or chains—what's stopping it from—

There's a black security bar against the base of the door handle and stretching down to the floor at an acute angle, firmly holding the door in place.

I twist the bar and pull it, wrenching it free from the door—then I spin and throw it down the hall. It twirls a couple times through the air like a baton and glances off the creature's left "shoulder" area, and this desperate act succeeds in making the thing step back.

When it whips its bulbous, pulsing upper area back toward me, I'm already out the door and up on the wood-slat fence Wahrheit must have installed against the chain-link one already bordering the trailer estate. I look back just before dropping over. I burst through the door so fast that it hit the outer wall and swung back to a mostly closed position. The newly cracked window shows a dimly lit hallway and an old, white-haired man walking down it.

Instead of contemplating the relationship between the nonexistent couple in the magical window camouflage, I drop to the dirt and patchy grass below and start running through a small forest of night-black trees on the periphery of whatever property I've crossed into.

chapter 21

I run out from under some tree cover near the fence and realize I'm in the cemetery I was really hoping to avoid. Some of the ghoulish flutter-stop creatures mill about the graves ahead of me.

I look back toward the fence and notice what must be some sort of vehicle resting on the roof of Wahrheit's main house. It's like a small hovercraft with no balloon thing on the bottom. I can make out a padded seat, thin antennae, and equipment with blinking lights similar in color and design to the stuff on the van I passed on the way in.

That must be how that damn thing got in past all Wahrheit's defenses.

From above. But how? And why?

I feel the vibration the creature gives off growing again and start running across the grass, then reach the nearest graves and run between them.

Take a quick look back over my shoulder and see the big, dark thing loping through the cemetery behind me.

As I snap my attention in front of me again, I see that some of the ghoul things have noticed me and are converging on me from all around. Their movements reveal their hollow stares and anguished, oozing faces as they get closer.

My legs are burning but I try to run even faster.

The apparitions in front of me bunch up and I can't avoid them. I run straight through them, and their half-there bodies and groping hands are colder than anything I've ever felt.

I make it through that group and zigzag between more of the pale, glowing things, seeing them best as they lunge for me.

Stealing another quick glance behind, I see that, instead of lunging for the big monster pursuing me, the wraith things make way, quickly clearing a path and shrinking away from it.

Even the scary things are scared of this thing!

I shift my direction enough to reach a path running between the plots and run down it until I have to cut through some more grave sections. Hillside Boulevard is less than a hundred feet away and the lights on the cars streaming by make me hopeful—until they start fading out.

Now what?!

The headlights on the cars, then the streetlights, and within a few seconds every artificial light in the area fades and blinks out.

The cars keep driving smoothly down the street like nothing happened. A person walking down the sidewalk doesn't seem fazed either, other than their glinting-eyed silhouette seeming to regard me with discomfort.

Make it to Hillside and run straight across the street, stutter-stepping before the last lane on the far side to avoid being hit by one of the ninja cars.

I see the signs for D Street and realize I'm farther south

than I hoped, so I steer more north as I cut through a cemetery and hop a fence into a cul-de-sac and beat my feet down it toward the station.

My muscles are filled with acid now and my mouth is filling with saliva from the adrenaline and workout. A third of the way down the street, I slow to a fast walk involuntarily, just not able keep up that pace.

As I run-walk, I look back down the strangely darkened street and see no sign of the horrible figure. Not seeing it is worse.

Looking around at all the dark windows, I notice people in murky silhouette in their living rooms and kitchens just going about their business like it isn't pitch black all around.

There's even a small swarm of darkened spiderflies that I can only make out from their strange movement and shape, fluttering and darting through the air above the houses.

Am I the only one in the dark? Is that thing doing this to me?

I catch a change in my peripheral vision above and to my left and look over.

The dark figure is on the roof of a house down the street from me.

It's already in front of me! How?!

I speed up and cut a wide path, crossing to the far sidewalk as I advance toward the next intersection. As I round the corner, I watch the figure for signs of pursuit.

It seems content to observe my retreat with its many eyes.

I start to feel the pull of the eyes and the constantly boiling, swirling limb-and-joint soup that makes up its filmy surface. Close my eyes and shake my head, clearing the hypnotic effect, but I'm unable to get rid of the images of split, ripped, sliced human appendages and organs recently seared into my mind.

Those images return some spring to my steps and I'm off running again, booking across six lanes of a busy street and narrowly avoiding being hit by a couple night-blackened vehicles.

As I rush up the gradual slope to the station, I look back and can't see the figure. Feels like it could come from anywhere.

I cross the street and hurry under a sidewalk overhang outside the station, slowing some to not look too suspicious.

Oh shit! There it is!

The dark creature is climbing onto the top of the overhang a little down the slope. When it climbs, it becomes an amorphous blob of malformed limbs, tentacles, and diseased organ slop that doesn't resemble a human form at all.

I break into a full run again, anticipating the creature's talons or claws—or whatever it has that can eviscerate a person so violently—sinking into me and pulling me away.

But that doesn't happen, and I find myself safely inside the darkened station. It's so dark, though, that I run straight into the turnstiles and double over, slamming my chest down into one and knocking the wind out of me.

"Hey! What's wrong with you?!" I hear the attendant yell from her booth. I look over at her, straining through my mild panic as I try to catch my breath.

As my eyes adjust to the shadowy artificial darkness, I can make out the woman's face as a kind of matte-black reduction with glistening black eyes. It looks like Delores from Fleischmann Medical Center. I'm almost sure.

The ground vibrates below my feet and I whip my head back to the station doors. My pursuer has stopped just outside of the station and watches me like before.

My breath starts to return and I stammer, "S-sorry. In a hurry."

She shakes her head and says, "You still have to pay!"

I take my pass out of my pocket and make a few attempts at getting it into the slot before it goes in and passes through the system inside the turnstile. Grab it on the other side and the pizza-slice barriers open with a thunk.

Without looking back again, I make a beeline for the stairs that lead down to the platform.

Behind me in her booth, I hear Delores say, "Fuckin' tweakers."

I run down the stairs and reach the platform.

Of course, there won't be a goddamn—oh hell yes!

The one time I really need it and I actually get it: a BART train is sitting at the platform, doors open and waiting for city-bound passengers.

I bolt down the platform and reach the train but the doors start to close. I lodge my arm in the closing doors and they open back up. I step in and grab a pole, then look at the doors, trying to will them into closing faster. After a long moment, the doors close and seal.

That vibration is back. I bend over and look out the windows. I can make the creature out down the darkened platform, many of its glowing eyes locked on the BART car as it watches from the base of the stairs.

–Okay, we're done checking the systems and ready to head on. This is a Pittsburg-Baypoint bound train.–

The figure takes a couple flowing steps down the platform but stops abruptly, its surface swirling all around it like liquid in a comically large, jarred punchbowl spiked full of animated decaying corpses—and Japanese-game-show large.

It seems to have noticed something farther down the platform or maybe in the train itself.

The train starts moving and I exhale slowly, unable to take my eyes off the creature as we pick up speed. I'm still staring at it when we round the first bend out of the station and I lose sight of it. There's a disorienting moment when we enter the underground tunnel and normal light returns with a shuddering, almost tangible, pulse, just as everything goes dark outside of the train car.

I have to squint but I am more than a little thankful for the return of normal light. I look out through the empty driver's compartment at the rear of the train just to be sure that thing isn't following somehow. Satisfied that it isn't, I slump down into a bench seat affixed parallel to the length of the car, drenched in sweat and muscles burning.

Looking around, I see that the only other passenger in this car is an elderly woman down near the doors to the next car who is trying to act like she isn't watching me carefully but mostly failing.

There's a vibration from my pocket and I jolt, almost jumping off the bench. Then I hear the theme from *The Third Man* and realize it's just my phone ringing. I take it out, see that it's Rudy, and answer.

"H-hello?"

"FELIX!" Rudy is breathing hard, and he sounds terrified.

"What's wrong?!"

"You have to get out of the city! Shit—I don't even know if that would do it!"

"What are you talking about, Rudy?!"

"Remember those things Wahrheit wouldn't talk about?! The thing I saw?!"

"Yeah! One just followed me from his place. I…I think Wahrheit is dead. I saw a hand—"

"Dead? Then we are *fucked*!"

"What is going on?"

"Those things killed Lacy! Fucking tore her apart! I didn't even tell her about this shit! I come home and she's all busted and sliced open and there's one of those things in our bedroom! I barely got away—they must be after everyone who knows!"

"Knows what? We don't *know* anything!"

"We can see them, can't we? That must be enough! Doesn't matter. We just need to get far away from this place! I don't know where it's safe, but we have to try for it...."

"Where are you?"

"I don't even know. I just ran out of my complex and kept going until I ended up in a construction site, I think. I need to find my way out and—"

Through the phone, I hear a loud shuffling and creaking and a hum like the figure that followed me made, then Rudy shouts—

"Oh fuck!"

What I hear next is chaotic. The hum gets louder, then there's heavy breathing and sounds of running and it gets quieter. Doors slamming. Creaking and splintering. Rudy yelps, then more running. Sounds like he's running across gravel maybe outside, then it gets quieter, and I can hear low steps and a door closing gently.

Rudy whispers, "I think I'm cool. I'll stay put until...."

There's a sizzling sound almost like frying bacon and the hum rises out of it fast.

Rudy's voice is meek and full of dread as he pleads, "I didn't say anything. P-please don't ki—"

Either the phone is knocked farther away or Rudy is, because his terrified yelps become more distant. What follows makes my hands shake and my stomach twist in a knot.

The hum rises in intensity and becomes a howl like a wavering turbine engine and Rudy screaming, then shrieking in pain. Slicing. Wrenching and snapping. Rudy squealing, then trying to scream through a thick gurgle. There's one last big slurching pop and Rudy is silent and the distorted turbine sound fades back down to the hum level.

I'm shaking as I listen in silence.

There is nothing but the hum for a long moment, then a wet sliding as the hum gets louder. The sliding stops and the hum is close to Rudy's phone. I feel a static tingling on my ear. The video call mode has turned on. I pull the phone from my ear and look at the screen and straight into several piercing, hollow eyes. Where they would be different shades of red on the creature that chased me, these are shades of unnatural green from British Racing to brilliant celadon and jade on up to bright candy lime.

I feel the hypnotic pull of the eyes and try to look away but can't. Everything other than the screen and those eyes swirls and fades away. The surface of the phone starts to bubble up and change, slowly becoming the shape of the eyes as it seems to push through into the train car. It takes all I have left but I close my eyes and shake my head.

I drop the phone on the floor of the train car and the wet, grotesque eyes search about before locking back on me. One of the eyes has formed almost entirely out of the surface of the phone screen.

I rise off the bench, lift and tuck my leg high, and kick down onto the phone hard, cracking it.

"FUCK YOU!"

I kick down again, slamming my foot down into it and shattering the screen.

"FUCK YOU!"

Another kick and it starts snapping and popping apart.

"FUCK YOU!"

I keep kicking down until it is a scattered pile of parts with no resemblance to a phone, cursing the whole way.

I'm breathing hard as I look down the train car and see the old woman staring at me, wide eyed.

I shrug and throw out my open hands wide as if to say, "What?" and the woman gets up and hurries through the doors into the next car.

I slump back down onto the bench and bury my face in my hands. I rub my eyes and slouch forward. I look at the pieces that were my phone, then lean back and slam my head back against the window a couple times before resting against it.

The BART train stops at Daly City station. My car

stays empty other than me. The train starts moving again.

I slide my head a bit against the glass and stare at the ceiling.

Carefully look over at my reflection in the window across the aisle for just a moment. I see dried blood from my nostrils down to my upper lip and fresh bruising where I hit my face against Wahrheit's dark hallway. Then I catch sight of the scar on my jaw and striking, different colored eyes for the first time in a long time and look down at my shoes to escape.

I bring a few fingers to my mouth and deposit some saliva on them, then rub the blood from beneath my nose.

My favorite song by the Pixies pops into my head, maybe for its haunting and playful absurdity, but also at that moment after many years listening to it and loving the song, it occurs to me that it reminds me of one of the last things my dad ever said to me.

So, I sing to myself.

"Hope everything is all-riiight…. Hope everything is all-riiight…. What's that floatin' in the water? Ol' Neptuna's only daughter. Pray for a man in the middle…one that talks like Doolittle. Got bombed, got frozen, got finally off to finally dozin'…. You can cry, you can mope…. But, can you swing from a good rope? hm-hm-hm-hm-hmmm… hm-hm-hm-hm-hmmm…"

I rotate my head against the glass while I sing and hum and look toward where the old lady bolted from. Someone is making their way from the next car back to mine.

Great. Bitch sicced the BART cops on me. Psych ward bound for sure.

Something about the man doesn't look right. I take my head away from the glass and lean forward for a better look. Definitely not right.

The man walks through the door at the rear of the next car. Not through it like it's open. *Through* it.

I jerk back in my seat and blink.

As the strange man continues through the closed door of my car, I turn my head and look up like I'm studying a route map. In my peripheral vision, I see the man take one casual glance at me, then sit on a bench near the far doors on the other side of the aisle.

That distant, not mortified part of me notes that we are now sitting perfectly opposite in the car. Myself on the bench by what are currently the southwest entry doors, the man on the other side of the car and on the bench by the northeast doors. He has even taken up the same pose and posture as me, looking up at the ceiling in the corresponding opposite spot.

The train slows to a stop at Balboa Park station and the doors open. A young couple gets on and goes to sit near me. I glance at them, then back at the route map.

Something about the look of me must bother them because they abort on sitting down, keep going down the train, and make their way through the doors into the next car.

The BART train starts on its way again, swaying and rocking on a long curve.

I steal quick sideways glances at the man down the aisle.

The song I was just singing still lingering in my mind, I can't help but think of this newly arrived fellow passenger as Grieves.

Grieves wears a thick, dark overcoat, dark pants, a blue and gray horizontal-striped sweater, and black combat or work boots. Dark is the best word because his overcoat and pants were probably black but now they are covered in a layer of fine, bright blue dust like glowing pool chalk. What really makes Grieves freaky is that what I can see of his flesh and body is translucent. Layers of skin, muscle, and bone on his hairless head and hands are all but see-through and in no particularly uniform way. His mouth and eyes are the worst. The big, wet eyes seem to be lidless or fixed wide open and his teeth can be seen through his closed mouth, which gives him this perpetual maniacal almost leering smile look.

He seems to vibrate at a varying rate and his "flesh" glows a faint but radiant blue and the internals past it glow pink and orange and red. The bright dust must continually flake off him.

I can't help but stare at Grieves's reflection in the window just behind him.

Grieves turns and lowers his head and meets my gaze. His unending stare is grotesque and terrifying. Depending on how the light hits Grieves's eyes, they look either dark-rimmed with pale orange irises and piercing black pupils or dead-shark black all over, much like freaky-face Audrey's.

I look back up at the map, hoping Grieves will too. He doesn't. Grieves is staring straight at me now and won't stop.

Grieves stands and begins walking down the aisle toward me. Fresh sweat is beading on my forehead and in my hair.

Grieves's movement is close to normal, but he will sporadically speed up or slow down for an instant. He makes it down the aisle and stops on my left.

Grieves just stands there for a long moment, then bends over and stares at my face.

I lock my eyes on the route map, hoping this glowing, see-through, manlike abomination will decide I'm not worth its time.

Grieves sits next to me on the bench, his face right next to my cheek. He just glares at me point-blank, his breaths smelling like a soldering iron.

I look over at Grieves without moving my head. From this close, I see that Grieves's orange eyes seep fluid the same blue as his glow and dust. I can also see what must be Grieves's sinuses through his translucent nose, nasal cartilage, and nasal bone opening.

There's also a glowing rectangular strip of fine, even lines of varying widths peeking out of the collar of Grieves's sweater on the right side of his neck.

In an odd, gravelly voice, which shares the speed-up, slow-down properties of his movement but occurs far more frequently, Grieves says, "I-its imp-olite to ss-tare."

I jolt and wince upon hearing this and look back up at the map.

"It-'s i-mpo-lite tt-o sta-rre. It'simpo-liiiiiiite to-oo stare."

I look sideways at Grieves again, and can see Grieves's mostly clear, Jello-mold brain through his skull and muscle. I could be imagining it, but I think I can just make out tiny pinpricks of electricity crossing synapses deep in there.

I look away and shut my eyes tight.

"Ar-re yoo-ou laik mee? Feel lai-kit. Areyoo?"

Grieves waits for an answer, then gives up and continues his verbal water torture, "Imp-olite…sss-tari-ng." He cocks his head a bit. "It'svery-yy im-politeto-staaaare. It is imp… polite to stare—"

I bolt out of my seat and run for the doors to the next car, then rush through them, looking back through the connecting doors as I hurry away. Grieves is still sitting but follows me with his eyes.

I keep going through this second car and through the doors into the next car forward and stop about halfway through to watch Grieves through both door windows of the car behind me. As the train goes around a curve, I can only see half of Grieves's head, but I can tell his mouth is moving and I assume he's still chastising me. He walks into the car behind, continuing about halfway before he comes to a stop, mouth still moving.

We pull into Glen Park station and stop. Grieves and I don't budge. I consider running out through the doors but I'm not too familiar with Glen Park and don't want to get caught so far from home and risk getting lost with this weird stranger on my ass. As the doors close, I feel a pang of regret at that decision.

The train leaves Glen Park and speeds on its way.

Grieves walks to the connecting doors and through them into my current car.

I back toward the doors to the next car.

Upon seeing me shrink away, Grieves stops in place. He seems to frown but it's hard to tell with his peculiar attributes.

His eyes pulse back and forth between the intense pupils and the dead-shark-eye black, seemingly unaffected by the angle of light now.

I stop and grab a pole.

Grieves stands between two homeless men arguing about something. The first man slaps the drunker one's arm across the aisle, his own arm passing through Grieves's midsection. Grieves doesn't seem to have noticed and doesn't seem to care if he did.

This world-class debate continues all the way to 24th and Mission station while Grieves and I have a staring contest that I know I can't win.

The train stops and the homeless drunks stumble off the train. The doors close and we continue on.

Grieves takes a couple steps toward me, so I back toward the doors and fumble with them before successfully backing through them into the next car.

Grieves stops again and his frown becomes more pronounced. If I'm being honest with myself, Grieves almost looks hurt.

I grab a pole.

We are frozen like this all the way to 16th and Mission, where the train slows to a stop.

As the train doors open, I just want to run out through them but the Mission, while I know it much better than Glen Park, is still not close enough for comfort. Plus that's where Rudy was just….

People get on and off and the train is on the move again.

Grieves takes another step toward me and I back away. Grieves takes another and I keep backing up, grabbing poles as I go.

Grieves's frown becomes a glower. He looks mad now. His eyes stay black and pulse, increasing his vibration to a degree that his flesh is blurry. As this gets stronger, that impossible "bright darkness" I've seen radiates from his head and hands, darkening and illuminating the area of the car around him.

I keep backing up, ignoring the normal passengers' confused looks. When I reach the doors to the last car, I search for the handle but can't find one. I look behind me and see the driver shooting a surly look back at me over his shoulder through the window in his control compartment.

Shit! This is the last car!

Grieves storms up to me, backing me up flat against the driver's compartment and forcing me to turn my head to the side. Grieves's movement has an added time delay now that he's upset. When he moves, trails follow him, flashing like still images here and there, then catch up, absorbed by his actual form.

Grieves's face is less than an inch from the side of mine when he says, "It isss rudeto ig-nuh...ooore someone.... Rudeto ignorepeepole.... Not niiiceto av-void someone."

I'm shaking as I see the signs for Civic Center/UN Plaza and I get an idea.

"Yoou-'re ver-ry ru-uude. Yesss, quoo-aight ru-u-oood."

Having said his piece (again), Grieves's many distortions calm to a gentle pulse in his pupils. He stares at me, judging me or maybe waiting for a response?

The train eases to a stop once again and the doors open.

I steel myself and push off the wall, going through Grieves and seeing a smooth, quick tour of all the parts in Grieves's head as I go. The feeling is indescribable, but my best effort would be something like getting your tongue piercing caught in a wall socket. I run out through the closest doors onto the platform and make it about fifteen feet before stumbling to a stop. I look back and see Grieves walking out through the open doors after me.

Perfect.

Grieves's increased upset intensity is back and he continues to harangue me, "How inc-reddiblly rhoood-dd!"

I let Grieves get about ten feet out of the car before I spin and run full speed for the next set of doors down the train's length toward the rear, dodging confused passengers that are leaving the train through them. I make it in just before they close, and the train starts off again. Grieves just stands there, frowning as he watches the train pick up speed. Just before it would pass him entirely, Grieves walks toward the train. I press myself against the windows to get a view of what I hope is Grieves being left behind on the platform—but Grieves walks into the rear section of the last car just in time.

No! Come on!

I push off the window and grab a pole to steady myself while I bend over and try to get a view down through all the cars. I see the moving sphere of darkness a few cars down.

Grieves storms briskly through the train toward the car I'm in, face ablaze with dark weirdness and mouth moving ceaselessly now.

I dance in place, not sure what to do next.

Powell-station signs flash by the windows and I take a deep breath and let it out. The train slows but not quickly enough for my liking.

Grieves has made it into the last car before mine.

When the doors finally open, I book it out onto the platform and pump hard to the stairs, then up them two and three at a time. I look back down at the platform over my shoulder and see that Grieves has left the train but is standing still watching me with a puzzling expression as the doors close behind me.

Is he actually smiling now?

I'm too over the edge to indulge curiosity, so I keep going without a second thought. I reach the top of the stairs and hairpin around the other side of the stairs, then hurry toward the turnstiles.

The top half of Grieves's head appears out of the station floor to my left. Grieves's glistening eyes follow me as I pass, alternating between the beady pale orange and shark black as the movement picks up the light at different angles again.

Now he almost looks amused?

I take my pass out of my pocket and send it through the turnstile with shaking hands, then take it from the other side and rush through the station to the stairwell up to Stockton. I go with the flow and reach the street level.

I look around as I walk up the street past the Apple and Disney stores but don't see Grieves.

As I pass the Fashion Institute, I notice Grieves across the street. He's sitting cross-legged on top of a Ghirardelli store overhang, peeking around from the company symbol, and following me with his eyes. He's mumbling something but the distance and street sounds all around make it impossible to make out what.

I speed up and start through the next intersection, looking back at Grieves as I go. Grieves descends into the overhang, disappearing. I scan the area for signs of him and notice something off in the window display on the corner of the sidewalk on the northwest of the intersection I'm walking through. The display takes up the first-floor corner of the building, and vertical support structures are the only obstructions.

Grieves is standing in the display but most of him is blocked by the outer tiles of the corner support structure. He follows me with one eye and tucks his body behind the corner interior. The slice of jaw I can see below Grieves's one eye is moving, probably still mumbling nonsense. Grieves sees that he's been caught and walks out through the corner of the building saying, "Fowned yoo-ou…. Ffoundyou…found yooouu toooo."

His amused excitement makes him look even more disturbing. I cut through the intersection diagonally, crossing toward the northeast corner instead.

Grieves descends into the sidewalk, saying, "I'llfindyou aggehn…. IwillIwillfin-dd you aggehn—" until his mouth and then the rest of his glowing, see-through head are gone.

I cut north up the sidewalk and see Grieves's head half poking out of the Macy's Men's Store sign above street level on the building I'm passing. I play it off like I don't see Grieves watching me and decide to try ditching him in the Macy's proper across the street.

A few cars honk as I jaywalk across Stockton. I make it to the sidewalk and rush through the doors.

Behind me, Grieves has come out of the sign and wall and dropped down to the street. Cars pass through him as he calmly crosses the street, practically beaming.

I run through the cosmetics section toward the elevators, then take one up to the second floor and hurry through the different departments. I see a pillar with a full-length mirror and hide behind it.

As I scan the floor for Grieves, I also keep a look out for suspicious employees.

A bougie woman walks by and stops with her back to me at a scarf rack. Grieves's head appears in the floor near the woman's shoe, looking away from me.

I back up and duck behind a circular rack thick with clothes, then peek around it.

Grieves rotates his head in my direction—

I bolt for the restrooms through the squat forest of dresses and jackets, crouched to stay out of sight. Open the men's room door, duck inside, and watch through the crack in the door until I'm satisfied Grieves didn't follow before letting it close all the way.

I look behind me to make sure I'm alone. I am not.

There is a bald, naked man standing in the restroom with his back to me, leaning his head against the first toilet stall. I flinch at the surreal sight.

What now?

There is a black burn mark on the right half of the man's back. It almost looks burnt from inside somehow. His body vibrates and hums.

I realize the man isn't leaning—his whole body is at a slight angle but seems to ignore gravity. The arms are at rest at the man's sides but at that angle, they would be hanging slightly in front of the body, not perfectly aligned with it as they are.

I look back at the door and wince, then back at the man. "Hello?"

I take a step closer and sees that the man's legs are fused into the floor at an angle just above where the ankles would be.

Okaaaay.

I lean to the side to try to see the man's face, but his head is fused into the toilet-stall wall like his legs. The left side of it ends just in front of the left ear, cutting down from the crown to along the jawline.

I get closer and examine the vibrating body, seeing another burn down the man's right forearm and one on his neck. I feel a strong urge to touch the man, just to see if he's there at all.

Or will it go through like Grieves?

I extend my shaking hand toward the man's left shoulder but hesitate.

"Ah, fuck it," I decide and go for it.

My fingertips start to turn translucent and little arcs of strange energy from the body bite at them. It feels like my fingers are asleep but there's an added sensation of something resembling extreme cold.

When I touch the man's shoulder, all at once the vibrating and hum stop and the body detaches from the head and leg fuse points—

Blood pumps and squirts out from the freshly severed parts and the body falls to the floor of the bathroom. The faceless, footless body jerks and twitches violently against the floor, causing more blood to spray and spurt.

I jump back, flattening against the bathroom wall.

Something hits the floor in the first toilet stall with a wet slap. I reluctantly bend down to see what it was.

It's the man's face from the bridge of the nose at an angle up to a bulbous section cut from the front part of his head, minus the width of the stall wall. It must have detached and slid a bit, then flopped down flat on the ground. The eyes are moving back and forth but with no will guiding them and they look mostly empty. One moves with less control and keeps twitching to the same side unnaturally.

Some eye-socket muscles must have severed on the eye closer to the stall wall and there must be just enough brain left in the front to....

I feel ill and the room rotates like a centrifuge, pulling me back against the wall. I double over, twist, and vomit against it. I spit a couple times, then cross back to the door, hugging the wall once I'm past my sick and watching the writhing mess as I go. I open the door but close it most of the way immediately—

Grieves is in sight. He's looking around, eyes changing as they catch the light.

I close the door all but a crack and look back at the thing behind me. Its spasms are still strong, and the blood keeps coming.

I look through the cracked door and see Grieves staring at the bathroom.

"This is not happening," I say.

I let the door close all the way and tiptoe back toward the toilet stalls, now trying to ignore the bloody, bucking mess in my peripherals. The last stall won't open when I push on it.

"*Occupado*," a smug, yuppie-sounding voice says. "You gonna clean up your fucking puke, man? That shit's disgusting. Maybe you should go drink somewhere else and pass out under a tree or something."

I ignore the man and enter the middle stall next to the one with the face/head chunk in it, then step up onto the toilet and crouch down. I close my eyes to focus on listening.

Abruptly, I hear Grieves's hum as he enters the restroom, then his heavy-booted footsteps. The footsteps become wet-sounding and then there are sounds of sliding and dragging. The face-chunk stall door creaks a bit and I open my eyes.

I look down and see one of Grieves's bloody boots and bloody prints leading to it. More blood is trickling down Grieves's lower pant legs onto his boots and pooling on the floor in parts. The bright blue dust gently snows down into the frothy blood too, resting like cocoa on a cappuccino or something.

There's a sound like strained urinating now and I see blood drizzling down the sides of the toilet and start to pool on and around the base. There's way too much blood.

I'm far enough gone that my curiosity momentarily overpowers my fear. I rise up from my crouch cautiously, steadying myself on the stall walls, and look over the top.

Where I expect to see Grieves's weird, grinning face, the diagonally cut head at the top of the still-writhing body is rolling back and forth with the jerking body motions. The glistening severed part hemorrhages blood from around the base of the cleanly cut rear-brain sections and out of the intact ears. I can see the bloody nerve roots in the bisected molar that lined up with the stall wall and the jagged cross-section of red-slick jawbone.

I take in a sharp breath—

The head turns toward me reflexively and it seems for a moment like it is looking toward me, impossibly.

I jolt back and my right leg comes off the toilet, my foot touching down in the growing pool of blood. I slip off the toilet and come crashing down on the floor of the stall on my side and, slamming the stall door against its lock, rattling the whole stall setup.

"Hey, what the fuck, junkie?!" the yuppie exclaims.

I'm eye-level with the floor of the first stall and I see the angled head chunk, now surrounded by the pool of blood and eyes still half-hollow and lolling around.

The yuppie says, "Maybe you should go jump in front of a bus! That might do the trick, you worthless piece of shit!"

Grieves's face appears upside-down at the bottom of the stall wall as he bends down at an impossible angle. His head shakes and blood drizzles down his face and into his big eyes, mixing with the fluid that already drools from them and dripping this mixture down onto my right forearm and the pool on the floor. He looks excited.

"Pry-vah-seeee shou-lld be re-sspected. Priiiiii-vasc-y sssh-oood be—re-specktedd. Fou-nnd youIfoundyou…. Imp-ooou-lite to sta-re."

I yell, "Shut up!" Grieves recoils and frowns.

The yuppie says, "Don't come near that door! I'm calling the police!" Digital tones and a nervous fart can be heard from the last stall.

I pick myself up, careful not to slip again, swing the stall door open, stumble out of the stall, and limp to the restroom door as fast as I can. Then I'm out through it and run through the store to the escalators, then down them round and round in a mad dash for street level.

chapter 22

I burst out through the doors of the Macy's and look back for any signs of Grieves behind me as I scramble toward a yellow cab cruising down Stockton toward Market. The driver gives me a cautious look so I straighten, trying my best to look normal. Apparently, it works, because the cab slows and stops.

Fighting my desire to fling myself into it, I walk with as little "holy shit get me out of here" showing as I can muster. I get in and sit on the padded bench seat. The cab drives down Stockton.

I watch out through the rear window and see Grieves materialize out of the wall of the third floor of the department store and fall smoothly to the street and land in a crouch. When he touches down, all of the blood from the body in the restroom cascades off of him all at once, most of it actually passing through his body on the way to the ground.

Grieves scans the area and sees me through the cab

window. He smiles big again.

Dammit!

Grieves stands and takes a few steps down the street before stopping and frowning. He descends into the street out of sight.

Finally!

I sigh hard and slump down on the seat, exhausted.

"Where we goin'?" asks the cab driver.

"Six forty-two Greenwich."

"Green witch it is," he says and chuckles to himself.

The cabby drives quick and smooth, and I don't care how long around he goes.

The back of the driver's head is covered in glowing flowers like those on the woman in the BART car. The translucent, bee-sized creatures flutter into them and crawl on them.

I feel the hum again before I hear it, coming from the bench seat next to me. The top half of Grieves's head comes up out of the seat and his big eyes look around, then fix on me. He rises up out of the seat and sits, then crosses one leg over the other in a casual manner that makes it weirder. Grieves leans over and stares straight at my face until I look forward.

Without looking away from my face, Grieves reaches over and plucks a few of the bee-things from a glowing flower on the back of the cab driver's head and puts them in his mouth. As he chews them up, the crunching and bursting is visible through his lips and cheeks and even a bit through his somewhat see-through teeth. Grieves swallows the little mushed-up creatures and I look away, not thrilled about watching the involuntary muscles work the food from the pharynx down his esophagus.

I don't know if I can take much more and watch out the windows, ignoring Grieves's incessant mumbling and whispering. As far as I can understand it, I'm participating in a macabre game of hide-and-seek that might just never end.

Is Grieves a symptom? Am I crazy?

But if I'm not, what can I do?

Light glints off a passing car's windshield and I squint, then notice a girl walking on the sidewalk with a satchel slung over her shoulder.

Wahrheit's emergency kit. Whatever's inside that pack—that's what I need.

I bide my time thinking about what might be in it until I see we are pulling onto my block. The cab pulls up and I pay the driver and get out, then walk up my steps.

I stop at the door and look back. Grieves is standing in the street where the cab was stopped before driving off, staring and mumbling.

I unhook my keys from my belt loop and open the door, then step in and close the door behind and look out through the high-set windows. Grieves just stands there and mumbles.

Please stay out there.

I turn around and creep down the hallway.

The I LOVE YOU FELIX sign glows in the hallway ceiling. It blinks on and off a few times and Audrey pokes her head out from inside the kitchen into the hallway and looks up at the flickering sign.

In a playful tone, she says, "Uh-oh! It's losing power! Maybe you should call when you're gonna be—" then stops abruptly and sobers when she looks at me.

She steps into the hallway, frowning and sizing me up.

I realize I must look awful. Covered in a few layers of dried sweat with a fresh one still beaded on my forehead and in my slick, messed up hair. My eyes must look wild and I have a few little tears in my clothing.

There are also mud stains on my pant knees and blood from Wahrheit's place and the Macy's restroom.

Can Audrey see that?

Somehow it hadn't occurred to me that Audrey might

be able to "see" too.

I notice tiny pinpricks of shark black pulsing in the centers of her pupils.

"Are you okay, Felix?"

"Fine—why?" I say, too quickly.

"You're a mess and…. You look scared to death."

"Oh, I'm fine—I thought a mugger was following me. This guy was like pacing behind me on the sidewalk."

Audrey studies me, eyes pulsing stronger now.

With her voice barely above a whisper, she asks, "Are you taking your medicine, Felix?"

"Yeah, why—"

"DON'T FUCKING LIE TO ME!" she screams, the distortions and blinding dark pouring out of her eyes and destroying her face more intensely than I've ever seen it.

The I LOVE YOU FELIX sign distorts and flickers for real now, parts of her burning mess of a head and face whipping up into it. The different layers of wire fluctuate in color and jumble and warp together, making nonsense abstractions of the A-U-D-R-EY and F-E-L-I-X letters. The intense darkness around her makes the glowing sign even more intense and contrasted, but it's almost obscured by the impossible brightness from the same source.

"AM I GOING TO HAVE TO WATCH YOU TAKE YOUR MEDICINE?!"

"I'm taking the pills—"

"I CAN'T TAKE YOUR WORD FOR THAT ANYMORE! IF YOU REALLY ARE, YOU NEED A HIGHER DOSE! IF YOU AREN'T, YOU NEED TO GO BACK TO THAT PLACE UNTIL YOU REALIZE YOU HAVE TO TAKE IT!"

I blink a few times, my face burning from that feeling like a blast of radiation. It stings and tingles.

Audrey storms back into the kitchen in a swirling huff of smoky distortion and the I LOVE YOU sign mostly returns to normal. I follow slowly, watching the wire letters glow and vibrate.

"SOMETHING BETTER WORK BECAUSE I CAN'T TAKE THIS SHIT!"

Grieves walks into the hallway through the front door.

"Oh, sorry. I actually forgot about you for five seconds," I say to myself. "Can you believe that?"

Audrey says, "WHAT? WHAT ARE YOU TALKING ABOUT?"

"Nothing."

I walk back down the hallway and into my workroom. Pick up a pile of drawings that have accumulated on the case Wahrheit gave me and set them aside. I'm still holding my keys so I flip through them, finding the small case key.

Grieves walks through the wall into the workroom and looks around at my drawings and paintings.

"Pik-tchersz au-rre neat. Pick-chersareneatt. I lai-kk themn."

I insert the key into the corresponding slot and rotate it.

When I open the case, there's a split second where it's just an empty case of charcoal-gray foam with professional looking cutouts. I furrow my brow and blink—and the cutouts are filled. A little music box that must be built into the case somewhere plays something like an Eastern European folk tune.

What fills the cutouts twists my stomach. I don't know what to make of it and the dread is back, bad.

The case now contains a large revolver.

Customized fittings, tubes, and ports like the weapons at Wahrheit's. The other cutouts in the case hold different types of ammo and those weird ampules filled with colored fluids I'd also seen before. Also, other custom parts, ammo quickloaders, and cleaning tools.

What am I supposed to do with this?

I pick up the pistol, ignoring neatly folded papers under it.

It's heavier than I was prepared for, even accounting for the foreign-experience factor. It feels real and solid, and it occurs to me that I'm holding something made for killing.

Grieves tears his attention away from the artwork to see what I'm doing. He sees the gun and recoils, then takes a step toward me and bends over.

Grieves whispers hoarsely, "Thossse a-rre dan-jurous! Thooo-se aredangerous!"

"Think so?" I ask, then point the pistol at Grieves's head and stand, letting the case fall off my lap onto the floor, scattering the contents.

I keep the pistol trained on Grieves as he yelps and throws himself back into the wall, seemingly terrified. I feel a surge of confidence from being able to scare the scary now too.

Then I realize what this new tool can get me.

Answers.

I take a step toward the hallway but stop when I hear the music box in the gun case on the floor playing a different tune. The case and its remaining, spilled contents distort in space like the light goes out on only them and they become matte and abstracted from the room, then they blink out completely and are gone.

I don't really care what that's about right now and continue out of the workroom, down the hallway, and into the kitchen. I keep the pistol behind my thigh, watching Audrey dice tomatoes with her back to me.

She glances back over her shoulder and her face swirls and breaks apart but it's not as freaky as it was a couple minutes before.

"WHY DON'T YOU TAKE YOUR CAMERA BAG AND JACKET OFF AND STAY A WHILE, FELIX?"

I raise the gun and point it at her back, cupping the bottom of its grip with my right hand like I've seen in movies and magazines to give it stability. It makes a satisfying clicking sound of shifting machined metal.

She looks back again, then does a double take and spins around, dropping the knife on the kitchen floor with a clacking sound. She yelps and extends her other hand in front of her. Her face twists and dances but it's different now. She's afraid, and that looks more like pulsing, living fractals sizzling through her moving cutouts of see-through flesh, muscle, and bone. Her eyes are almost visible in the shark black, and they glint, reflecting the kitchen light strangely. Her voice changes too. Still strange, but not as shrill or vibration distorted. "Felix! Wha—"

"What are you?!" I demand, trying to mask my fear and desperation.

"What do you mean?!"

"What are you?! A vampire?! Some kind of ghost?! A fucking alien?! What?!"

"I don't understand—"

"Quit acting! I can see what you are! I just don't know *what* I'm seeing!"

"Please put that down, baby! Please."

"Don't call me that! Tell me what you are, or I'll shoot!"

Audrey's expression changes and she narrows her eyes at me. "No, you won't."

"Shut up!"

I cock the hammer.

Wait, is this thing even loaded? I didn't check! Don't look at it—she'll know you aren't sure!

Audrey looks scared again. Not like she's new to being in this position, though, which unnerves me. I try not to show it. She blinks a few times and her eyes dart around in thought. She closes her eyes and sighs.

She opens them again and says, "Okay. I am…different, but I'm not any of those things, Felix. There's a lot you don't know. Put that down and I will explain it to you, baby."

"Quit calling me that! Explain it now!"

She's bothered by the gun, but looks like she is becoming more angry than scared. The anger distortions start to blossom slowly, and her eyes go all shark black again as she speaks.

"I'll explain it when you…" her face erupts into a

burning dark star of organic chaos as she continues, "…
PUT THE FUCKING GUN D—"

I jerk in reflex and the gun goes off.

The kick is so strong and the sound so loud that I drop
the pistol out of shock and in a moment it's going to make
a heavy clunking sound as it connects with the kitchen
floor.

Before that can happen, a .45 Long Colt bullet hits
Audrey just above what would normally be her perfectly
plucked left eyebrow, more out of sheer proximity than any
skill on my part.

Her skull cracks, the distortions cut out instantly, and a
good portion of her brain comes out the back of her head,
hitting the wall behind her above the sink.

The pistol hits the floor as Audrey crumples back against
the sink and her body goes limp, sliding down to the floor
and ending up propped against the lower cupboard with
her legs splayed out unnaturally. Her body undulates and
twitches like she's having a seizure. Her now normal eyes
go blank and blood pulses out of the hole in her head in
time with her last few heartbeats before it becomes just a
slow, steady trickle. One of her eyes half closes and both
of them stare down through the floor at an angle, hollow.

I watch the blood trickling from the entry wound on
Audrey's very recently flawless forehead slow to a stop and
the spasms and twitching subside. Audrey's body is still. I
hear the sound of the *Flower* intro screen music from down
the hall in the living room.

I hadn't noticed that.

Was she playing it because I like it so much? Did she
set it up for me because she thought I might have had a
hard day?

I'm not sure if anything could make this worse, but that
comes close. I lose all my strength and my legs buckle,
collapsing down without stopping myself and landing hard
with my legs half tucked under me. I lean forward and prop

myself up with my arms, swaying.

Grieves's face appears out of the upper kitchen cupboards, and he says, "Tolld yew…. I tould yooooo—danj–urous."

I ignore Grieves and he leaves after a few seconds.

It's hard to look at her—her body. She's—

She was so beautiful.

’ . ’ . ’ . ’ . ’ ’ . ’ . ’ . ’ ’ . ’ .’
,· ,,·, ·,, ·,, ·,, ·, ·,, ·,,· ,, , ·,, ·,,
’ . ’ . ’ . ’ . ’ . ’ . ’ . ’ .’
, ·,,·,· ,,, ·,, ·,, ·,, ·,,·,· ·,, ·,,,
’. ’ . ’ . ’ ’ . ’ . ’. ’ ’ .
,· ,, ·,,· ,,·,, , ·,, ·,,,· ,,· , ·,

I get mad. This time, though, it's at myself. I sway back and forth on my arms, hurting in ways I never have before. An enormous sob is caught in my chest but it won't come. Lost. Angry. Twisted up inside. Something switches off in me and I reach a state of ineffable clarity.

The only way to not feel the way I do about myself is to not feel. Anything. Ever again.

You can keep your babbling, see-through weirdos, pregnant blob eye monsters, and solarized surgery-collage-face beauties, Universe™.

One day seeing what I'm sure is just a sample platter of what you've really got to offer and I'm through. This place is just a fucked-up mess of pain, horror, selfishness, and bullshit. I'm cashing in. "Picture Me Rollin'" and "So it goes" Vonnegut style, and all that.

My eyes roll over to the big pistol on the kitchen floor. I walk with my hands and pick it up, then rest back on my legs.

’ . ’ . ’ . ’ . ’ . ’ . ’ . ’
, ·,, ·,, , ,,·, ·,,· ·,,· ,,· ,,,

I raise it toward my mouth and insert the hot barrel between my teeth. Looking down my face, consider the best angle to achieve instant brain death and adjust accordingly.

We wouldn't want to experience some extended fever dream of diminished perception due to major brain damage, now, would we?

When I'm satisfied, I look at Audrey's body one more

time to steel myself, then up at the ceiling before closing my eyes.

I cock the hammer slowly.

The darkness in my mind swirls and pulses.

```
  ’. ’. ’. ’. ’.
,. ,,, .,,, .,,, .,,, .,,,
  ’. ’. ’. ’.
, .,,, .,,, .,,, .,,,,
  ’. ’. ’. ’
., .,,, .,,, .,,, .
  ’. ’. ’.
, .,,, .,,, .,,,
  ’. ’. ’.
, .,,, ., ,,
  ’. ’.
, .,,, .,,,
  ’. ’
, .,,, .
‘
  .
,.,,,
  ’
., ,
,—
```

How do you say goodbye to yourself? Scratch that—who cares?

Fuck. It.

My left index finger curls a bit and I apply gentle pressure to the trigger—

What is that damned sound?

It's like bugs flying into a zapper put through a chorus pedal and reversed.

My eyes flutter open and roll languidly around in search of the source.

Oh, come on….

The sound is coming from the kitchen wall above the sink. Specifically, the brain matter Audrey unwillingly parted with a few moments earlier. Every little zapping sound corresponds with a small bit of it disappearing off the wall.

I watch this for a moment before gingerly taking the gun out of my mouth. It's still up by my head, just out of my mouth and a bit to the side and ready at a moment's notice. I can't look away from the popping and vanishing brain mush.

That is, until Audrey's body starts twitching again. Similar to the seizing undulations at first, then the back arches a bit and her muscles tighten. Then it arches again like when someone gets shocked with paddles in trauma-room shows. The third spasm is so hard that the whole upper body is pushed upward and supported by the backs of Audrey's palsy-clenched hands before slapping back down. The body is mostly still for a long moment.

Then the hardest spasm hits and the whole body arches and twists up from the floor.

A sound like a scream being pulled backward out of thick liquid rises quickly out of the near silence and organic struggling. The scream forms into a screeched word.

"FFFUUUUUUUUUUUUUUUU-GCCK!" Audrey screams, vibrating the whole room, especially the oven and fridge coils.

I flinch and the gun goes off again. My coffin-nail bullet blows past my face and head, striking the kitchen wall, passing through at a ricochet-altered angle, and slamming into the I LOVE YOU sign in the hall ceiling with a shower of sparks and an explosion of luminous gas.

Audrey's body jerks hard and her clenched hands slap repeatedly against the kitchen floor as the body violently convulses. She moans and mews like a tortured, injured animal. The hole in her head starts seeping blood again and her eyes roll all around, trying to focus again. They finally lock onto me and life flows back into them, immediately followed by the pulsing shark black and crackling, warping distortions.

"YOU MOTHER— F-FUG-CKER! NNNNHN-HUHN—HURTSS!"

She swallows and breathes in and out like she's trying to breathe through and past the pain. She moans in agony and writhes. The brain matter continues to leave the wall and I have to assume it's reforming in her skull.

The see-through prisms of flesh and blinding darkness

calm down and she coos, "My head hurt*ss ssso* bad. Feels *ssso* weird."

Still twitching and not in full control of her movement, she rolls onto her stomach and shoots her icy gaze toward me again, shimmering black pulsing in her pupils. The one eyelid is still half closed and one side of her lower lip droops. She presses her still partially clenched and hooked hands on the floor and rises on her arms.

"You *ss*-shot me. How cooth—couldth you do that?"

"I'm so sorry, baby," I say like I forgot an anniversary. This is a *little* worse, but I don't know what else to say.

"I didn't do anything to de*ss*serve—" Her skull reforms with a crunchy pop and she cringes, collapses on the floor, and her face goes slack while her eyes lazily dance around without focus for a moment. She shuts them tight and exhales hard before she rises back up on her arms and starts to slide across the bloody floor toward me.

"Why didjhyou do that? I wasth going to eckss-plain it to you."

As she inches closer on her hip, thigh, calves, and hands, I slide backwards on my hands and butt, still clutching the revolver. I back up into the hallway and the wall stops my retreat. I wince as my right hand comes down onto some shards from the nixie tubes.

Audrey gets mad again watching me shrink away and jabs, "YOU SSSHOULD TRY THAT AGAIN WHEN WE BUH-BOTH HAVE GUN-SSS....MORE SS-SPUH-NNNH-SSPORTING."

Her face breaks open and the luminous shadows whip around and through her head.

"I didn't m-mean to, Audrey."

"BULLSSHITT!"

She slides and flops closer and makes it to my feet, then calves. She leans over my thighs, then inches forward and hovers over my chest, blood drizzling down from her rhythmically leaking wound. It's just a trickle now.

My face burns from the radiant distortions.

"Wh-what are you?"

Audrey glares at me but the freaky subsides some. The leaking has stopped and eyes and face almost look normal again.

"'What are you? What are you?'" Audrey mocks. "I'm not the one who just sshot their loving ssignificant other, I can tell you—" she cringes a little and closes her eyes, "nhn…that."

"I d-didn't mean to," I stammer, almost blinded by her proximity. She opens her eyes.

"Believe me, I've been through wors-se."

She looks up at the shattered remains of the I LOVE YOU sign and says, "Oh dammit, Felickss—look what you didd to the ssign."

I look past her at the wall where the brains and blood were.

Almost clean now. Gotta make a move before she can follow.

Audrey frowns, looks back down at me, and her eyes dart back and forth in thought. They start pulsing stronger again.

"Wait—thiss better not be about thAT TRAS-SHY QUIM AT THE FISH STORE. I DON'T KNOW WHAT SS-SHE'S TOLD YOU BUT I CAN TREAT YOU BETTER THAN SHEE EVER COULD HAVE."

I furrow my brow. "S-Siobhán?"

Oh, this could be bad.

"YOU DO KNOW HER!"

Shit! Throw her off-balance somehow!

"Yeah, 'cause she works at the fish store!"

"DON'T RAISS-Z YOUR VOICSSE AT ME! YOU'RE THE ONE IN TROUBLE HERE! 'SSSHIV-AWN,' HUH? SOUNDSS LIKE A FUCKING MICK LUXURY CAR! YOU THINK SHE'S PRETTY WITH ALL THOSE TATTOOS AND TRIBAL GANGSTER BULLSSHIT AND FUCKED-UP HAIR? I'VE SEEN SOME OF THE PORNO YOU HIDE IN YOUR COMPUTER, FELICKS. I KNOW

YOU LIKE THAT EDGY BULLSHIT.

"YOU THINK SHE'SS PRETTY? YOU WANNA FUCK HER? YOU WANNA FUCK THE SSTREET TRASSH WANDERER HOOKER?! IF I THOUGHT YOU HAD, I WOULD CUT YOUR—" The storm calms dramatically and it's more like the paisley fractal pulsing through her.

"You…you haven't, have you?"

"Wh-what?"

"HAVE YOU FUCKED SSHIV-AWHN?!"

"No!"

"I DON'T BELIEVE YOU! YOU DID, DIDN'T YOU?! I BET YOU WENT DOWN ON HER AND EVERYTHING!"

The burning radiance is so strong now that I can't keep my eyes open.

Do something!

I tuck my left leg up toward my chest and Audrey looks down as I'm tucking my right leg up the same way. Audrey's face whips back up.

"DON'T YOU DARE—"

I kick Audrey off of me and into the kitchen. She slides through what's left of the blood on the kitchen floor and slams into the cupboard under the sink.

I crawl into a crouched run toward the front door and hear a whirring sound and a *thunk* in the hall wall behind me. I glance back and see the kitchen knife Audrey was dicing with and dropped near the sink stuck halfway into the hallway wall where I just was.

"FELICKS, YOU *PUSS*-Y!" Audrey screams from the kitchen. I open the front door and go through it.

"GET BACK H—"

I slam the door behind me.

It only takes a half a block for me to realize I'm running with a loaded gun in my hand and I step into a darkened doorway long enough to stow it in my camera bag, dancing in place out of fear that Audrey is behind me.

Then I'm off again, running up Greenwich toward Coit

Tower, thankful the cops haven't shown up yet.

Two gunshots—they'd have to come, right?

I run without a destination. I just run. Pioneer Park at the base of the tower is almost empty as I book through it in the dark, half expecting Audrey to pop out from behind a tree or drop from the sky and cut me in half with her eyes or something.

I breathe hard and my muscles sting with acid as I run for my life for the third or fourth time today.

I decide to cut down the Filbert steps, a long staircase of wooden and some concrete steps down the other side of Telegraph Hill between the houses and flanked by bushes and trees.

As I'm skipping down the gently creaking steps, a loud, shrill cry from behind and above me almost stops my heart and I spin, rolling my ankle. There's another cry and another and it becomes a cacophony of maddening cackles as I gasp and fall over the wooden railing toward the dark, damp bushes.

The distant part of me realizes it was just those "World Famous" wild parrots of Telegraph Hill and I'm about to chuckle in relief when my head connects with equal parts wooden fence base and dense-packed earth.

Then it's all deep, inky black and gentle, edgeless oblivion.

part three

"And we may never know how much we have done for them...just as they will never know how much we have sacrificed."

chapter 23

Two homeless gutter punks, Adrian and Sharky, stride with purpose down a sidewalk bordering the Panhandle offshoot that stretches east of Golden Gate Park.

Adrian says, "So, what's this big tech piece that can net us so much pony?"

Sharky's eyes scan all around.

"It's a sick video camera. I call this guy Camera Man 'cause I've seen him in different parts of the city just filmin' stuff. Or video-ing, I guess. I think he's fuckin' crazy or somethin' but his camera's real slick. Real new. I hadn't seen him in a while...but he's back now and right down here."

Adrian nods as he looks around too. "Oh, okay. Shasta's mentioned seeing that guy too. Also said he seemed familiar."

"Why do you still hang out with Shasta? She bugs, man."

Adrian scoffs. "Watch it, man. She's special to me."

"Yeah, whatever."

"Hey, if he's crazy, how do we know the camera even works?"

"I seen the lens zoom in and out and stuff. It works, man, don't worry. I seen it."

Sharky stops and pats Adrian on the shoulder, then points toward a grove of trees in the Panhandle. Adrian can make out a supine form resting on a rucksack in the shade from a few of the trees.

Adrian follows Sharky through the park, both of them forcing a casual pace. As they reach the shade of the trees, they become stealthier, sneaking up while looking all around for observers.

"Camera Man" has a black-on-black SF cap over his face and he snores lightly.

Adrian sees several weeks of facial growth on a part of the young man's jawline poking out from one side of the cocked cap and a scar of some kind through the tangled thick of it.

A rectangular bag under one of his arms is promising, though. Looks like a professional camera bag and has a company name stitched into it, but the words have been written over repeatedly with permanent marker to match the black of the bag material.

Adrian looks at Sharky and they make eye contact. Adrian points at Sharky, then the bag before pointing at himself and making a circle with his finger as in "you grab it, I'll keep watch."

Sharky thinks for a long moment about this, then seems to catch on. He creeps over to the Camera Man and crouches by the bag. Adrian looks around, not seeing anyone other than the cars driving down Oak and Fell. Sharky gently lifts Camera Man's arm and his head moves under the hat.

Sharky freezes.

Camera Man mumbles, "Nnnhn…sosorryaudrey. Nnhn…."

The sleeper is still again. Sharky lifts his arm and sets it on the ground and gingerly picks the bag up.

Adrian salivates a bit when he sees the satisfying weight of the bag Sharky is lifting.

Sharky rises to his feet and starts walking quickly but quietly away from the former Camera Man. Adrian lets him pass, then looks around again and turns to start walking toward the edge of the shade.

Sharky looks back toward him and mouths the words, "Too easy," but has to close his eyes as a red dot plays across them. Adrian watches the little bright dot dance around on Sharky's face, then his upper back and back up to his face. He furrows his brow in confusion.

Behind them there's a hacking cough.

"Hey, Sid an' Fancy!"

They look back and freeze. Sharky breathes in sharp and puts his hands up, camera bag dangling from one of them. Adrian just takes it in, unable to move at all.

Camera Man is awake and pointing a large pistol at them with one hand. He's propped up on his other hand but still half on the ground. His hat has dropped to the dirt and grass and the whites of his eyes are red, which makes their contrasting blue and brown irises look even more distinct.

He looks spun on something, Adrian thinks.

"Drop my shit and walk," he says in a gravelly voice, then coughs again. He coughs harder, his eyes close most of the way, and the gun droops a bit.

Adrian looks sideways at Sharky, who gets that he's thinking about running, he's pretty sure.

The red-blue-brown eyes lock on Adrian and he feels the dot dancing on his chest whether he's imagining it or not.

Camera Man cocks the hammer on the revolver.

"Bullets go fast, junkie fuck-stick. That thing in the bag is more trouble than it's worth."

Adrian is trying to see if there are bullets in the cylinder. Thinking through the fear now, he remembers the fixed hunting knife he has strapped on the inside of his left shin. Camera Man must notice because he raises the pistol a bit and the laser dot forces Adrian to blink a few times.

"Oh, it's loaded, bitch. Now…. Drop. My. Shit. And. Walk."

Sharky slowly sets the camera bag down and steps back, raising his hands again. Adrian raises his too, deciding that risking a rush assault would end badly either way.

Camera Man gestures with the gun for them to go and says, "Get the fuck on!"

They spin and walk quickly back to the sidewalk and book out of sight.

I lower the pistol and my hand starts shaking. There's only one live round left in the cylinder. One would do some damage, but maybe not enough.

That could have gone very badly.

That's what the gravelly voice was for. I put on my most genuine sounding (Solid) Snake Plissken / Adam Jensen / Dirty Harry, and did my best not to dip over into *Dark Knight* Batman voice. That would have been a tad too much. The voice wasn't too hard considering how much I've been smoking since diving off the wagon. Back up to a pack and a half to two some days from almost none for a long while.

I tuck my revolver back into a black leather holster I stitched into the reinforced lining of my hooded German Army parka. In the interest of blending in, I've cobbled together a decent Uncle Salty cosplay from military surplus shops.

I take a Kamel out of its red and tan pack in my BDU pocket and light it with a vintage trench lighter I acquired yesterday after deciding to return to the City.

I've been bumming around Concord, Antioch, Bay Point and on around to San Mateo and Burlingame, and even Dublin and Pleasanton just recording weird shit on video for several weeks. Basically, any spot on the BART line I wouldn't be in normally and that also wouldn't be too uptight about a homeless guy sleeping around outside.

At first, it was just to escape Audrey and Fleischmann and everything I'd seen in the City. Then it became aimless wandering and coming to accept that as far as I went, it was the same. It wasn't that San Francisco was infested with all the weird creatures and plants and monsters and all of it—it was like that everywhere I went. Eventually, I was struck with a new purpose—to document.

I charge my camera at coffee shops and libraries and keep up on the news. There's still nothing about a manhunt under way for the whole…Audrey thing.

I guess if I could survive a gunshot to the head, I wouldn't go around advertising it either. I imagine the torches and pitchforks would come out PDQ.

Yesterday, I chanced going to a barber in Palo Alto. My hair got trimmed down to a four all around, which makes it about even with my facial growth. The barber had to hold his breath a lot, but it got done. Even with my liberal use of spray deodorant, I'm a little ripe from sleeping out and only rarely making use of showers and other resources made available for the homeless.

My surplus ensemble is probably a little silly but I look nothing like I normally would and that's the idea, right? If this goes right, I'll be in and out anyway.

My hand is still shaking as I drag on the cigarette and hold the smoke in my lungs before letting it pour out of my mouth.

I haul myself up, pick up my SF cap, and cross to the HDV-426 in its bag. Pick it up and walk back to my rucksack on the ground and set the bag down. Put the cap back on and look around this currently sleepy end of the

Panhandle.

Time for another pill? Certainly.

I take three to four Wahrheit pills a day now. Even got pretty high at first when taking that many but now just have a lot of nervous energy and don't sleep much.

"Steall-ing isz wronhng…thie–vhz arestealers—that's– wraaauu-ung."

Grieves is sitting up in the tree I was sleeping at the base of and he's lambasting the two young street punks for trying to make off with my property.

I assume Grieves can still see them from his higher vantage point and imagine him "crushing their heads" *Kids in the Hall* style with his index finger and thumb in a little vertical pincer motion in front of one of his big, wet eyes.

I sling the camera bag over my shoulder and put the rucksack on. Then flip the hood up over the SF cap and put on my other surplus store accessory: a pair of mirrored aviator sunglasses to complete my little Uncle Salty look. I've been going pretty home/free of late, after all.

"Good morning, Grieves."

"Nammesnaught that. Ayethink so nn-ot. Or maybe…."

Grieves keeps babbling while watching the punks, but trails off into a quieter volume, thankfully. He does that sometimes. He'll start to whisper things while he stares at you. He seems to think you are still in the conversation and will even make little jabs about how you are rude for not responding.

I look up at the fluffy, patchy clouds, then to the horizon. A wall of huge, dark thunderheads is coming in from the west.

Hella rain coming in. Should be a big one. Maybe even some lightning.

I start walking east toward the end of the Panhandle and look back over my shoulder and watch Grieves mumble up in the tree.

Grieves looks down and sees that I'm not where I was.

He looks all around, his neck phasing a bit into itself and rotating past a natural turn.

He looks like a damn owl when he does that, and even more freaky.

Grieves sees me walking away and frowns.

I wave for him to follow, knowing he would anyway but it never hurts to make Grieves feel wanted. It's better than when he gets all sullen and butthurt that I don't seem to want him around every second.

Grieves's body rotates to line up with his head as he descends into the tree trunk, disappears completely for a moment, and then strolls out of its side at ground level smiling like a puppy.

He follows me out of the Panhandle and down Oak, heading east toward downtown.

chapter 24

Colorful tentacles and bulbs and knobs of translucent, glowing strangeness filled with little organs and fluid conduits pulse and slither on most of the people in the area. People covered in small patches on up to whole planter's worth of the glowing flowers and as many little beelike buzzers. Almost every person driving down the street or walking or riding a bike has some form of hitchhiker or growth in them or on them. Spiderflies, slints, burrowpedes, little see-through crab things I first noticed a couple weeks ago I call "grabbits," and moving, organ-filled ooze blobs I just call "amoebas" because that's what they struck me as.

The amoebas are Kaiju-sized by regular amoeba standards but similar in look and movement. A girl walks down the sidewalk with one in her face, dense enough that her left eye can't be seen through it as it writhes and undulates. Another person with one in their head and neck passes her and the two amoebas stretch to reach each other, successfully intermingling their long, bulbous pseudopods for just a moment before being pulled apart like parent and child or star-crossed lovers or street fighters. Hard to say which.

I cruise east through the intersection at Divisadero and Oak and watch two air-swimmers—the dolphin- and small-whale-sized creatures I've seen chasing the big blimpwhales around—play with each other under the overhang at a gas station. They twist and whip around, chasing each other and nuzzling their head regions together when they make contact. It's like a dogfight between squishy, organic jets. They interact with each other just fine, colliding and such but they glide clean through the bored and impatient people pumping gas into their cars.

I chuckle to myself and wonder if the fumes get the creatures worked up.

I'm tempted to take out my camera but the drive is almost full. I've been busy these past weeks in between stoned accidental trespassing adventures and narrowly escaping the secret enforcement teams I'd first noticed after starting to take more than one pill a day. If people start to seem like they can see, the vents open up like in Rudy's footage and gas them back to oblivious bliss—but a few times, I noticed the gas didn't work. And a couple times, I caught glimpses of the intended targets wearing clear, barely visible breathing masks with tubes that disappeared down into their jacket or into a satchel that must have contained air canisters.

When the gas vents were circumvented, vans—like those I'd seen outside Wahrheit's place the last time I was there—would roll up and spill out what I came to think of as monster cops.

Most of them I thought of as Snow Globers and they looked like something between a combat soldier and an early astronaut—their sealed body armor resembling the interior pressure suits Apollo astronauts wore under the EVA coverings more commonly associated with moon shots. Complete with a fixed-glass or plexiglass bubble pressure helmet on top—only instead of breathable air, the monster cops' helmets contained faintly glowing fluids that swirled around their decaying dead-eyed heads—heads that also had something like padded cloth Soviet tank helmets on them inside too, increasing the old pressure suit similarities.

While stealthily observing these SGs whenever possible, I had also noticed that detritus from their decaying heads and faces would detach like big dandruff flakes and float to the bottom. So, if they moved quickly and stopped, those flakes would get kicked up and float around their heads like snow. Once there was a certain amount of the buildup, some sort of vacuum port inside seemed to suck the necro-dandruff out of the bubble from below, another topping it off with more of the glowing fluid.

These monster cops even had two-inch-thick tubes connecting their suits to a weird machine inside their vans, and if they had to go farther from it than about a hundred feet, the tubes detached and retracted back into the vehicle, and they had tanks of whatever that tube had been supplying on their backs that activated, but those didn't seem to last long. Reminded me of the "mechs" in *Neon Genesis Evangelion*.

Then there were the bigger ones, like a tactical baseball-umpire cosmonaut five feet across and nine feet tall. Those big ones carried gas guns connected to big tanks on their backs—and their snow-globe helmets had external add-ons with sets of clicking lenses and diopters on wire-pulley rigs. Their globes were harder to see into and their heads harder to make out, causing shadowy glimpses of layered, pulsing somethings squirming around, even less human than the SGs. I'd never seen eyes in those globes, but I figured all the lenses and such had to be for something. I dubbed those Fat Boys.

I got footage of all this, and much more. That's actually

what brings me back to the city—

A young woman almost hits me with her candy-pink, days-old paper-license-plated Bentley Continental as she blows through a red light. I'm pretty sure the interior is black and pink zebra striped. Zebra of all things. She's talking on her mobile phone and seems oblivious to anything else. I try to kick the rear panel of her lovely, expensive automobile to wake her up but she's going so fast, I miss and stumble and have to take a few steps to regain my footing. She never stops.

I yell, "Crazy bitch!"

She's almost to the next intersection down the way already. I shake my head and continue on.

Blimpwhales moan and sing to each other in the sky above downtown, and a few of them swim through the air between a patch of the dark chunks of asteroid belt weirdness. Different sets of chunks seem to revolve around unseen points of what I assume are gravity wells from objects in different layers of reality.

About the time I started taking too much medicine with my nips of the ol' Irish, I could swear I saw a tiny silhouette of a human shape standing on what looked like an artificial cutout on one of these larger, slower ones. I was just lying down on the side of a small mountain above Colma watching all the different chunks glide and slam around amidst fluffy thunderheads. Whistling the tune of "Voices" from *Macross Plus* for some reason I couldn't place. Something about watching things float in the sky brought it to mind.

This chunk's orbit caused it to come closer to the ground than usual and I was just high enough up on the mountainside to make out the little guy or whatever it was. I guess he would have been normal size, just real high up. Probably my imagination, though, anyway. I was soused, not gonna lie.

The chess games on Market Street are going strong

at several sets of neatly arranged plastic tables and chairs arranged in rows. When not in use, each table has a chessboard and set of pieces ready for play. Right now, they are all in use. Some of the players are homeless. Some are locals with homes. Some are tourists that must have heard about the Market Street chess arena and decided to stop by and get whooped on by the genuinely wicked-skilled regulars.

I sat down for a game once. It lasted one minute and nine seconds. I think he took an extra-long time checkmating me so it would end up at "69" seconds.

In amongst the regulars and noob suckers today, there are two men I haven't seen before playing each other. They look homeless but a little strange too. Their big duffle bags and thick, warm clothes are normal but there is something off.

I'm walking up the sidewalk perpendicular to the table arrangement so I can only see the face of one of them. That one is a small white man with light brown hair and large blue eyes. They are a little too large, which makes them look odd. He looks kind of like caricatures I've seen of the actor Peter Lorre. The man across from Big Blue Eyes with his back to me has graying blond hair and is larger.

A trio of blimpwhales soars over Market Street moan-singing and I look around for onlookers before casually looking up and watching through my mirrored shades. I tilt my head and scratch my ear just in case. I smile a bit at the playful frolicking of the behemoths.

As I look down, I see that Big Blue Eyes is watching the blimpers too. He looks back down and locks eyes with me, having obviously just looked down from them also. It feels almost like he's looking straight through my aviators. He studies my face and clothes, then mumbles something across the chessboard to the taller man.

I try to look natural as I shift course toward Market Street itself with the intention of hurriedly jaywalking across. I don't know what their trip is and surely don't want to. The F Market streetcar is cruising down the center of Market toward us from the Embarcadero end.

The taller weird hobo looks back at me and does a double take. His eyes are the same too-large orbs with rings of unnatural, plastic blue. On casual inspection, the eyes look real if not a bit big. Closer scrutiny reveals them to be subtly odd and unsettling.

Upon seeing me, the taller man stands up, jostling the chessboard and knocking over several pieces. In a raspy, low voice, the man says, "Hey! You there!"

The shorter man stands and slings his duffel bag.

Uninterested in waiting to see what they want, I bolt across Market Street, weaving in between swerving, honking cars. I look back as I reach the south sidewalk and see the taller man sling his duffel bag and take a few steps toward the street but then stop. Something concealed under his long coat was moving too freely for his liking and he adjusts it before continuing to give chase.

Oh, that can't be good….

I run down the sidewalk as fast as possible, which isn't one hundred percent. I need to cut down on the smokes, damn. Haven't had to run for a while and all the smoking is catching up with me. Just hope that doesn't make it so they do the same. But my pace is strong enough that they aren't gaining yet at least.

The tall man yells, "Stop! We just want to—shit!"

I look back and see the men dodge the honking F Market streetcar, the small one juking over to my side and the taller one having to rush parallel to us on the other.

I just keep hoofing it hard and make it to the corner of 10th, then cut south around it and run across the street at an angle heading southeast. See an alley street and run into it without looking back.

I run through puddles in the asphalt in the shadows of the buildings. About halfway down the alley the southern building is only one story, as opposed to the twelve or so on the corner I came in on, and bordering the far end. The dim light trickling from the overcast sky brightens a bit and the shadows seem to grow darker as the contrast intensifies. The light goes from a dim trickle to a vibrant pour.

I slow to a gasping stop in the bright patch of sidewalk and outer building wall, then walk slowly through it using the wall to steady myself and enjoy the warmth for once.

Fighting to breathe through a hacking cough, I look back down the alley, hoping to watch the strange men pass quickly by—and the smaller man does!

But the taller, older-looking man glances into the alley and shuffles to a stop. Shit. He calls to his faster, smaller comrade before entering the alley.

I force myself back into a medium run and hurry into the shadow of the far building, missing the warmth almost instantly. Look back and see the men approaching the big rectangle of brightness and imagine them burning and sizzling in it like creatures of the night or maybe even being literally flattened against the lit-up wall by an invisible trash compactor wall of power.

I need to cut down on the smokes and the pills.

As if to spite my fantasy vision, the clouds swallow the warmth and light back up just as the men run through it.

Booking out of the alley and down the sidewalk bordering 9th, I see the intersection with Mission and what I hope is a stop for the 14 bus. I throw all I have into running down and across 9th, backed by a chorus of angry honks. Make it down to Mission and see the walk sign so I start to run across the crosswalk between a few other people stepping off the curb—

And get upended by a car attempting to run their red light and slam into its windshield with my bad left shoulder and that side of my face. Shoulder doesn't pop out again, but it doesn't feel good either as it strains against its bonds.

Come on—the one time I use a crosswalk?

The car squeals to a stop and I'm thrown off onto the street and roll over a couple times. I groan deep as I haul myself off the asphalt. Pick up my hat and replace my aviators back over my blue left eye from their new hanging position over my right eye and mouth. I don't want to wait for the apology from the mortified-looking man who is getting out of the car, so I put my hat on and turn toward the bus stop.

The man is large and muscular and has a crew cut, which seems to squirm and wriggle with popping veins. Not to mention the tentacles writhing like ferns in the wind in the surface of his head and chest.

"What the fuck is wrong with you?!" the man demands. As he yells, the tentacles flutter and writhe on the side of his face, a smaller part curling into his mouth and squirming like the arm of a small living octopus.

Okay, so apology was a bit much to expect, I guess? Oh, I gotcha: sleeveless Tapout shirt to go with Vanilla Ice mustang and crew cut.

I wave him off and say, "Don't worry about me. My fault, my fault." I see the 14 bus coming from down near 8th and try to head for the bus stop but the man grabs my jacket by the hood and the strap of the HDV-426 bag and pulls me back.

"You're lucky you didn't crack my fucking windshield, faggot!"

I don't appreciate the man grabbing my things so roughly like he is and I start to get mad. I spin around, wrench the man's arm off my jacket with a wide swiping motion, and say, "Suck my dick, bro-beef."

The tough guy is ready to go now and says, "Whatthefuck-yousaytome, bitch?!"

The man raises his arms to push me but out of reflex I've already brought my arms up between the man's with my hands close together like I'm making a steeple with my fingers and I whip them outward, throwing the man's arms wide to his sides. Then I lift my leg and drive my boot down at an angle into the man's right knee and it bends the wrong way and pops.

Shouldn't lock your legs, coolguy.

The man screams in pain as he collapses and his head hits the front-left windshield on his car, a little spiderweb appearing in the surface as he flops down to the ground.

I want to kick his face and gut until he stops moving but I fight it off. I bend over and get real close to the man's face, which he's covering defensively with his arms now.

"There's your crack, you big pink bitch! And I said 'suck…muh *deeeiiiick*'!"

RIP ODB. Big Baby Jesus forever.

I remember myself and why I was running as I notice the two weird homeless guys watching from the sidewalk back up 9th, apparently wary of the small crowd forming near me.

The bus pulls in on the other side of the street and I limp around the back of it and up to the doors.

People are calling for me to deal with the man on the ground. Some are calling for justice in my favor and some in the man's. I ignore them and pay the fare in the machine as the bus driver eyes me cautiously. I look through the windows as I walk down the aisle and see the two hobos at the corner watching me and arguing about what to do. I sit as the bus speeds off.

Those weird bum guys can fuck off along with the lookie-loos. Okay, back to business. After a few stops, I'll double back and get off around 8th.

The sky darkens as I get off a few stops down and get on the next 14 going back the way I came. As I pass the next 14 coming the other way, I duck down in my seat and scan the passengers as it blows by. Sure enough, the weird hobos are standing up in it, holding poles as they watch out the windows all around for signs of me. They don't spot me, and I rise up in my seat again.

Then the bus passes the intersection where I was hit and fought the meathead. He's on a gurney being lifted into the back of an ambulance.

I feel a pang of guilt through the anger and self-righteousness I initially felt in the haze of adrenaline right after the fight.

Really, though, if you're going to hit someone with your car by running a light, then try to fight them, maybe you earned that limp.

I'm actually more concerned with reaching my destination without being spotted now than any perceived slight from these strangers who watched me defend myself / attack that poor, poor bro-hemoth.

I have so much to do.

It's sprinkling by the time the bus pulls in and stops at 9th and Mission. I flip my hood up over my hat and let the light droplets speckle on the outer surface of my aviators as I walk down 9th watching for cop cars or the occasional SFPD beat officer.

I step into a doorway overhang and light a smoke, then continue on, taking drags from it occasionally, holding it by the butt and keeping my hand cupped around it.

chapter 25

I walk down Rincon until I come to a big warehouse vehicle door. The blue light bulb in the fixture above the smaller entry door of the warehouse is on. Probably from the night before.

Press a button by the door and hear the muffled sound of a B-movie actress screaming in terror inside the warehouse. I shift on my feet for a full minute, then press it again. Another, different scream. I wait another minute and reach for the button again but hear shuffling steps and grumbling in Japanese about stupid nuisances and the value of patience.

Hirofumi unlocks the door and swings it open, squinting out from the dark warehouse interior like he's staring at the sun. His hair is wild and unwashed and he's wearing royal-blue silk pajama bottoms with bare feet and an old Mickey Mouse shirt. The feeling of familiarity almost chokes me up. I've been out of the loop with normality for a decent bit and Hirofumi is a very welcome sight.

Hirofumi scowls, rubs his stubbly chin, and demands, "What do you need? I don't pay beggars!"

I smile sheepishly.

"Well? I don't need smiles! Go away, man!"

I realize my disguise must be more effective than I thought.

"Hiro, it's me."

Hirofumi scowls and says, "Get away from here!"

I take off the aviators and tilt the SF cap up a bit as Hiro says, "I will call the police—" Hirofumi squints, cocks his head, and says, "*Hontou ni*...Felix?!" His face brightens and he widens his eyes. "*Doushita no?! Genki desu ka?!*"

I laugh. "*Genki desu!*"

Hirofumi wraps himself around me in a bear hug, even lifting his legs around my back so that I have to hold him up. Hiro gyrates up and down on me and yells, "*Iroppi!*"

I laugh and help Hirofumi down.

Hirofumi grabs my shoulder and leans against it at arm's length, looking me up and down. He smiles and screws up his face as he says, "Your clothes are stupid! You look like my game characters!"

"I know, I know. It worked, though, didn't it?"

Hirofumi looks a little confused by that answer but nods, pulling me into the warehouse by my shoulder with a big smile on his face.

Hirofumi closes the door behind us and locks it. We walk in through the old administrative and control rooms on the first floor below the "house" upstairs. Hirofumi's office and studios are down here.

As we enter the warehouse proper, I see that the projectors have been hooked up around the warehouse again like the night of the beta party months ago. Seems like years at this point.

The different projectors are currently throwing moving images of the Disney version of *Swiss Family Robinson* from the '60s and direct *Home/Free* feeds from different players exploring the looming, stark city in search of colorful recyclables or comically large bottles of alcohol. The audio from both sources is audible but the movie is loud enough to make out over the sounds of the city's different locations. Low under both I can hear a Portishead track. Probably coming from their "house" upstairs.

"Wandering Star," I think it's called.

The rows of computers in the rough center of the warehouse are still installed too and there are several people sitting in the rows with laptops hooked up next to the desktop stations they are playing *Home/Free* on.

Must all be working on the game in some way.

Oscar sits at a workstation drawing with a digital tablet hooked up to one of the computers. He looks up from his hobo variations and sees me.

"Holy shit! You alright?"

I nod. "Yeah, I'm cool."

"I'm glad!"

On the end of one of the rows sits Yevgeny, Weyland-Yutani–symbol-emblazoned knit cap hanging casually off the top and back of his head like a reservoir tip on a rubber. He's wearing a PC headset that wraps around the back of his head. His red-ringed crystal-blue eyes leave his screen and land on me and his face slowly forms into a relieved smile.

Yevgeny takes off the headset and rests it around his neck. "Hey, Felix! I knew you'd show up. These fools were worried. I told them you just need to go on walkabout to finish *Brain Wrap* script!" Yevgeny laughs until he coughs for a bit.

I notice glowing spidermites crawling languidly in and out of Yevgeny's nose and mouth. Some disappear into his face through his jaw or cheek. Others seem to be waiting for something. Yevgeny picks up a small bong from near his keyboard and hits it with a lighter. As he takes a nice-size hit, the spider things on his face quickly crawl back into his nose and mouth. He holds it and lets it out slowly, mouth open in a big oval.

The spiders come, tumbling out of his nose and mouth, some lazily grabbing for a hold on his face at the last moment while the others just roll down onto his lap and thighs. Yevgeny chortles in short bursts as the last of the hit burps out of his mouth. This sends a last wave of stoned spiders pouring out, their glow pulsing now.

Trippy.

I try to match Yevgeny's enthusiasm and say, "Yeah, that was totally it! *Brain Wrap*! How you been, man?"

Yevgeny gestures around at the pipe and the computer in front of him as if to say, "How could I complain?"

I nod my understanding and follow Hirofumi to the stairs up to the house inside the warehouse.

Hirofumi says, "Zhenya, come on. I need you to keep stress-testing those new features."

"Just saying hi to a good friend I thought might be dead somewhere in ditch, master."

"I thought he was writing his screenplay," Hirofumi retorts.

Yevgeny raises his eyebrows. "One or the other, yeah?"

Hirofumi swats the air in disgust, then pantomimes someone using a mouse and keyboard in deep concentration. Yevgeny sets his bong down and flips Hirofumi off with one hand as he lifts his headset back up over his ears and mouth with the other.

I follow Hirofumi up the stairs into the living area. The soothing sounds of Portishead get louder as we climb, especially when Hirofumi opens the shop door at the top. He holds it open, and I enter past him.

Shortly after moving into the warehouse, Hirofumi and Kaori installed a bunch of thin-panel monitors around their livings areas and finished them off with mock window frames, some even with curtains. These artificial windows make the building's industrial confines feel less cave-like.

The first one I see is a view out onto Machu Picchu in Peru. Huayna Picchu looms in the background as Hirofumi leads me to the big bedroom. Windows in here now look out onto an ice floe in the arctic. Kaori is lying on her back on the big bed, head obscured by a big manga anthology magazine she has propped on her stomach.

That one has her favorite serial, *Hook-up Battle Fight*. It's about a competitive underground crocheting league. Crochet to the death! There's also a subplot about a shady organization needing an intricate mandala thing crocheted to bring about heavenly peace or damnation or something.

Hirofumi crosses to the bed and gently tugs on Kaori's sock-covered toes. She makes a cute sound of annoyance and disapproval. He tugs again. She slaps the magazine down on her chest and exclaims, "*Fuzakeru na!*"

Kaori sees me and she drops her comic on the bed, rolls off it, and wraps herself around me, hugging tightly.

"Don't do that! You are mean to worry us!" Kaori says half into my chest.

Hirofumi says, "Yeah, jerk. You're not cool."

"I'm really sorry, guys. I had to get away. Audrey—" I stop myself when I realize I have no idea how to explain what's going on with her or if I should.

Plus, I have no idea myself.

Kaori asks, "Where is Audrey? She's not here with you?"

"No. I haven't seen her in a while."

Kaori pulls her head away from my chest and frowns a little, then looks sideways at Hirofumi but he ignores it.

Instead, he asks, "So, why are you here, man?"

"I need your help with something."

"Have you talked with Audrey at all?" Kaori asks.

I think for a second. "No. We…. We had a fight."

"Felix, it's been weeks since you—"

Hirofumi interrupts Kaori, "What kind of help?"

Hirofumi and I enter his editing and programming

computer room on the first floor. Kaori stands at the threshold. Other than the light from some blue bulbs in the hallway it's almost pitch black down here. Kaori breathes in and out deeply and deliberately and makes a little nasal cooing sound until Hirofumi notices and he flicks the switch to a soft bulb in the ceiling.

Kaori is super nyctophobic. They have silly nightlights in their bedroom and installed anywhere with a plug from there to the bathroom they use.

Hirofumi's main workspace was installed within the old main electrical room for the warehouse and, unlike the heavily altered upstairs, most everything down here is original besides a few framed movie posters and three computers and a cable patch bay installed on a long metal table they slid in from the warehouse floor.

There are also racks of video and film equipment against the far wall and a long, puffy green couch against the wall opposite the computer table.

There's only one chair in front of the computers at the moment, so Hirofumi grabs a padded folding chair from against the wall, opens it, and sets it down a few feet down the table from his throne of an ergonomic computer chair.

Kaori flops down on the couch, I take the folding chair, and Hirofumi sits in his master-control throne.

Hirofumi rotates back and forth in his chair like an impatient child and says, "Okay, what do you want to show us?"

I unsling my pack and camera bag. I set the packs down on the floor near the folding chair and the camera bag on the metal table. Then unzip the bag and say, "Proof."

"Of what?" Hirofumi and Kaori ask, one starting right after the other.

"That I'm not delusional and I'm not hallucinating. I was in the hospital for the wrong reasons."

"You are joking," Hirofumi says with a frown.

Kaori lets out a disappointed sigh and looks at the

ceiling.

"Seriously. Listen, you are the closest friends I have. Give me one chance."

Hirofumi and Kaori look at each other. Kaori's face is a mask of guarded disapproval, but she doesn't say anything.

"Please."

Hirofumi looks away from Kaori and nods affirmative to me. "One chance."

I open the bag and take the HDV-426 out, then set it on the table.

Hirofumi studies it and asks, "What kind of tape?"

"Solid state drive. They went with USB three-point-oh."

"I have that," Hirofumi says as he presses a few switches and re-hooks a BNC-tipped cable from one spot to another on the patch bay to his left. I hook a cable to the camera and hand the other end to Hirofumi. He hooks it to an extension, which disappears behind his patch bay.

Hirofumi gently slaps the spacebar on his keyboard, shooing away his animated looping screensaver depicting Winnie the Pooh doing calisthenics in front of a mirror.

"Okay, where do I go?"

"It saves in separate raw files. They can be opened as AVIs. Just access it like a drive."

Hirofumi navigates to his drive list and opens "HDV-426," then peruses a set of folders for firmware and PDFs of instruction manuals. He double-clicks the "CLIPS" folder icon. There are hundreds of them on the drive. Hirofumi right-clicks on a blank spot in the window and switches the view to thumbnails. The small images themselves aren't that strange. He looks at me with his "Well?" expression.

"Just open one, man," I say, anxious about getting past the convincing part and on to my planned task at hand.

Hirofumi double-clicks on an image of people walking down the sidewalk near a busy street. This should be good.

That's a shot from Walnut Creek. I was crossing through an intersection and some of the dolphin-sized swimmers flew into view from inside a Fuddruckers building and chased each other through the air over the street and then a parking lot before disappearing over the Target it serves.

Hirofumi frowns and says, "What am I looking for?"

The sights and sounds of the swimmer's frolicking are clear as day to me. "Are you serious? Play it again."

Hirofumi restarts it and I lean forward. When the swimmers emerge from over the Fuddruckers, I extend my hand and trace their movement on the screen, careful not to touch it and piss Hirofumi off. One of his other huge pet peeves.

"See that? Either way, don't you hear it?" I ask.

Hirofumi's eyes follow my fingers and he concentrates. "I see something like blurry swirling. Hear what?"

I hear the swimmers chiding each other clearly in their strange ways.

I shake my head. "Try another one."

Hirofumi does. The image is of a field. The me of that moment is panning as if to follow something.

A bulbous creature with tall, spindly legs lopes awkwardly, the thin appendages disappearing into the ground at different angles like it's walking on a different surface the ground conceals. I remember one of those things coming at me and Grieves on a hill like it was going to eat us—which is where my other few remaining pistol rounds were spent, other than that last one. Grieves hopped up and wrestled it like it was a big dog until it shook him and shambled off in apparent terror. Grieves was bummed to lose his new buddy.

I watch Hirofumi examine the screen with a look of skepticism.

"I don't see anything."

I point at the thing and follow its movements with my finger.

Hirofumi says, "There's some blurring or something like the other but I would not call it proof of anything."

It occurs to me that you might have to look through the camera or be on Wahrheit meds to see it like I do.

But I haven't seen anything in the warehouse other than those things using stoned Yevgeny as a thrill park. That probably wouldn't be a good place to start.

"Try another."

Kaori makes a scoffing sound of exasperation from behind us on the couch. She gets up and walks toward the doorway. Hirofumi stops her with a sound in his throat and a kind of whine sound. She turns back and looks at me. I can't take the expression so I look away and pretend to check cables on the patch bay. She's looking at me like I'm another person. Someone she doesn't like.

In my peripheral vision, I see Kaori spin her index finger around near her ear while mouthing "*kuru-kuru…*," then make a fist and flick all of her fingers up and out like a little explosion, mouthing a big silent "*PA!*"—a Japanese expression similar to the western finger spinning gesture for "cuckoo" or "crazy."

Then she whispers something low in Japanese about Hirofumi trying to see something that isn't there and how she loves me too but wanting to see something doesn't make it real. Hirofumi tries to protest but she's already gone down the hall by the time I look over.

Hirofumi shakes his head and looks at the screen. He takes a cigarette out of a pack on the table and lights it, then takes a big drag.

As he exhales, he says, "You said one chance."

"Hiro, come on. Maybe if we go outside and you look through the camera."

"No, I don't think so," he says before taking another drag. I take my pack of smokes out and light one.

Hirofumi notices and says, "Audrey is going to kill you."

"Yeah, we'll see. I don't know how to make you see this shit other than the camera, but I'm not going to fight you in the alley over it." I imagine picking up Hirofumi, throwing him on the ground, and laying an elbow drop down on him before trying to force him to look at a passing swarm of spiderflies through the viewfinder.

Then the last part of Kaori's scolding of Hirofumi reminds me of something Rudy did the first time I went to Wahrheit's house.

"Okay, play another one," I say.

"Why?"

"Just play one. If this doesn't do it, I'll let you drive me to the FMC. Hell, I'll drive."

"Yeah, right. You get the sweats on Autopia, Felix."

"Look, there's not much for me out here if my best friends don't believe me."

Hirofumi takes another drag, exhales, and opens another clip, all while staring into my eyes like he wants to slap me. When the clip opens, he rolls his eyes toward the screen.

A man sits in a Mr. Pickle's Sandwich Shop in a strip mall in Dublin (CA). The view a telephoto zoom from table level across the shop.

Hirofumi looks over at me again. He raises his eyebrows in mock expectance.

I say, "Okay, you see this guy. He's loving this sammich like it's his first time stuck up in someone. Normal looking guy, yeah?"

"Exactly."

"There are glowing, see-through tentacles all over his face that are swatting away smaller glowy see-through bug things."

"Bullshit."

"Glowing, flicking tentacles. Glowy bugs."

"Not that I can see."

"Now...." I extend my hand again and do a quick continuous sketch of the moving tentacles and the movement of the bugs with my index finger. "Glowing tentacles and bugs."

"I see blurring still."

"Let your eyes relax a little. Glowing tentacles and bugs all in and around his face."

"I don't see it." Hirofumi seems to be really trying now.

"Let them relax like a stereogram. Remember those? Kinda like that."

I continue to follow the movement of the tentacles and bugs on the screen. Hirofumi blinks a few times, then tries to relax.

"Yeah, but I sucked at those things—what the…?"

"What?"

Hirofumi leans forward for the first time, blinking and squinting at his screen. "I think I see them."

The clip freezes, paused at its end. He restarts it and silently watches the whole thing again.

Hirofumi turns and looks into my eyes, waiting for a smirk or anything to relieve his confusion. I just stare gravely and nod in the affirmative that Hirofumi saw what I wanted him to.

Hirofumi opens another clip, this time a view of the sky above the Carquinez Bridge, part of a toll road on the way up to Glen Cove and Vallejo.

Hirofumi asks, "Alright, what's in this one?"

I trace and follow the movement as I describe what I already see to a newly fascinated Hirofumi.

"It's a blimpwhale. That's what I call them. See-through and glowy like the tentacles and a lot of the other stuff out there. It's floating through the air and like barrel-rolling around the bridge. They love that. They fly around whatever they come across. Chase each other too. I saw one—"

"Just tell me what it looks like," Hirofumi interrupts as gently as he can in his state of cautious excitement.

I realize I got ahead of myself and trudge through my embarrassment, describing and sketching until Hirofumi's eyebrows slowly rise and his eyes widen.

"*Masaka.*"

Hirofumi restarts the clip and watches in amazement.

He blinks deliberately a few times before relaxing again. He starts another and I sketch the scene of a bulb pumping through the air with my words and hand. Then a clip of a few swimmers racing each other down a street, diving in and through cars on their way to an unseen finish line. A zoomed-in close-up of spiderflies buzzing around a big dog's head trying to claw burrowpedes out of its face. The zoom pulls out a bit and the oblivious owner pulls the dog on a leash.

I guide Hirofumi through a few more, always leaving out descriptions of the myriad black chunks looming in the sky and why once in a while there's a shot of a white van that seems out of place without explanation of the blue-black equipment and antennas on top or the monster cosmonaut cops they haul around inside.

A clip of a luminous amoeba roughly ten feet across crawling through a vacant lot with beams of bright light pouring out through intermittent breaks in its surface comes to an end. Hirofumi looks down at his keyboard, eyes darting back and forth in thought. His excitement has become confusion and maybe a little fear.

"You had this done by someone? Professional effects hidden in optical interference pattern or something? Like an illusion?"

I shake my head. "Those are raw shots. Haven't touched a computer that could do anything like that in weeks. Not that I would know how to anyway. Not like this."

Hirofumi grimaces and keeps searching his mind for a rational answer. "Then it's in the camera. Automatic motion tracking, rendering, and some kind of visual encryption. A big practical joke by disgruntled designer?"

"Sure, except that I see this stuff *without* the camera."

Hirofumi locks eyes with me. "No way. That's bullshit."

"I shit you not."

Hirofumi thinks some more, then gets out of his throne and crosses to the hallway. He leaves the room and I hear him yelling at Yevgeny.

"Zhen-ya! Don't ignore me, shithead! Come back here. I said come back here! Oh, and you too please, Oscar."

I hear Yevgeny grumbling in Russian.

Hirofumi comes back in and sits, and Yevgeny enters a moment later, holding his small bong and lighter in one hand and an unopened bottle of Anchor's Old Foghorn in the other. He sits on the big couch behind us and sets his piece on a metal end table. Oscar comes in and sits on the big arm of the couch. Yevgeny uses the lighter to pop his bottle top and sets it next to the pipe. The bottle cap hits the concrete floor with a tinny sound and I wince. A memory I don't want tries to pierce its way to the fore. Yevgeny puts the bottle under his nose and inhales, holds it, and lets it out with a squeak.

"That's the shit, man," Yevgeny says before taking a swig off his bottle.

Oscar shakes his head. "Well, I guess it's five o'clock somewhere."

Hirofumi says, "Get serious."

Yevgeny nods. "Okay then. Hey top, what's the op?"

"Just watch this," Hirofumi says, then double-clicks the sandwich guy with the tentacles and glowy gnats clip.

Hirofumi raises his hand like he intends to start describing and sketching the weird stuff for Yevgeny like I did for him—but before he can, Yevgeny laughs and says, "Woah, that's crazy-looking shit, dude!"

Hirofumi and I look back at him and he goes back and forth with a "what?" expression on his buzzed face. Oscar frowns and leans forward a bit.

Hirofumi asks, "What do you see?"

"The smooth squid arms all around his face and the bugs. I love the translucence and light and color, but it looks kind of fake animating. His hands and sandwich go through the arms like they aren't there. And the bugs."

Hirofumi looks at me and I shrug, unable to help with

an explanation of why Yevgeny can see the weird things on video already. Oscar squints at the screen.

Yevgeny takes another swig, swallows, and says, "There should be, like, collision or something. Did you use Blender or finally just torrent Maya or something, you pirate fucks?"

I wonder if Yevgeny being quicker to see is related to his inebriation. Like, his eyes are more relaxed and so is he?

Oscar shakes his head and says, "Huh? I don't see it."

"Don't see what? It's so clear." Yevgeny asks.

"Homie, I see a guy eating a nasty sandwich. I don't see any squid arms or bugs or anything." Oscar shakes his head.

Yevgeny continues, "Oh, forget you. You're playing me. The compositing is fucking great, though, dude. I should switch *Hudson Lives* over to whatever you used, foreal!"

I frown. "*Hudson Lives?*"

Oscar chuckles and shakes his head. "He has a new hobby, or therapy outlet, I call it. He's re-editing and using mapping and compositing to make a version of the movie *Aliens* where the character Hudson lives through the whole thing."

I can't help but laugh and shake my head.

Yevgeny says, "It's like *The Crow* sort of but not so IRL sad." He takes another pull off the beer and sets it down, then picks up the bong and lighter to take a hit. "If it goes good, I am going to make Hicks and Newt live through *Alien 3* and add Hudson to the whole thing!" He takes a big hit.

"That should keep him busy," Oscar jokes.

Yevgeny exhales as he says, "In *Aliens*, my shots where Hudson is firing on eggs in queen chamber with Ripley is my challenge right now. I have to use shots from the first cocoon chamber part and—"

"Zhenya," Hirofumi interrupts. Yevgeny will go on and on if you let him. I watch the little spidermites crawl around on and in Yevgeny's face waiting for his next hit like a wave at a big pool in a water park.

Yevgeny says, "Sorry," and takes another hit.

Hirofumi stubs out his cigarette and lights another. He starts the blimpwhale barrel-rolling around the bridge clip again and just watches it silently, dragging on his smoke a few times. After it ends, he says, "Okay. This is spooky shit, and you aren't imagining the video part at least. So, what do you want me to do about it?"

"Spooky? These are the fun parts!"

Yevgeny exhales, "What do you mean? Who made this?" and sets the bong back down before picking his beer up. He takes a big swig.

"Felix says these are raw shots taken with his weird, haunted camera."

Yevgeny does a genuine spit take and chokes on his beer. As it sprays back out in bursts, I watch the stoned spidermites being flung off of his face and across the room. A few land in Hirofumi's hair, not that he notices. Oscar slaps Yevgeny's back a few times and Yevgeny twists away and gestures that he's fine.

Oscar shakes his head. "Oh, whatever."

As he recovers Yevgeny says, "*Hhgt—hk—hwhat* about camera?"

"You heard me. Haunted camera," Hirofumi repeats.

"You shitting me?"

I say, "It's true. Haunted isn't what I'd call it, but the camera does pick up things we can't normally see."

"Like what?" Yevgeny says through an incredulous smile.

Hirofumi nods. "Yeah. Like what? What is this shit?"

I take a deep breath and exhale. "Well, I don't know anything concrete. What I do know is that we are surrounded by all these strange things. Some are really cool—beautiful even. Some are more messed up. Like, disturbing, scary shit.

"So, these things are all around us all the time. It's like there are other dimensions merged with ours partly? I really don't understand it myself. I just see the results of whatever happened or just how things are? There's all kinds of creatures from little bugs and jellyfish-looking things on up to whale-sized things like the one in that bridge shot. There are competing asteroid belts of black chunks floating all around. Sad ghouls or ghosts or something. Big, formless sacks of nasty muck. Monster cops in cosmonaut suits. Patches of glowing plants or flowers on buildings and cars and people here and there like pulsing moss and the bugs fight each other to pollinate or eat stuff from them? Maybe they...." I get lost in my thoughts.

Hirofumi raises his eyebrows. "You alright?"

"Yeah, just a lot to process."

Yevgeny laughs. "You need medicine again."

Oscar scoffs. "Really? This is from the guy who thinks the moon landing was faked and there are Nazis living in bases on the inside of the empty Earth?"

"Hollow Earth. Both true—"

"Guys," I say.

Hirofumi takes a drag and lets it out. He asks, "Okay, so what? What do you want?"

"You remember that one night we were all coked out in Osaka, and you slapped on a multiple proxy thing and hacked into those porn sites?"

"Yeah, and I replaced the videos with slowed down clips of Adventure Time," Hirofumi says, smiling at first, then his expression changes. "*Chotto*...."

"You said if you felt like it, you could hack a satellite."

Yevgeny laughs on the couch. "No way."

"I was joking. Mostly."

"Hiro, I need you to help me flood the airwaves and web with this stuff. Force a wakeup call."

"Do it! Do it! *Price*-less!" Yevgeny exclaims.

Oscar looks nonplussed.

"Can you do it?"

Hirofumi rubs his face. "You've really lost it, Felix."

I gesture toward the screen with my flat, open hand. "You've seen it yourself—and believe me, there's more! People need to see this stuff!"

"Do they? Even if I could do it, what's the point? I saw it and I can't see it's done me any good."

"But—"

"I have too much going right for once to risk it on some wild goose fuck. That shit is federal, Felix. No chance."

"Hiro, I need your help. I can't...." I trail off.

Was that a door opening? Hiro seems to have heard it too. He seems relieved?

"No, the way I see it, you've got a weird glitchy camera and mental health problems. Zhenya is right. You need your medicine."

Footsteps. Two sets?

Kaori walks in, still concerned but now with a touch of apprehension. "I had to, Felix. I love you but you need more help from that hospital."

My stomach balls into a fist and I swallow hard.

"No...."

Audrey steps into the threshold behind Kaori, face undamaged and with a concerned, cautious expression.

chapter 26

Audrey takes a step in, wearing sweats and sneakers like she was doing chores at home, but looks great to me—even through my shock and fear.

That doesn't stop me from jumping out of my seat and backing deeper into the room, hand raised reflexively to keep her at bay. "Kaori, what the hell?"

Audrey stops and stands just inside the room.

Kaori has a guilty expression but remains earnest.

"You need to go back to see doctors. We love you but you need more help."

Oscar says, "Agreed. I think she's right, Felix."

In a calm, careful tone Audrey says, "Felix, I love you, baby. I just want you to get better."

I know I'm in a concrete cave with no exits but I glance around anyway. Nothing! No way out! You are so stupid, Felix!

Audrey continues, "Please, baby. Let me take you back there. Just until they can change your dosage or medicine or whatever works."

"You know damn well they won't change the medicine, Audrey. Harmonia is for *special* cases!"

"I don't know what you mean, baby. But I know they'll do whatever it takes to—"

"Whatever it takes? Whatever it takes to stop me from seeing and shut me up, right?"

Hirofumi sighs. "That's not what she's talking about. You need help. When you say those things, it is obvious."

I know I've lost Hirofumi already and that Kaori was obviously never mine to convince. Hiro must have just been humoring me to buy time. I look at Yevgeny.

Motherfucker looks like he's at a movie. Smiling and trying not to laugh. I should slap the glowing mites off that shithead's face.

Oscar's already shared his agreement, but I look at him again.

"You just mean so much to us, Felix."

A hum builds in the wall to my right. Grieves walks out of it and up to me. I ignore him like I've learned to do around others.

Grieves leans in, getting right in my face.

"Ff-ounddyou—I fou-ndd yoooooou."

I say, "Congratulations…," under my breath.

Grieves makes a disappointed, duck-faced frown in response to my rudeness and looks around the room, completely unconcerned with the situation at hand. He starts inspecting all the old built-in warehouse equipment and controls in the walls that Hirofumi left installed as decoration.

As Grieves passes between me and my other friends, Audrey's expression changes but she holds her composure. I look back and forth between Audrey and Grieves, watching her like a hawk as she struggles to keep her pleading "let me help you" expression up.

Audrey begins, "Just let me take you. Let me take you

back...." She trails off and I notice her doing something with her fingers by her side. Little glowing characters kind of like Wahrheit's bullet-calligraphy equations cut the air by her moving fingers and burn out, twinkling into nothing as they fall toward the floor.

The warping and pulsing starts in her eyes but stays relatively calm. She seems quite collected and in control of it now. Been practicing?

Audrey looks at Grieves, then back at me, and says, "Okay, what the fuck is that?"

Grieves is too busy with something on the wall and doesn't notice her giving him the once over. Neither do H&K, Yevgeny, or Oscar.

I narrow my eyes. "You can see him?"

"Of course I can. But what is it?"

I point at Audrey and flail my arms, jabbing towards her as I yell, "There! There! She can see him!"

Hirofumi and Kaori look more and more concerned. Yevgeny wears an amused expression and watches me with his red eyes as he takes another hit. Oscar closes his eyes and sighs, then shakes his head.

"Oh, they aren't hearing this, baby. They're hearing something like 'Puh-lease let me help' and all that. The responses they hear will sound roughly in context, so we have privacy. Well, I do. You sound like a lunatic. So, what *is* that?"

I let out something between a whimper and laugh and close my eyes.

"Grieves is what I call him. He just follows me around."

I open my eyes.

Her distortions pulse a little stronger and darker.

"That's how you've been spending your time after trying to kill me? I've been at home furious with you, *and* worried about you—and you're out making home movies and hanging out with a glowing gelatin-mold anatomy-model man?"

"I didn't try to kill you."

Hirofumi, Kaori, Oscar, and Yevegeny raise their eyebrows. They start to fade into a vague blur where they are and it's all Audrey and I. Well, Grieves is still glowing and mumbling over by the wall. He must not be affected by her hypno-spell or whatever.

"Really? Seemed like it. It's not like I was there or anything. So why did you shoot me, Felix?"

"I didn't mean to. I saw all these photos and—"

"Photos? Of what?"

"You from all different times. And paintings before that."

"So, you shot me. Because of some pictures?"

"I didn't mean to. You scared me—"

"Oh, sorry about that. Sorry I scared the boy with the huge pistol in my face. Suppose I believe you didn't mean to do it. I'd really like to believe that. But what were you thinking coming here? What's your big plan?"

I consider lying and start, "I came here to…," but realize Kaori probably told her about the camera and footage already and, in a resurgence of purpose, I belt out, "I'm going to blow this wide open!"

Audrey looks genuinely confused. "Why?"

"What?" I ask, already disarmed.

"Why would you do that?"

"Because nobody knows what's really going on!"

"Why would they want to?"

"Because…it's the truth."

"And they're better off not knowing it."

"But—"

"Is that all this is about for you? Show and tell? Whistleblowing? You want to drop some knowledge on all these blissfully ignorant yet somehow still miserable wretches? Like they don't have enough going on in their little self-constructed rat mazes? 'First world problems' doesn't cover how out of it all of these *Homo inermis* are.

Wow, that bastard really doesn't have anything to worry about."

I frown. "What 'bastard'?"

"They have such a short time. If they only knew what's coming.... Just let them fight their wars and worship their celebrities and politicians and porn stars and religious idols without knowing they're pretty much all the same false thing. All they have are fears and distractions from them. Promises of unattainable peace of mind.

"Let them check out with drugs and alcohol to escape a world they think they understand *too* well. Let them eat themselves to death. Let them screw so they can have little oblivious babies." That last part makes her stop herself and she looks genuinely sad for just a moment before returning to her confident smugness. "Let them enjoy themselves before their hearts stop and their brains let go for the last time. Why rob them of that?"

I don't know what to say and let my defeat sink in deep, sighing big and letting my shoulders slump down and my arms dangle. I figure I've been beaten. Coming down from my pill high, and exhaustion creeping in, I let out a meek, "Okay."

Audrey beams with glazed, pulsing eyes.

"So you'll come then? You don't really have much choice after they heard all of that on your end. But you understand now? I mean, I've taken Harmonia for years to be like them—"

"You what?"

"I only stopped recently so I could keep an eye on you and figure out what you could and couldn't see. I grew to hate seeing things as they really are a long time ago, but that's how much I love you. Now, once you forget all this, we can both take the medicine and be happy together like these sheep. We'll have nice, little sheep problems."

Forget?

Audrey's eyes take on a subtle gleam of desperation

and the swirling strangeness in and around them looks different than I've ever seen it. She looks like she's going to cry thinking about all of this. Then her face brightens into a visage of pure, willful denial.

"Or better yet—like cats! Compared to what's coming, our biggest problems right now will amount to which angle to stretch to make best use of sunbeams coming in through the blinds." Even through the weirdness, she looks like a little girl trying to reconvince herself there's a Santa Claus after catching her father arranging presents.

I don't know the hows or whats, but seeing Audrey like this forces me to realize that I'm dealing with a broken, miserable creature. The happy, vibrant, beautiful girl I love is a mask this bitter, old, scared thing wears to forget something, or a lot of somethings.

"Audrey, what's coming?"

Audrey's eyes pulse differently.

"He's going to wake up the gods. I tried to convince him not to, but I don't have sway like I used to. Not now that he has that revolting doll."

"Gods? What gods? Who—"

"It doesn't matter who. Or what. Or anything. It just doesn't."

"Fine. What do you mean by 'forget'?"

"The center has machines. They can make you forget. We can be happy again."

As I consider this, my eyes dance around and my gaze falls on Grieves. One of his hands is phased through a panel on the wall and he appears to be rubbing something inside.

"What if I don't want to forget, Audrey?"

"You have to. I need you to."

"But what if I don't? Do I have options?"

"Past a certain point, they aren't mine to decide."

"What's to decide? What are the options?"

"I thought that would be obvious. You all but said it

yourself."

"Just say it."

"Forget or…die."

She says it so matter of fact and without any malice that I'm waiting for her to crack a smile or something.

I chuckle mirthlessly. "You're serious. Just kill me?"

"Not 'just.' It won't be quick or easy like, say, a bullet in the brain." She shoots a quick poison-tipped smile before returning to genuine concern. "Trouble cases get fast-tracked to the top of the quote, unquote *donor* list. It could take years for you to die, and I can't bear the thought of you in that much pain. Not you. You hurt me bad, but you still don't deserve that."

"Why can't I just move away or something? Play dumb? Start over?"

"Believe me, I know how this all sounds but this is not a game to them. They don't leave things to chance or choice. I've done all I can and this is your last option."

"'Donor list'? 'Them'? Audrey, what are you?"

Her distortions glitch and pulse with more intensity.

"Still so curious? I haven't forgiven you yet, boy. I don't really owe you anything, do I? But it really doesn't matter now. You should have just taken your medicine. Let me take you there before this last kindness is revoked."

"So, what? I just go with you, and they zap me and we're happy ever after?" I ask, trying to fight the ton of bricks feeling of defeat pressing against my chest. I look at Grieves playing with the panel in the wall again.

Grieves looks back at me and smiles.

"I-iht's ttinguhlly…it'stingly-tingly—it's tingly, I like it."

The last part becomes clearer than usual—more normal sounding, which makes it odd. I look at the panel more closely.

Audrey looks at Grieves and makes a disgusted face, then back at me and answers, "Yes. Simple as that. It won't ever come up again. We'll go and I can give them that awful camera and that will be the end of it."

"What about the camera?"

"They thought they got them all with the recall and had teams buying or stealing the rest to destroy them. I won't ask where you got that one. As long as you don't have one, I don't care what happens to them."

I look at the HDV-426 on Hirofumi's metal desk and Hirofumi is a little more visible as a result but still looks more like a partially filled-in silhouette. I can just make out his bewildered expression and it hits me how strange my side of the conversation with Audrey must sound without context of the full thing. She's right. I'm finished. Only one thing I can do.

I bow my head a little and start walking toward Audrey and Kaori like a scolded child. Audrey smiles, relieved. Kaori seems to relax a little too but it's hard to tell with Audrey's spell or trick making everything but herself fuzzy and dark.

I gently grasp Kaori's upper arms and say, "I'm really sorry." Then pull her in and kiss her forehead. "Just remember to breathe."

"*Nah-zhay?*" Kaori asks, curious why she should.

I throw Kaori onto the puffy couch next to Yevgeny, lunge toward Grieves and the panel, pry it open, and throw a set of main breaker switches Grieves has been toying with.

The room goes pitch black and I hear frustrated and confused murmurs from the people out in the warehouse at the *Home/Free* terminals. The only lights are Audrey's swirling distortions, a faint glow from Grieves's head and hands, and the buttons on the HDV-426. Grieves looks around like he noticed a change but can't place it.

Kaori starts screaming and won't stop, Yevgeny chortles, and Hirofumi yells, "FELIX!" Oscar groans and it sounds like he's sliding his hands on the wall behind the couch to keep his balance on the couch arm.

I can't tell if Audrey can see in the dark but I hope not. Her pulsing eyes are reflecting the burning glow from around her face and head but they are darting around the room so I might have a shot.

I jump back to the metal desk and wrench the camera from its connected cables and fumble for the power switch to extinguish the little lights but can't find it.

Fuck it—just go!

I cradle the camera like a football and go for my best interpretation of the Heisman Trophy. Grab my pack in one hand, sling it over a shoulder, and barrel through the room toward the door, fumbling through Oscar's and Hirofumi's flailing arms and legs.

Hirofumi yells, "Felix, you ASSHOLE! My SERVERS and my—FUUUUCK!" Then he's so mad he's cursing in Japanese.

Kaori can't stop her high-pitched screaming and Yevgeny can't stop laughing about it. Through his laughing he says, "You sound…like Newt…in water sublevel part!"

I can see the little mites glowing around his mouth and nose like bioluminescent deep-sea fauna and it makes his laughing face look like a dim mask in the dark.

As I'm trying to brush past Audrey, her shark eyes lock on the little lights of the camera, and an industrial hydraulic clamp locks around my wrist, or it feels that way. I keep rushing for the door but my arm stays behind, with my hand now through the camera's carry grip.

"REAL CUTE, FELIX!" Audrey chides in her shrill, room-vibrating angry voice. I pull with everything I have but she won't let go.

"OH, SORRY. DID I GIVE YOU THE IMPRESSION THAT I'M WEAK?! I'M GOING TO DRAG YOU OUT OF HERE AND LOCK YOU IN MY CAR! I'LL CALL FOR A RESTRAINT GURNEY WHEN WE GET TO THE CENTER AND WE'LL GET YOU DEALT WITH PROPERLY!"

Her other machine claw of a hand locks on my forearm and she starts pulling me back to her.

I strain and yell, "Fuck you! Let go of me!"

I'm almost crying from the frustration and pain of pulling against her grip.

"I'M NOT HURTING YOU! YOU'RE HURTING YOURSELF PULLING LIKE THAT, FELIX!"

Grieves notices that I'm upset and that seems to make him upset. "Thatt- iss ver-ry rhooood. HowrudeIdon'tthinkHe–Liiikes yooudoingg-that."

Grieves storms over and passes through both of us with a static electric buzz and a flash before grabbing my free hand and pulling me away from Audrey. Her grip is still incredibly strong, and it just becomes a tug-of-war game.

She sounds breathless.

"GA! THAT FELT SO WEIRD! KEEP THAT THING AWAY FROM ME!"

Grieves looks back at her hands and I start vibrating. I can feel it in my bones and pores and then pretty much everything. My body goes almost numb but the lack of normal feeling is replaced by the metal-in-a-wall-socket feeling. Then I can see through the now translucent camera and then the bones and tendons in my hands, and they're glowing—then Grieves pulls me out of Audrey's grip through her fingers. He keeps pulling me along and pulls me through the wall that Hirofumi's table and computer are set against. I get a visual flash of the wiring and pipes running through the wall before we are through into a room Kaori uses for fashion design and drawing. It's jet black inside but I know the rough layout.

"Okay, okay! Thanks but let go!" I yell, my word echoing in my head and reverberating strangely.

Grieves stops and lets go and I'm instantly opaque, filled in, and solid. Other than the definite astonishment, I'm just glad my feet were out of the floor. Then a wave of nausea crashes on my stomach and I retch on a loose spool of yarn on a chair I can see faintly in the glow from Grieves.

"Oh, maaaaan...," I moan.

We hear Audrey and Hirofumi stumbling into the hallway and Grieves grabs my arm again.

As I go all translucent and glowy again, I try to protest, "No don't—" but I'm already looking through my clothes and skin and muscles again at my luminous bones and marrow, and Grieves is leading me through the room.

Audrey and Hirofumi hurry down the hall perpendicular to Grieves's path through the room he and I are in. I can hear Kaori sobbing and taking in stuttering breaths as she tries to stumble her way out of the dark maze and I feel terrible. Then I hear Yevgeny mocking her through his amusement and it sounds like Oscar is trying to guide her out of the computer room. "It's okay, sweetie. Come on."

Grieves pulls me through the wall and into the hallway. Audrey must hear or feel the vibrations and looks back. She slows down as she watches Grieves steer me through the hall behind where she just was and through the other hallway wall and out of sight. Grieves keeps going through the dark room on the other side and into another before veering toward the south wall, and I have to squint as we emerge out onto the street and the dim but blinding light of the gray, rainy day.

I watch the rain shower down through my clothes and body before bursting on the concrete under my luminous, see-through boots and feet. Grieves lets go of me and I become solid again, forcing the rain out of my space with a shuddering spray. I stumble toward the asphalt of the street itself but the nausea is worse this time and I retch hard down onto it and crumple to my hands and knees.

Through teary eyes, I see the Swede parked at a bad angle on the wrong side of the alley and realize Audrey must have been upset and anxious to see me to show such a lack of control. What if she really does love me, whatever she is? For a moment, I regret what I just did to escape her and any hope I had of forgetting all of this.

Grieves walks back through the corner of the warehouse over onto the covered walkway between it and the next one over and chastises what sounds like Audrey and Hirofumi as they rush toward—shit!

As I haul myself off the drenched street, I take my pack off my shoulder and release the top flap. I jam the HDV-426 down in between my clean socks, a T-shirt, and a bag of Double Stuf Oreos, then take my first few painful steps. Hirofumi whips around the corner of the warehouse and beelines for me with bare feet.

I forgot how fast Hiro is!

I pick up speed and go into a dead sprint to keep some distance between us. We're in a mad dash and the distance between us gets shorter, then longer, then shorter again.

Hirofumi yells, "Stop, you shit! I'm hungover—agh!" He runs over some sharp gravel on the street and sucks in air as he tries to keep pace through the pain. He slows to a limping jog and I look back.

Hirofumi is slowing, but down by the warehouse Audrey is already starting up the Swede. This keeps me pumping my legs and I near the corner of a building at an intersection. As I'm rounding it, I look back and see Audrey driving up to Hirofumi and slowing down to let him in.

I slip and stutter-step onto the intersecting street and beat my feet toward the next intersection.

The Swede squeals around the corner behind me and quickly catches up by going against traffic on the one-way street.

She seems a liiiittle upset.

Audrey swerves to avoid the cars I'm running between and paces me as she and Hirofumi yell and plead through open windows. I ignore them. She steers in close, and Hirofumi stretches to try to grab me but I juke away. She curses and speeds up some, getting a little ahead of me.

She's going to cut me off!

I cut at an angle to the sidewalk on my right and Audrey's swerve maneuver misses. Face stinging from the pelting rain, I haul ass up the sidewalk while she tries to pace me again.

I notice the light for the cross traffic streaming through the intersection turn yellow and hope that she didn't. Then sprint full speed like I'm going to run through the intersection so she speeds up to cut me off again.

I'm running so hard my hat shifts on my head and meets some resistance. It's blown off onto the wet street behind me and I imagine the Swede's wheels crushing it like as under a tank tread.

The light turns red and the cross traffic eases to a stop as the cars lined up like stomping bulls start pulling into the intersection toward them. The first row of the motorized phalanx starts honking at the speeding Swede and Audrey looks forward.

She screams, "Shit!" and slams on her brakes too fast, sending the Swede into a slide. I can just see Hirofumi bracing his arms against the dash.

The tires lose all traction, and they hydroplane, barely missing the evading oncoming cars and only slowing when she trades paint with the side panels of a parked Escalade just past the intersection.

I put on my brakes too or rather try to and slip again, this time slapping down on the concrete full on my side and onto my holstered pistol.

I claw myself up and back to my feet with hands shaking from the pain and make a break northeast up Folsom perpendicular to my initial path.

Audrey wrenches the Swede free from the Escalade and tries to turn around amidst a cacophony of honks and yelling from drivers and onlookers.

I keep hoofing it and desperately search for a way off

this street before she catches up. I see a DEAD END sign near the entrance to a street on my right.

I cut around the corner and run down a line of cars parked on the left side of the dead-end street.

They'll see me if I'm just running down the street like an idiot.

I crouch by a hybrid car's front bumper and tuck myself in to hide—except there's a middle-aged man sitting at the wheel reading something or playing a game on a tablet. Damn it! I just need a few seconds.

The man is pretty sucked into his tablet so—nope. The man notices me. He's just confused at first, then seems scared.

I raise my hand and gesture "it's cool, just need a minute" but the man seems to misinterpret it and get mad now. He locks his doors and honks reluctantly. It looks like he's never used his horn but right now it's his only weapon against the mongrel hordes, myself their representative.

I give him a "what the hell, man?" look, but it occurs to me how strange my panting, wide eyes, and sneaky crouching must look.

The Swede barrels down Folsom, Audrey driving so fast Hirofumi only barely glances down the dead-end street and doesn't see me at all.

I rise and lean over the angry, terrified man inside his car. Then flip him both birds, slap them down on his windshield and knee the front panel above the wheel well.

Yeah, he'll probably call the cops but fuck him.

When I reach the corner, I peek around and up Folsom. The Swede is already two blocks down and speeding up the street. Even that far away, I can see the glow of Audrey's freaky-organic-swirl-prism-face burning.

She's really pissed.

The Swede cuts down a street about a block farther down on the right.

Must have noticed I wasn't in sight. Gotta get gone.

I cut across Folsom and head down to the intersection where Audrey just had her demolition-derby show. Hurry around it and head up the sidewalk toward Market, keeping an ear and eye out for signs of the Swede.

Okay, think…think…. Where can you go?

Where is it safe?

Europe? The UK? Japan? Hong Kong would be cool. No, you'd have to deal with visas and passports and shit.

I reach Howard Street and head through the crosswalk.

And for all you know, it's like this there, or worse. What's far from here but not so touchy ID-wise?

Hawaii? Fuck yeah, Hawaii. Just chill.

As long as you're frugal and don't piss off the locals, you could be okay there probably.

Reach Natoma Street, wait, then cross.

I should have enough saved to get a last-minute ticket and enough fundage to keep me going until I can find like an under-the-table dish-washing job or something.

Hell, I could probably sleep on the beach. People do that there, right? Actually, maybe not. We'll see.

Minna Street.

Man, for all you know, they've got all this spooky weirdo shit over there too. How could they not?

It's worth a shot, though. Just act normal. Quit taking the pills and just let yourself forget. Or maybe start preachin' it in public and get gassed on purpose. Then it's all surf wax and sunsets. Nothing to keep me here.

Mission Street.

Okay, it's settled. Jump on the BART and head to SFO.

I continue up to Market and cut up toward Civic Center Station.

Audrey's after me. Friends don't believe me and probably never will. No family left who live here anymore.

I reach the stairwell and start down the steps to the station.

Forget or die, huh? I think I'll go hide somewhere and

forget my own way. Everyone else I know who could see is dead already. Nothing's keeping me here—

I stumble to a stop on the stairs and grab the handrail. Oh. Shit.

chapter 27

I take another pill while I'm hustling up Grant toward Chinatown.

Can't miss anything right now. Gotta stay sharp. Get in and out and fly the hell away.

As I pass through an ornate Chinese-style *paifang* arch, known as the Dragon Gate, and continue up Grant into Chinatown, it occurs to me that my disguise is a dead giveaway now.

I hike up to a cheap, touristy store and grab some black track pants with white stripes down the legs that are probably a bit too big; a colorful mesh-back trucker hat that says "California" right below a long wave curling off from a couple of palm trees; and a shiny dark-blue baseball-style jacket with red dragons curling down and around the sleeves.

As I'm being rung up, I add an umbrella and a pair of white plastic shades with a thin, curving slit to see out of to my pile. I figure they're supposed to resemble Inuit snow goggles.

Pay with cash that I take out from ATMs just before leaving one area for another—just in case there's anybody keeping track.

The man behind the counter grabs a plastic bag and the track pants. I say, "It's cool. Don't need a bag. You have a bathroom, actually?"

The man shakes his head and eyes me cautiously.

I change in an alley down the street, then secure my revolver in my pack with my camera.

I open the big *kawaii* octopus-printed umbrella I also purchased, put on the Inuit sunglasses, and set off down the sidewalk in the rain.

From the corner of a building at Grant and Sacramento, I watch the fish-store entrance and rest of the block for signs of an ambush. A swarm of spiderflies flutters and darts across the intersection. Some pinks walk by me with bulbs and glowy, mite-infested moss half visible under pulled-down umbrellas.

In and out, Felix.

I start up the hill.

The bells strung from the interior handle clank and tinkle as the shop door closes behind me. "Sing Your Life" by Morrissey plays on the record player as I walk the front of the store looking down the aisles.

I close my umbrella but don't bother shaking it out.

She's on the end of the far-right wall, feeding something in a tank. She glances at me and the light from the aquariums makes her weird contacts flash opaque and reflective as she sizes me up with three eye twitches. She looks back at the tank in front of her.

Her blue and black mane is down for once, some of it curling down her chest and some to about halfway down her back. The quarter-inch hair on the front half of her head has been re-dyed deep black recently, with nickel-sized dayglo multicolored dye-stamped skulls scattered around in it.

I take a few steps down the aisle. The colorful tanks glow even more than they normally would due to a lovely haze that last pill has placed me in and the optical acuteness caused by the thin slit in my plastic eyewear.

"Hey, Chauncey, we try to keep the water in the tanks," Siobhán says, more sarcastic than playful. "Oh, and the wannabe triad auditions are a few blocks up at the Happy Donut on Columbus. You've got promise. Those goggles should help you see as you hike up there through the blinding, sun-drenched snow. Very tactical." Lower, but obviously still loud enough to hear, she says, "Idiot."

"Siobhán."

She doesn't look at me but there's a subtle movement of her left arm that's out of sight and just a hint of stance change.

"If the hog leg in your bag is for me, you should have fired it already. Won't do you any good back there. Also, you could use a shower, Stucky. Are there no professionals left?"

"It's me," I say as I take the silly specs off and tuck them in my jacket pocket.

She glances back up, then does a double take and points toward the door.

"*No.* I don't know what your damage is, but you need to go. Get your aquatic-care products elsewhere. I hear Petco has a better selection anyway. I think there's one in Potrero."

"What? Why?"

"I reserve the right to refuse service and I am refusing to serve you. Considering the circumstances, I think I'm also pretty reserved. Now, as you and your computation-box friends might say, git-foh."

"What did I do?"

"You? I'm not sure. But if your girlfriend ever comes in here again, I swear I might just lose my temper."

"Audrey? When was she here?"

"Weeks ago. She said you had a fight the night before and to tell her if I saw you. I almost felt sorry for her but then she flipped out about me being a slut or whore. It wasn't polite."

"Why did you feel sorry for her?"

"She looked like you gave her a once-over. Too much makeup. Bruises and bumps and a couple Band-Aids on her forehead. Eyes worked funny like she had a concussion or something."

"I didn't touch her."

Siobhán studies my eyes and lingers on the brown one before looking down at the tank again. There are turtles flopping at the surface trying to snag the food she drops sporadically.

I notice that her nose chain is on the right side of her face for once, strung through little sets of tiny red and black hammers that silently swing back and forth on swivels between them when she moves her head.

"Yeah, you really don't seem like the type, if there is such a thing. I get the vibe that you did do something you feel guilty about, but it wasn't pummeling her like a drunk hoobilly. Either way, though, I don't need the drama. I've had enough to last a while, believe me."

"None of that *matters*. Listen to me, okay. We have to go—and I'm thinking now would be prudent."

"Go? What are you on about? I think *you* should go." Siobhán caps her turtle food and replaces a mesh top on the tank. She scoffs and shakes her head as she walks down the aisle away from me.

I say, "'I know you see them too.'"

Siobhán stops but doesn't turn around.

"See what?"

"I got your notes. The braille. If you can see them, and

they figure out that you can—"

She spins on her heel and throws her arms wide, just missing the tanks on the end of the aisle.

"What? What are *they* gonna do, Felix? Do I strike you as someone who's incapable of self-preservation? Do you think I give a fuck what your *theys* and *thems* have against me?"

As she yells this, the tanks all around vibrate hard in time with her syllables and the fish and other creatures in them swim in loose, erratic patterns.

I feel my own fear and desperation to escape the city couple with a confusingly deep desire to keep her safe and I snap.

"You think you're so fucking tough, right?! What's after me is tougher! If it's after you too, you're fucked! Swallow your bullshit bravado and let's go!"

Siobhán is instantly disarmed by my anger and her eyelids flutter. She lowers her arms and studies my face and eyes again.

She starts to speak and stops herself. Then starts again and her "American" accent falters a little as she says, "Okay, Felix. What's so important? Why are we in danger or whatever you're getting at?"

There's that Irish again. Why does she always hide it?

I pull myself together, taking a deep breath and exhaling.

"I…I got this camera and it made me see all this stuff that's around. Forced me to. Since then, I've seen that Audrey is some kind of scary, old creature with a dark, burning face that gets all messed up and distorted. I've seen all the bugs and jellyfish bulbs and flying, crawling, floating things. Monster police teams, old-guard spaznoids, and big, writhing bags of muck covered in spooky eyes and shaped like a large, warped person—until they need to move quickly or attack. Those might be the worst."

"What's a spaz…noid?" Siobhán asks, genuinely curious and back to her put-on accent.

"Doesn't matter. The reason I'm here is that everyone I have met who could see this stuff is dead. Killed. And I don't want that to happen to me, or you."

"That's kind of sweet, Felix." She cocks her head. "You know what I think?"

"What?"

"I think that you are hitting on me. Which is flattering, but I know full well that you have a lady friend."

"I think it's pretty safe to say we're on a break. But—no wait, it's not like that."

Siobhán chuckles as she turns away and walks toward the back counter area.

"Now we're getting somewhere."

"What?" I ask as I follow her.

"Freshly broken up and you want a piece of this as rebound ass. Listen, I may be a tease, but I am not a slut or a home-wrecker. Golden rule and all that."

She steps around the counter, spreads her hands out and leans on them, curving her back a little like a southern girl in Daisy Dukes maybe. "This is more fun, though, with you sort of single and all. Now you just have to convince me that I'm not just another floozy in your harem and that you…are a…worthy…suitor."

"It isn't like that, Siobhán. She's one of them! Can we just go?"

"Simmer down, Felix. This is just getting interesting. You have me intrigued but if you're trying to scare my little undies off, it's not going to work. I don't scare easy, undergarments or otherwise. Come to think of it, we never finished that conversation. Anyway, I might be convinced to run away with you, but you have to be honest."

"I'm not trying to fuck you, Siobhán!"

She frowns as a clown might.

"Why not? Is it my fashion sense? Or—" She takes a sharp mock breath in. "Or do you not find me lovely? Am I not a pretty princess? You know, I never have seen a

Barbie that looks like me! Where did I go wrong? Quick—play some eighties music and put a bright bow in my hair. Give me a frilly boring dress, you bastard! Where's Molly Ringwald when you actually need her? I'm a basket case!"

I can't help but laugh. Somehow the whole horrible death at the hands of evil forces thing melts away when I look at Siobhán right now. That last pill has got me rolling balls.

"No. It's not that! I mean, I'm not gonna lie. You're incredible looking. Gorgeous. I've never met anyone quite like you. You are…really beautiful." *Jesus, how do you really feel, Felix?*

Siobhán waves her hands at her face.

"Ooh la la, a little gushy, but you are good. Can you tell I'm blushing?"

She bends over the counter and leans on her elbows, interlaces her fingers, and rests her chin on top of them. She bats her eyelashes and sways a bit to make her backside smoothly slide back and forth through the air behind her.

I hear a hum from the wall behind her by the record player. Siobhán's eyes flash from playful to sharp and aware and she cocks her head back toward the wall before looking at me with a question on her tongue.

Grieves strides out of the wall leering gleefully and chiding me, "F-foundyoouAgai-hn! I–foooooooooouuundd yooouu!"

Before I can figure out what's happening, Siobhán has whipped around and has one of her weird butterfly knives fanning open, then locked in her grip with the tip pressed to Grieves's neck where his major arteries are visibly pumping. Grieves must have stopped out of reflex.

And where the hell did that knife come from?

Grieves shifts phases and takes two steps up to Siobhán's face, allowing her knife and arm to pass through his neck and upper body.

"Ihmp-pouliiiiite!"

With just a thought from Grieves, Siobhán's arm is thrown through his body and out to the side with incredible speed and her knife is flung out of her hand, thunking into the wall next to an aquarium at the end of the far aisle and vibrating in place.

Grieves reaches up to grab Siobhán but she's unfazed by his strange qualities and whips her arm up in a sweeping block of his solidifying hand and forearm before making a quick, circular corkscrew movement with both hands from her solar plexus area to Grieves's.

I feel air rushing past my ears toward Siobhán, then there's a blast of pressure that throws Grieves off his feet and back through the wall he came from—and it's so strong that just the blowback knocks my stupid hat off.

Siobhán assumes a defensive stance from a martial art I'm not familiar with, watching the wall and glancing around for hints of another attack from her flanks.

"Was that thing talking to you?!" Siobhán asks as her eyes dart around.

"Yeah. That's Grieves. He's harmless. Mostly. I think. He probably assumed you wouldn't see him and wanted to tell me once again how great he is at hide-and-seek."

"'Hide-and-seek'? Are you kidding?"

"Long story. Grieves! It's okay now! You startled her is all!"

Siobhán relaxes her stance a little and looks back at me.

I look around at the walls and ceiling. After a few moments, the top part of Grieves's head appears in the ceiling above us in one of the colorful, black-lit fish paintings and he watches Siobhán with wide, cautious eyes.

She does the same to what she can see of him.

Siobhán leads me up the stairwell I had seen at the back of the store, that Miss Long came down when I met her.

Siobhán says, "If we're going on a trip, I'll need a couple things." Lower and to herself, "'Cause there's obviously more to you than good looks."

We reach the top floor and enter a dingy, dimly lit hallway with funky old carpet. She leads me to a door halfway down and takes out her keys.

Miss Long appears from a different stairwell at the end of the hallway carrying a big laundry basket. When she sees Siobhán and me, she stops. Siobhán speaks to her in Cantonese. Miss Long looks older than I had originally thought. There's a look in her eyes I initially mistake for concern but from her short responses and demeanor, I get a weird feeling it's more like jealousy.

Miss Long slowly carries her basket to an apartment a few doors down and across the hall.

Siobhán opens the door and lets me in first. I step in a few feet and listen to Siobhán explaining something to Miss Long, who doesn't seem pleased but isn't arguing exactly.

I'm not sure what I was expecting of Siobhán's apartment but it wasn't this.

I guess maybe a messy, lived-in place with poster-covered walls and empty food packages lying around on sticker-tagged yard-sale furniture. A feel to match her devil-may-care appearance.

This place is something else entirely. Minimal, elegant, tasteful, strange. Plus, if I hadn't entered from that door in that hallway, I wouldn't have believed I was standing anywhere near a bustling metropolis. Just being in here is calming.

Siobhán steps in behind me and closes the door. She takes one of those big, red beedis of hers from a pack on a small table near the door, lights it, and takes a drag.

As she exhales, she says, "I probably shouldn't let you in here, but I think it's safe to assume you aren't completely in the dark."

Her strange abode is dimly lit, but it's hard to discern the source.

There's a strange orb on a small table near the door that I realize is a scooter or motorcycle helmet with a mirrored faceplate like something out of a 1970s sci-fi movie.

Besides the small kitchen to my left and an old Sony component stereo with record-filled milk crates to my right, this place is unlike any living space I've ever come across.

Every inch of the floor is covered in a few layers of thin silk rugs with beautiful, intricate designs.

There's a low table not unlike a Japanese dinner table made of a dark wood I couldn't name and one mat at its head. There's a single Lily of the Valley in a thin vase placed on the opposite end in place of a mat. Next to the table is a beautiful multi-stemmed hookah or nargileh. In the corner near the table there's a shrouded, round object on a tall rod with a clawed base.

There are lush mounds around the living room that look like luxurious velvety bean bags and near them there are musical instruments resting, some of which I have never seen before. Wind instruments, stringed ones, and something that looks like a beautifully crafted cross between bagpipes and a hurdy-gurdy.

Every inch of exposed wall is covered with hanging, vertically parallel rods of dark, translucent Plexiglas. They have a strange appearance, but I can't place what bothers me about them.

I step toward the wall to my right to examine the rods. As I get closer and study them, I become disoriented.

They're shiny but there's no reflection. Instead, I see ghostly, dimly glowing images of what look like buildings and pathways and cherry trees filled with blossoms, and all of this appears to be suspended somehow. I step closer and my perspective shifts like it would if I were looking at something in reality.

That's not Plexiglas.

The room fills with soft, bright light and I have to

narrow my eyes as I look back at Siobhán. She has taken the opaque shroud off the object in the corner, which is a smoke-tinted glass orb containing the strong yet soothing light source.

"Sorry," she says, and covers it with a translucent shroud, which lowers the intensity and increases the soothing effect. Through this shroud, I can see that the orb is filled with white flower petals that glow intensely.

Riiiiiight…totally normal.

I look back at the rods on the wall and let my eyes adjust. The strange town or village appears to have been built into the underside of a huge, almost horizontal cliff overhang, which must have necessitated building downward from the ceiling of rock.

There are downward-extending sets of watermills that supply each other like symbiotic generators. Also, old machines that resemble ancient diesel generators with big rotating wheels and they're pumping out smoke or steam from pipes, bellow, and vents. Some of the lowest reaching buildings have small dirigibles with deflated and secured air bulbs and balloons moored on dock-like pathways. There are other skiff-like ships as well, which don't have a visible means of floatation but rest at the docks just the same.

I realize I can't tell what all this is built over and step closer to the wall. I look down and see rushing, crashing waters of a stormy sea as far in each direction as I can see, other than darkness in the distance and to my right, which I guess must be the rest of the cliff or mountain this place is built into.

"It's like a snapshot of a memory, I guess you could say," Siobhán says behind me.

I look back at her, head full of questions—then notice the ceiling, or rather what's on it. Installed across and in the entire ceiling is a patchwork of hollow logs and glowing moss and flowers, which I realize must have been the source of the light when I first walked in. There are butterflies and translucent creatures hanging around on it and fluttering about or crawling across.

Siobhán makes a high-pitched chirping sound and I hear movement in the ceiling tunnels followed by a squeaking, tittering sound.

An animal pops its head out of a dark opening I hadn't seen in the tunnels and moss. It pulls itself back out of sight when it sees me.

Siobhán keeps chirping, then says, "Come on, Billie. He's not so mean."

She stretches her hand up toward the hole.

The creature cautiously peeks out and examines me from the safety of the hole. It decides to trust Siobhán and crawls out of the hole, down her arm, and gently wraps itself around her neck and shoulder before pulling itself around and landing in her cradled arms.

It resembles a marbled polecat but with larger dark blue eyes and rainbow-speckled markings on its almost comically long body.

I watch Siobhán stroke and tickle the long ferret thing. "You're not...."

She looks up at me and raises her eyebrows in expectation.

"You're not just some punky goth girl that works at a fish store, are you?"

"Well, I *do* work at the fish store." Siobhán's expression takes on a hint of pleading. "Can the rest wait? I can't tell you how much I could use a real vacation, Felix. From myself, especially."

My curiosity competes with mental images of burst open, eviscerated bodies and the horrible animal sounds Rudy made while being killed by one of those nasty, amorphous monsters. That, combined with the pill high plateauing for the moment, returns the twist to my stomach and the urgency to my mind.

"Okay. If it gets us on the road and in the air, it can wait. But we do have to—"

"Go. Yeah, you mentioned that."

Siobhán kisses the head of the long, adorable creature writhing in her arms and squeaking. She gently drops it to the floor, and it crawls toward me. Near my feet, it starts arching its long back toward the butt and jumping back and forth on its back feet while making a little squeaky barking sound.

"She's harmless. Don't let her scare you."

"I'll try not to." I look around the apartment again and ask, "How do you keep this hidden? Like if you needed a plumber or the landlords needed to get in to check something?"

"Oh, I own the building. Plus, plumbing is one of my many hobbies."

I decide to let this go too in the interest of a timely escape from this crazy town.

Siobhán says, "Okay. What to wear?"

My face contorts and I'm about to protest but Siobhán extends her hand toward me and pantomimes like she's zipping my mouth closed.

She gently kicks off her brocade slipper shoes and nudges them toward the nearest wall into neat parallel, then strides toward what must be the bedroom.

I follow her but stop near the doorway out of respect.

She takes another drag off her beedi, then stubs it out in a glass ashtray on an old mahogany dresser and tucks it behind her ear.

Instead of a bed or futon, Siobhán's bedroom has a wide, luxurious-looking padded hammock strung from one end to the other on gyroscopic mounts of some kind about head-level on the walls, the hammock itself drooping down to only a couple feet above the floor. Billie runs into the room and jumps up into the hammock and squeaks at me like a guard, warning me to stay out of its softness.

In a corner near the door, I see a strange easel with a mechanical supply and wrapping spools for working with vertical scroll paper. The paper is like dark blue vellum and there are painted images and vertical strips of characters in a bright orange ink or gouache around them that resemble Chinese Hanzi characters—and their descendants, Japanese kanji, Korean Hanja, and Vietnamese Chữ Nôm—but have obvious differences and a flourish to them I've never seen. It's like if you sprinkled in some Arabic style and added in strips of organic barcode intermittently.

I look a little closer and see that the painting in progress on this stretch of material is of a long creature amidst fluffy clouds that appears to be whipping back on itself to attack a tiny figure in the air that looks like a man wearing a wide *sandogasa* hat and pack and wielding a very long, curved sword. I've never seen anything quite like this in the worlds of painting or illustration.

Siobhán says, "Chronicling the adventures of an old friend from way back, from stories they told me…and things I saw myself. Another hobby."

Against the far wall on the other side of the hammock I notice a long, black table covered with a variety of religious idols and symbols I recognize and, as I've come to expect recently, many I don't. Glowing on the wall above this table is a large, intricate diagram that resembles the I Ching but seems subtly different and more complicated.

I raise my eyebrows and whistle.

Siobhán chuckles. "I like to think of those as my Assorted Saints. I just figure, it's not worth taking chances. Gamble enough and you learn the importance of hedging your bets when possible."

I nod. "Plus, this way you can divide the blame more evenly for all this nonsense."

"That works too."

She grabs her knee-high atom-bomb-and-nuke combat

boots from against the wall near the easel and sits on the edge of the hammock, swinging the side she's not on up as she settles low into the edge.

"So where shall we go first, young adventurer?"

"First?"

"I've been enjoying my boring little fish store, teacher life but once I start traveling, I don't stop in one place for too long."

"I only have like twelve hundred left in my savings—"

Siobhán raises her finger. "When you travel with me, money is not something you need to worry about." She starts separating her longer hair and dreads into two loose braids. "Okay, so where?"

"Um, I was thinking Hawaii?"

"Ooh, tropical. A weakness of mine, not gonna lie. My sub is in drydock and my nearest ship is in Singapore, last I remember…so how shall we travel?"

"Take BART to SFO and take a plane?"

She nods. "Boring but effective."

Siobhán stands up, letting the hammock swing some, and pulls her orange sweater off over her head as she crosses to a closet.

I finally get a glimpse of more of her tattoos and I'm not disappointed. Other than the physical beauty that was their canvas, the imagery and designs are detailed and fascinating. I take in what I can before looking away to give her some privacy, although it didn't seem like she was overly concerned about that.

All the skewered and sliced open semi-humanoid sea-monster imagery frames an isometrically angled representation of an archipelago with some writing like I'd seen on her scroll artwork, almost like an old map.

Siobhán throws on a black Alien Sex Fiend T-shirt with sleeves cut off at the seams and a printed image of Nik Fiend with a 13 on his forehead, big nails in his noggin like Pinhead, and hands pressed together like he's praying.

She puts on a hoodie, zipping it halfway. Then she crosses to her Assorted Saints and starts applying some sort of face paint or makeup that was near all the idols.

I sigh and shift restlessly.

She says, "What?"

chapter 28

Siobhán and I reach the base of the stairwell and enter the fish store from the dark rear section. Chinese pop music plays on a small tape player that has been placed on top of the closed record player. Mrs. Long is behind the counter and does her best to ignore us as we cruise toward the front door and out through it onto the sidewalk.

I put my Inuit snow-goggle specs back on and open my rainbow umbrella.

Siobhán scoffs. "You look so silly with those on."

"I'm not worried about it. Disguise is the idea."

"Yeah, those are pretty low profile. Very subtle."

I shake my head. "Says the woman who just had to take the time to put on skull face paint...."

Siobhán tucks her thick braids behind her neck and back and pulls the hood up over her head, letting it droop a bit over her forehead. This combined with the quick makeup job she did before finally leaving the apartment makes her look a little like the grim reaper.

If I'm being honest with myself, the whole look is subtle enough and I can still make out her freckles. Overall, she's still stunning, but her reflective contacts make the hint of ghoulish countenance look more pronounced as they reflect gray sky and pouring rain all around.

She takes a pair of dark driving gloves with cut fingers out of her back pocket. As she's pulling them on, I notice those little slivers of curved metal on the top and bottom of her left ring finger again.

She opens her own umbrella as we start up the hill toward Stockton.

"Aren't you a little worried about airport security? Looking like that, I mean."

Siobhán chuckles. "Not at all. Oh, one thing—I need to stop in Colma and pour one out on an old friend's grave if you don't mind. Tradition. That's what the spooky face is about. It's on the way out of town."

"Yeah, nothing bad ever happens in Colma. Fuck it, sure. Once we're out of the city proper, we can have a picnic there if you like."

We reach Stockton, take a left around the corner, and continue down the hill.

"Is, uh, Billie gonna be alright on her own?"

"Definitely," Siobhán replies, apparently uninterested in elaborating.

I hear a little humming and Siobhán looks behind us, so I do too. The top half of Grieves's head is following us down the rain-pelted sidewalk about ten feet back, eyes even wider than usual. I look ahead but Siobhán keeps watching him as we go.

Siobhán asks, "What is his deal, anyway? You don't seem too bothered by him, freaky as he looks."

"Oh, I was at first, believe me."

We close our umbrellas as we enter the Stockton tunnel and I raise my voice to compete with the roaring cars and honking.

"Near as I can tell, he was real lonely before we ran into each other! Now we're like BFFs or some shit! He does his own thing sometimes but never stays gone long!"

"Smashing!"

Grieves seems to notice we're talking about him and comes up out of the sidewalk, taking steps like he's getting out of a pool. He mumbles about how rude we are as he walks behind us.

"I don't know what he has to do with all the other stuff going on, but he has grown on me!"

We leave the tunnel, open our umbrellas back up, and continue down Stockton.

"Felix?"

"What's up?" I ask while I look around for any signs of danger from here to Market Street. Bulbs, fliers, blimpwhales, glowing moss on a passing bus. Nothing out of the norm.

"What is it that you think is going on?"

I frown. "Why do you say it like that?"

"Uh, I guess I just mean, what's going on? What's got you so spooked?"

We cross the street and walk past the Hyatt.

"The only ones I knew who I could ask look kinda like big smashed jars of strawberry jam right about now."

"What?"

"They're dead. Killed. I told you this already."

"Yeah, I heard you. Chill, alright? People die or get killed all the time. Stay alive long enough, you get used to it."

I stop at the corner of Stockton and Post and face Siobhán.

"I don't know who you really are or how you can say something like that and make it sound fucking casual—but I'm a freelance artist and wannabe filmmaker, and my last straight job was at a video-game store! This real mutilation and gruesome death shit is *new to me!*"

"Okay, sorry. You're not real experienced and still

sensitive, I get it. Really, you should hold on to that as long as you can."

I shake my head and we continue down Stockton toward Powell Station past Union Square in silence.

Grieves babbles behind us incessantly.

As we approach Geary, the light changes and we wait at the corner. Grieves mumbles about Siobhán's martial arts prowess and throwing him back through the wall. He doesn't seem mad. More like surprised and impressed.

The light changes again and we cross Geary and continue down the sidewalk.

I watch the rainwater rush through the gutters on the sides of the street. Feel light-headed as a new pill wave crashes on me and I go all tingly and euphoric. The water streams through the gutters and I imagine it rushing faster and faster until it's a tsunami of rainwater washing the cars and everything else down toward Market and slamming it all into the Diesel store and Old Navy at the intersection. Siobhán and I just tread in place impossibly under the surface, watching it all rush and crash and we laugh and laugh....

I stop walking.

Siobhán notices and stops too. "What?"

Something's missing. What is it?

Grieves's mumbling.

I look back at the intersection of Geary and Stockton.

Through the slits in my goggle specs, I see that Grieves has stopped in the middle of the intersection and is staring down Geary to our right. He's saying something but I can't make it out. The light has changed, and cars pass through Grieves as he stands and stares.

I take a few steps back up the sidewalk toward the intersection. Grieves turns his head toward me and the look on his grotesque face stops me in my tracks.

Grieves looks scared.

The last of the cars pass through him and I can hear

what he's saying now.

"Yoou're-in tr-ouble bbig-troublein bigg-trou-ble-ssshould go you—shouldd g-go…."

Grieves continues reiterating this as he descends into the street.

"Wait! What do you mean?!"

A few people walking up the sidewalk notice me yelling and give me strange looks but I don't care.

Siobhán steps in with, "He's a little drunk, sorry. He can't get enough of that Zima shit. It's a real problem, y'know?" The people move on and Siobhán stares them down as they hurry away up Stockton toward Grieves, unknowingly. "I've tried everything. I even…," she trails off, then says, "What…the actual…fuck?"

I'm still focused on Grieves, who has stopped descending and is still visible, but only from the eyes up.

I feel a tug on my dragon sleeve.

"Felix."

Grieves's hand emerges from the rain-pelted street and he jabs a finger a few times in the direction he was staring, then he descends out of sight into the asphalt.

"Felix!"

I hear a strange whirring sound rising in volume but I'm pretty high so I'm more concerned with Siobhán's attitude.

"What?!"

Siobhán grabs my silly snow-goggle specs and whips them off my face and tosses them onto the wet street. She covers my mouth with her gloved hand. I shrug in protest but she just points at the source of the whirring sound I've been ignoring.

Siobhán whispers, "Be. Quiet."

A blue-black vehicle is hovering about thirty feet above the street and gliding toward the Geary-Stockton intersection from down Geary to the east.

I recognize it—the hovercraft thing I saw on Wahrheit's roof, or one like it.

Seeing it now, I realize it's more like a "flying jeep," a competitor with helicopters for the affection of the US Army and Navy in the late 1950s and early 1960s. They were abandoned for a few reasons but this one looks to be an evolutionary descendant of the idea.

The main structure is canted near the center of its length and houses two shrouded, downward-facing rotors front and back like a bent figure eight. A thick black mist swirls through the rotors and around the vehicle sporadically. A long cylinder struts from an articulated hydraulic support on its underside. Antennae and arrays of monitoring equipment resembling those on top of the monster-cop vans are built into it near the center.

Sitting in what serves it as a pilot seat amongst all this and between the rotors is one of the big, human-shaped blobs of deep black madness. Its eyes are all gray and cloudy, unlike the different shades of one color in the others' I've seen.

Monitoring arrays are clustered like barnacles all over the main structure of the vehicle and look like dense patches of baseball-sized artificial eyeballs as if crafted by Swiss clock makers. They catch light as a cat's eyes would, glinting from deep inside as they twitch and roll around, scanning.

Siobhán lets her hand slide off my mouth as she watches the thing floating by above the street.

There's a faint, colorful glow on the surface of the horrible mess in the pilot seat, which must emanate from visual displays in front of it. Its eyes barely move, like it's entranced by the visual feeds from the monitor eyes. Rain pelts its languidly squirming muck surface while it just watches its screens or projections like a couch potato watching *Family Feud*.

I'm high enough that I've already forgotten Siobhán's warnings and say, "You have got to be fucking kidding me!"

"Shut up, *idiot*."

One of the intricate mechanical eyes scans toward us, then away, but lolls back, examines us, and locks in place. The rest of the eyes swivel and pan toward us and lock on in an automated wave of glinting movement.

The vehicle eases to a forward stop, hovering in place as the gray-eyed muck creature's articulated seat shifts it closer to the displays.

The eyes on the squirming creature twitch and pulse as they fill with blue coloring from almost black up to matte cobalt and vibrant electric. Some are left gray and stupid, but the rest become intensely focused. After poring over the glowing displays, it shifts and twists in its seat and looks directly at me and Siobhán down on the sidewalk.

I swoon as the eyes pierce into my own. Even from up there, the eyes are almost hypnotizing me. The combination of the pill high and those mesmerizing eyes makes my whole body tingle and I feel like I'm in a pool of thick, warm fluid—

NO!

I flood my mind with images and sounds and the remembered smell of these creatures and their handy work. Sewage, urine, blood, burst organs, bile, shit, stomach acid, screams, animal moans, pain, snapping, and ripping!

I shake my head. "Not today!"

I grab Siobhán's hand and pull her the other direction so hard that she drops her umbrella, then toss my own and haul ass down the sidewalk with her in tow.

"Hey!" Siobhán yells and tries to pull her hand out of mine.

"No time!"

I look back at her and something in me softens her glare. She leaves her hand in mine and runs with me. Past her above the intersection the vehicle maneuvers to follow, then glides swiftly through the air after us.

I pull Siobhán through the O'Farrell intersection crosswalk.

The whirring gets louder behind us, but I don't look back.

We get confused looks from impeccably messy techsters inside the sleek, shiny Apple store at the corner of Stockton and Ellis as we run past it toward the Powell Station stairwell it shares a wall with.

I drag Siobhán around the Apple store corner into the stairwell and chance a look back up as we jump down a few steps at a time. The flying jeep slows to a stop above the street outside. I wonder what the techsters in the store would think if they could see that.

The gloppy sack rolls and pours itself out of the vehicle and reforms into its rough humanoid form with surprising grace as it reaches the sidewalk.

We rush down into the bright, drab beige entry level of the station past a guy playing bongo drums with a hat out.

As we run between and weave through throngs of rush-hour cattle down the long stretch toward the paid BART area and turnstiles, the station goes dark. The lights are still on but that same artificial, murky darkness I was caught in running through Colma is swallowing all the light coming out of them.

"Shit! Speed up, boy!" Siobhán exclaims. She effortlessly pumps past me and starts pulling me by the hand down the stretch instead. I can barely keep up and almost stumble.

Siobhán lets go of my hand. "If you didn't look like that, I'd leave you here!"

"What?! What does that mean?!"

"Keep up!"

I run with all I have toward the BART paid area and stairs.

I can't help but admire Siobhán's preternatural grace and agility even while terrified or as close to even uncomfortable as I've seen her. The humming and wet slapping sounds of the nasty monster rushing through the station behind us clears my head though.

Dense packs of silhouetted people all around watch Siobhán and me running and their eyes glint strangely, reflecting the unseen light as they seem to frown or stare or shake their heads.

Siobhán reaches the BART-fare-paid area and vaults the waist-high glass wall without hesitation like a gazelle, continuing toward the stairs to the platform. She glances back and sees me fumbling for my transit card.

"Fuck your card, Felix—oh shit!"

I try to look back but all I see are silhouettes of people and inky darkness. I hear the hum right behind me and the smell makes my eyes tear up.

Siobhán slides to a stop, whips around, and snaps her fingers—which cuts a symbol in the air for a moment before it glints and twists into itself.

There's a flash behind me that all but blinds me the rest of the way and I almost run straight into the low ticket-stall barrier wall. I hear a shrill wail behind me that vibrates through my teeth and bones.

Siobhán says, "Yeah, I got tricks too, you sloppy bitch!"

I throw myself over the ticket barrier but botch the landing and slip, slamming down onto the smooth, hard station floor.

Before I can gather myself, Siobhán has me up and she's pushing me along in front of her down the stairwell to the platform.

"Why is there a porker after you?!"

"I told you we were in trouble!"

"I thought you were exaggerating!"

She keeps nudging and guiding me down onto the dark platform. It's a long open stretch to the other stairwell on the far end—which I can't see right now but know it's there from my many trips into and out of this station. The only cover down here are sets of cylindrical metallic columns that run parallel down each side of an island platform.

That and the dense herds of rush-hour commuters on

each side and patches between.

I hear the slapping sounds of the "porker" moving again above and behind us upstairs and can just make it out coming down from the top of the stairwell as a big dim silhouette with its glowing blue eyes. I can see the swirling 3-D fractals messing with the air around the larger, brighter blue eyes.

I break off my gaze before it can pull me in and concentrate on the platform in front of us. There are more people than usual. Even for rush hour.

Siobhán's gloved hand gently but firmly grasps my shoulder from behind and she starts guiding me through the crowd on the SFO-bound side of the platform.

There's a shudder and creak from the walls on both sides of the platform and vent-slats appear and flap open in them. Glowing green gas starts belching, then pouring out of them full blast.

Siobhán says, "Oh, that can't be good…," and takes a silky, purple-black bandanna out of her back jeans pocket and quickly wraps and ties it around her face before clasping my shoulder again. I try to cover my mouth and nose with my dragon sleeve but already feel a little dizzy from the gas. It's cool and sweet like nitrous at a dental office. The gas is cool in my lungs, but my chest feels warm and kind of nice, which is confusing. My limbs start to feel a little heavy and tingly too.

I remember a torn green T-shirt in my pack and try to slip it off. Siobhán releases me for a moment, and I take the pack off to rummage through it. I take the torn T-shirt out and tie it around my face. As I go to close the pack, I feel the weight of the camera and pistol. This pack is probably just going to slow me down.

I cover myself with the pack and slip the gun from it into my waistband, then take the HDV-426 out by the carry grip on the top and drop the pack on the platform.

Siobhán seems to hear something that I can't and grabs

my shoulder again. She guides me down into a crouch and says, "Stay low. It can see a lot better than we can, but the chatter will confuse it."

From her voice it sounds like she's watching behind us as she pushes me through the forest of silhouetted people. There are comments and disapproving grunts from the forest as we push through.

I cringe. "What'll these people think?"

"Don't much care."

One of the trees says, "Fuck you too, weirdo."

Another says, "Yeah, what is this—Occupy Powell Station?" and a few of the other trees chuckle or scoff.

I'm confused by this for a moment until I visualize what we must look like in the light with the cloth over our faces.

The gas is still getting in through the T-shirt and I'm feeling hazy and stupid but it's almost pleasant. The platform is getting brighter, and I can see the faces of the people more clearly. With each breath, the people pulse between silhouetted forms covered in grayish translucent flowers, bulbs, and amoebas and normal people looking at us with disgusted or nervous eyes. Is that the gas? It feels nice....

Siobhán slaps the side of my face to clear my head and pushes me onward. It stings but that's the point and it gives me a moment to get back with it. It gets a bit darker again but continues to brighten as I breathe. Things are clearer and more normal. For a moment, I'm relieved but then I realize—

If I can't see the darkness, can I see the monster?

I look back through the crowd and can only vaguely see the black, human-shaped blob down by the stairs. With each breath it becomes less defined, and I can see through it more.

I feel the beginnings of panic trying to make me run screaming any way I can.

If I can't see it, I can't get away! It's going to eat me! It's really going to fucking eat me!

I blink a few times and realize I can't see the blue-eyed muck thing anymore at all. I stifle a yelp but drop my camera and stop, crouched in place and shaking.

Siobhán whispers, "What's wrong you?!"

I shudder. "I c-can't see it!"

"Neither can I but we have to keep going!"

"I can't!"

Siobhán digs her fingers into my shoulder with such effortless strength that they feel like talons. Her makeup job and hood combine with her eerie, mirrored eyes into a genuinely fearsome scowl and for just an instant I'm more frightened of Siobhán than the monster down the platform. I still can't force myself to move, though.

She locks the depth of her claws but starts to twist them in my jacketed flesh.

"Oh, yes you can...," Siobhán growls with a flash of malice I hope is just to drive her point home.

I look down away from her intense gaze and see the camera next to my open hand on the platform floor. The piercing pain focuses me. I only grabbed the HDV-426 from my bag out of habit and to save the footage maybe, but it hits me that I'm holding a peephole into bizarro-world.

"Let go, shit!" I whisper hard.

Siobhán releases her death grip and I turn on the HDV-426 and pop open the little monitor screen from the side of the camera body. I press the button on the lens and there's that familiar static pop. The view clears and the screen shows the murky black platform. It's tinged green from the gas but the vents are hard to see because the camera isn't as clear as fully dosed eyes.

I tilt the screen almost totally down, then raise the camera to over shoulder level of the tree people and point it behind through the crowd toward the nasty creature. The camera catches the impression of the muck figure as it looks back and forth into the crowds of tentacle- and bulb-covered people from near the foot of the stairs they came down.

Siobhán whispers, "Clever boy."

We creep through the forest of disgusted and confused normals, watching the porker for any evidence that it has seen us. We make it to one of the metallic columns about halfway down the platform and she pulls me up against it. I adjust the little screen to be seen from hip level, then press the camera against the column and slide it around enough to watch the creature. Siobhán peeks around and studies it on the screen too.

Siobhán says, "*Blech*—worse than I remembered. On the very short list of things I'm afraid of, porkers are almost at the top."

"I'd hate to see what beats them."

"Yeah, you would." She looks around the platform. "And here I am without my goddamned peacemakers." She looks toward the tunnel. "Won't matter in a minute though."

The creature starts pouring itself into a slow stride down the platform as it looks around.

I feel like urinating on myself for a moment but fight it off.

Okay, just keep your cool and the BART car will—

—This is a service advisory message—all trains are delayed to clear some debris from the track. Be about five to ten minutes. Sorry for the inconvenience.—

Siobhán says, "Bullshit! We won't last two minutes down here like this." She looks around the normal platform, then back at the muck monster coming toward us through the weird darkness on the little camera screen. "Okay, get low and keep going. We'll sneak to the stairs, haul ass up out of here, and try to catch a cab or something."

"What if there aren't any?"

"Hell, we can roll a messenger for his bike. You can ride on the handlebars." She grasps my shoulder again and says,

"You got me into this—so whatever it takes, got it?"

"Alright, alright."

I crouch and start through the rest of the rush-hour crowd. My shoulder hurts from her claws before and I shrug for her to let go. I glare back at her too and something in my eyes makes her let go but she gently places her hand against my back to stay in contact. I decide I can live with that and move on.

Siobhán and I are almost to the stairs in the cover of confused strangers when I see two men coming down them. It's the weird, samey-looking homeless guys with the stuffed duffle bags and overcoats, and they're scanning the platform with their big fake-looking eyes as they descend. They have faintly glowing, plum-sized orbs stuck to their overcoat chests.

I stop and rest on one knee. I look at the men and back down the platform through the camera.

"Felix, I'm not fucking around. If we don't get out of here—"

"*Shhht!*"

A high-school-aged skateboarder to our left notices us. He's swigging off an open tallboy in a brown bag and looking sideways at us. Finishes his pull and lightly slaps his two cronies on the chest and shoulder before loudly announcing, "Hey! Is someone looking for these two fuckin' freaks?!" He points at me and Siobhán. His friends laugh and he continues, "They lookin' hella shady, kid! Yo, check this isht right here!"

I watch the muck creature on the display screen. Most of its eyes lock on the skater, then examine the area where he's pointing. Nonono....

Siobhán says, "Shut up, dickhead," and takes a small, round pebble or BB out of the coin pocket of her jeans. She curls her index finger behind the inner tip of her thumb with the BB between and lightly flicks it at the lower third of the bag-covered can below the jerky skater's hand. It goes through the bag and can and I hear it hit the other side of the can interior as it stops. A yellowish fluid drains out of the hole in the can, soaking the bag and streaming down onto the expensive-looking shoes the skater is wearing.

The skater exclaims, "What the fuck?!" and hobbles about trying to stop the flow. He doesn't seem smart enough to figure out Siobhán is responsible, but I'm damn sure she wouldn't care if he did. The troll was successful, though.

The muck monster stops about twenty feet down and stares through the crowd between me, Siobhán, and itself.

Siobhán sees this on the little screen too. "Damn."

It's hard to make out fully on the video screen, but the diseased-organ-and-amorphous-limb surface undulates and writhes more intensely. Parts of it break and split open revealing what look like misshapen, asymmetric chasms of jagged, obsidian teeth between the eyes. It lets out a wail from all of the openings, and its whole form rolls and whips around atop two asymmetrical base limbs like it's trying to start up a few Hula-Hoops at once. That mostly comes through on the little playback speaker in the camera body but I can still hear some of it reverberating off the platform walls like it's huge and far away.

The creature breaks apart again and different-sized parts of it become long, eye-covered appendages like pulsing, obsidian-bladed whips that swipe through the air with the sound of a heavy scythe going through thick grass.

The wail is now a shrill, maddening howl and I can't handle it. It's getting so loud the playback speaker is blowing and it's almost deafening. I keep the camera locked on the creature as I stand and turn toward it and try to pull the pistol out of my waistband. Instead, the hammer hooks on the bottom of my dragon jacket and the heavy pistol drops to the platform floor with a metallic thunk.

The muck sack's gyrating and pulsing slows and the whipping of the tentacles and thicker, eye-covered appendages in its chaotic storm of psychedelic madness calms enough that it's almost human shaped again. It watches me fumble to pick up the gun with its livelier eyes.

A group of commuters shrieks and yells at the sight of the pistol and others look to see why. Like an ocean parting, the frightened rush-hour crowds shrink away and bunch together near the platform edges.

The mucky figure forms something like a twisted arm out of matte-black organ-and-sinew slop and digs the end of it into the stormy ocean of its main current trunk. Then it pulls it back out, producing a plum-sized sphere not unlike the one the weird hobos have on their coats. Wait, where did they go? Doesn't matter now—

The straining filth limb's end closes around the sphere and I hear a little click. Then the muck creature releases its grasp on the sphere and drops it. Before it can hit the ground, it starts spinning so fast that it hovers in place and glows brighter as it picks up more and more speed. I don't care to see what the sphere is for and start to raise the pistol to make the point moot.

"No, Felix!"

Siobhán lunges toward me fast enough that her hood falls back, almost freeing her two big braids. She grasps my jacket collar and pulls me toward the stairs like I weigh a fifth of what I do, and her braids whip free and are flung around like the legs of a gymnast performing an aerial. My feet leave the ground and she hauls me through the air almost parallel to the ground lengthwise.

I'm so focused on survival that I don't really think about how Siobhán is defying gravity or how I've achieved liftoff—I just struggle to train the camera and pistol back on the mucky form in its darkness but all I can see as the viewing angle of the little screen changes is it whipping back up into a murderous fury, and the bloodcurdling wailing is blowing the speaker again.

The whirling muck monster starts toward us taking

steps from one malformed pseudo-leg to the other. As Siobhán pulls me along with her long, powerful strides, I desperately try to aim between my own legs and feet, which are flailing round.

Then things get *really* weird.

There's a flash in the core of the glowing sphere hovering above the floor behind the advancing porker and for just a sliver of a moment it feels to me like I'm slowing down and the creature is speeding up. What I can see of it on the video screen becomes even more blurred and vague.

Before I can even panic all the way, I slap down on the floor of the platform on my ass and it feels like someone has pulled down my ripped shirt mask and is holding something to my face. My pistol clatters down onto the platform next to me.

I can barely see, and everything is blurry and pulsing. I struggle and can just make out that it's the smaller of the weird Peter Lorre–looking hobos and he's wearing what looks like a clear plastic dust mask with rotating valves over the nose and mouth and short cylinders jutting at downward angles off each side of the jawline. Is that what's on my face?

Something bright is on my chest. I look down and see one of the spheres like the hobos have—and it occurs to me again that they look similar to the one the creature used. It's blurring but the insides look like spherical clock parts whirring into and around and through each other like a little impossibly intricate and complex machine.

There's a beep and I feel the breath come out of me, so I struggle more. Feel pressure on and then in my neck and realize the small hobo is injecting something into me. By my third heartbeat, I can breathe again and whatever the hobo shot into me has dropped the cloak of the inky blackness back down onto everything and I see the fearsome muck monster whirling in the platform-wide green gas and can hear its wail with my own ears again. It's advancing and almost right on us.

Ten feet maybe.

All of the movement in my vision takes on surreal, warping properties—as the smaller hobo moves to put away his syringe, his form takes on the shape of all the space it fills as it moves. When the movement is finished, the warping catches up and it looks almost normal until he moves again.

The shot in my neck has brought back my high and I joke in my mind, I bet there's some Futurists back in the day who would've killed to see this.

Through this disorienting effect, I see the larger hobo step in front of us and throw his overcoat open toward the creature.

He raises a metal, cloth, and flesh blob from inside his coat, which reveals itself after a moment of stillness to be a heavily-modified old submachine gun with tubes, ampules, and spheres pumping glowing fluids through it—and a long box magazine jutting out to the left perpendicular to the gun's length.

The hobo aims it toward the barreling muck abomination and yells, "*Deine mutter geht in der Stadt huren, sheisskerl!*" his words warbling and twisting like the sound equivalent of the warping movement.

The hobo fires the gun and the muzzle and breach flash a brilliant indigo as blinding white rounds sear the air like tracers, then shred into the trunk and whipping stalks of the charging monster.

As the casings leave the ejector, they become glowing strips of solid light until they vanish a few feet from the gun and the trail catches up and it all blinks out.

Some of the fluids in the gun's strange add-ons boil now as they course through their tubes from ampule to bulb, and an exhaust port burps dark smoke or mist out and back over the hobo's shoulder in time with the bursts.

The smaller hobo stands, steps toward the creature, and

produces two machine-organic limbs, which catch up and become long-barrel machine pistols with drum magazines, and similar strange modifications.

He fires full-auto into the wailing blue-eyed muck sack, and I see the hobo's elbows bulge backwards in time with the shots—then I realizes he must have some kind of recoil-dampening cylinders concealed by his coat sleeves.

As the rounds tear and shred into and through the thick, oily nastiness that makes up the porker, the holes left behind start to suck and rip the creature into itself.

Its wails take a turn toward pained and fearful as the psychedelic black sludge that holds it together is pulled into the negative space, leaving piles and puddles of partially digested and corroded organs, deformed teeth, warped bones, limbs, eyes, and fluids sprayed and slapped all over the platform.

The creature's eyes go gray and dead again, and its wailing cuts out abruptly as the last of the muck is sucked away into the air over the sickening collection of glistening parts left behind.

The thick darkness just vanishes when the last bit of muck is gone but the green gas and spinning hover ball remain.

The hobos stop firing their smoking weapons but scan the area before lowering them. The larger one turns around and becomes a moving Duchamp painting in my mind for a moment before catching up with himself as he stops and examines me on the floor.

The man's big blue eyes and roughly cropped blond hair poking out from under a dark gray knit cap look even more fake now.

He thinks for a moment, then chuckles and says, "What was it you said? 'Scientists would say sure…. Philosophers would say who knows…,' and then what? I've been trying to tell that one to Sujit and I can never remember the last part."

I just look at him in a daze.

The hobo says, "Oh, sorry. The hot shot's got you looped a bit."

He takes off his mask, sticks a gloved finger down his throat, and retches a small black ball into his hand. It looks like an obsidian bouncy ball.

As soon as the ball leaves his mouth, the kind-of-fake-looking blond hair, blue eyes, and pale skin become roughly cropped, coarse black hair where he must have cut off his dreadlocks; dark skin; and rich brown eyes. The gap between his chops has filled in and become an unkempt salt and pepper beard. He puts the clear mask back on without taking a breath and exhales into it.

"Wahrheit?"

Wahrheit tucks the little ball into a coat pocket and makes a "thumbs up" gesture with his hand.

"Got it in one."

chapter 29

I am not convinced this man is Wahrheit but I decide to keep that close to my chest. Nauseated, I partially burp out, "What's—what's going on?"

"Not much now that the cavalry showed up, am I right?"

The smaller man who must be Sujit snorts an acknowledgement of Wahrheit's joke through his artificial Peter Lorre stomach-ball face. These guys seem pretty soused themselves.

Wahrheit looks past me. "Who's the frail?"

I look to where Wahrheit's gaze is falling and see Siobhàn. She looks like a statue for a moment, then I realize that she's just moving incredibly slowly. There is definite movement, but it only seems noticeable because she was moving so quickly. Or still is, I guess? This is too much.

I look around the platform and notice that the rush-hour commuters are practically frozen in place. The faster movement is progressing, but you have to pay attention to see it.

"Felix, I need your attention! Who is this woman to you? How do you know her?"

"I met her at a party. She works at a fish-supply shop. She has a fuckin' weird apartment in the same building in Chinatown. That's pretty much what I know."

"Is she kosher? Can we trust her?"

I'm still unsure who I can trust at all but I say, "I mean, I *think* so. Not a hundred-percent sure, I guess."

Wahrheit narrows his eyes at me, then looks back at Siobhàn and considers. He cautiously crosses to Siobhàn's slow-running form. I notice that her expression is changing ever so slowly into a mask of confusion and her head is turning almost imperceptibly. Has she noticed I'm not at the end of her arm anymore?

Wahrheit opens his slung duffle bag and takes out another of the clear masks and an ancient-looking syringe from out of a velvet-lined case. He takes a few steps around her like he's looking for the best spot.

Blond-blue Sujit says a few phrases in what I decide is probably Thai and Wahrheit grunts like a long-married husband, seeming to convey an "I know, I know."

"What did he say?" I ask.

"Uh…," he says as he calculates, "…he told me to be careful."

"Why?"

"Well, what you have here is what you might call a wolf among sharks, or a shark among wolves. Either way, she's out of her element but still deadly as hell if you get too close."

I shake my head. "Please just make sense for five seconds!"

"She's a member of the Thae'st Ra'yho tribe of the A'uhlt-Yha diaspora. I honestly have no idea what she'd be doing on this side of Junction Town right now, though. How'd you meet her again?"

"At a party. She just showed up high off her ass and I think I reminded her of somebody. I think she has maybe a crush on me."

"Lucky you."

"Why?"

"Tribal women of the Thae'st Ra'yho, especially warrior idols like this one, are known for their...marital talents, let's say."

"Are you serious with this right now?"

"Totally. They're fiercely romantic ladies," he says and chuckles. "And they're even better in a fight."

I decide not to explain what I meant and just say, "You know that from experience?"

Wahrheit ignores my question and continues his examination with the calculation of a naturalist.

"She has the distinct queue-esque hairstyle. That particular one is the oldest, least used, and most recognizable across the tribes. The braids are a cute touch. The dyed markings scattered around on her hair seal it as Thae'st Ra'yho, though. She's toned down what would normally be intricate and striking face paint into this Halloween-y makeup job, and this particular style makes me think she was going to pay respects to a fallen comrade. I would have to assume she has extensive tattoo work in a roughly Asian style. Most likely with a focus on monstrous creatures, dirigibles and airships, flowers and/or wind- and watermills?"

"I saw sakura and slithery sea-creature people."

"Mm-hmmm. These contacts are new to me, though. Not common by any means. You met this woman...at a *party*?"

"That's what I said," I half growl, getting tired of re-answering questions.

"Must have been quite the soiree."

Wahrheit looks like he's decided on a plan of attack. He gently inserts the needle into her neck and empties the smallish tube. Then he pulls down the silky bandanna from over her mouth and nose and detaches the chain with the little hammers on it from her nose ring, lets it dangle down her neck from her ear lobe, and places the mask over her face. It sucks into place as he produces another of the plum-sized spheres from his duffle bag. He presses a button and lets it spin up a bit before gingerly placing it against the left side of her hoodie. He steps back just in time.

Siobhàn is pulled out of what I can only think of as normal time with a sound like distorted suction, then platform-wide shuddering, and she makes it a couple long, warped blob strides before gagging and choking for breath. She collapses against the first few rows of stairs but catches herself on the way down and succeeds in whipping around into a cautious crouch with her feet and hands supporting her on different steps.

She fights to catch her breath and her eyes dart around, taking in the situation and strange warping of space in time.

"Not…again…," she says as she finally gets some air. She grimaces as a wave of nausea washes over her. She lifts one of her hands and watches it warp into a blob as she wags it back and forth. "God, I hate this shit."

Her eyes dart around again and she blurts out, "Where's the fucking porker?!"

Wahrheit answers, "We returned it to the primordial abyss."

"Good riddance," Siobhàn replies.

She notices the clear mask on her face and starts to take it off.

"You'll need that. The gas is still on."

She looks around at the vents and thick green fog and seals it back in place. She stands and scans the platform, ready to run again given the slightest hint of a reason.

"Who are your friends, Felix?"

"I'll tell you in a minute."

Wahrheit walks over to where I'm still sitting on the platform and offers his hand to help me up.

"You're in a lake of shit, man."

I take his hand and Wahrheit pulls me to my feet.

"I've got to get you to—"

I put the business end of my revolver against Wahrheit's forehead. "Wahrheit's dead! Who the fuck are you?"

Wahrheit raises his eyebrows and then his hands in surrender.

Sujit detaches and secures one of his modded guns in his coat, then pulls out an unmodified semiautomatic pistol and points it at my head down the platform.

In strained English Sujit says, "Bad…plan."

Wahrheit says, "Wait," and I realize he's addressing Sujit and not me, the person holding a gun to his head.

I can feel Sujit deciding the best angle to shoot me with any chance of not killing Wahrheit but I don't care anymore.

Siobhàn laughs. "Ooh-ooh, *quien es mas macho*?" and mock fans herself. "You're givin' me the vapors!" She shakes her head. "Idiots."

Wahrheit says, "Felix, I know all this is confusing but—"

"I saw Wahrheit's body—what was left of it! Who are you?"

"Felix, ask yourself what you saw. I know you didn't see my face, 'cause I didn't die in that trailer park. You probably saw Chucky C.'s body, sad as I am to say it. I had some of my street-team sergeants over for a meeting when we got raided. Only Sujit and I made it out. For all I know, there's parts of Kveta and the rest of 'em in that mess I just made. Look in my eyes, Felix. It's definitely me."

"After all the shit I've seen, I don't trust your word or your face!"

"Fair enough."

Wahrheit starts vibrating and with a shudder he becomes a moving blur—

I'm slammed flat on my back on the platform with my legs kicked up and Wahrheit is standing above me holding the revolver that was just in my hand.

Wahrheit watches my legs crumple back to the floor and looks down into my eyes. "Please, don't do that again. The Ref is already fixin' to give me a yellow card, so the less I do that the better. It's bad enough we're using these booster spheres. These are a big no-no."

He releases the cylinder on my revolver and examines the spent and unspent rounds.

"One bullet? You were going to try to ace a fuckin' *Albtraum soldat* with one normal bullet? What are you, John McClane? And that fool had two." He laughs and empties the cylinder into his open duffle.

"Yippie-Ki-Yay...," Sujit quotes, then chuckles and holsters his normal pistol and goes back to scanning the platform. He focuses on the ceiling and floor, which is strange to me but what about this isn't?

Wahrheit extends his hand down to me.

"Shall we try again?"

I take Wahrheit's hand and I'm hauled to my feet.

I cough to clear my throat. "Okay, you're Wahrheit. But what are you doing here?"

Wahrheit takes my revolver apart, grabs mods from his bag, and deftly installs them. Securing brackets, ampules, pressure button to the right rear of the chamber.

"Well, I'm here to make sure that *Albtraum* doesn't kill you. Oh wait, did that. Other than that, I've got to get you to Walt and Izzy in Sausalito."

"What? Who?" I ask.

"Best hackers in this or any remotely close layer. If I had known you were the kid they always talk about, I wouldn't have let you out of my sight."

I ignore the stranger parts of what Wahrheit just said and ask, "Why?"

"Because you're...special."

I laugh. "Oh, stop it! Don't even start!"

"I know, I know…but it's true. They've been protecting you from a distance since you were young, after your father died. From what they've said, there's even some layers where they stepped in and pretended to be related to you so they could guard you even closer. They didn't know what you were, but they knew it was important to the Refs and maybe even whoever they answer to."

I sigh, defeated. I guess you can't fight a dream with logic from within, right? Even one this lucid.

"Okay, from what? What would I need protection from?"

"Hard to say. Maybe they didn't even know themselves, but either way they failed. All that time keeping you safe and you end up bumpin' uglies with none other than Obrist's little witch."

I shake my head. "Obrist? Witch? You don't make any sense, man."

Siobhàn seems interested now.

"The man you know as Doctor Fleischmann is actually Albrecht Obrist. He made the FMC and Harmonia to control pinks and keep them from seeing, like I told you at my house. That's more like a hobby, though. He does a lot more than that."

"Like what?"

"Just to name a few things, he also made those vents that materialize, this gas, and the creatures your friend here calls 'porkers'—that I know from their official project designation in the 1940s as Obrist's *Albtraumsoldaten*. Nightmare soldiers, as the spooky-ass Nazis called them."

Siobhàn narrows her eyes. "Made them? How is that possible?"

"They're basically golems of flesh, organs, bones, and fluids held together by a nasty glop he siphoned from the Big Black. He perfected the process in the fifties after moving his previously Nazi-funded research facilities from the Vosges Mountains in France to northeastern Greenland."

My head is spinning for a few reasons and I'm just trying to keep up. "So, he's like a Nazi scientist?"

"Not really. He took funding and resources from the krauts for work on highly advanced weapons, vehicles, and super soldiers to help them beat the Allies, but mostly used it on his obsession with immortality. He did make huge advances in all these things but he either kept them for himself or gave the Nazis all but faulty or useless prototypes for his own amusement. He was able to make most of these advances with the help of his witch."

I shake my head. "Okay, you keep talking about this witch, but I don't remember stickin' it to a witch. I'm no choirboy but it seems like something I would recall."

Siobhàn chuckles. "You're cute but you're not that smart, are you, Felix? I barely know you but even I can see he's talking about your girlfriend."

"Audrey?"

Wahrheit says, "Yes, Audrey. Now, as far as I've been able to glean, Audrey and Obrist have been on the outs for decades but you getting your hands on the four-two-six camera and flipping out must've made her desperate. She probably went to him for your treatment knowing what you had seen. What she is. When it comes to re-pinking people, 'Fleischmann' is the best."

"Why do you keep calling her a witch?"

"It's what the soldiers called her in the camps and 'research' lab. She knew things she *couldn't* know about science and technology and many other things, and to them that meant magic and evil, ironically enough."

"Okay, what is she then?"

"She's an immigrant. As far as the Refs are concerned, she's an illegal—only they can't touch her. She can't be deported or punished. She's unstuck from time and impervious to their abilities because of the crude yet powerful method that was used. She has something like a reluctant amnesty."

Siobhàn turns her head away and looks like she might cry for a moment. It's the strangest look I've seen on her face and even in profile it reminds me of the hollow look she gave me the night we met. It's just a flash, then she's back to her predatory feline observation and confidence, but I feel like it told me how little I actually know about her, or any of this, really.

I shake my head. "The more you tell me, the less I understand—or *care*. Can we just get out of here? I don't want to die today."

"I don't think you're the one in danger," Wahrheit says.

"What? Of course, I am!"

"No, I think you're under Audrey's protection."

"I thought you said Audrey was Fleischmann's witch. Why would he listen to her?"

"I said that's what they called her. I always got the distinct impression that *she* was in charge. Obrist is in love with her, or was. I don't think she's been active for decades, so he's basically king shit now, but I don't think he'd risk upsetting her further by letting you get hurt."

Wahrheit finishes modifying my pistol and releases the cylinder again. He takes a quickloader out of his duffle, which holds six translucent rounds similar to the ones he was making the day we met, inserts them into the chamber and releases the quickloader, dropping the rounds in place.

"'In love'? Great. So who *is* in danger then?"

Wahrheit whips the revolver cylinder closed and looks at Siobhàn, so I do too.

She scowls. "I don't even know this kid! I came here to get away from bullshit like this!"

Wahrheit nods. "I was wondering about that myself. Why are you running around with him anyway? In this realm, no less."

Siobhàn's glinting eyes slowly roll from one scared, all-but-frozen commuter on the platform to another as she says, "Not that it concerns you, but I came here to get away from the tribes…and my lover. She's too impressionable and if I'd stuck around, she'd end up worse than me. The tribes have become so self-serving, cold, and brutal, and it's my fault."

Wahrheit laughs. "I knew it! You're not just a lesser warrior idol—you're the Thae'st Ra'yho idol queen!"

"What of it?" Siobhàn says with a sneer.

"No offense meant. I am curious, though…."

"About what?"

"What led you here, at this particular time? Honestly."

Siobhàn seems to fight off a sarcastic retort, then furrows her brow and thinks for a moment. "I was in Lower East Junction getting ready to take a small rented amphibious air skiff through the locks to Wei-Tshi on Iya Prime. My loose plan was to go sky fishing in low atmosphere storms for a while to clear my head, then do some climbing in the mountains and maybe even get a monkey to pick some tea for me. I've never pulled that off, even to this day."

Wahrheit narrows his eyes. "But something happened and then you had a different plan?"

Siobhàn studies his face and eyes.

"Yeah, actually. I passed a small aquarium and remembered my shop in Chinatown here. It belonged to an old ex of mine 'cause I gifted it to her, but it's still mine. So, I came here to relax instead. Should've just gone sky fishing."

"And something called your attention to the aquarium, right?"

I scoff. "Who gives a shit?"

Siobhàn ignores me and says, "Now that you mention it, a fight broke out in a tavern on the other side of the street between two Sken'ghi pirates. In the reflection of the tavern window, I saw the colorful aquarium and looked over. How did you know?"

"I've been kicking around this hypothesis that the Refs are guiding us. They can't directly influence anything that doesn't break the rules, but beings capable of doing that are rare at this point. So, I think they use little tricks of circumstance and association to guide us. They're bringing us together for a greater purpose. I think that's maybe how Felix ended up with Audrey. We just have to—"

I say, "That is fucking fascinating, but if we don't get out of here, we'll all get the Rudy treatment!"

"What happened to Rudy?"

"I thought you knew everything!"

The strange, inky darkness descends upon the platform again and we all look around. The light from the glowing spheres on all our chests is enough to give off a dim illumination not unlike that of a strong glow stick. As our eyes adjust, the light is more than enough to see several feet around in front of us but drops off dramatically past that. The eyes of the frozen-silhouette commuters reflect the glow of the spheres, and they look like a huge pack of animals lurking just outside the periphery of a prairie campfire on a night with no moon.

Siobhàn shakes her head. "Not more porkers...."

A hum grows in the ceiling. Wahrheit readies his submachine gun again with one hand and aims at the spot where it seems to be strongest.

He flips the revolver in his other hand and offers me the modified pistol, grip first. I take it and examine the new additions to make sense of them.

"You have to press this thumb button to prime the catalyst fluids every time or it won't fire."

The hum gets louder and more familiar to me—

Grieves drops from the ceiling, his head and feet rotating counterclockwise around his center as he descends.

"More-troubble com-ming! Morre trou-ble coooooming!"

I yell, "Don't shoot!"

Wahrheit tenses and steadies his gun with his other hand as he aims at Grieves's descending center-mass but doesn't fire. Sujit also refrains from firing but doesn't look happy about it.

"More mons-turrs onn the w—" His speech is cut off as his head rotates down and into the floor and then his body follows, phasing out of sight.

"What the hell was that?!" Wahrheit demands.

"My friend Grieves."

"Friend? How does he...." Wahrheit trails off for a moment as he tries to get his head around what Grieves must be.

Very different shuddering and groaning vibrations grow in the ceiling above. It darkens unnaturally in one spot, then another several feet away. Wahrheit aims at one dark spot and Sujit at the other.

Siobhàn looks around for a way out. She takes a few steps toward the stairs Wahrheit and Sujit came down but stops and crouches.

"Felix."

I hear fear in her voice and cross to her side.

Colorful, psychedelic circles of blue and green and red dance in dense patches near the top of the long, dark stairwell back up to the station and multiple sets of splashing, slapping steps can be heard.

I shudder. "So many...."

Then look back toward Wahrheit and Sujit just in time to see the dark spots in the ceiling disgorge most of their contents like huge boils being lanced. Malformed blobs of translucent, gore-filled muck strain like huge black larvae being birthed out of the ceiling and their myriad eyes glow in the dark as they loll around—then they find and lock onto Wahrheit and Sujit.

Without dropping from the ceiling, the writhing sacks break apart and begin whipping and thrashing around. Sujit tucks and rolls as one obsidian talon-tipped appendage slices the air over the spot he had just occupied.

Wahrheit and Sujit fire up at the hanging and swinging nightmare things, dodging the deadly whips and blades of squirming black flesh and obsidian. As the first two creatures are sucked into nothingness in a shower of organs, rotting bones, and filth, more dark spots and straining larvae appear. Wahrheit and Sujit dispatch their targets as they writhe out of the ceiling only to be sucked away leaving a nasty mess—but the spots keep appearing.

Siobhàn stands. "Oh, fuck this noise."

In warping, liquid strides, she hurries down to the BART tunnel on the left.

I say, "Wher- -re you goi—?!" trying to compete with the gunfire and failing.

The shots are louder than I would have thought, having only really heard automatic fire in movies. It rattles through my skull, and it feels like my bowels are shuddering. My hand is shaking too, which makes my revolver click and clack a little, when I can hear it.

I look back up the stairwell and see that the muck monsters are climbing and rolling down every surface of it—some pouring between and around the all but frozen silhouetted commuters—descending quickly now and wailing as they come.

The futility of their fight almost causes me to drop my pistol. I fight off paralysis and yell, "Wahrheit! They're comin- -own the stairs!"

"How many?!"

"I- -on't kno- dozens?" I respond.

"Dozens? Did you say *dozens*?!" Now Wahrheit sounds scared.

Siobhàn looks at me. "They're go--- t- get you kil--- -own here! We need to ke-- -unning!"

She pulls her silky bandanna off her neck and drapes it over her glowing orb, dousing its light. By the movement of her dim silhouette, it looks like she ties the bandanna off below the orb to secure it.

The dark figure down the platform says, "Trust me, Felix," in Siobhàn's voice.

I look back up at the howling madness coming down the stairwell and raise my gun, which is heavier now with the mods and my arm wavers a bit. I can probably get one or two before they eat me—

"Felix!" Siobhàn's voice booms from the darkness by the tunnel mouth.

I look back toward her but don't lower my big pistol.

"I need yo- t- -rust me," the featureless female silhouette says. There's that vulnerable Irish girl again? The movement of her mouth and jaw are all I can make out in the dark as my eyes adjust and it reminds me of a dream I had, what seems like years ago now.

"Felix, please."

"Okay, sure," I say like she asked me to pass the dinner rolls.

She grabs the metal barrier that blocks the tunnel-access path and smoothly swings herself around it like she's hanging onto a merry-go-round bar. Then she's out of sight and I hear her soft but strong steps padding quickly down the access path away from this nightmare, in between the booms and rat-ta-tats.

I look back up the stairwell and see a living wall of psychedelic eyes, undulating black flesh, and flashing obsidian teeth and talon-blades. The 3-D fractal abstractions pouring out of the blue, red, and green sets of eyes become blinding white when they overlap from all the grotesque, almost obscene slapping and slithering.

For a long moment I just watch, detached and fascinated—

Then the smell hits me and my fear returns—and I can't get to the tunnel mouth fast enough. I run for it, unable to force a look back, out of overpowering fear there's a monster already behind me. As I'm climbing around the metal gate,

I see Wahrheit and Sujit spin toward the stairwell and start firing at the living wave of horror spilling out of it.

Sujit sweeps his two autopistols back and forth, tearing into the disgorging mass of layered muck creatures and subtracting dense chunks from them—but nowhere near enough.

A neglected muck-monster larva spills out of the ceiling behind the two men, slapping a gloppy mess of slender appendages like anemones' sucker-less tentacles around Sujit's upper torso—

He's still firing as it sinks talons between his ribs, lifts him off the platform, and pulls him into one of its larger toothy mouths. As it bites into his head and shoulder, another larva that's dropped out of the ceiling latches onto Sujit's legs, pulling them into its own mouths as it tugs his abdomen apart with its own tentacles and warped appendages. Sujit's entrails tumble out as his spine detaches.

Sujit is devoured between the two nightmare creatures in the most obscene, stomach-turning version of the spaghetti scene from *Lady and the Tramp* I've ever witnessed.

I collapse onto the narrow service path, then haul myself up and run as fast as I can.

chapter 30

I secure my revolver in the large left pocket of my jacket and fumble with the torn T-shirt wrapped around my neck as I run, in an attempt to cover up the glowing orb on my chest. The shirt is thin, so it dims the light some but won't douse it. The sphere gives off an eerie pale green glow now from the shirt as I run down the service path, and the pistol swings back and forth in the drooping left front of my jacket.

I hear wailing and gunfire and screaming behind me in the tunnel or back in Powell Station and, because of that and the adrenaline pumping through me, I can't hear Siobhàn running ahead at all. I can't see her either but imagine her running just up a ways.

An explosion booms behind me and the tunnel shakes and groans and the gunfire and screaming stop.

I slow to a jog and look back, then shuffle to a stop and listen. There's nothing but silence in the complete darkness past my green glow at first, then I hear sliding or shuffling down the tunnel that I can't make out.

And I'm lit like a fucking Christmas tree right now!

I start running again and try to pry the sphere off my chest so I can tuck it under my jacket. I expect it to feel hot or at least warm but it's actually a little cold. I twist it and it pops off of my chest. I'm careful not to drop it because I have to assume that would suck me back into normal time, and I know that wouldn't be good right now.

I let it suck onto me and close the green torn shirt and my jacket over it. I start popping the buttons to keep the jacket closed, which gets rid of most of the light and keeps my pistol from swinging so much. It's a mostly straight shot from Powell to Civic Center but I manage to catch the edge of a slight curve in the narrow service path and stumble before falling onto my hands and knees hard. My palms are raw and wet as I rub them together.

The path and tunnel to my right start to vibrate and shudder and there's a rising hum.

I look back down the tunnel, hoping my eyes can adjust now that the glow isn't a problem. I put my hand on the tunnel wall to steady myself as I start to get up. As I'm rising, the wall feels different. It moves and changes against my palm and between my fingers and they're too wet now.

I pull my jacket near the top and the buttons pop as it opens, bathing the tunnel wall, my right arm, and hand in the green glow.

The wall is covered in eyes. Dead and gray and red and orange. Amorphous black blobs of organs, sinew, arteries, muscles, and bulbous, malformed bones flutter and pulse and squirm out of the wall in a swirling storm of oily, translucent, flashing muck.

I have never seen one of these things so close and I'm entranced by it even if the better part of me is screaming to run.

The eyes between my fingers loll and dart around moving my hand a bit, then the part it's on swells obscenely and breaks open, revealing those translucent, glinting black teeth.

As I finally pull my hand back, the newly opened chasm of teeth tries to keep it, bulging out and slamming together with the sound of metal and glass crushing and grinding together in a high-speed car wreck.

I jolt back and throw myself off the service path and land hard, my tailbone connecting with the closer rail.

"Gahnnn!"

I grit my teeth together to focus through the pain and go for my pistol. It was great a moment ago that my pocket fit the whole pistol but that's a problem now. With my hands shaking and mind going from watching the huge, swirling mass of psychedelic organ slop and eerie lightning suck and pull itself out of the tunnel wall, I can't get my hand into the big pocket. The fabric is cheap and smooth and bunches together like it doesn't want me to retrieve my gun.

The porker is out of the wall now and looms over me, large enough that it must alter its form to conform to the upper curve of the tunnel. Parts of it bulge and protrude but it keeps the talons and blades tucked in as it wraps thin tendrils around my feet and legs. The rancid casket-butter-and-vomit-feces stink of the creature almost turns my stomach.

I finally get my left hand into my pocket and tug and fight with the pistol until I have it free, then struggle to see through tears brought on by the muck monster's stench. Then swing the gun up and steady it as best I can one-handed and try to squeeze the trigger—

But it won't move.

FUCKFUCKFUCK!

WhatdidWahrheitjustsayaboutthisfuckinggun?!

The thumb thing!

But before I can press the button that releases what must be a safety to ensure the mods are primed, the porker wraps more of the thin muck tendrils around my arms and wrenches the revolver arm away from its aimed position.

The nasty creature holds me in place as it forms a rough armlike appendage, plunges it into its main trunk, and produces a different kind of sphere. It shares the Swiss-watch interior but it's larger and has multiple adjustable translucent dials on the outer surface that directly alter the shapes of the intricate watch-part formation in the sphere as the porker moves them.

I'm transfixed by what seem like impossible configurations of the intricate, shifting machinery in the sphere and there are balls of deep black energy forming at junctions of the whirring, rotating blobs of delicate-looking metal.

In between pulses of distorting strangeness, which cause them to glow and warp, I can see that the wheels, balances, gears, springs, pinions, regulators, rollers, and other less recognizable parts are polished hematite black, shiny cobalt blue, and bone white, and as I examine them, I decide I'm not sure if they're metal at all.

The porker must be satisfied with its adjustments because it stops tinkering with the sphere and holds it in place as it wraps more tendrils of glistening muck around me.

I struggle against the slithering bonds but, despite their oily fluid and treacle appearance, they're as strong as thick braided steel cable. I fight the bindings with all I can muster but more latch around me, holding me tight like a swaddled baby.

I also fight a profound terror that wants me to give in. It's trying to overwhelm me like the black threads and tendrils and it's going to succeed.

"Leave the kid alone, Fritz!" Wahrheit yells from the darkness down the service path—before firing his submachine gun and lighting up the tunnel brilliant indigo as the blinding white rounds burn through the air into the porker.

A burst hits the sphere it's holding, knocking it out of the creature's reach and sending it through the air before it hits the floor of the tunnel and bounces back and forth between the train tracks as it rolls away to Civic Center Station.

Wahrheit empties his magazine into the vile monster with a thick mechanical click and thunk as the muck is sucked into the entry and exit wounds the searing white rounds created in the thing's disgusting body. Rotting fluids and body parts cascade down onto me as the creature howls in fear and agony. The tendrils binding me detach and shrink up into the larger appendages—which collapse into piles of organic detritus as the maddening nastiness holding them together is forcefully subtracted.

Wahrheit noisily collects a mouthful of mucus, takes off his filter mask, and spits the phlegm on the last concentration of muck just before it's sucked away into the air above the mess on me and the tunnel floor. Wahrheit puts his mask back on and grunts.

I fling the dissolving filth and organs off as I roll over and try to haul myself up. Then slip in a pool of the cast-off fluid and land in it on my right hand and knees. I tense my left arm and keep the revolver just above the surface.

Soft white, blue, and green light appears and mingles with my light as Wahrheit removes an opaque woven shroud from the sphere on his chest and another from the glowing fluid bulbs and ampules on his gun. He tucks the sphere cover into a pocket on his plaid thrift store pants but the flap that was over the gun is attached to it with straps and Wahrheit drapes it down off the stock.

I notice that Wahrheit is covered in blood spray and spatter and his face is laced with streaks of it. It looks fresh and human.

The humor Wahrheit's eyes and face usually exhibit is completely gone as he hops down off the service path and crosses to me, then helps me up.

"Sorry about Suj—"

"Shut up. We need to move."

Wahrheit roughly pushes me in front of himself, guiding me toward Civic Center station between the tracks. I slip and almost fall again but recover and trudge forward.

There's a ruckus in the darkened station up ahead and what sounds like a distorted PA system.

"Quick and quiet," Wahrheit whispers as he ejects his spent magazine and tucks it in his duffle bag.

I look back and watch Wahrheit release and adjust a modified variable feed slot and mechanism on his submachine gun. Wahrheit takes a dripping snail drum magazine out of what I see is the blood-soaked left pocket of his overcoat, whips it and stops his arm to fling the excess blood off, then slots it into the feeder on the gun. He chambers the first round and crooks his arm, pointing the gun at the ceiling of the tunnel as we quickly advance.

As we hurry up the tunnel, my foot connects with a hard ball and it rolls forward several feet. I close the distance and pick up the sphere the muck creature was prepping to use. It's gone into a standby mode of some kind and the glowing and movement inside it are almost imperceptible.

Wahrheit reaches around me and take the sphere out of my hands. He grumbles, "The way this is going, we might need this," and squirrels it away into his trusty duffle bag.

We keep moving and the distorted PA sounds are met with yelled rebuttals from somewhere down the platform. I'm pretty sure I've never heard the language they are arguing in even though it's not totally clear yet. As we get closer, I decide the language is completely alien to this planet. The sound makes me think of it as Cantonese by way of Farsi and Russian, with a dash of Zulu popping and clicking? But it's none of those things at the same time.

"What are they saying?"

Wahrheit whispers, "Can't make it all out. Not great

with Junction Pidgin, but it's something about deportation and a lot of curses and sarcasm in response."

Just before we reach the tunnel opening into the Civic Center station and platform area, Wahrheit grabs my shoulder to stop me and steps ahead of me. He secures the flap back over the glowing fluid bulbs on his gun, snuffing the light, then takes the other shroud out of his silly old pants and covers the sphere on his chest. He fishes in his duffle bag and takes out another shroud and hands it back to me, so I place it over my sphere and button my jacket.

"Stay on me."

Wahrheit crouches and uses the waist-high station platform as cover, sneaking along its length through the dark along the train tracks. I follow closely. Wahrheit stops about every ten feet to pop the top half of his head up above the level of the platform and scan it for signs of what's happening. It reminds me of Grieves popping his see-through head out of inanimate objects and surfaces. Where is he off to anyway?

The forest of silhouetted rush-hour commuters in this station is more naturally grouped, being completely oblivious to the troubles down the tunnel and the amorphous beasts lurking all around.

The support pillars on this platform are square instead of round and there is just one row of them that runs down the center of the platform.

Wahrheit pops up again and stops. I cautiously pop the top of my head up too and see bright blue light beaming through the green dumb-dumb gas all around and the limbs and trunks of the dark forest. Wahrheit tucks his head down again and shuffles down several more feet before popping up again. I follow and take another look too.

The source of the distorted "PA" and what now sound like alternating angry and playful responses becomes clear: There is a phalanx ten across and three deep of the spooky Snow Glober monster cops with padded riot shields on the platform. One of the big umpire bomb disposal-naut Fat Boys looms behind them. Instead of the gas guns I've seen before, this one has something like a big net gun. The monster cops are flanked by ranks of almost unmoving silhouette tree people as if they somehow shifted them cleanly out of the way to create their phalanx. That was nice of them?

In the ceiling above the monster cops is the source of the blue light, a biomechanical camera-and-speaker array, which is hard to see clearly because it is densely layered with 3-D fractals similar to the ones over the muck monsters' many eyes. Its form is an asymmetrical, bulbous shape like maybe a huge mutant pear with Swiss-watch eyes. The speakers are nothing more than shiny, opalescent plates in its surface with concentric circles of tiny holes in them, and the blue pours out of three big spotlights on articulated arms, two jutting off the bottom at different angles and one near the top of the horizontal pear shape. I choose to think of it as an "Observer."

The Observer's lights are all aimed at one of the central square supports running down the platform closer to me and Wahrheit and I see that in the shadows created by the overpowering lights, Siobhàn is pressed against the dark side of the support, shoulder against it and peeking out of the shadows sporadically as she curses and retorts. The Snow Globers' phalanx is posted up about thirty feet down the platform from the support and Siobhàn.

As Siobhàn continues to argue and joke with the weird PA-and-camera-system creature, she slides back and forth on her back across the support, seeming to glean structural details as far as I can gather from the brief glimpses when her face leaves the shadows. The next glimpse I get is of her face a few feet lower and she must be crouching.

My eyes adjust to the shadows created by the support as I focus on it and can just make out Siobhàn scanning the platform. Her view locks on one of the dark tree people several feet away from her. Something about that changes her posture and demeanor.

Siobhàn peeks around the edge of the support toward the Snow Globers and Fat Boy again but instead of looking around she makes an almost inaudible whistling sound. She seems satisfied and slides back into the shadow. In half silhouette, she takes off her brocade bag and sets it on the floor. She pops the still-shrouded time sphere off her hoodie and presses it against her chest, then unzips her hoodie, takes it off, and drops it gently onto the bag. She slides back up to a standing position against the pillar.

Siobhàn's retorts go from playful and sarcastic to two steps louder and threatening. The distorted voice from the Observer increases in volume and intensity in response.

There's a pregnant pause, then the light goes from bright blue to pulsing blood red and the Fat Boy shifts and seems to be prepping the net gun. The Snow Globers activate more red lights and what look like electric shock or stun nodes embedded in the surfaces of their padded riot shields and start to advance at a cautious, slow pace.

"She needs help, man," I say.

"You will do nothing," Wahrheit commands.

"I'm sorry about your friend, but—"

"'Friend' doesn't cover it, you little prick. But that's got nothing to do with this."

"So, what is it? Are you studying her? This doesn't seem like the time for that."

"Felix, has it occurred to you that she doesn't need any help? Now shut the hell up and let me watch. Probably won't ever get another chance on this side of the breach."

I look over at Wahrheit but he doesn't return my hard, questioning glare. He's practically entranced by whatever it is that has him so fascinated by Siobhàn. Then I look back at the platform in time to learn a little of what Wahrheit already knows.

Siobhàn closes her eyes and breathes slow and deliberate. There's a long moment that's hard for me to take when she seems to be meditating against the support as the Snow Globers continue to advance, then her eyes open and reflect the red light pouring around the sides of the pillar.

She seems to study the changing layers of the light cones as they advance. They're only about fifteen feet from the support now and I'm really getting anxious. I keep squeezing the pistol grip of my revolver like an unyielding stress ball.

Back still against the pillar, Siobhàn lets out a last taunt in that weird language, then raises her hands up and out so that they jut out from the sides of the pillar on the ends of her tattooed forearms and she flips the Snow Globers off double. Then she curls her fingers so that the middle and thumb press together—

Remembering her move up in the station before, I close my eyes just as she snaps her fingers. It's enough to avoid the full blast of light and heat I didn't feel when running from the muck thing upstairs but I'm still half-blinded by the light through my eyelids. I flutter them back open as Siobhàn is dive-rolling across the platform toward the tree person.

Siobhàn rolls up onto her feet and pries something flat and rectangular out of the slowed-down person's grip and there's a raspy sucking sound. It looks like a touch-screen tablet, but the screen is a dull blur from the artificial darkness. She turns back toward the SGs, takes a long step for momentum, then flings the tablet hard and it arcs up toward the platform ceiling, but she's put so much English on the spin that it curves back down and whirs down over one of the SG's riot shields. It connects with a hollow thud and crack but the snow-globe helmet stays intact.

Siobhàn whistles a note that quickly becomes a harrowing shriek in her throat and Wahrheit and I have to cover our ears. The Snow Glober's helmets vibrate and shudder and when she hits the highest part of her rising shriek, the helmet she struck with the tablet shatters, exploding out like a glass bomb and shattering most of the others' helmets too. She shifts the note and rises again and the helmets that were cracked open and shattered by the first one explode too, destroying the last of the helmets in a blast of cascading translucent obsidian.

The SGs spasm and collapse, some dropping their shields and some keeping them half raised as the contents of their helmets come out like liquid noise made real and swirl like chaotic, fleshy smoke or CO_2 haze rolling down off of dry ice and pouring across the floor. I can't look directly at the leaking mess of light and solid/fluid/smoke madness because I can't get my mind around it existing. The intensity of the synesthesia is too much, and it defies what I've come to accept as physical laws even more than some of the really dicey stuff I've seen.

The chopped up, distorted voice on the Observer goes apeshit.

When the Snow Globers hit the ground, a few of their mottled, pickled heads just splash apart like organic slush and others come apart more in chunks. One of them claws up at its own head, accidentally taking it apart while it tries to keep it together and another's exposed head connects with the top edge of its riot shield on its way to the floor and breaks open like a rotten melon dropped from a height.

The Fat Boy growls bubbly in its shifting diopter-filled helmet and most of its eyes lock on Siobhàn. It advances and levels the big net gun at her, stomping with a pronounced malformed-limb limp through the pulsing red light, haze of green gas, and organic noise liquid rolling and spreading across the floor like living mercury smoke.

Siobhàn lowers into a half crouch and raises her right hand to snap again. The Fat Boy stops and presses something on its helmet, which causes a black mirror cover to slide down over the mostly transparent central faceplate.

Unfazed, Siobhàn spreads her arms wide and starts running toward the Fat Boy. I duck my eyes below the level of the platform as she slaps her hands together hard in front of her face like a Buddhist monk minus the big prayer beads. I feel a blast of heat roll across and over my head. The sound of this mighty clap vibrates the platform and it's immediately followed by what must be the sound of the big gun firing its net projectile.

I look back up. The net is sprawled out and empty by the stairs toward the Powell side of the platform, Siobhàn is gone, and the Fat Boy is jerking what serves it as a head back and forth in its space helmet trying to find her.

Then I spot Siobhàn sliding upside down across the ceiling on a painted concrete beam like she's on a flat waterslide. Her feet, butt, and hands are the only contact points as she glides down the beam underside above and past the Fat Boy. She slows herself somehow, tucks her head to her knees, and flips down to a low crouch on the platform floor facing the back of the Fat Boy.

I don't know how she did it, but those mean-looking butterfly knives of Siobhàn's are in her hands now and she's gripping them reverse-hand, slight sickle-curved edges out.

Siobhàn spins up out of the crouch with knives outstretched and whirls like a demented ballerina jumping into a pirouette, then ends back down in a half-crouched defensive stance. The Fat Boy roars and wobbles around to face her but she's already attacking again, flipping the knives to forward grip and whipping them from arms wide to across her chest, then whipping them back out wide, slicing across its bulk in a squat X-on-X pattern. I can see more of the organic mercury CO_2 haze stuff seeping out through gashes on the creature's padded back armor and it starts to do the same from the chest slices. She goes to slice again, and the Fat Boy raises the net gun up in defense and she cuts into its matte-metal surface, leaving visible gouges.

What are those made out of?

The Fat Boy swings the big gun toward her, and she throws herself back. It swings it again, advancing this time. Siobhàn throws herself back again as well, but this time arches her body and spins, slicing the thrice-thick arm the Fat Boy has closer to her in its swing before landing in a defensive stance again.

More of the weird stuff pours out of the arm slits and the big suit of padded bomb-squad/cosmonaut armor is becoming more misshapen and asymmetrical as it loses its grotesque filling.

The Fat Boy tries to reload the net gun, but Siobhàn has other ideas. She flips her knives closed and drops them to the floor, each one sending warped ripples flowing through the crazy smoke juice on its surface. She gracefully brings her arms up from her sides, raises them above her head, and brings them down and together at the pinky-side edges with palms toward her face. She takes a deep breath and holds it.

I notice the air distorting and warping like a mirage on her exposed arms and face and it occurs to me that it must be doing this over the tattooed patterns I first saw in the black lights of the fish shop.

She presses the tips of her fingers together and begins turning her hands away from herself, then opening and thrusting them toward the Fat Boy as she exhales smooth and slow.

Instead of a flash of heat and white light, the living mercury closest to her ignites and blinding white flame burns across all of it like a pool of gasoline. The Fat Boy drops the net gun and actually turns to run away from Siobhàn, but she finishes her forward thrust, grabs her knives from the floor, and flips them open as she runs after it.

The white flames chase the Fat Boy too like he's carrying a leaking gas can. Siobhàn gets ahead of them and springs up onto the Fat Boy's back, then sinks the blades into its thick shoulder armor. She climbs it like a little moving mountain and when she has footing on part of the flopping less-filled parts of armor, she proceeds to stab and cut into it until geysers of the synesthesia-inducing pseudo-matter are spewing out at all angles.

The white flames catch up as the creature slows down, and they ride the spraying weirdness into the suit, burning it away from the inside as it tries to crawl away. It crumples to the ground and writhes a bit as the last of it burns and melts into nothing, leaving Siobhàn standing atop a smoldering empty suit of padded armor. With her visage of sheer menace turning to triumph with each hard breath, Siobhàn looks like a master huntress atop fresh kill. Then a perverse smile stretches across her face, and she looks to be in a kind of murderous afterglow.

I don't want to interrupt her moment, but I figure we don't have much time before another wave of evil nightmare people and things descends upon us, so I raise my mouth over the platform edge and whisper, "Siobhàn."

Siobhàn whips her head and right knife in my direction and glares hard before recognizing me and pulling back her intense malignance. She fans her knives and flips them closed, then tucks them in the back pockets of her jeans.

Wahrheit climbs onto the platform and I follow. He takes the shroud off of his glowing sphere, so I do the same.

Siobhàn steps off the empty Fat Boy armor and walks back to her bag and sweater by the support. She slings the bag and drapes the hoodie in over it loosely.

The Fat Boy and Snow Glober armor, riot shields, shattered helmet glass, and net gun start decaying and breaking down and the Observer seems to be the cause but it's unclear how. Then a pulse from it blasts them apart like piles of black ashes and dust before a second pulse zaps the ash away entirely, leaving only scorch marks and boiling fluids. I think of the lawn outside Wahrheit's mobile home compound.

The Observer is still directing threatening comments at Siobhàn in the Junction Pidgin, as Wahrheit called it, but one of its eyes locks on Wahrheit and follows him.

Siobhàn shakes her head. "They're sending more. We should skedaddle."

The Observer stops ranting abruptly and for a few seconds only a pulsing tone and clicking can be heard. Then the eyes flutter back to life and focus on Wahrheit and a different distorted voice with a German or Swiss accent says, –Kendall? *Einfach unglaublich*! My, this is serendipitous!–

"Yeah, we'll see," Wahrheit responds in a cold, defiant tone as he approaches the Observer and pulls an unmodified pistol out from under his coat while still holding the modified submachine gun by its pistol grip in his other hand.

He flips a selector to burst fire, then flicks the safety off and unloads several sets of almost deafening triplets across the thing's psychedelic-projection-warped surface.

The voice just laughs in a menacing tone, which is served well by the distortion and ascends into what I can only equate to a shimmering "Acme hole orifice" in the ceiling that swallows it up and disappears immediately after. The inky darkness disappears with the Observer, and we're left in the sludge of crawling time with the almost-statue people instead of dark trees.

Wahrheit reloads the pistol and re-engages its safety. As he's tucking the pistol back under his coat, he says, "Okay, new plan."

"I don't remember agreeing to your old plan," Siobhàn says.

"Does she speak for you, Felix?"

"N-no—"

"Yes. He's a child. He doesn't know what's going on here."

Wahrheit blinks. "Where is this coming from? What's

your interest in him anyway?"

"Not your concern. That squawk box knew you. Someone on it did. This kid owes you nothing and I don't need more drama, *fehr-shtayst doo*?"

"Cry me a river, stretch! I'm the one that should be upset! I get this close to Obrist, then I meet this 'kid' and most of my crew and higher associates are wiped out in less than a week!"

I look at Siobhàn. "Let's hear what he has to s—"

"This man doesn't care about you."

Wahrheit narrows his eyes at her but says nothing.

"What do you—what does she mean, Wahrheit?"

Siobhàn says, "You are a pawn here. That's all I know."

"Wahrheit?"

Wahrheit seems to consider lying, then says, "Listen, Felix. You seem like a good guy...."

"This isn't a confession session, man! What does she mean?"

"Okay, she's right. I'm not helping you because I like you. I broke some of the rules recently and I got a yellow card from the Refs. Then I broke another one getting away from the *Albtraumen*...and I'm facing a red card now."

Siobhàn nods. "So, this is more like a plea bargain or deal for you."

"Accurate enough."

I furrow my brow, confused. "You work for the spaznoids?"

"'Spaz' what?"

"Yes, he works for the 'spaznoids.'"

"A red card is a ticket to oblivion, and I have too much to do before I can die."

Siobhàn chuckles mirthlessly. "At least you have purpose."

"What purpose?" I ask.

"He wants revenge."

Wahrheit locks his eyes on her. "Very perceptive. I want

it, I deserve it, and I'm gonna get it. But I will protect Felix because I must and because it's the right thing to do. You're right, he owes me nothing. If anything, I owe him for messing up and giving him my pills without proper supervision. I was busy and didn't know he had straight up got himself on the bad side of Albrecht fucking Obrist himself. I won't be that sloppy again."

Siobhàn softens some upon hearing this.

Wahrheit studies her eyes. "Nice lenses. Never seen 'em quite like that. How many homes can't you go back to, sister?"

This time Siobhàn narrows her eyes. "You have no idea, flyboy."

Wahrheit says, "How'd you figure that one out?"

Siobhàn just winks at him.

"So, new plan?" I prod.

Siobhàn nods. "Why not? Mine are all about running away and/or killing and such. You got something else?"

"I'd love to watch all of that. For research purposes, I mean," Wahrheit says.

"I bet you would."

I shake my head. "You guys should break each other off and be done with it, damn."

"Can't say I'd complain, but she's made her choice in the courting department for the moment."

Siobhàn's eyelids flutter, then her eyes dart in my direction but she stops herself from looking at me and looks away like she's scanning for danger.

I think I see a slight reddening in her cheeks but before I can be flattered or maybe happy about it, Wahrheit is tucking something small and round into my hand and closing his fingers over it.

"Hold that until I say when."

Wahrheit gives another of the small spheres to Siobhàn and she takes off one of her gloves to hold it in her gently clenched fist.

"New plan is this—you two get to Walt and Izzy's in Sausalito without me and explain what's going on. That's if they don't already know. They'll know better than I do what should be done either way."

I say, "What is going on, though? Is all this about some kind of…uh…gods?"

Wahrheit looks at me. "Why would you say that?"

"Audrey said, 'He's going to wake up the gods,' last time I saw her. I guess maybe she meant Fleischmann or Obrist? She seemed pretty shaken up by the prospect, and she's no slouch in the scary department"

Siobhàn frowns. "She doesn't mean…."

Wahrheit and Siobhàn share a look before Wahrheit locks his attention back on me.

"Did she say when?"

"N-no."

"Did she say how many?"

"No."

Siobhàn grimaces, accentuated by what's left of her skull face paint. "Any is too many."

"Too true. Okay, you two get to Sausalito double-quick then. If things are really that close to going *that* bad, they are the only ones who can make sense of it."

"What are you doing?"

"Obrist knows I'm here now. He raided my house for hoarding the four-two-sixes and spreading knowledge with my street teams, but I doubt he had any idea it was me. If he went after you with that much of his nightmare brigade, he'll go ten times harder for me. Just the fact that he's using hack spheres at all is a disturbing sign. He knows something I don't and it's big enough to risk that much. Or maybe—anyway, I'm a liability to my own mission now and you need to get gone."

"Oh fuck off, man! What, you're gonna make a last stand down here?"

"Simmer down, spunky. Hell no, I'm not making a

last anything. I'm on borrowed time already but I've got something to do before I give it up, like I said. Apparently, a few things, if what you say is true. Don't worry about me. With this plan, I go from liability to vital mission element."

I cringe. "What?"

The little spheres in Siobhàn's and my fists vibrate and beep in a pleasant tone.

Siobhàn lets her sphere drop from her hand and roll across the platform away from us and says, "Decoy," as the sphere rolls to a stop and beautiful, layered symbol equations flitter and spray up out of it and swirl around above it into a five-foot ten-inch glowing tornado. It swirls into itself in different ways and forms into an almost perfect facsimile of Siobhàn standing above the sphere. "He means decoy."

I shake my head, still able to be amazed after all I've seen. Then look back and forth between Siobhàn and faux Siobhàn and notice that the only real obvious difference is that the faux version is brighter in color all around like a setting was off.

I roll mine gently across the floor, but it doesn't get very far and I'm met with a bright mirror image that unsettles me for multiple reasons. At least it doesn't move with my motions—or is that worse?

Wahrheit steps closer to Siobhàn and looks in her eyes. "Will you protect this kid?"

"Not for you...but I will, yes."

"Whatever it takes, I guess."

Siobhàn nods.

Wahrheit lets his submachine gun dangle under his coat from its sling and fishes through his blood-laced duffle bag. He produces a Webley revolver with brass tubes and fittings and a mostly shrouded brass ampule compartment running along and below the barrel with holes down its length to show how much of the glowing fluids are left. He hands it to Siobhàn grip-first, and she takes it and nods in appreciation. Then he hands her a few quick loads and a thick cigarette case that must contain a few more ampules. She squirrels them away into her own bag and tucks the pistol in her waistband against the small of her back, then covers it with her shirt.

Wahrheit says, "That's a Polish Stan original and I will want it back."

Siobhàn nods. "Understood."

Next, he takes out and holds up two vacuum-sealed plastic baggies each containing a small, shiny black ball.

In those bags the small spheres look like Wahrheit is selling homemade Atomic Fireballs or something.

Wahrheit says, "These are an old design. Far from perfect but they should do what's needed of them. Didn't have the scratch for new, good ones. These are probably more for fetish role-play or simulated cheating with your spouse or something than disguise, but it's what I could get. To pinks you'll look great, but those that can see will notice distortions and odd details if you get too close."

He offers them both up in his open hand and Siobhán and I both reach for them at the same time. Our pinkies brush together and we each nervously take one. The moment makes me think of weddings abstractly and I blush.

"Naturally, you can't be seen running out of here all normal speed, so you'll have to turn off them pretty boosters, slow down, and play dumb. After that, I'm sure you'll do fine."

Siobhán takes her mask off, squeezes her little package from the bottom, and pops the ball straight into her mouth. She swallows and after a few seconds she grimaces, moans, and doubles over. She puts her mask back on and keeps moaning through it. Her black, blue, speckled, and little skull-stamped hair becomes blond wavy locks of the same rough shape and outline. She stands up with a scrunched-up face and her hand over her stomach. Her quarter-inch front half of hair on back to the strip of it around the base of her skull at the neck looks like it's long and pulled back by an invisible Alice or headband. Her face is the same rough shape and proportions, but her eyes are a bit too large and candy blue like Wahrheit and Sujit going incognito, and her makeup, piercings, and creamy pale skin and tattoos are gone, replaced with a mild case of lip gloss and fake tan. She swallows, shakes her head, and says, "Ugh. Never had to use one of these myself but they're worse than I heard."

I cringe. "Great."

I take a breath, then remove my mask and pull the little plastic package apart. Pop the ball into my mouth and roll it around. It tastes like stomach acid already, which makes me doubt its newness. I try to force it down a few times, but my throat fights me.

"I can't swallow it," I say and accidentally take in a small hit of the gas before holding my mask against my face.

Wahrheit takes a flask out of his duffle bag, unscrews and flicks aside the hinged top, then hands it to me. I grimace a bit.

"It's the only liquid I got on me."

I take off the mask and down the ball with a shot of that fine, warming whisky. Then replace my mask and breathe out raspy and hoarse—but the shot is already mixing nicely with the pills in my system. Before I can enjoy it, the sickly pressure and nausea creep up and now I double over. I watch my shaking hands take on a bronze tint and feel a slight numbness all over my body and face that subsides quickly, taking the nausea and pressure with it. I straighten back up and become light-headed from the pills, whiskey, and hit of gas—

The light head and other pleasantness almost cause me to miss the platform vibrating and shuddering. Then the darkness rolls down over everything again and I fight to regain my fear. I know I'm in trouble without it but the best I can muster now is an abstract assurance to myself that I need to get out of this place immediately. I still can't take it all seriously, though, and that's the part that I'm trying to fight the most. I titter at faux Me and Siobhán cowering and shaking on the platform while their eyes dart around in terror. Then I remember again that there is something to be that scared of on its way down to us.

Wahrheit says, "Put the pistol away, Felix. This is where you blend in."

I tuck my revolver back in my big jacket pocket.

Siobhán puts her hoodie back on to cover her booster sphere.

Wahrheit hands us each a pouch containing another booster. "You won't need these if you're sneaky, but they never hurt to have around. I'm gonna run with the assumption that my probationary pass on getting in trouble for hacking extends to you right now too."

"You better be right. Take it easy," Siobhán says and walks toward the stairs. She stops at the foot of them, looks up the darkened stairwell, and back at me expectantly.

The vibrations are becoming strong enough to be hard to hear over, so I raise my voice. "Uh…thanks?!"

The whole platform seems to shift and buck.

Wahrheit takes back the flask that I forgot I was holding. "Don't thank me until I do something nice for you!"

I walk over and join Siobhán at the foot of the stairs. The ceiling in the station up above is glowing in overlapping colors near the top of the stairs, which must be from dozens of psychedelic distortions over colored eyes.

Siobhán sighs and nods. "If we get past this part, we might have a chance!"

Wahrheit yells, "Hey, Felix!" and I look back.

Siobhán keeps watch on the approach above. I can barely make out Wahrheit in the darkness because it's becoming even thicker than the times I've seen it before—it's like a fog and the glow from his booster barely cuts through it.

"The falling tree does make a sound! But with the right chemicals, you can choose to ignore that fact for a while!"

Wahrheit raises the flask as if in a toast just as Siobhán reaches over and engages a pressure button on my shrouded booster in unison with her own.

The darkness, time sludge, and Wahrheit warp and blink out all at once. I feel dizzy for a moment and the sudden sounds of rush-hour commuters, tourists, and high-school kids on the platform create a cacophony when compared with the relative silence and sound warping of the slowed-time effect.

As I blink, there's a fluttering of layered darkness, which I hope is the muck creatures passing and ignoring me and Siobhán. I also hear a buzzing sound not unlike a loud gnat, which could be Wahrheit's gun going off really fast—then it's gone.

Let's just get out of here.

Siobhán starts up the stairs with a convincing casual air about her and I follow, trying my best to act as casual but even in my chemically enhanced state I'm still expecting *Albtraum-soldat* talons or a blow of some kind to meet me. Then I realize that it probably would have happened already based on my mental estimates on the relative time difference the booster spheres cause. We're practically statues right now if anybody's watching in Boosterlandia. At this speed, it would be an hour or two after anything happened to Wahrheit and they would have moved on—I think? Hard to keep my head around it.

We make it to the top unscathed and cruise through

the station seeing nothing weird other than open slatted gas vents filling the station. It's actually weirder to see so many people looking almost happy at once, dopey as they are from the gas.

As we approach an open-air stairwell, which leads up to UN Plaza, I see rain pouring down into it. I could use a shower, sure.

The gas is thrown around in tiny, wispy tornadoes around the rain-impact points and all of it swirls like smoke in an LZ as a chopper is dropping in to pick up the last of a shot-up platoon.

I follow blond Siobhán up an escalator to the right of the stairs and enjoy the feel of rain pattering down onto my face and head. The surface of my disguised skin and hair make a slight sizzling sound I assume is in reaction to the moisture but I feel no heat.

UN Plaza is mostly empty, probably due to the rain. Buildings and trees line it north and south and gas pouring out of more vents in the buildings is clinging to their branches and lightly fluttering leaves.

There are open gas vents as far as I can see in all directions and a layer of the glowing miasma slides across the streets and sidewalks like green fog. People walking by under umbrellas or raised newspapers breathe it in and exhale dark blue as they calmly shuffle to their destinations.

Siobhán throws her hood over her fake blond locks and struts through the plaza and starts up Hyde on the sidewalk. I follow, watching a swimmer gliding through the air above the rising gas like a sleek, graceful seal while another dips down into the gas and swims more erratically through it.

Siobhán looks back. "Alright, let's hike up to Bay Street and start working our way over to the Golden Gate."

"Why not just take a—"

"Taxis are risky 'cause they trap us in a small space with prying eyes. You never noticed the little black cameras hidden in them? They're made to look like rivets or rounded bolts in the door frames and ceilings. This town has become a surveillance nightmare for the not-so-normal. I thought London was bad, but this Obrist has been working overtime hooking in all these vents and cameras. Wasn't nearly this bad in the eighties. No, slow and steady and we act like tourists. We'll hop on some tourist bus that crosses the bridge. Shouldn't raise any suspicion. I just hope your pilot friend is right about these 'hackers.'"

"Pilot? Anyway, I couldn't tell you. So, you think Wahrheit's alright?"

Siobhán nods. "He seems to be good in a fight. I have a feeling he's in a big hot bath downing a fifth somewhere right now, sure."

I'm not sure she believes that, and I definitely don't.

As we reach the corner of Hyde and Turk, I hear a whir and look east—

I grab Siobhán's hand and yank us both back around the corner. Before I can flatten back against the wall, Siobhán has pressed herself against me and firmly clamped a gloved hand around my throat.

"I am not a *doll*, Felix!"

She's only inches from my face and her expression softens as she studies me up close. I can feel her breath coming out of the filter ports onto the parts of my face the mask doesn't cover.

I bend my arm and jab back toward the east around the corner. Siobhán loosens her grip but still holds me against the wall while she leans over and sneaks a peek. I exhale sharply into my barely visible mask and my eyes roll around. Dim, gray light glints off the trim of a passing car and I wince. My eyes land on something west down Turk. Siobhán watches two gray-eyed porkers atop flying platforms hover through the air above the intersections of Taylor and Leavenworth that run parallel to Hyde to the east, equipment and clockwork "eyes" scanning civilians for an ID hit of some kind. One is heading north and one south.

"Okay, maybe they're focusing on downtown…so we just play dumb and keep going," she says.

I pry her hand off my throat. "Or not."

I spot what I decide is our salvation and walk into the busy street without looking around for cars at all. I hum a little tune, then say in a sing-song way, "Let's do…the time warp…agaaaain," and press the sphere on my chest back into action just before I would be hit by a speeding SUV. The driver has just enough time to start laying on the horn before—

The booster sphere warms back up and I'm hit by a wave of thick, invisible sludge that breaks over me, then releases its pull almost entirely as it passes, allowing me to casually stroll out of the path of the now slowly creeping vehicle.

I look down at my warping organic goo hands and chuckle as I wave them around, watching their true shape catch up after a moment.

I look back up at the object of my desire, that damn candy-pink Bentley Continental with the pink zebra interior. The driver was running out of a bodega, packing a fresh box of Virginia Slims against her palm lightly with the filter side up, the opposite of how you should, when I hit the slo-mo button. There she is now caught in an almost frozen pose of shifting her weight from one "fuck me" wedge platform to the other as she rounds the back of the car.

As I approach the Bentley and its soon-to-be former owner I say, "Hey, how's it going? I'm gonna take your expensive, stupid pink car now."

I take the pack of skinny cigarettes out of her hand with a little crackling sound and flip them over. As I'm tucking them back into place just a bit further into her packing motion I say, "Oh and just to put your nerves at ease, I'm mortified by cars, I've never driven, and I'm pretty sure it's a bad idea to start today, but—what's that? Yeah, exactly… fuck it! I knew you'd understand."

I stride up to the driver-side door, open it, and slide into the zebra-print bucket seat. Take the extra booster sphere Wahrheit gave me out of its pouch and press its activation button. After letting it warm up a bit, I press the booster against the dashboard and it sucks into place. The sound of the running engine revs up to normal speed and the rain pelting the outside explodes strangely against the surface.

"First time for everything and all that? Okay, so, in theory…."

I adjust the mirrors, start the wipers at medium speed, shift in the seat until I'm comfortable, and move the seat back with an electronic button on the left side of its base. The wipers cause a beautiful, hypnotic series of waves to roll across the surface of the windshield as the water fights two time states. Survey the relatively slow-moving traffic for a moment, then press the brake in, shift it from "P" into "D" with the polished auto stick, and gently grasp the wheel at 2 and 10. Release the brake pedal and depress the accelerator—but nothing happens other than a loud rev from the engine.

"What am I not…?"

Then it hits me.

I find the parking brake release and use it—

The powerful Bentley screeches as it lurches forward and accelerates toward the intersection and the back of the statue of blond Siobhán still standing at the corner watching the slowly cruising flying platforms that can be seen hovering over the street down the way.

"SHITSHITSHIT!"

I slam on the brakes and the Bentley hydroplanes through the intersection, narrowly missing two cars. I jerk the wheel right a bit too much to compensate, though, and the Bentley fishtails around, barely missing a car parked on Turk as the big, pink car slides to a stop now facing west and Siobhán's all but frozen face peeking around the corner.

I just sit with my foot jammed down on the brake pedal and hands locked in death grips around the steering wheel, breathing heavily as I try to calm down.

Okay, don't do that again.

When I've recovered enough, I ease my foot off the brake and gently down onto the accelerator. Pull up to the corner slow and deliberate and put it in park, then get out and walk up to Siobhán. I gingerly uncover the booster on her chest, then press its button on and step back before she can break my arm or something.

Siobhán shudders into pace with me and pulls her hood down off her head as she whips her head toward me in a flurry of blurred goo.

Siobhán stomps a foot down. "Jesus! Don't *do* that!"

"Relax, alright? Damn."

"Don't tell me to relax, child."

"'Whatever it takes,' right? I got us a car."

Siobhán squints at the Bentley and says, "That? It looks like a Hello Kitty store exploded on it. You aren't much for subtlety, are you?"

"It's fast and we're in a hurry."

I turn and walk back to the open driver side door and get in.

"Felix, that thing's atrocious. It's basically the opposite of stealth. And who said we were in a hurry? We could show up in Sausalito tomorrow if these disguises hold up."

I glare at her from the driver's seat.

"Wahrheit said—"

"If what your better-really-be-ex-girlfriend said is true, we're all fucked anyway, Felix. Your 'Var-height' knows that."

"I'll die *trying*, thanks."

"Fair enough."

Siobhán walks around the front of the car and gets in,

throws her bag in the back, settles her rear end into the bucket seat with a touch of exaggeration, and looks at me expectantly with her big fake eyes.

"Let's go, then, Suddenly Assertive Felix."

I shut my door without returning her gaze and put the car back in drive, then start off through the slow traffic, weaving and swerving quickly but carefully. Even chemically elevated and enhanced as I am, I have trouble hiding my anxiety about driving. I catch Siobhán noticing my white-knuckle grip on the wheel.

"You want me to—"

"I've got this. It's cool."

"If anyone is, I don't know, sped up like us right now, we stick out badly. I think you can sync these glow-y balls. Here."

She places her left hand onto my booster and feels around while doing the same to hers. I drive with one white-knuckled hand while she fiddles. "Uh-huh. There."

There's a little beep on both boosters and I feel mine vibrate like a video-game controller for a moment. Then she does the same thing to the sphere on the dashboard.

"Alright, good shit."

"How did you know about that?"

"I've never used these things myself, but you hear stuff. Met a girl in Junction who used to shtoop a guy that used this kinda stuff to rob banks. Artsy prick. Bad business, that. Especially if your supplier had shoddy workmanship. Not worth the punishment or side effects. I will say that your friend is fucked already if he's on the Guardian's bad side."

I steer us north around the corner of Turk and Van Ness Avenue and almost directly under a boosted porker flying platform hovering in place about thirty feet over the gently upward-sloping street. The porker and front of the vehicle are facing north above us and it being that high makes it harder to see us down in the car if it tried, but one of the eye cameras on the body of the platform is rotating slowly towards us.

Siobhán hits the booster power button on her chest, and me, her, and the Bentley shudder back into normal speed. I hit the brakes but not as hard as last time. There's a little slippage caused by the shifting friction of the two time streams, the rain, and the smart-brake system being profoundly confused for a moment. It recovers with a fluttery screech and eases us to a stop behind the naturally slowing normal-speed traffic.

I try my best to look casual as I scan above the street out the driver window. There's a vague, dark fluttering like something staying in one place longer than other things in a time-lapse film clip, then it's gone.

"Anything?"

I look around above the street up and down Van Ness. "I…think…it's gone."

She cringes some, looks around out her windows faux-casual and grumbles, "I hate this. I like things that fight fair—it's easier to trick them."

I close my eyes and breathe in and out slowly, concentrating on my body high and trying to forget that I'm terrified of driving and that there's a fleet of horrible monsters flying around the city trying to find and hurt us.

A honk from behind opens my eyes and I see the line of cars ahead has already moved twenty feet on up the gentle slope of Van Ness.

"Go, Felix, and keep it cool. Not too fast, not too slow."

"Gotcha."

I accelerate and ease us into a medium pace up the slight hill, trying to focus on just what I'm doing and ignoring the cars changing lanes and zooming past every which way all around us.

We both silently scan the streets and skies through the haze of green gas as I drive us up Van Ness.

Nothing strange besides bulbs, fliers, spiderflies, etc.,

and those barely seem strange at all to me now.

chapter 32

I break into a fresh sweat as we wait at a stoplight to turn left and continue on the 101 up to Golden Gate Bridge and the salvation it hopefully represents.

The light turns green and we're still alive and unmolested, so I go, driving us toward the bridge.

Siobhán shifts in her seat like she's uneasy. I glance over, then look back at the road. She looks nervous in a way I haven't seen.

"What's wrong? I mean, besides the obvious."

"Okay, before we get up there, I need to know something."

"I'm pretty easy right now. Ask away," I say, chuckling nervously like a kid in line for a rollercoaster I keep having to watch tear by full of terrified, screaming riders.

"Am I familiar to you?"

"Of course. I mean…what do you mean?"

"When we met at that party, was I familiar?"

"How could you be?"

Siobhán starts, "Do you—" but cuts herself off.

There's a pause as Siobhán closes her eyes and seems to meditate, clenching her jaw repeatedly as well. She hums and wiggles her jaw around like she's prepping for a stage play or trying to relax from being in one.

In an entirely unrestrained Irish accent Siobhán asks, "*An chuimhin leat mé?*"

"What?"

I'm confused but not just because she's opening the floodgates of some vulnerable place I've only seen hints of. Her undisguised voice and foreign speech vibrate through my mind like a memory I can't have.

"D'yeh remember me?"

"I don't understand."

"Is that you, Ciarán?"

I'm struck by that name said by that voice and it makes me profoundly uncomfortable. I concentrate on the road, steering us north up the highway and the stretch called Doyle Drive, the last curving section of road north out of the city, which is flanked by trees and brush with the bridge as its terminus.

"*An chuimhin leat an meaisín*, Ciarán?"

"Don't call me that. I don't know what you're getting at—"

"Y'sure y'dohn remember? The name means nouthin' to yeh?"

I surprise myself by racking my brain to figure out if it does mean anything. Then glance at Siobhán, who is now staring at me with her fake, candy-blue eyes. I'm glad I can't see her even eerier contact-covered eyes at that moment and look back at the road.

As the tree flanks thin out, a line of tollbooths for people heading south into the city stretches over the road just before the bridge begins. To the right of this is a roughly two-lane northbound bridge entrance, so I stay in the farthest right lane.

The Golden Gate Bridge looms over the choppy,

swirling strait below, majestic and ominous in the mist and heavy rain. There's a large fog bank rolling into the bay above and below the bridge, and the south bridge tower is intermittently obscured by it as it meets with low-lying cloud cover.

"I…I d-don't know…."

"Yeh have'teh. Y'canna leave me alone agehnn, *a ghrá*. Not now that O-eh johst have'yeh back. *Tá tú uaim*…."

"Siobhán, I have no idea what…what you—is that Grieves?"

Siobhán joins me in staring out the front windshield at the figure standing with its back to us in the road about thirty feet ahead in the next lane over to our left. Dark coat, pants, and boots—check. Glowing, translucent, and Jello-mold-like head and hands—check.

The rain runs down Grieves's head, clothes, and hands as he turns back toward us, mumbling already. Upon seeing the pink eyesore speeding toward him, Grieves's eyes seem to get even bigger as his almost invisible, useless eyelids widen around them. His mumbling becomes excited yelling and he takes a few steps over to stand in our lane. He waves his arms back and forth in the air like he's still trying to get our attention.

Grieves bends over halfway as we pass quickly through him and in the short window of time he's phasing through the Bentley's interior he is able to ramble in an exaggerated whisper yell, "DDon'tgofurthuuuur—thersBad—"

My eyes dart repeatedly from the cars and bridge ahead to Grieves in the rearview mirror waving his arms. I realize that Grieves wasn't waving to get our attention, but to warn us. We watch Grieves out the rear window as he runs after us a few long strides, then stops and descends into the road by the tollbooths.

I notice vents flapping open in the surface of the bridge road, walkways, and towers and the glowing green gas comes out faster than usual. "What now?"

As Siobhán looks at me again, she falls back into the American accent, which must be a subconscious or trained habit at this point, and says, "What was that about—" but cuts herself off when something down the bridge grabs her attention.

I look at her, then follow her gaze.

A young woman stands on the east pedestrian walkway. She is stock-still and dressed for a funeral in the nineteen forties, black shoes, skirt, jacket, tilted topper hat, and lace-net veil drenched and dripping from her lack of an umbrella. She seems to have something in each hand, but I can't see what.

That's when I realize there's something very strange about her. I can't really look directly at her face and once again I'm reminded of Wahrheit's house. It's there like a soft-focused, high-contrast version of a face, but as we come around the curve toward her, I see a subtle disturbance in what I can't help but think of as the surface of a form-fitting moving projection. The un-woman raises her left hand to her waist level and its contents glow.

Siobhán instinctively presses her linked booster sphere and goes for the pistol against the small of her back with the other hand as it warms up.

As the linked spheres sync roughly with the booster the strange woman engaged, there is a bone-vibrating shudder and everything goes distorted and gooey for a flash. Then the flash subsides, and I'm faced with the fact that I am speeding us toward slow-moving walls of cars, trucks, and vans caught in the time sludge as they crawl across the bridge heading north and south. That distant part inside of me is able to joke, they should add this to the driver test.

Something about the boosters synergizing causes the strange woman projection to glitch and cut out.

The figure is actually in a form-fitting blue-black body suit with antennae-sprouting equipment on her upper back between her shoulders. The head is encased in a sleek, contoured full helmet with a glowing, pale bluish-white tinged transparent faceplate—a vertical oval starting below the wearer's lower lip and bubbling out a bit over the forehead before curving back down and terminating near the top of the head.

It's Audrey. Her black hair is pulled back tight and glowing symbols dance across a kind of readout display glowing in the faceplate over and around her eyes. She stares coldly through the streaming data and pulsing diagrams at the car until she locks eyes with me.

Audrey's eyes initially convey something between "I knew it" and "how could you" before transforming into "you did this" as she raises her other hand. She shifts her glare onto Siobhán, and her shark eyes pour out, pulling and melting and tearing her face apart in the helmet while she aims what looks like a Makarov pistol with a long suppressor attached to the end.

Siobhán can only whisper, "Oh fuck y—"before the first shot goes cleanly through the windshield and through her neck, causing her curse to end in a loud gurgling moan. It makes a perfect 9.22mm hole in the glass without cracking out from it all, so Siobhán's neck doesn't stand a chance.

"Silencer" would for once be far more accurate as a description for whatever the attachment on the end of the gun is. The pistol makes absolutely no sound and there's no flare at the end of the muzzle either. The ejected cartridges are caught in a black velvet pouch, which pooches out on the side as they hit its interior but sags back down with each shot as they fall to the pouch bottom.

Audrey fires three more shots in through the passenger window as I try to maneuver us behind a large crawling moving van. The first two crack Siobhán's head open with a sickening one-two pop, spraying blood, skull, and brain matter all over the pink-zebra interior and me. I put the van between us but the third shot comes through the entire van—then Siobhán's right shoulder, upper torso, and left shoulder—and out into my right shoulder, then comes out clean before exiting the Bentley and, at that velocity, presumably cutting through the whole rest of the bridge and ending up somewhere out in the Pacific.

"Hnnnnngh–Fuck–ghnn!" I blurt out through clenched teeth.

I've never been shot before but I'm not sure even that would have prepared me for this kind of getting shot. It feels like the cylindrical path the bullet cut through the back of my shoulder is still forcibly open to the air and sizzling and it burns like hell. I'm bleeding but not like it hit an artery. The weirder sensation is my muscle trying to clench around the cylindrical section that's no longer there, and the strange, searing pain makes me tear up.

Through the pain, I turn my attention back to steering the Bentley as best I can. I nearly strike a Ford Ranger as I steer us through staggered rows of crawling vehicles, but I squeak by just barely.

I sneak a peek at the rearview mirror in time to watch Audrey fire another shot from back on the walkway that goes through the cars I just maneuvered around, through the back of the Bentley, through Siobhán's heart, and out through the side of the engine, catching the radiator on its way out to cut low into a minivan on the bridge ahead.

The Bentley keeps going and fast, but steam starts wafting back from the front where the bullet exited.

I can't bring myself to look at the mess that's left of Siobhán in the seat next to me but, mercifully, her bucking and twitching is subsiding. To keep my mind from cracking any further for just a bit longer, I decide to forget she's even there. It helps that the task of speeding between and around all these vehicles in the rain in fast-motion is taking most of my concentration.

I can't see Audrey in the mirror anymore but I'm not slowing down for anything.

After avoiding a grouping of southbound cars as I steer

between them and a northbound truck, I see something dark moving downward in the upper fog bank ahead from behind the south-bridge-tower horizontal strut one down from the top.

The fog clears for a moment, and I see a muck-monster flying platform descending from its ambush hiding spot in a controlled fall. It's obscured as it drops past the next strut down and when it comes back into view, the thrusters and rotors are spinning back up. After dropping behind the lowest strut, the vehicle smoothly eases itself down to a floating stop about twenty feet above the bridge surface. The long, cylindrical tube that juts from the ball on the bottom of the flying platform shifts from its fixed position and smoothly aims toward the speeding Bentley.

A blue light strobes from the Swiss-clock eye cameras and I assumes it means for me to stop and go peacefully.

Not feeling I have a choice, I decide to ignore it and steer my pink chariot so that a pack of crawling cars is between me and the menacing turret.

The lights strobe red, and it fires a beam of impossible black, cutting the cars I'm currently hiding behind in clean diagonal sections along the path of the beam, but seems to miss me intentionally like a warning shot.

It's like a foot-diameter cylinder of subtraction, which cuts matter into nothing in its path. The cars and SUV come apart and collapse slowly toward the bridge road surface and I have to fight the urge to visualize what just happened to the people inside as I swerve around their diagonally bisected vehicles.

The oblivion turret trains itself on the Bentley again as I guide it around the falling vehicle chunks and there's a long moment in my mind where I consider just letting it blank me out to avoid the risk of anymore pain or worry…

,.' ,., ,., ,., ,., ; —

…which is immediately followed by a cold fury and the overwhelming sentiment, "I still want some answers and you ain't shit, motherfucker!"

I jam the accelerator down all the way, steer horribly with my burning right arm, and try to get the revolver out of its big pocket again. The blue strobe starts again but I keep going.

As I get closer, the light strobes between blue and red in what must be a last warning signal.

I decide to swerve at the last second and don't let myself think about what's going to happen if that doesn't work. I almost have my big pistol free but its hammer is hooking on the edge of the pocket.

Not again! Fuck—FUCK!

The mechanical eyes start to strobe all red and I realize that the turret will just follow me if I swerve.

So, this is it then.

Tendrils of energy that look like silhouetted electrical arcs build on the ball and cylindrical length of turret barrel and I think about my mother and father with me at the beach when I was about seven years old and wish I was there.

Stupid, right? Can't help it.…

I want to play with my bucket in the wet sand just out of reach of the frothy tides and chase crabs near a set of human-placed concrete rocks that were covered in mollusks and anemones. The clouds were fluffy and huge as they crept over the coast and it rained for a month after that, but that time at the beach just before the storm is the only thing I've ever been able to think of as perfect. Simple, pure happiness I have never felt since and the last thing I think about is what my life would be like if things had continued like that—

The crackling black turret buckles and fires wide, missing everything but the rear driver panel of a southbound car. It buckles more and sags before falling off the bottom of the flying platform onto the bridge.

My eyes catch some movement and are drawn to the

rearview mirror—Audrey is standing atop a slow-moving minivan in her weird stealth suit with her silent pistol still aimed at where the turret was. Then the vintage-funeral-goer projection seems to fold around and into her, and then she's gone from view.

The red-eyed muck golem on the vehicle wails and detaches what must be a large nothing-beam rifle from next to its seat with a few oily, malformed tentacles, plunks a thick cable into a socket on it, and aims down at the Bentley to finish the job.

A dark object falling from a couple struts up on the bridge tower registers in my upper peripheral vision but I'm more concerned with the business end of the beam gun aimed right at me in the driver's seat.

Then my eyes flick up and I see—GRIEVES!

He's thrown himself out of the south tower from somewhere up high and he's falling toward the floating muck-monster mobile platform like a grotesque flying squirrel. Grieves's head, face, and hands are burning dark and sketching out from whipping distortions and he's falling fast enough that the glitching follows him down like the tail of a comet.

The muck creature fires but I swerve and the beam subtracts the passenger mirror and part of the windshield on that side, leaving overlapping circular cutouts in the glass and metal.

Before the nightmare-soldier creature can fire again, Grieves lands strangely on the flying platform's front half—

He lets himself phase mostly through it, but his hands solidify at the last moment and grab the rotor shroud, using his weight to pull the vehicle's front end down and the muck monster has to let itself roll down partially into a blob to keep from falling off. It keeps a hold of its beam gun with a few of its thinner warped appendages but isn't able to use it for a moment.

Grieves pulls himself up through the vehicle and stands

on the self-leveling front end in a hunched ready stance. The muck thing whips up into a fury, sending rain cascading all around as it breaks apart and takes its first few swipes at Grieves. The obsidian-taloned tentacles fail to connect as they pass harmlessly through Grieves and he just pushes the big sack of swirling muck back into its seat, taunting it like this is a slapstick movie.

Dammit, Grieves! This isn't playtime!

The porker's eyes lock on me quickly approaching the area of road below its vehicle and it roll-climb-pours itself off in time to plop down onto the hood. Grieves drops down onto it and wrestles with it.

I can barely see around Grieves and the wailing blob of teeth, eyes, and whipping tentacles but I try to fling it off by driving even faster and swerving back and forth.

But it's moored itself into the hood with a few dedicated talon-tentacles it has pierced the hood with, and it isn't going anywhere.

The swerving does clear my view some on each side for an instant each time, so that's something. I steer by inexperienced instinct and memories of the quick flashes I see of the crawling-car-and-truck patterns on the drenched bridge ahead. As I swerve, I hear Siobhán's vacant body shifting back and forth in the bucket seat against the seatbelt tension.

The revolver comes out of my pocket finally with a last twist and pull, and I press the priming button. There's a blow-off valve spurt and a hiss.

The muck golem is holding full-blown distortion-swirl prism-cutout-face shark-eyes Grieves up and away with a few weird appendage growths like an older brother keeping a sibling from landing a blow with his superior reach.

It presses itself against the windshield and part of the roof and they start to warp and bubble where it's trying to pass through into the car interior. Between its variably tinged and aware reddish eyes, several of its many mouths flap open and form flat against the vibrating, rain-slick glass and gape, revealing those rows of nasty transparent obsidian teeth like a pack of warped, bloodthirsty lampreys. A thin black tendril squirms its way in naturally through the first bullet hole Audrey made and it writhes against the sizzling inner surface of the windshield like a sucker-less squid tentacle.

Grieves phases through the nightmare spawn, turning as he does, and he ends up in the dashboard inside the car facing the creature on the hood and windshield. He grabs blobs of teeth and eyes in two big bunches and phases out of the interior of the car, pulling himself out through the solid matter of the glass. When he's done, his back is on the windshield and the muck monster is held away from it as much as Grieves can manage. Grieves has to keep phasing different parts of himself in and out to avoid the mouths and talons striking out for him while keeping it at bay.

I try to aim the revolver through the windshield but the Bentley rakes and crunches against another vehicle on the bridge and my first shot goes wide. Seeing that I have what I assume is the one type of weapon that can hurt it, the creature tries to pull away. Grieves switches tactics and tries to keep the creature on the hood, phasing himself down into the engine compartment and pulling the big monster down with him.

I prime again and fire through the windshield and this time my aim is true enough. The weird glowing equation rounds blast out of the chamber, igniting the colored fluids somewhere inside and flaring up to that blinding white as they come out of the barrel and go through the windshield into the porker's closest blob of gnashing madness.

The muck is blown out through the back of the nightmare soldier's bulk—then starts sucking back in, pulling and twisting it into the nothing around the path the bullet made through the creature's body. The porker wails but isn't done for yet.

Grieves can't see from his straining position down in the engine compartment and he holds onto one blob section too long. The closest tooth chasm closes into the nasty mess and reopens around Grieves's sleeved hand and arm, slamming closed on it and sending his weird glowing blood spraying out all over. The porker wrenches the mouth that has Grieves's arm completely closed, ripping, breaking, and slicing Grieves's forearm off about four inches down from the elbow. Grieves howls in pain and his cries are muffled but reverberate through the body of the car.

I prime the revolver and fire, then prime and fire again. The wounds suck the porker into itself as it wails.

The eyes go gray as whatever force it is that takes control of the creatures leaves this one. What's left of the oily, fetid muck slumps down and, as the black sludge is sucked away, pickled organs and unnaturally warped bones slide down the hood and fall to the bridge surface speeding by below.

Grieves arches back up and begins searching through the last of the muck for his arm. He finds it but it's already half sucked into one of the nothing-maker wounds. He seems to be trying to phase it by touch, but it just keeps disappearing into the gap. He pulls at it until all he's holding is the pinky, then he's forced to let go as it's sucked in too. Grieves turns and leers back at me through the windshield with an expression that seems to mix triumph and sadness.

With the creature mostly gone and Grieves's desperate struggle for his appendage finished, I look past them and finally notice that I'm driving us straight into the first curve just past the bridge at about ninety miles per hour.

With the weak left arm at the end of my burning shoulder and my revolver-filled left hand, I try to steer the car away from the curve but overcorrect and we veer between two cars toward the metal barrier at the foot of the western walkway and grind against it. I panic and slam on the brakes. The crunching slide only dissipates some of our forward momentum and hitting the brakes causes the

Bentley to hydroplane almost straight toward the eastern walkway at over sixty miles per hour.

Grieves reaches his intact arm in through the windshield and tries to phase me like he did in the warehouse—but it's not working.

Grieves looks up at me and rambles something apologetic. Then phases through the car and I watch in the mirror as Grieves ends up in a trot across the wet bridge behind the sliding car, waving toward the Bentley before grabbing the glowing stump poking out from his torn coat sleeve at the end of his other elbow.

Thanks for trying?

I look back down at the quickly approaching curved walkway and have just enough time to think, Oh, this is gonna suuuuck—

The Bentley hits the base of the walkway at an angle and the front end of the passenger side starts to crumple but something about the objects being in different time streams causes a kind of shuddering vibration and extra resistance. The rear end was already kicking up, but the resistance amplifies it, and the silly pink car is thrown up over the walkway and flips end-over-end as it flies off the last curved stretch of bridge.

I'm sucked back against my seat due to the Bentley's vertical rotation and a twirling the angle caused, and I can only wonder if I will vomit, pass out, or die on impact first.

My money's on dying instantly, for the record.

Mercifully (depending on who you ask and their existential comfort at that moment), the Bentley slams upright into the hill just down from Vista Point, an outlook spot near the bridge to the northeast, at about a hundred-and-ten-degree angle to its slope.

The engine compartment and front end crumple safely enough in theory, but the particular way they do at this off angle causes something in my left upper leg to crack on impact, and the airbags instantly inflate.

chapter 33

I come to, looking up through shattered safety glass at gouges and tracks that the Bentley must have made as it slid down the hill it landed on. The deflated airbag is on my lap.

Rain crawls down from the sky to pour on the resting Bentley, then bursts when the vibes of the two time streams collide. Raindrops fall slowly like clear molasses through the bullet holes Audrey made in the windshield and passenger window and burst on Siobhán's body.

The car ended up about thirty feet down from the impact point facing up the hill and askew with the driver's seat just a bit more downhill than the passenger's. At least we didn't roll down—

"AGH–NK!" I shift in my seat and discover that my leg is broken. I keep it still until the sharper pain goes away but the pounding ache isn't going anywhere unless shock kicks in. Won't that be fun?

Between the broken leg and strangely shot shoulder, I'm

not feeling so hot. I turn gingerly to my left and see the gap we sailed across, then chuckle through my pain at our magnificent twisty-twirl.

Shuffling and loud sounds not unlike thick logs popping in a campfire grab my attention from the passenger seat.

Siobhán is moving.

It doesn't seem deliberate. Her body jerks and shakes as if in a palsy and the movements get stronger for a moment with each pop from her head, neck, and chest. Other than that, she still looks dead. The blood, bone bits, and brain matter on Siobhán, me, and a great deal of the car interior are buzzing and popping.

Okay, that's it. I'm officially done playing now.

One especially loud pop reforms the shape of her head back to what it was before Audrey's bullets had their way with it, and Siobhán moans long and low. Her head lolls around weakly atop her neck and she seems to be looking around, but the fake blue eyes move at slightly different times and angles. Then her face goes slack like her nerves are messed up before tightening back up and forming into a grimace.

After a little flopping, she succeeds in bringing her hands to her face and head and moaning like a maimed animal. There are cracking sounds in her neck and chest and a last pop from somewhere in her head and she whines and cries in agony. Her eyes flutter open and they're synced again but she looks confused. She pulls her hands away and looks at them, then realizes what the problem is and pulls the clear mask off her face. She clumsily sticks a couple fingers down her throat, then retches into her mouth and spits some fluid and the black ball at the cracked windshield.

She appears as herself again as the ball ricochets off the cracked glass, falls to the rain-slick dashboard, rolls down it, and drops down onto my broken leg.

It hurts but not enough to distract me from this horror show.

Siobhán looks over and down a bit at me and I see that the weird contact lens that was over her right eye has come out. A brilliant, emerald-green eye peers at me along with its translucent, reflective companion on her left. The piercing black pupil is…pulsing?

Siobhán struggles to say, "You mmade iht? That'sh grand."

Her whole body tenses up and she cringes hard before going slack against the seatbelt and sighing.

Siobhán murmurs, "Oooh, I'm gonnah need sho mush morphine thish time," then closes her eyes and tries to breathe through what must be excruciating pain.

That's when it all clicks for me that I've witnessed this process once before. "You're one of them!"

Siobhán winces and raises her hand, "Shh-sht. Q-quieter, pleash…."

As I try to shift away from her without moving my leg too much I yell, "Fuck you! Fuck! Yoooooooouuuuu! How's that for quiet?!"

Siobhán's eyes snap open and the right one explodes, pulling that side of her face into a warped, melting organic mess of solarized psychedelia. In a flash the only part of her head that's not a part of the swirling pulse is her left, contact-covered eye.

She grabs me by the throat with her left hand in an upside-down grip but not hard enough to choke me. She strains a bit against the seatbelt to bring her right hand down and puts her fingers against my clear mask, then pulls it off and tries to put two fingers in my mouth but I close it tight.

I can feel her prying my lips and teeth apart with her superior strength and I can't do anything about it. I try to shirk her arms off too and have no luck. Siobhán's fingers start to enter my mouth. "IF YOU BITE ME, I'LL HURT YOU," she says calmly in that shrill yet booming way, and I know she's not bluffing. She has recovered her motor skills quicker than Audrey did and seems able to recover from the crazy-face flare-ups faster too. It's still a weird, distorting mess, but I can make out her face in it already.

Siobhán forces her fingers to the back of my throat, and I gag. She keeps doing that until I hurl out my own black, nasty stomach ball onto the deflated airbag, then the tilted zebra floor. I hear a clink right after it's out of my sight under the seat and figure it hit the other stomach ball.

Siobhán lets go of my throat and shakes her other fingers off, then wrenches the rearview mirror off the shattered windshield, making a hole and letting in more clear molasses. She puts the mirror in my hands and raises them to my eye level. "You are 'Them,' Felix."

I glare at her and try again to struggle out of her grasp.

Siobhán yells, "LOOK AT IT!" and the car vibrates hard around us.

I won't look so she grabs my chin and gently but powerfully forces my face toward the mirror. I try to fight her hand but feel my jaw trying to pop out and relent. I keep my eyes on her, though, as my last act of defiance.

Siobhán's intensity lessens, and she says, "No more games, Felix." She gives a little nod and eye roll toward the mirror.

I give up and look myself in the eyes for the first time in almost fifteen years. I blink hard from the sheer oddness of it. I've had to imagine what I look like for over half of my life and seeing the reality now—

Then it starts as pinpricks of impossible black in my pupils. It's stronger in my brown eye but not by much.

I start breathing hard and the harder I breathe, the more I freak out and the more I freak out, the larger the black pulsing gets. I have fractal shark eyes now and my face starts to melt and break apart and go all prism-cutout on me.

It's like my body, head, and face are connected abstractly to my emotions. It fuses in a kind of synesthesia with the visuals into something like an unseen cosmic butcher touching and showing you your prime cuts with lasers, clear hyper-prismic blades, and a sonic see-through acid-thrower. There's a mixture of dissociation and perception-altering hallucination but the difference is it seems to actually be happening in front of me and the weirdness comes from my mind actually grasping that it's real—or a layer of the reality, more like. I can see through my new shark eyes but my peripheral vision is all shifting layered fractal symbols I don't recognize.

I tear my eyes away from the mirror and look at Siobhán and her chaos-surrounded, lens-covered left eye.

Siobhán nestles back into her bucket seat and says, "Trippy, yeah? You get almost used to it a few decades in. It can even be fun sometimes if you're bored and have a mirror around." She cracks her neck and moans as she massages her temples.

"What does it mean?" I ask, and my voice echoes around inside the Bentley and my head.

Siobhán produces the crimson beedi from behind her ear and lights it with a snap of her fingers this time. I'm far too gone to care how it was still in place all this time and just watch her drag off it, then let out a huge cloud and a sigh.

"You're one of us."

"What are we then?"

She considers her words more than usual.

"Your…lovely, not-the-least-bit-homicidal Audrey and I are one thing, you're something close but I don't know how close, and I'm still trying to figure out what your Stretch X-Ray–lookin' friend is. I say us 'cause we're all seeds spread by the machine."

"STOP IT! JUST TELL ME WHAT THIS MEANS!"

Siobhán cringes from my yelling and what I realize is my own shrill and booming bizarro-voice.

"Okay, but keep that shit down, man." She breathes in

and sighs, then says, "We're 'unstuck,' as Wahrheit put it with surprising accuracy. I am curious where he gets all that information.

"You and I are from Cork, originally, but I guess that's not proper literal and not at all true, get me? Not sure myself. You look so much like him, other than that blue eye.

"The only fact I can give you is that less than fifty years from now, our version of this place gets lit up bad. It starts over water and other resources, then religion and jingoist nonsense comes back with a vengeance to take away any progress we had made since now. My favorite part is that we were days—*days*—away from completing the orbital-and-ground-defense mesh when the fuse was lit.

"It's getting weirder for me the closer it gets to then, 'cause it's looking more and more like the world of our childhood and this city as it was…and will be then. It's a little different here, but mostly the same."

I'm glitching on my cutout-riddled hands and the strong echo and reverberation of my breathing and only caught a bit of that, but it was enough to ask, "But you're that—what was it? 'Taste raw yolk'?"

"Thae'st Ra'yho."

"Yeah, and you're their princess," I say, quietly to lessen the echo.

"It's even more religious than that, sadly. It's my own fault in a way. That's what I am now and what I've been for a while. But I've been so many things."

Her voice is different on the last part. Distant. Sad.

I look over at her through my fractal-pulse eyes and her distortion is slowly shuddering more than fracturing.

She chokes up sporadically as she continues, "I wasn't even sure until I saw you with that 'Grieves' thing. I can't imagine what it's been like for him, considering what I've endured. But when you're close to him, I can see it clearer.

"I'm not the same woman anymore. It's been so long.

I've done so many things because I thought—" She has to stop for a moment.

Why does this busted car feel like a confessional all of a sudden?

"I've seen so much darkness, pain, and cold brutality. I tried to be good, but I caused my share too, if I'm being honest. I've stolen and tortured and murdered and… enjoyed it, God help me, whatever you may be.

"I've f-fucked so many people. But what's worse is I've loved others too. Deeply. I won't apologize for that because you were gone. And I don't expect forgiveness 'cause I don't deserve or want it. I won't betray the memory of those others as I betrayed you, unknowing as that was."

I can just make out mascara tears sliding down her lightly freckled cheeks through the pulsing weirdness.

"But I've seen so much beauty too, each time like a bright, warm oasis in the dark. And part of me always wanted to share those moments with you, no matter what man or woman I loved at the time. Now I don't know how to feel."

She cries openly for a stretch before I ask, "Who are you talking to?"

"My husband, Ciarán. From another life I guess you could say. Many lives ago now. I don't know how but you're him."

"No, I'm not."

I look back at my shark eyes in the mirror and a glowing section of bone and sinew I can see through a prism cutout in my right hand that's holding it.

"It's you. You're in this boy somehow, but it's you, Ciarán."

"My name is Felix Brewer."

"Your name is Ciarán Aodhan O'Shea. We were born in Cork City, County Cork, and were lifelong friends, then lovers. I taught you Braille so you could write me emails on a special keyboard when you were blinded by a low-altitude nuke and in the hospital, then rehab for a while. Eventually, they gave you new eyes and you studied physics in school."

"None of that's true."

"Your science prowess and my own talents got us selected along with about five thousand others to get in that horrible machine and come back here to stop our lovely mushroom holocaust from happening again. These people's worst nightmares became our reality.

"They sent us back selfishly to warn these idiots not to make the same mistakes so that our layer would be fixed. But smart as they were, they didn't account for parallels. A nightmare it will stay."

"BULLSHIT!" My distortions flare and the layered fractals fill my vision until I breathe through my anger and confusion. "If we made it here, why don't I remember any of this? Why did I grow up in this time?"

"Because you didn't make it. I don't know what you are."

"I don't believe you. None of that is possible. How did this machine work then, huh?"

"I don't know how the machine worked and if I ever did, I can't remember. But it did work, and phase one was a success, if you factor in the unpublished estimated survival rate. But after what happened to you, I just didn't care anymore.

"I've been drifting since then. Longer than you can comprehend. Then after all this time not caring, I find you again at a stupid party. I just crashed it to find some stranger to fuck into a coma to get over my silly, young Viohl'ta. Let the healing begin, so to speak. Imagine my surprise finding you there."

She curls her fingers and flicks the last of the beedi out through the hole in the windshield where the mirror used to be and watches it slow down abruptly as it hits the sludge of proper time a few feet from the car.

Then she looks at me. I'm staring at the mirror and

looking around once in a while but it's like she's not even there.

I'm entranced by my warping image in the mirror and by the organic see-through mercury rolling down through my hands and arms. Nothing Siobhán said after "phase one" properly registered in my mind.

"What's wrong with you?"

Quietly, I answer, "I *am* crazy. You're a delusion and I'm crazy. I guess they're wrong about knowing when you are...."

"No, you're perfectly sane."

"Blah, blah, delusion, blah. I'm not listening. You aren't real," I whisper. Then I whisper more words but those are more to myself and almost probably inaudible to her. My eyes roll back and forth between my hands and the mirror and the raining clear molasses pelting the hill outside the car.

"Felix, stop being stupid and—"

But I start singing a song to myself to drown out her voice, so she cuts herself off. It's something about hoping things are 'alright' and I'm singing it like a mantra.

My singing seems to backfire because I start tripping on my own voice again but don't stop or get quieter this time. I just repeat the same line, changing my tone and pitch and glitching on the intense, layered reverberations.

Siobhán just watches Felix for a while before realizing what she has to do.

"This was too much for you. I'm sorry I hit you with so much at once. I just couldn't hold it back anymore. Maybe in a way you're right. Maybe you aren't him exactly."

She looks out through the shattered windows for signs of activity and sees none.

"It definitely seems like they're more after me, at least from my achin' head and body. If you're still alive, your girl couldn't have been *too* sore at you."

She unlatches her safety belt, reaches toward Felix's chest, and pulls his booster sphere off.

Felix is instantly pulled into the sludge and his shark eyes take several seconds to blink once and his mouth barely changes shape while forming the words to his mantra.

She kisses him on the right temple and holds there for a long moment before saying, "I'll see you later, *cushlamachree*. I promise you that."

It takes me a moment to realize I'm back in normal time but the fast-pouring rain is my first clue. It's falling down into the car through the holes in the windshield and bursting explosively against the vague pink-and-black surfaces inside the Bentley, which is vibrating and blurry all around me.

There's something in my right peripheral vision—

A second later, the car shudders into normal speed and the passenger door is open.

Siobhán is gone.

If she was there at all.

I look back down at the mirror in my hands. My warping image starts to pull me in again but this time I'm not having any of it and fling it at the passenger-side windshield. When it connects, half the safety glass that was held in place precariously collapses and showers onto the passenger seat, followed by the rain.

But if this isn't real, how did I get here?

I open the driver door and start to crawl out, nursing my hurt leg. My right foot connects with something heavy on the floor of the car.

The revolver.

Crazy or not, better take it in case there be more monsters about.

I pick up my pistol and gingerly pull myself out of the

car, sliding backwards out onto the wet grass and brush. I scan the area through the haze of pain.

Down the hill a ways there's a path of some kind.

Up the hill the heads of tourists and their umbrellas and cameras are visible once in a while from the scenic-view park on top, but they are distracted by that scenic view.

Don't know where that path down there leads. I could die getting lost if there's bleeding or something.

I roll onto my stomach and start up the hill, going between a heavy limped walk-crawl and sliding up on my stomach and chest. I make it about a third of the way up, but fatigue and a growing nausea, dizziness, and weird chest pains halt my progress. It feels like I'm sweating a lot too, but the rain confuses that.

I decide a rest would do me some good and I roll onto my back, letting the rain pelt me all over. It keeps me with it, I decide. The fractal layers are still at the edges of my vision but after some unrelated blurring and light-headedness clear, I can see the bridge and almost the whole city.

The rain and fog make the view a little dim, but I can see a large cloud of the green gas peeking between and even above some of the buildings all around downtown. I look over at the Golden Gate Bridge and the cars zooming north and south through the still-growing clouds of the gas coming from and clinging to it. A few low-cruising black chunks of whatevertheyare pass through the air between the bridge towers and I'm pretty sure they subtly disturbed the gas cloud where they passed through.

If I didn't know the purpose of that gas, these might almost be beautiful sights. Like some spooky fun Halloween-parade accompaniment.

Watching the chunks slowly rotate in their different revolutions is calming. My eyelids start to droop and I almost give myself over to my overwhelming exhaustion. I feel something near me and force my heavy head back to look up the hill from my lying position.

Something impossi-black is watching me from up the hill. I don't suppose that's a good thing.

I strain to aim the revolver up the hill but the thing disappears. I blink a couple times and look around. The thing looms at my feet. Without thinking, I swing my pistol down to fire at the dark figure. The revolver is much heavier to my weakened arm and almost smacks my left leg as it passes my intended firing spot. I use everything I have left to raise it back up and fire—

But as the revolver's hammer comes down, the pistol collapses in on itself like an imploding, revolver-shaped Rubik's Cube. I look at my empty hand in disbelief, then at the figure that I now see, from its shimmering outline and the absolute dark of its vague human form, is a "Ref."

The next part starts silently in the distance as a light from the southern horizon. As it approaches, it swallows the South Bay, the City, and the bay into a stratosphere-high tsunami of blinding liquid light, then the bridge implodes into complex, abstract shapes and my vision goes the way of the revolver, everything left in sight collapsing into itself like fractalized 120-cell planes.

chapter 34

I feel my weight shift as the surface of the hill becomes flat ground.

The fractal mesh dissipates, and my vision returns, and I can see that I'm somewhere quite foreign—bordering on alien.

A desert at the base of a valley between large dunes. The sand is fine and gray with specks of black. Almost too fine and it seems to come apart as I rub a handful.

I stand and look around.

The white cat with the obsidian eyes is poised atop the big dune on my right staring down at me. It patters away out of sight. My leg doesn't hurt anymore so I start up the dune after it. It's slow going but I reach the top and survey the area.

The sky is huge and black. Not like night. Like an overcast sky of inky black thunderheads and storm clouds. Rays of swirling, kaleidoscopic light break through the clouds sporadically only to be swallowed up again. There's thunder in the distance and lightning cracks but it's silhouette-black like the arcs across the Albtraum flying platform's turret, so the bolts are hard to make out at first amidst the varied shades of black and dark gray in the sky.

I can't see the cat anywhere.

Behind me, the dunes stretch to the horizon like an ocean of frothy gray waves. Ahead, the dunes get smaller, and I see red past the lowest one. It looks like a red salt flat.

"Sure, why not? I've got nowhere else to be today, since I'm probably dead or something like that. Walter and Izzywhatsit will have to try a Felix from another layer of the old glass onion, I guess."

I slide-hike down my dune and up the next and continue onward like that until I'm almost down to the flat.

Across the flat in the distance and on to the horizon there are what look like oil fires burning but the flames at the base of the diagonally leaning plumes of deep black smoke are brilliant white.

As I reach the flat and take my first steps across, my feet splash gently into six inches of red fluid. The liquid reflects the swirling of the clouds in the big, black sky but not their darkness as it stretches to the horizon. The liquid reacts to disturbance strangely, not giving the level of resistance I would expect.

Plus, it smells awful.

The surface of the flat that can be seen through the odd fluid is like an endless patchwork made up of translucent fossils of amorphous creatures of all structures, shapes, and sizes formed together and filling in each other's gaps, then frozen together. Malformed organs, tissue, and bones are visible in the layers closest to the surface, sometimes shared between the suggested separate bodies. It's like organic nonsense aged, then eroded to be flat and smooth as alabaster.

"Nhhnnnn-kay...."

Something in the distance catches my gaze. It looks

like two sharply pointed artificial structures or smoothed angular obelisks. It's the most obvious landmark in sight and I can see a white speck near them that could somehow be the cat, so I start off toward them through the ankle-high liquid, trying to ignore the weird forms suggested in the fossil surface.

A few miles on, I notice a dark, circular plate in the ground off to my right. I stop and look at it from where I am but something about it I can't place keeps my curiosity in check and I err on the side of caution, even now.

As I continue toward the pointed structures in the distance, a slight breeze kicks up and I get a chill and shudder. Button my dragon-sleeved jacket up all the way but soon it's a bone-biting cold wind that cuts through the smooth fabric and I wish I could get to the structure faster to take cover. Little ripples spread across the red fluid like on a lake.

I see that the ripples ahead of me have a different pattern and, upon closer examination, I see through the reflection on the surface of the pseudo-fluid that it gets darker in a gradual arc. When I near the edge, I can see that the fossil-slop marble drops off dramatically at an angle like a continental slope might. It gets darker almost immediately below the surface and I can barely see past about ten feet into the dark red murk below.

The wind is getting stronger.

To my left and right, I can only see a gradual curve to the slope edge leading me to believe that this lake of sorts must surround whatever those obelisks are and they must be at the center of it.

Well, gosh, that's too darn bad. I'm not going in there for anything, homie. If it's my death-dream delusion, can't I make changes, like a lucid dream or something?

The thunder rolls behind me, louder and closer now. I look back toward the dunes and see a sky-high storm of the ashy sand blowing toward me where they were. The desert is coming for me.

"Forget I asked, spaznoid!" I yell toward the white speck near the obelisk in the distance.

I can only watch as the roaring wall closes in across the flat and it stretches as far left and right as I can see. I shake my head, trying to think of any other option than swimming through the weird liquid.

I mean, who knows what that shit is? It smells like rotten animal carcass baked in acetone and vomit.

I have to shift my footing as the wind blows me about on the edge of the drop. The ground beneath my feet shudders, then rumbles as it vibrates and shifts up and down in time with the howling storm approaching.

I hold off until the storm is less than fifty feet away, the wind throwing me almost off my feet, and all the red fluid in the shallows is whipping around in spirals.

Even though every little bit of my being is against it, I dive into the red murk as the storm passes over—and immediately learn that I was right not to trust the fluid—it doesn't resist like water and I lose little speed as I dive-fall down into the obelisk lake, but it also doesn't let me drop like I expect after experiencing the lack of resistance. I tuck and roll a bit and go into a gradual tumble, which slows me enough to start descending toward the surface of the slope.

My eyes adjust and on the upturn of the tumble I watch the storm above roll over the lake, obscuring what diffuse light there was from the black sky. On the downturn I can see that the surface of the slope isn't smooth like the flats. The jumbled, chaotically grown or formed bodies are bulbous here and jagged there but vague enough through the murky liquid that I convince myself that I see parts of the bodies in the slope moving.

My tumbling slows and I see that the red fluid becomes more of a dark blue near what must be the "lake" floor.

I'm getting deeper fast and I'm almost at the end of my breath, so I try to swim back to the surface. The low resistance works both ways, though, and I can't gain any purchase. I just keep falling deeper and closer to the slope.

I realize I'm going to drown but I keep flailing in hopes of catching some friction to no avail. I hold the last of my breath as long as I can, then my mouth opens and I breathe in against my will. The red fluid enters my nose and mouth and fills my chest and I kiss my ass goodbye.

Then I start breathing again. The fluid is hard to get used to the first few times I let it in, but I can breathe it.

I let himself float down to the slope and guide myself the little bit I can, touching down on the distended, entrail- and organ-filled belly of a warped, horse-sized trunk of abdomen. Its head and limbs are lost in the seamless continuum of organic alabaster.

I look up the slope and consider trying to climb back up what looks to be about a half mile of angled weirdness, but I see from the rolling darkness above that the storm has made it almost all the way across the lake.

That didn't seem like a friendly, nice ash storm either. Down then?

Like an astronaut on a low-gravity planet or moon, I make a series of long, slow jumps down to the foot of the fossil slope.

I can barely see into the foggy blue layer over the lake floor but there aren't any moving forms, so I chance going straight into it on my last jump. I break through, disturbing the blue mist but touching down safely about ankle deep into some kind of sediment on the entire lake floor.

The base of it is blue and gray silt and multicolored pebbles but there are broken white shells as well?

I crouch and scoop up some of it in my left hand, then examine it as I stand.

The blue and gray sediment is the shredded remnants of decayed, soaked carpet fabric. The colorful pebbles are wet, waxy chunks of crayons. The shells are crushed and shattered teeth.

I rub the scar on my jaw through my Uncle Salty facial growth and let the sediment run through my fingers and drift to the lake floor before flinging the last of it down and scuffing my hand against the side of my soaked track pants a few times to get the residue off.

"Real classy, spaz."

I can make out a dark, skyscraper-tall form in the distance through the murky blue and decide that must be the bulk of a form that is topped by the obelisks. I set off toward it, shuffling through my deconstructed childhood living room and hundreds of thousands of my father's broken teeth.

I see a few more of the plates like the one I saw on the red flat poking up partially through the sedimentary junk but ignore them as best I can. As I near to the looming form ahead, there are more and more of the plates randomly scattered around and I can't help wondering what they're for.

Through the blue haze, the form ahead is becoming clearer. It looks almost like a Gothic cathedral with a very tall main structure and two main towers jutting up past that. There's a suggestion of many flying buttresses building from a wide base and climbing the main structure walls and a bit up onto the higher towers and even between them. It's like a warped, vertically stretched caricature of the Reims cathedral in France.

I get closer and see that the cathedral comparison is spot on but not the whole picture. The structure is a dull matte orange due to its main building material being what looks like rusting machines of all kinds.

Some machines are still pumping and turning and slamming together slowly and awkwardly but most are just fused together and/or seized up. There's the suggestion of the internal workings of cars, trucks, turbines, generators, pumps, etc., but none of it is clear. Some pipes still let out smoke or steam that hits the strange blue fluid and looks like a vent on the deep ocean floor. The whole thing sways a bit back and forth and creaks and moans. The rust and metallic ash of decay continuously flakes and falls off or clings to different parts, giving the towering structure the look of a pickled creature in a formaldehyde-filled jar.

I hear a thump and spin toward the source. All I can see is one of those plates. There's another thump and I turn toward that one.

It had to be from that plate over there.

I creep to the plate and crouch down. As I brush the carpet, crayons, and teeth aside I realize it's not a plate at all. It's a transparent porthole looking down into a dark tube about three feet in diameter. All I can see down in the tube is a bluish-black sludge, which catches the dim light a bit with a touch of iridescence on its surface.

I brush more of the sediment off the porthole and see a long barcode on the curve of the part closer to me. There's another thump as I watch something move in the sludge. The thing writhes and twists and a grotesque, sludge-covered human face emerges, then sinks back down out of sight. I can hear a low moan and see thick bubbles form at the surface, then more thumps.

"Uh...."

Thumps start coming from another tube behind me, then another—and soon dozens of them are thumping.

The humanoid thing in the tube I'm crouched at forces itself up and slams the porthole with its face, causing me to straighten up and take a step back. It slams the porthole repeatedly and the other tubes start to make the same wet, meaty slapping sounds.

With a final thump and slap, the thumper closest to me pops the top of its tube off, then drops back down. Wet sliding and wriggling sounds are followed by the human thing squirming its way up out of the tube into the faux-fluid of the lake bottom through undulation and lubricated sliding alone, and it flops its upper half out onto the crayons, teeth, and carpet mush.

The malformed humanoid flops around like its muscles are badly atrophied but, once it sees me, starts to flop and slide across the lakebed toward me, so I back away.

More tubes pop open and each produces a similar creature, and they join in the pursuit. I have to keep changing the direction of my retreat. Soon, there are dozens of the things crawling all over and I have nowhere to escape to. They converge on me, clawing and pulling and a few get a hold of my feet and lower legs and upend me.

Yeah, I probably should have just jumped.

I try to fight them off but they've dogpiled onto me, all of them trying to get a piece. They seem to be attacking me but they're too weak to succeed in rending me limb from limb like they want to. If it weren't so disturbing to be the focus of this so far less-than-deadly attack, I might laugh.

Then I do laugh. I laugh hard in their muck-covered, ghoulish faces and say, "If this's gonna be that kinda party, I'ma stick my dick in the mashed potatoes!" and keep laughing.

The would-be killer human-creatures stop like someone pressed pause and proceed to collapse in on themselves with that hyper-prism puzzle implosion effect and I can see the light-sucking silhouette of the Ref standing in front of me. It's not as tall as I originally thought.

The creatures disappear completely but I'm still covered in their muck at first. As I haul myself off the lake floor, the liquid I keep forgetting I'm surrounded by pulls some of the oily residue off.

I glare at the gaping black of the Ref's head region.

"Is this supposed be scary or profound or something?"

It cocks its head a bit but I'm not sure if it understands or just finds my mouth sounds puzzling/amusing.

"I mean, I think I get what you're trying to do. Metaphors and symbols and shit get you hard. I can respect that."

Its head cocks the other way and now I'm sure it doesn't

understand me.

I can see that the border of its form that has the light-sucking effect is like a constantly decaying and replenishing mesh of something like fractals.

"The thing is, I just don't care anymore. I don't need to know. I don't want to know. What you're doing isn't going to work, get me?"

The Ref observes me a moment longer, then straightens up and its form collapses into the lake floor like an illusionist disappearing under a dropping sheet.

There's a long moment in which I feel like maybe I got through to the Ref but that's immediately followed by another that feels like I'm alone and stranded.

The floor of the lake starts to vibrate and rumble and it's strong enough that I have to half crouch to keep my balance. Parts of the rusted cathedral fall off and glide down to the crayons and teeth, making little clouds of the carpet mush puff up.

"Now what, spaz?!"

The floor of the lake starts rising with incredible speed and force—collapsing impossibly upwards as if the lake was trying to fill itself in—and rushing up toward the red surface like a set of locks was released on an amusement-park ride.

I'm pulled down into an unintentional narrow X shape in the lakebed. There's enough force for me to feel crayon shards and bits of busted teeth digging into the back of my head.

With effort I turn my head and see that the fossil slope is breaking apart all around as the lake floor collapses upwards and myriad shattered parts of the amorphous frozen creatures are being forced toward the cathedral like waves toward a circular island—some of them freed from their stonelike state but into the reality of their severed parts, now writhing and spasming like the unfortunate man Grieves had freed similarly in the restroom before.

They keep coming and I decide for the fourth or fifth time today that I'm about to die.

Just before the huge wave of translucent statue parts converges on me and the cathedral from all sides, the lake "floor" reaches the red flats level and stops.

The force of it stopping explodes the cathedral and its rusted machine parts; the fossil creature chunks, the teeth-crayon-carpet mush, and the fluid that made up the lake all explode up and out from the now level flats and into the ash storm.

I'm thrown up through all this at remarkable speed and I scream the fluid out of my lungs only to have my mouth fill with ash as I reach escape velocity toward the black swirling clouds in the sky. I'm swallowed by the stormy black abyss and my body goes cold from the wind as I fly sightless through the inky abyss.

There's a shift in the pull on my stomach I can only feel as my scream finally trails off.

The clouds and wind fade out and I'm moving through a black void. Then in the periphery of my vision dim specks of light appear. They get brighter and I realize they are stars, planets, moons, comets, asteroids. White, yellow, blue, red, etc., and I see them everywhere save for a huge circle of black that remains in front of me and seems to be growing.

The circle becomes illuminated as if with a celestial dimmer switch and reveals itself to be not just an enormous orb, but Earth itself. It's not as blue, green, or white as I'm used to seeing it, but it definitely has the right continental outlines.

I pass myriad orbiting satellites as I keep rocketing toward the looming planet. I hit the first layer of atmosphere and start to fall more than fly. Fortunately, even though my clothes and face are fluttering some it's looking like I don't have to worry about all that re-entry burn stuff.

As I fall into the lower atmosphere, I can see hundreds of spears of shiny gray and white metal arcing over the planet below me and, as I fall closer, my pace matches their downward curves. I look back and forth and every time I blink the sky fills with dozens more of the thermonuclear phalluses, all falling toward Earth in a cartoonish yet incredibly ominous shower of doom.

Another blink and now there are Fat Mans and Little Boys; then Fat Man–like Mark 4s, smaller but similar Mark 5s, and Mark 6s; the longer, smoother Mark 7s and stubby Mark 8s; girth-blessed Mark 14s, 15s, and Mark 36s with ribs for Mother Earth's pleasure; enema-tip Naval sub-launch W47s; B28 anal intruders; and everything else from M29 Davy Crockett–fired W54s on up to dunce-cap spurting MIRV LGM-118 Peacekeepers and the foreign equivalents and alternatives of all of the above. And who could forget the John Holmes of bombs and Peter North of nuclear ejaculation, the Russian Tsar Bomba? There are dozens of those throbbing monsters too.

Grieves is sitting cross-legged on one of these big boys, perpendicular to its length and facing the rear fins. He's holding something like a newspaper in both hands but its thick, orange-ish pages are transparent and the block letters of the headlines glow bright blue. In between flaps I can see that the headline is in multiple written languages and the English reads:

THE END IS NOW

I become aware that I'm wearing a parachute when the yellow-and-black-striped pull handle starts flapping against my jacketed chest. I pull it out of instinct and the wad of parachute is pulled straight up out of its pack and opens, slowing me considerably.

As the bombs keep falling, Grieves notices me, smiles in his strange way, and waves as he drops away with them.

The bombs fall until they reach Earth and explode in blinding balls of light as far as I can see in every direction.

I can feel the heat on my face and hear a crackling and sizzling sound from above and look up. The parachute is disintegrating as if from invisible flame. I drop faster as a hole forms in the fabric and quickly grows. In only a few moments, the parachute is useless, and I drop unhindered toward the incredible heat of the continuous explosions.

I scream again as I fall into the blinding light of the ceaseless nuclear blasts.

With no perceptible transition, I'm standing in a line of people six across that extends as far as I can see in front of me. The phalanx is flanked by large blue military-and-refugee-style tents and from the asphalt at my feet this all seems to be in what used to be a huge old lot around a large dark structure in the center.

It's a bit cold but I've already forgotten why that's a welcome change. My hand is warm, though, and I look down to see why. There's a hand in mine so I look up at the owner.

Siobhán is holding my hand. Her beautiful green eyes twinkle with anticipation and nerves and she looks so much younger. The Siobhán I know always looks physically young, but her eyes belie that youthful appearance with a look of profound worldliness and suppressed melancholy. This Siobhán has raw hope and real fear in her eyes.

Her hair is a natural auburn and cut short into a loose, wavy bob and she wears no makeup, so her light freckles are obvious. Actually, all she is wearing is something between a robe and a smock made of matte rubberized plastic with a barcode down its left front in a vertical strip and slippers of the same material. I decide the getups must have something to do with the thin arcs of weird electricity biting at the ground all around and jumping from one small puddle on the asphalt to another.

That's when I realize that I'm Ciarán, at least for the moment.

I get flashes of memories that aren't my own and close my eyes:

I remember meeting Siobhán while she was kicking a ball against a wall in Cork City when we were children. We play tag. We wrestle. We kiss. When we're older, we make love for the first time and we're clumsy and nervous. We get better. I see an otherworldly flash, then have a whole chunk of memory that is black with swirling imagined images and things I could only hear, smell, touch, and taste. Then more sighted memories of making love, walking, reading. Then more bombs and almost nothing else.

Siobhán squeezes my hand, and I open my eyes. In her natural Irish accent she says, "I think the line's movin' agehnn."

I look at her, then at the wide line ahead. There's a heavy vibration and a snapping sound and the structure at the line's terminus lights up with an unnatural glow.

It looks like a heavily modified baseball stadium with a huge metal dome built into its center, which is visible even from out here in what had to be its parking lot. There are large machines moving on the outside surface of the dome in almost obscene pumping motions giving them at quick glance the appearance of oil derricks trying to bleed a comically small planet. On the lowest part visible that isn't obstructed by the old stadium structure from this angle, I can make out the top of a huge object slowly moving around the dome. From the bit I can see, I imagines it's a huge train engine pulling a machine the size of a large, squat building around the base of the convex metal half bubble.

Siobhán and I go with the flow of the line and enter a large mouth of an opening into the stadium. This leads to an angled, rubber-lined ramp wide enough for six across, which leads up into the base of the dome. They are under it now and I can only imagine what the whole dome and machine look like.

The people in front of us remove their smock-robes and place them in pneumatic chutes on each side of the line path that carry them away. They also take off necklaces and rings and place them in the tube.

The nude people have intricate reflective tattoos in rectangular strips down the right side of their backs from shoulder blades to hips. There are thinner strips down their right forearms and calves and horizontal ones on their necks I hadn't noticed before because they are subtler. When the row in front of me and Siobhán disrobes, I can see that what I took for tattoos are more like embedded holograms of cylindrically concentric, layered coding. I know this has a purpose but my memory of it is hazy.

Siobhán and the rest of our row take off our smocks but I hesitate. I'm confused by a mix of remembered familiarity and an excitement. From what I've seen of her arms and posture, I can tell Siobhán is more toned and strong as I know her, but this Siobhán is very lovely in a softer way that lacks her later toughness and predatory qualities. She gives me a nudge and I remove my smock and deposit it in the tube closer to us.

Siobhán takes off her wedding ring and seems to place it in the tube but I remember our plan. I take mine off too and let the shim I've had around the band's inner circle fly into the suction tube instead, as she just did. I close my hand tightly around the ring, hoping it won't set off the detector due to the special film we sprayed our hands with.

It works. We follow the rows in front of us up the rubber-lined ramp.

We emerge onto the rubber floor and move in sync to disperse evenly around the circular plate and I remember we were trained for this moment, and it has been well rehearsed. When we are all inside and in our places, the angled walkway closes and locks in place flush with the floor.

I look up and study the inner surface of the dome. The

lower ends of the pumping derricks enter the dome above them in offset rhythms and disturb a layer of steam or mist collecting near the dark inner apex.

Siobhán says, "Y'think the food'll be better at least?" and lets out a little laugh so she doesn't seem scared to death.

In an Irish accent that surprises me with its natural easiness I say, "I hope so. I could punish eh fuhkin' cheeseburger."

There's a pulsing sound, then a digital PA crunching on noisy and distorted until something catches up and clears some and what must be a scientist in an unseen control room says, –What we do here today is for the good of our ancestors and, in the course of time, our children.–

This voice strikes me as oddly familiar but all I can associate it with is electricity and mumbling and that makes little sense to me at the moment. The scientist voice says more but I'm distracted by the feeling the voice itself gives me and miss the meat of it.

After a few minutes of silence, another, less poetic voice says, –The Engineer of our salvation has joined you in the chamber. Prepare yourselves. Preparatory sequence commencing in five... four... three... two... one.–

I hear more machines warming up all around. Humming, whirring, and shuddering. The floor vibrates under us and rises in intensity until I can't feel my feet.

A sound rises above all the rest and with it the strongest reverberation and shuddering and it goes around the entire outer base of the dome, increasing in speed, volume, and intensity with each pass. I can feel it vibrating my bones and numbing my muscles.

Siobhán squeezes my hand, and I know it's time. I offer her my left hand and the ring in it. She takes the ring and slides it back onto my ring finger. She offers me her left hand and ring. I take it and gently slide it back up into place at the base of her ring finger.

We kiss.

The machines are all deafening now but the thing going around the dome base is like the ever-intensifying roar of a city-sized monster lion. The room shakes violently.

Light starts bending and warping all around. The shape of the room changes in a pulsing rhythm with the revolutions of the unseen lion, and it feels to me like we're inside a transforming psychedelic heart.

The sound warps and bends now too and I hear Siobhán say, "I love you," before she says it. I say it back in my mind, but I don't say it for a long moment and then it's drowned out in the roar and screaming. Screaming?

I open my eyes but don't remember closing them. People all over the chamber are screaming because they can see through themselves in flashes like they're translucent and some are sinking into the floor or passing or falling into or through each other when it happens.

The roar hits a new peak, and everything explodes into a chaotic mess of organic madness and bent light.

I can't think right. I can see forward but can't look around. We're in a forest greener than any I've ever seen. I can't move or think…think right? Everything's vibrating and glowing strangely still but all I hear is a humming in my head. In his head?

I see Siobhán a ways away flopping around between some trees. It looks like she's screaming but I can't hear it. She's almost bald and steaming or smoking all over her reddish naked body. Her hair seems to be burning on her head but there's no visible flame. I'm forced to watch her scream herself tired and start sobbing silently.

Eventually she hauls herself to her feet and walks around like a rickety-legged baby calf, falling and getting back up on her unsteady legs a few times.

Siobhán scans the area and spots me but her expression is not one of relief. She runs as best she can and collapses to her knees in front of me silently screaming, "Ciarán," but

I can't figure out why she's upset.

Tears flow down her face as she slowly reaches her shaking left hand toward my face. I can see that her wedding ring is embedded in her finger like it shifted in transit and fused into the proximal phalange of her left ring finger. I wonder if that happened to mine as well, but can't feel my hand so I'm not sure.

When Siobhán touches my face, the glow, vibration, and humming are instantly gone and my view drops to the forest floor and slaps down looking straight up. Siobhán looks down as my view quickly fades and her eyes are wild. She looks like something snapped in her mind. My view goes black as the blood drains out of Ciarán's severed forebrain and eyes.

There's an ineffable peace for an immeasurable interval before I perceive anything else I can get a handle on, then there's a flood of bio-conscious concurrent time-lapse experience in which I grow from sperm and eggs into embryos and into an army of boys, turtles, girls, dogs, men, cats, women, fish, lemurs, old men, alligators, old women, a blue lobster, a suicidal hermaphrodite, a particularly playful beluga whale, and a stupid, yet happy, zebra.

There are many other things I experience having been, but I don't have the frame of reference to grasp what they are, so they feel more like a myriad of dramatically varying psychedelic feedback loops than lived lives. Alien creatures of varying types and from different planets, I'll come to decide later.

This all collapses closed spherically in my mind as—

I'm slammed into my own nine-year-old body, which is currently trapped under my father's lifeless body, screaming, and trying to fight out from under the heavy empty vessel to the tune of *Voltron*'s intro music out in the living room.

The experiences mesh together, and young and old Me

use the same vocal chords to scream for different reasons.

My father's body and room implode into blinding white fractal fun and I'm free, but I keep screaming anyway—

My consciousness returns and I'm still screaming as I'm wheeled down a hallway on a moving gurney. I'm curling up against straps and doctors and police officers keep pushing me down on my back.

One of the officers has seething, pumping bulbs on his neck and red mist pours from his nose and black-toothed mouth. Through a small jungle of translucent, glowing tentacle parasites on her face, a doctor yells that I am going to have to relax.

"What happened?!"

"Fuck if I know! He was fine, then flipped a bitch fit!"

"Sedative! Get a damn sedative!"

I lie in a hospital bed. My leg is in a cast and it's raised up by a cushioned sling. The television is on but I stare at the ceiling, uninterested. A police officer is sitting in the corner doing a crossword puzzle.

I sit with my leg raised onto another chair and stare through a plate of lovely food in the Fleischmann Medical Center dining room.

I sit on a bench out on an island in the big pond at the center of FMC. I look at my leg cast, then watch a koi gracefully swim by.

I look up at the infinite-seeming reflections of the mirrored patio walls around the small lake and stare at a descending loop of my form and the back of it alternating as they get smaller into the distance. Dozens of my own eyes watch me and dozens of my close-cropped heads ignore me.

"Good morning," I say, causing dozens of meaningless conversations to begin.

I look down at the slightly darker ring of skin around the base of my left ring finger. What I thought was a birthmark, now more like a cosmic echo.

Good morning.

Doctor Fleischmann presses play on a remote in his left hand and the camcorder starts recording. He starts a player with a different remote and readies his expensive pen over a notepad on his desk.

I see myself. I'm sitting in almost exactly the same spot. I look drowsy and complacent but my eyelids flutter as I watch footage of another Felix—a much more elevated Felix.

The elevated, unseen Felix yells, ——of a bitch! He knows all about you! You can blank my brain all you want! I might forget, but he won't, motherfucker!" and the complacent Felix that I see on the screen winces in shame and embarrassment. I watch this with almost no emotion.

On the video Fleischmann says, "Let's not get nasty, Felix. So, you still believe all of this? After everything I have presented you with?"

"You might as well just blank me, 'cause I don't give a shit what you 'presented,' Obrist!"

"My name is Heinrich Fleischmann. I wasn't even born until nineteen forty-nine. I am no more an immortal evil scientist than you are a Vietnam veteran, Felix. I also never met your girlfriend before that day in the hospital and I wouldn't 'blank' you if I could. I am trying to help you live with the luggage of your real life, not burn out one that has no basis in fact.

"Let me give you a few more things you might 'give a shit' about. In the interests of patient confidentiality, I have withheld information about your 'Wahrheit.' For your well-being, I will temporarily forgo my integrity. His name is Dwayne Kendall. I believe his middle name is Aloysius. He was a patient of mine who fixated on me… quite obsessively. I have even had to have him arrested for stalki——The Fleischmann in the complacent Felix's video presses either the stop or pause button.

I remember that it was "pause," because when I was complacent Felix, I had to watch my own snarling, indignant face in freeze-frame as roll bars traveled down the screen.

Off screen, Fleischmann says, "Now, you understand that I have only played you this back to show you how much progress we have made."

Complacent Felix says, "I understand."

"Wonderful. Now, I believe you are ready for a discussion of your revised diagnosis."

Complacent Felix nods on the screen.

"Severe schizo-dissocia aggravated by narcotic-induced psychosis and post-traumatic stress disorder."

"Chemical psychosis and PTSD? How so?"

"After toxicology analysis, it was determined that Kendall gave you pills containing a mixture of rare herbal stimulants and psychedelics. It was quite powerful."

Complacent Felix considers this, then says, "And the PTSD?"

Fleischmann sighs. "That is more complicated. Other than the obvious damage caused by your father's suicide and your unfortunate…proximity to it, it has become clear to me over the course of these sessions that you have repressed an even more powerful and hurtful memory. It would explain many things, not the least of which is your need to create a young woman capable of…'coming back to life' in a damaged automobile in your presence."

"I'm sorry. I don't follow you, doctor."

"Felix, you were in the automobile with your mother when she died."

Complacent Felix blinks a few times and becomes

Confused Denial Felix.

"She was driving you home from a Taekwondo class when you were struck by an inebriated driver in a larger vehicle. You were trapped in the auto with your severely injured mother. From what I have seen in the files there is little chance she would have survived, but you witnessed an overenthusiastic emergency worker wrenching your mother free without being aware of her impalement by a poorly designed safety strut. She exsanguinated in front of you."

Felix's eyes dart around on the screen.

"That's not true. I'd—I would remember!"

"It is true. I am sorry, Felix."

Felix breaks down. We hear Fleischmann leave his chair and cross to Felix, blocking the shot for a moment before he's past the camera and can be seen placing his hand on the shoulder of Emotionally Destroyed Felix.

I wonder if there'll be another Felix watching me and what his title will be to that one and then what that one's would be to another and on into infinity like that damned mirror-lined lake.

The Fleischmann in the office with me pauses the player, this time causing the roll bars to travel down EDF's face. Fleischmann gestures to the screen with his expensive pen.

"And once again, you have made progress."

I nod. "I'm glad you feel that way."

"I am hoping this will be our final session."

"So am I."

"How is the adjusted dosage working?"

"Fine."

"Have you had any more visual or auditory 'distortion'?"

I smile a bit. "None at all."

Doctor Fleischmann looks over his notes.

I look over at EDF on the screen and watch the visage pulse and warp ever so slightly.

Well, almost none. Nudge-nudge.

Fleischmann says, "Everything appears normal?"

I look back at him. "Perfectly. You're very good at what you do, doctor." *Wink-wink.*

"Are you having any more anxiety about the auto-theft-and-property-damage suits?"

"Should I?"

"As I have said, not at all. You have my full support, and my lawyers are quite possibly the best in the world."

"Then no."

Doctor Fleischmann studies my face.

I half smile.

Fleischmann says, "This is going quite well. You've really come so far."

"Thanks to you, Doctor Fleischmann."

Fleischmann narrows his eyes ever so slightly at me like he's unsure if he's being patronized. "Last step then?"

I nod.

"I am going to present you with a hypothetical situation. Please respond honestly."

"Of course, doctor."

"Imagine for a moment that everything you believed in your delusional, intoxicated state is in fact real."

"But…it isn't."

"Of course not. Please indulge me."

I nod but my smile is gone.

"If those things were real, would you be happy?"

"Pardon?"

"Would it make you happier?"

I shift in my seat. "No."

"Felix, you needn't feel uncomfortable. I'm just curious. If you had to make a choice between running around through a glowing, creature-filled world most can't see on some dangerous, absurd quest…and living in this boring, safe world, which would you choose? Aware and in danger or oblivious?"

Now Fleischmann is half smiling.

"I would choose to be normal."

"In the hypothetical I am describing, 'normal' would mean oblivious."

"Whatever you call it, I want to be happy. Being normal will make me happy."

Happy zebra time.

"You are sure of that?"

Eating grass, leaves, shrubs, twigs, bark.

"I have worried and hurt everyone who loves me. I've become a…a criminal by doing things I could have controlled if I had just kept taking my medicine. In my psychosis, I thought I needed answers to big questions no one really needs answers to. And those answers wouldn't have even been real. I have all the answers I need.

"I am completely sure. I want my life back."

Ev'rything's alright.

Fleischmann studies my face again.

"That is wonderful. End hypothetical, Felix. I apologize for making you uncomfortable."

"I'm fine."

The doctor opens a drawer in his desk, takes out a few pieces of paper, and sets them on the desk in front of me.

"Perfect. All I need is your initials and signature, and you are free to go home to lovely Audrey."

I wince just a bit at the unnecessary "lovely."

"Great. Can I have a pen?"

"Of course."

Instead of handing me the expensive pen in his hand, Doctor Fleischmann takes a blue-black quill pen out of an ornate yet tasteful holder on his desk, dips it into an inkpot, and extends it toward me.

As I reach for the pen, Fleischmann accidentally jabs my finger with the sharp writing tip.

"Gah!"

Fleischmann jolts back as my finger starts to bleed.

"Good Lord! I apologize! Here, take it and sign while I

get you some ointment and a bandage."

Fleischmann extends it to me again with the tip facing away from me and I take it blue-black-feather-first. I can see that the tip is bloody.

"I...I might make a mess."

"That's not a problem. It's more of a formality than anything else."

The doctor rises from his chair and crosses to a cabinet to search for bandages.

I initial the first page. Then I can see that the writing seems to burn in subtly and the blood is sucked into the letters. The type on the paper flutters and ripples and the font becomes an unfamiliar handwritten language for just a moment. I sneak a look at the Doctor.

Fleischmann seems to be watching my progress in his peripheral vision as he searches the cabinet.

I look down again and the paper is normal. I hesitate, then initial the next page and flip to the last.

Fleischmann returns to his desk with ointment and bandages. "Just sign and I will fix you up."

As I sign the last page, I feel my finger go a bit cold as blood trickles out of my cut like it's being sucked into the signature. I see that strange handwriting again as I sign and the lights in the office dim slightly. I finish signing and everything is normal again.

Fleischmann smiles pleasantly.

"Now, let me dress that wound."

I use my crutches to limp up to the internal reception desk. Peggy is at the desk and Raymond is leaning against the counter. Raymond notices me and smiles.

He nods toward the entry doors and says, "A pretty young thing came in and signed your discharge but said she didn't want to wait in here."

Then what did I just sign?

"What did she look like, Ray?"

"Like I said, pretty. She's right outside the doors."

I look toward the translucent and reflective doors and see a vague human form made of mirror standing just on the other side holding what must be one of those Macy's bags full of my effects.

"So, you ready to get back out into the world, man?"

I notice something change in the ceiling just inside the doors. After I let my eyes relax a bit, I can just make out the top half of Grieves's head poking out upside down from inside the ceiling. I look back down at the where the face would be on the mirror girl.

"I guess that depends on how I look at it."

SEE YOU SPACE COWBOY ...

STAY STRANGE
PUBLISHING